INSATIABLE

MEG CABOT

HARPER
Voyager

HarperVoyager
An imprint of HarperCollins*Publishers*
77–85 Fulham Palace Road,
Hammersmith, London W6 8JB

www.harpercollins.co.uk

This paperback edition 2012
2

First published in the USA by
William Morrow 2010

A catalogue record for this book is
available from the British Library

ISBN: 978 0 00 746212 4

Set in Sabon by Palimpsest Book Production Limited,
Falkirk Stirlingshire

Printed and bound in Great Britain by
Clays Ltd, St Ives plc

MIX
**Paper from
responsible sources**

FSC **FSC™ C007454**
www.fsc.org

INSATIABLE

Chapter One

9:15 A.M. EST, Tuesday, April 13
Downtown 6 platform
East Seventy-seventh Street and Lexington Avenue
New York, New York

I t was a miracle.

Meena hurried onto the subway car and grabbed hold of one of the gleaming silver poles, hardly daring to believe her good fortune.

It was morning rush hour, and she was running late.

She'd expected to have to cram herself into a car packed with hundreds of other commuters who were also running late.

But here she was, still panting a little from having run all the way to the station, stepping into a car that was practically empty.

Maybe, she thought, *things are going to go my way for a change.*

Meena didn't look around. She kept her gaze fastened on the ad above her head, which declared that she could have beautiful, clear skin if she called a certain Dr. Zizmor right away.

Don't look, Meena told herself. *Whatever you do, don't look, don't look, don't look. . . .*

With luck, she thought, she might make it all the way to her stop at Fifty-first Street without making eye contact or having any interaction at all with another human being. . . .

It was the butterflies—life-size—that caught Meena's attention at first. No city girl would wear white pumps with huge plastic insects on the toes. The romance novel (Meena assumed it was a romance, based on the helpless-looking, doe-eyed young woman on the cover) the girl was reading had Cyrillic writing on it. The giant roller suitcase parked in front of her was an additional clue that the girl was from out of town.

Though none of that—including the fact that she'd pinned her long blond braids onto the top of her head, *Sound of Music* style, and had paired her cheap yellow polyester dress with purple leggings—was as dead a giveaway to her new-in-town status as what the girl did next.

"Oh, I sorry," she said, looking up at Meena with a smile that changed her whole face and made her go from merely pretty to almost beautiful. "Please, you want sit?"

The girl moved her purse, which she'd left on the seat next to her, so that Meena could sit down beside her. No New Yorker would ever have done such a thing. Not when there were a dozen other empty seats on the train.

Meena's heart sank.

Because now she knew two things with absolute certainty:

One was that, despite the miracle of the nearly empty subway car, things definitely weren't going to go her way that day.

The other was that the girl with the plastic butterflies on her shoes was going to be dead before the end of the week.

Chapter Two

Meena hoped she was wrong about Miss Butterfly.

Except that Meena was never wrong. Not about death.

Giving in to the inevitable, Meena let go of the gleaming metal pole and slid into the seat the girl had offered.

"So, is this your first time visiting the city?" Meena asked Miss Butterfly, even though she already knew the answer.

The girl, still smiling, cocked her head.

"Yes. New York City!" she cried enthusiastically.

Great. Her English was basically nonexistent.

Miss Butterfly had pulled out a cell phone and was scrolling through some photos on it. She stopped on one and held it up for Meena to see.

"See?" Miss Butterfly said proudly. "Boyfriend. My American boyfriend, Gerald."

Meena looked at the grainy picture. *Oh, brother,* she thought.

Why? Meena asked herself. *Why* today, *of all days?* She didn't have time for this. She had a meeting. And a story to pitch. There was that head writing position, vacant now that Ned had had that very public nervous breakdown in the network dining room during spring sweeps.

Head writer was really where the money was on a show like *Insatiable*. Meena needed money. And she was sure the pressure wouldn't cause *her* to have a nervous breakdown. She hadn't had one so far, and she had plenty of things to worry about besides *Insatiable*'s ratings.

A woman's voice came over the subway car's loudspeakers to warn that the doors were closing. The next stop, she announced, would be Forty-second Street, Grand Central Station.

Meena, having missed her own stop, stayed where she was.

God, Meena thought. *When will my life stop sucking?*

"He looks very nice," she lied to Miss Butterfly about Gerald. "You're here to visit him?"

Miss Butterfly nodded energetically.

"He help me get visa," she said. "And—" She used the cell phone to mimic taking photos of herself.

"Head shots," Meena said. She worked in the business. She understood exactly what Miss Butterfly was talking about. And her heart sank even more. "So you want to be a model. Or an actress?"

Miss Butterfly beamed and nodded. "Yes, yes. Actress."

Of course. Of *course* this pretty girl wanted to be an actress.

Fantastic, Meena thought cynically. So Gerald was her manager, too. That explained a lot about the baseball cap—pulled down so low that Meena couldn't see his eyes—and the number of gold chains around his neck in the photo.

"What's your name?" Meena asked.

Miss Butterfly pointed at herself, as if surprised Meena cared to discuss *her* as opposed to the ultra-fantastic Gerald.

"I? I am Yalena."

"Great," Meena said. She opened her bag, dug around the mess inside it, and came up with a business card. She always had one handy for exactly this kind of situation, which unfortunately came up all too often . . . especially when Meena rode the subway. "Yalena, if you need anything—anything at all—I want you to call me. My cell phone number is on there. See it?" She pointed to the number. "You can call me anytime. My name is Meena. If things don't work out with your boyfriend—if he turns out to be mean to you, or hurts you in any way—I want you to know you can call me. I'll come get you, wherever you are. Day or night. And listen . . . ," she added. "Don't show this card to your boyfriend. This is a *secret* card. For emergencies. Between girlfriends. Do you understand?"

Yalena just gazed at her, smiling happily.

She didn't understand. She didn't understand at all that Meena's number might literally mean the difference between life and death for her.

They never understood.

The train pulled up to Forty-second Street station. Yalena jumped up. "Grand Central?" she asked, looking panicky.

"Yes," Meena said. "This is Grand Central."

"I meet my boyfriend here," Yalena said excitedly, grabbing her huge roller bag and giving it a yank. She took Meena's card in her other hand, beaming. "Thank you! I call."

She meant she'd call to get together for coffee sometime.

But Meena knew Yalena would call her for something totally different. If she didn't lose the card . . . or if Gerald didn't find it and take it away. Then give her a fist sandwich.

"Remember," Meena repeated, following her off the train. "Don't tell your boyfriend you have that. Hide it somewhere."

"I do," Yalena said, and scrambled toward the nearest flight of stairs, lugging her suitcase behind her. It was so huge, and Yalena was so small, she could barely drag it. Meena, giving in to the inevitable, picked up the bottom of the girl's incredibly heavy suitcase and helped her carry it up the steep and crowded staircase. Then she pointed Yalena in the direction the girl needed to go—the boyfriend was meeting her "under the clock" in the "big station."

Then, with a sigh, Meena turned around and headed for a train back uptown, so she could get to Madison and Fifty-third Street, where her office building was located.

Meena knew Yalena hadn't understood a word she'd said. Well, maybe one in five.

And even if she had, there wouldn't have been any point in telling the girl the truth. She wouldn't have believed Meena, anyway.

Just like there was no point in following her now, seeing the boyfriend for herself, and then saying something to him like, "I know what you really are and what you do for a living. And I'm going to call the police."

Because you can't call the cops on someone for something they're *going* to do. Any more than you can tell someone that they're going to die.

Meena had learned this the hard way.

She sighed again. She was going to have to run now if she wanted to catch the next train uptown. . . .

She just prayed there wouldn't be too many people on it.

Chapter Three

"Professor?"

Lucien Antonescu smiled up at her from the enormous antique desk behind which he sat, grading papers. "Yes?"

"So is it true," Natalia asked, grasping at the first question she could think of, since she'd completely forgotten what she'd meant to ask him the moment his dark-eyed gaze fell upon her, "that the oldest human remains ever found were discovered in Romania?"

Oh, no! Human remains? How disgusting! How could she ask something so stupid?

"The oldest human remains found in *Europe*," Professor Antonescu said, correcting her gently. "The oldest human remains ever found were discovered in Ethiopia. And they're roughly a hundred and fifty thousand years older than the remains found in what we consider modern-day Romania, in the Cave with Bones."

The girl was only half listening. He was the sexiest of all her instructors, and that included teaching assistants. On the University of Bucharest's equivalent of Rateyourprof.com, Professor Lucien Antonescu had been given all 10s in the looks category.

And justifiably so, since he was over six feet tall, lean and broad shouldered, with thick dark hair that he wore brushed back from his temples and a smooth, gorgeous forehead.

As if all that weren't enough, he had dark brown eyes that, in certain lights, when he was lecturing and grew excited about his subject matter—which happened frequently, because he was impassioned about Eastern European history—flashed red.

Surely the posts on the message boards were exaggerated . . . especially the ones hinting that he was related to the Romanian royal family and was a duke or a prince or something.

But since taking Professor Antonescu's class, Natalia could see why he—and his course—was so popular. And why the line of girls—and some boys, though when he showed pictures of ancient Romanian art, Professor Antonescu spoke so appreciatively of the lush lines of the female form that there was no possible way he could be gay—at his office hours was so long. He was a gifted orator, with a regal yet very engaging presence. . . .

And he was so very, very hot.

"So," Natalia said hesitantly, taking in the way his perfectly tailored black cashmere blazer molded those shoulders. She wondered why she couldn't see his eyes—those dark, flashing eyes—better and realized it was because he had the shades to his office windows pulled down. She hoped he'd still notice that she'd worn a new shirt, one that showed off her cleavage to its best advantage. She'd bought it at a steep discount at H&M, but it still made her look irresistible. "It would be correct to say that Romania is the cradle of civilization in Europe."

This, Natalia thought, sounded very intelligent.

"It would be a lovely idea, of course," Professor Antonescu said, looking thoughtful. "Certainly there have been human beings living here for over two millennia, and this land has been the site of many bloody invasions, from the Romans to the Huns, until finally we had what today makes up modern-day Romania . . . Moldavia and Wallachia, and of course Transylvania. But the cradle of civilization . . . I don't know that we can say that." He was even better looking when he smiled, if such a thing were possible.

"Professor."

The smile caused her to come undone. She knew she was not the first. His bachelor status was legendary, the intrigue heightening whenever he was spotted with a woman—never the same one twice—in the posher restaurants downtown. How many had he asked back to his castle—he owned a castle!—outside of Sighişoara, or to his enormous loft apartment in the trendiest district of Bucharest?

No one knew. Maybe hundreds. Maybe none. He didn't seem to care to marry and start a family.

Well, all that would change when he tasted her cooking. Iliana, behind her in line to see him just now, had teased her for saying she was going to invite him over. So old-fashioned! She said Natalia should just offer to sleep with him right there, in his office, like Iliana was going to, and get it over with.

But Natalia's mother had always told her she made the best *sarmale* of anyone in the family. One taste, her mother said, and any man would be hers.

"Yes?" Professor Antonescu asked, one of those thick dark eyebrows raising.

Natalia wished he hadn't done this. It only made him look more attractive and made her feel more foolish for what she was about to do.

"Would you like to come to my place for a home-cooked meal sometime?" she asked, all in a rush. Her heart was beating wildly. She was sure he could see it thrumming behind her breast, considering how low-cut her new blouse was.

Something in the dimly lit office made a chirping sound.

"I beg your pardon," Professor Antonescu said. He reached into the inside pocket of his expensive coat and produced a slim cell phone . . . top of the line, of course. "I thought I'd turned this off."

Natalia stood there, wondering if she ought to say something about the *sarmale* or perhaps undo another button of her blouse, as Iliana would have done. . .

. . . but she hesitated when she saw Professor Antonescu's expression change as his gaze fell on the name on the caller identification.

"I'm terribly sorry," he said. "This is an important call. I have to take it. Could we discuss this at another time?"

Natalia felt her cheeks growing red. It was merely because he was looking at her . . . and yet had never once lowered his gaze below her neck.

"Of course," she said shamefacedly.

"And please tell the others," Professor Antonescu said as he accepted the call, "that unfortunately I'll have to end office hours early this evening. A family emergency."

Family emergency. He had family?

"I'll let them know," the girl said, pleased. He trusted her! That would put Iliana in her place!

"Thank you," Professor Antonescu said politely as she slunk from the dark, lushly decorated room, all in richly appointed leather-trimmed furniture and filled with manuscripts that were many centuries older than she was. Even Professor Antonescu's office was different from the offices of her other instructors, which were as barren as a politburo's and just as grim.

She opened the door, slipped through it, and turned to close it. . . .

But not before she heard him say, in a voice she had never heard him use before, and in English, "What? When?" Then, "Not again."

Natalia turned then to see a look on his face that made her heart turn over in her chest.

But not in the joyful way it did when she spied him coming down the corridor toward the lecture hall.

Now she was afraid.

Deathly afraid.

Because those beautiful eyes of his had gone vermilion . . . the same color her shower water ran when she accidentally cut her leg while shaving.

Only this wasn't a trickle of water. It was a man's eyes. His *eyes*.

And they'd gone the color of blood.

His gaze was boring into her as if he could see straight through her blouse, past her bra, and into the most intimate places of her heart.

"*Get out*," he said in a voice that she would swear later, when she told her mother about it, didn't even sound human.

Natalia turned, threw open the door, and flung herself through it, flying with a face as white as death past the other students waiting to see their professor.

"Well, that obviously went well," Iliana said with a sneer.

But when Iliana tried Professor Antonescu's office door, she found it locked. She knocked and knocked, finally cupping both hands around her eyes and pressing them to the door's frosted glass.

"The lights are out. I don't see him in there. I think . . . I think he's gone."

But how could the professor have left a locked a room from which there was no other exit?

Chapter Four

ood morning, Miss Meena. The usual?" Abdullah, the guy in the glassed-in coffee stand outside her office building, asked her when it was finally her turn to order.

"Good morning, Abdullah," Meena said. "Better make it a large. I've got a big meeting. Light, please. And don't bother toasting the bagel today, I'm running really, really late."

Abdullah nodded and went to work as Meena narrowed her gaze at him. She could tell he still hadn't seen a doctor about his out-of-control blood pressure, despite the talk she'd had with him about it last week.

Seriously, *she* was the one who was going to stroke out one day if people didn't start listening to her. She knew taking time from work to go to the doctor was a pain.

But when the alternative was *dying*?

Precognition.

Extrasensory perception.

Witchcraft.

It didn't matter what anyone called it: In Meena's opinion, as a skill, it was totally useless.

Had it been particularly helpful when she'd finally managed to convince her longtime boyfriend, David, about the tumor that she could sense was growing in his brain?

Sure, she'd saved David's life (had they found the tumor any later, it would have been inoperable, the doctors said).

But David had left Meena immediately after his recovery for one of his perky radiology nurses. Brianna healed people who were sick, he'd said. She wasn't a "freak" who told them they were going to die.

What had Meena gotten out of saving David? Nothing but a lot of heartache.

And she'd lost half the down payment on the apartment that they'd bought together. Which she still owed him. And which he was being a total jerk about her paying back on her pittance of a salary.

David and Brianna were buying their first house together. And expecting their first baby.

Of course.

Meena had learned from that experience—and all the ones before it—that no one was interested in finding out how they were going to die.

Except her best friend, Leisha, of course, who always listened to Meena . . . ever since that time in the ninth grade when Rob Pace asked her to that Aerosmith concert, and Meena told her not to go, and Rob took Angie Harwood instead.

That's how Angie Harwood, and not Leisha, ended up getting decapitated when the wheel of a semi tractor-trailer came spinning off and landed on top of Rob's Camaro as it was cruising down I-95 on the way home from the concert.

Meena, upon learning of the accident the morning after it occurred (Rob had miraculously escaped with only a broken collarbone), had promptly thrown up her breakfast.

Why hadn't she realized that by saving her best friend from certain death, she'd all but guaranteed another girl's? She ought to have warned Angie, too, and done anything—*everything*—to stop Rob from going that night.

She swore then that she would never allow what had happened to Angie Harwood to happen to another human being. Not if she could help it.

It was no wonder then that high school, torturous for many, had been even worse for Meena.

Which was how she got into television writing as a career. Real kids may not have enjoyed the company of the "You're Gonna Die Girl" so much.

But the people Meena discovered on the soap operas her mom liked to watch—*Insatiable* had been a favorite—were always happy to see her.

And when the story lines on the soaps she liked didn't go the way she thought they should, Meena started writing her own.

Surprisingly, this hobby had paid off.

Well, if you call being a dialogue writer for the second-highest-rated soap opera in America a payoff.

Which Meena did. Sort of. She knew she'd landed what millions would kill for . . . a dream job.

And given her "gift," she knew her life could have been a thousand times worse. Look what had happened to Joan of Arc.

Then there was Cassandra, daughter of the Trojan king Priam. She too had been given the gift of prophecy. Because she hadn't returned a god's love, that gift was turned by that god into a curse, so that Cassandra's prophecies, though true, would never be believed.

Hardly anyone ever believed Meena either. But that didn't mean she was going to give up trying. Not on girls like the one she'd met on the subway, and not on Abdullah. She'd get him to go to the doctor, eventually.

It was just too bad, really, that the one person whose future Meena had never been able to see was her own.

Until now, anyway.

If she was much later to work, she was going to lose any chance whatsoever she had at convincing Sy to take her pitch seriously.

And forget about that promotion to head writer.

She didn't need to be psychic to figure *that* out.

Chapter Five

7:00 P.M. EET, Tuesday, April 13
The hills outside of Sighişoara
Mures County, Romania

Lucien Antonescu was furious, and when he was furious, he sometimes lost control.

He'd frightened that young girl in his office nearly to death, and he hadn't wanted to do that. He'd felt her fear . . . it had been sharp and as tightly wound as a garrote. She was a good person, longing, like most girls her age, only for love.

And he'd terrified her.

But he didn't have time to worry about that now. Now he had a very serious situation that was going to require all of his attention for the immediate future.

And so he was doing what he could in an attempt to calm himself. His favorite classical piece—by Tchaikovsky—played over the hall's speakers (which he'd purchased and had shipped from the U.S. at enormous expense; quality sound was important).

And he'd opened one of the truly exquisite bottles of Bordeaux in his collection and was letting it breathe on the sideboard. He could smell the tannins even from halfway across the room. The scent was soothing. . . .

Still, he couldn't help pacing the length of the great hall, an enormous fire roaring in the stone hearth at one end of the room and the stuffed heads of various animals his ancestors had killed leering down at him from the walls above.

"Three," he growled at the laptop sitting on the long, elaborately carved wooden table in the center of the room. "Three dead girls? All within the past few weeks? Why wasn't I told this before now?"

"I didn't realize that there was a connection between them, my lord," the slightly anxious voice from the computer's speakers said in English.

"Three exsanguinated corpses, all left nude in various city parks?" Lucien didn't attempt to keep the sarcasm from his tone. "Covered in bite marks? And you didn't realize there was a connection. I see."

"Obviously the authorities don't want to start a citywide panic," the voice said fretfully. "My sources didn't know anything about the bite marks until this morning. . . ."

"And what attempts," Lucien asked, ignoring this last remark, "have been made to discover who is committing these atrocities?"

"Everyone I've spoken to denies any knowledge whatsoev—"

Lucien cut him off. "Then obviously you're not speaking to the appropriate people. Or someone is lying."

"I . . . I can't imagine anyone would dare," the voice said hesitantly. "They know I'm speaking on your authority, sire. I feel . . . if I may, sire . . . that it isn't . . . well, one of us. Someone we know."

Lucien paused in his circuit around the room.

"That's impossible," he said flatly. "There's no one we don't know."

He turned and approached the wine decanter, which was filled with rich ruby liquid. He could see the reflection of the firelight against one side of the perfect crystal globe.

"It's one of us," Lucien said, inhaling the earthy fragrance of the Bordeaux. "Someone who has forgotten himself. And his vows."

"Surely not," the voice said nervously. "No one would dare. Everyone knows the repercussions of committing such a crime under your rule. That your retribution will be swift . . . and severe."

"Nevertheless." Lucien picked up the decanter and watched as the liquid inside left a deep red film against the far side of the crystal bulb. "Someone's savagely killing human women and leaving their bodies out in the open to be discovered."

"He *is* putting all of us at risk," the voice from the laptop ⌐ hesitantly.

"Yes," Lucien said. "Needlessly so. He must be discovered, punished, and stopped. Permanently."

"Yes, my lord," the voice said. "Only . . . how? How are we to discover him? The police . . . my informants tell me that the police haven't a single lead."

Lucien's perfectly formed lips curved into a bitter smile. "The police," he said. "Ah, yes. The police." He glanced away from the decanter he held, toward the face on the computer screen a few yards away. "Emil, find me a place to stay. I'm coming to town."

"Sire?" Emil looked startled. "*You?* Are you certain? Surely that won't be—"

"I'm certain. I will find our murdering friend. And then . . ."

Lucien opened his fingers and let the decanter fall to the flagstones beneath his feet. The crystal bell smashed into a thousand pieces, the wine it contained making a deep red smear across the floor, where, centuries before, Lucien had watched his father dash the brains of so many of their servants.

"I will show him myself what happens when anyone dares to break a vow to me."

Chapter Six

Meena was wolfing down her bagel when Paul, one of the breakdown writers, poked his balding head into her office.

"I don't have time to help you update your Facebook page right now, Paul," Meena said. "I've only got a minute before I have to meet with Sy."

"I take it you didn't hear, then," Paul said morosely.

"Hear what?" Meena asked with her mouth full.

"About Shoshona."

Meena's blood went cold.

So it had finally happened. And it was all her fault for not saying anything.

But how did you warn someone that her advanced state of gymorexia was going to kill her? Treadmills were not widely known to be fatal, and Shoshona was so proud to have gotten down to size 00.

The truth was, Shoshona had never been one of Meena's favorite people.

"She . . . *died?*"

"No." Paul looked at Meena strangely. "She got the head writer position. I guess it happened last night."

Meena choked.

"Wh-what?" She blinked back tears. She told herself they were tears from a chunk of bagel going down the wrong tube.

But they weren't.

"Didn't you see the e-mail?" Paul asked. "They sent it around this morning."

"No," Meena croaked. "I was on the subway."

"Oh," Paul said. "Well, I'm updating my résumé. I figure she'll be firing me soon anyway so she can hire one of her club-hopping friends. Would you mind looking it over later?"

"Sure," Meena said numbly.

But she was only half listening to him. They'd passed her over for *Shoshona*? After all the hard work she'd done this year? Much of it *Shoshona's* work, because Shoshona was forever leaving the office early to go work out?

No. Just no.

Meena was standing in the door to Sy's office exactly two minutes before their appointed meeting, anger bubbling over.

"Sy," she said. "I'd like to speak to you about—"

That was when she noticed Shoshona was already sitting in one of the chairs in front of his desk, wearing, as usual, something from Crewcuts, the J.Crew children's section; she was *that* skinny.

"Oh, Meena," Shoshona Metzenbaum said, tossing some of her long, silky dark hair. "There you are. I was just telling Sy how much I love the little treatment you gave him. The one about Tabby being in love with that bad boy from the wrong side of the tracks? So sweet."

Sweet? Up until today, Shoshona's only job responsibility at *Insatiable* had been, like Meena's, to write the dialogue for story breakdowns, especially those featuring the show's biggest and longest-running star, Cheryl Trent, who played Victoria Worthington Stone, and now her teenage daughter on the show, Tabitha.

Except that Shoshona had rarely been able to handle even that, always leaving early to go to the gym or calling to say she'd be late because her convertible had broken down on the way back into the city from the Metzenbaum family weekend home in the Hamptons.

Or the decorator who was redoing her downtown loft hadn't shown up on time.

Or she'd missed the last flight out of St. Croix and was going to have to stay another night.

Not that anyone who mattered ever got upset about these things, considering who Shoshona's aunt and uncle were: Fran and Stan Metzenbaum, *Insatiable*'s executive producers and cocreators.

It would have been different, Meena thought, if Shoshona had actually *deserved* this promotion. If it had been Paul or any of the other writers who actually showed up to the office once in a while, Meena wouldn't have minded.

But Shoshona? Meena had once overheard her bragging on the phone to a friend that she'd never even watched the show until her aunt and uncle had hired her to come work for them . . . unlike Meena, who'd never missed a single episode—not since she turned twelve. Shoshona didn't know the names of every single one of Victoria's ex-husbands, the way Meena did, or why they'd broken up (Victoria was insatiable, it was true, but not terribly lucky in love). Or that Victoria's beloved teenage daughter, Tabitha, was following in her mom's footsteps. (So far they'd managed to kill off every single one of Tabby's love interests. The latest had just been blown up in a Jet Ski accident intended for Tabby by a spurned stalker.)

"I'm glad you like it," Meena said with forced patience. "I thought throwing in a bad boy for Tabby might attract a younger demographic—"

"That's exactly what we're hearing from corporate," Shoshona said, flinging Sy an astonished glance. "We were just sitting here discussing that. Weren't we, Sy?"

"We were," Sy said, beaming at Meena. "Come on in, kid, and take a seat. You heard the great news about Shoshona?"

Meena couldn't bring herself to look at Shoshona, she was so furious. She kept her gaze on Sy as she sank into the other Aeron chair in front of his desk.

"I did," she said. "And I was really hoping to have a word with you in private this morning, Sy."

"Nothing you can't say to me in front of Shoshona," Sy said jovially, waving a hand. "Frankly, I think this is just fantastic. We're going to have some real estrogen power going on here!"

Meena stared at him. Had Sy really just said the words *estrogen power*?

And could he actually not know that Meena had been the one doing all of Shoshona's work for the past twelve months?

"Right," Shoshona said. "So I think Meena should be one of the first to know about the new direction the network would like to see us start heading in."

"The network?" Meena echoed bewilderedly.

"Well, our sponsor, really," Shoshona said, correcting herself.

To Meena's knowledge, Consumer Dynamics Inc.—*Insatiable*'s sponsor, a multinational technology and services conglomerate, which also happened to own Affiliated Broadcast Network—had never once lowered itself to bother with the show.

Until now, apparently.

"In a word," Shoshona said, "they want us to go vampire. All vampire, all the time."

Meena immediately felt the bagel and coffee she'd had for breakfast come back up.

"No," she said after swallowing hard. "We can't do that."

Sy blinked confusedly at Meena. "Why the hell not?"

She ought to have known. Her day, which had already started off so badly, could only get worse. Lately her whole life had been headed in a steady downward trajectory.

"Well, for one thing, because there's already a soap opera on a rival network with a vampire story line that's killing us in the ratings," Meena said. "A little show called *Lust*. Remember? I mean, we have to have *some* pride. We can't just outright copy *Lust*."

Shoshona pretended to be busy straightening her patterned hose as Meena spoke. Sy, peering over his desk, couldn't take his eyes off her long, coltish legs.

Meena wished she had a mini-Butterfinger for sustenance. Or to smash into Shoshona's flat-ironed hair.

Flat-ironing! Who even bothered anymore?

Certainly not Meena, who had hacked off most of her dark hair at Leisha's command—Leisha's "gift" was that she could look at anyone and immediately tell them exactly the most flattering way they ought to be wearing their hair—and who had enough problems making it to work on time without having to worry about flat-ironing, even when she wasn't busy trying to save young girls on the subway from certain death by white slavery.

"We'll look like total fools," Meena said.

"I don't think so," Shoshona said coolly. "*Lust* is obviously doing something right. It's one of the few soaps right now that hasn't been canceled or been forced to move to L.A. to shoot to save money. It's actually going *up* in the ratings. And like you said, if we're going to survive, we need to pull in a younger demographic. Kids don't care about soaps. It's all about reality shows to them."

"And what's so real," Meena demanded, "about *vampires*?"

"Oh, I assure you, they're real," Shoshona said with a catlike smile. "You've read about those girls they keep finding, drained of all their blood, in parks all over New York City, haven't you?"

"Oh, for God's sake," Meena said sourly. "They weren't drained of all their blood. They were just strangled."

"Um, excuse me," Shoshona said. "But I have an inside source who says all three of those girls were bitten everywhere and drained of every drop of their blood. There's a real-life vampire here in Manhattan, and he's feeding on innocent girls."

Meena rolled her eyes. Okay. It was true some girls had turned up dead lately in a few city parks.

But drained of their blood? Shoshona was taking vampire fever— which, yes, gripped the country, there was no denying that; it was obvious enough that even Consumer Dynamics Inc. was aware of it, and they were so oblivious to trends that they still thought having a MySpace page was cutting-edge—too far.

"So let's give the show a pulled-from-the-headlines feel," Shoshona went on, "and have a vampire feed on the girls in *Insatiable*. Tabby's friends. And let him brainwash Tabby, and let Tabby be his vampire bride."

Sy pointed at Shoshona. "Vampire bride," he yelled. "I love it. Even better, CDI loves it!"

Meena contemplated getting up, walking over to Sy's office window, opening it, and jumping.

"And you haven't heard the pièce de résistance," Shoshona said. "I can get Gregory Bane—"

Sy gasped and leaned forward. "*Yes?*"

Meena moaned and dropped her head into her hands. Gregory Bane played the vampire on *Lust*. There wasn't a single person on earth who was sicker of Gregory Bane than Meena.

And she'd never even met him.

"—to get Stefan Dominic to read for the part of the vampire," Shoshona went on.

Sy, looking disappointed, sank back into his chair. "Who the hell is Stefan Dominic?" he barked.

Shoshona smirked.

"Only Gregory Bane's *best friend*," she said. "I mean, they go clubbing together practically every weekend. I know you've seen his picture with Gregory in *Us Weekly*, Sy. The press we'll get from hiring him will be huge. I can't believe no one's snatched him up already. And the best thing? He has his SAG card, and he can come in this Friday to read with Taylor." Shoshona looked like the cat who'd swallowed the canary. "I already talked to him about it. He goes to my gym."

Suddenly, Meena knew exactly why Shoshona was spending so much time on that treadmill. And it didn't have anything to do with fitting into those Crewcuts.

"There is no way," Meena said, fighting for inner patience, "that Taylor"—Taylor Mackenzie was the actress who played Tabby—"is going to agree to play a vampire bride."

Taylor had recently gone on a macrobiotic diet and hired a personal trainer, shrinking herself down to Shoshona's size. Although Taylor was delighted about this—and the attention the tabloids were paying to her because of it—she needed to watch out if she too didn't want to end up in a coffin . . . something Meena had been trying to warn her about by leaving large deli sandwiches in her dressing room. Not exactly subtle, but the best Meena could do.

"Tabby will like it if the network tells her to," Shoshona said. "This is what ABN wants."

Meena was trying very hard not to grit her teeth. Her dentist had already chastised her for doing this in her sleep and prescribed her a mouth guard. Meena dreaded wearing it, because it wasn't exactly the most romantic thing to show up wearing to bed. She looked like a hockey goalie.

But it was that, the dentist said, or a new, less stressful job.

And there were none of those to be found. At least not in television writing.

And since Meena was currently sleeping alone, she guessed it didn't matter what she looked like anyway.

"Cheryl isn't going to like it," Meena warned them. Cheryl was the veteran actress who'd played Victoria Worthington Stone for the past thirty years. "You know she's been hoping this is the year she'll finally get that Emmy."

Thirty years, ten marriages, four miscarriages, one abortion, two murders, six kidnappings, and an evil twin later, and Cheryl Trent still had never won a single Daytime Emmy.

It was a crime, in Meena's opinion. Not just because Meena was one of Cheryl's biggest fans and getting to write for her was the thrill of a lifetime, but because Cheryl was one of the nicest ladies Meena had ever met.

And part of Meena's plan, in the story line she'd submitted to Sy—but which he'd just passed over for Shoshona's vampire plot—had been for Victoria Worthington Stone to fall for Tabby's new boyfriend's father, a bitter police chief Victoria was going to help reunite with his wayward son . . . giving Cheryl a sure shot at that golden statuette for which she so longed.

But a *vampire* story line? No one was going to be handing out Emmies for that.

"Yeah, well," Shoshona said, narrowing her eyes at Meena, "Cheryl can cry me a river."

Meena's jaw dropped. *This* was the thanks she got for having saved Shoshona's butt so many times with her late scripts?

Why had she even bothered?

"I love it," Sy said, snapping his fingers. "Run it past your aunt and uncle. I gotta go, I've got a meeting." He stood up.

"Sy," Meena said. Her mouth felt dry.

"What?" He looked annoyed.

"Don't . . ."

There were so many things she wanted to say. Felt as if she *had* to say. For the good of her soul. For the good of the show. For the good of the country as a whole.

Instead, she just said, "Don't take Fifth. There's congestion. I heard it on 1010 Wins. Have the cabbie take Park."

Sy's face relaxed. "Thanks, Harper," he said. "Finally, something useful out of you." Then he turned and left the room.

Meena swiveled her head to stare daggers at Shoshona.

Not because she was irritated that she'd just saved Sy's life—if he took Fifth, his cab would, indeed, meet with congestion that would so irritate him, he'd get out and walk, causing him to jaywalk injudiciously at Forty-seventh and be struck by a Fresh Direct truck—and he wasn't the least bit grateful, but because she knew what "Run it past it your aunt and uncle" meant.

It meant Shoshona had won.

"*Vampires*," Meena said. "Real original, Metzenbaum."

Shoshona stood up, slinging her bag over her shoulder. "Get over it, Harper. They're everywhere. You can't escape them."

She turned and walked out.

And for the first time, Meena noticed the gem-encrusted dragon on the side of Shoshona's tote.

No. It couldn't be.

But it was.

The Marc Jacobs tote Meena had secretly been lusting after for half a year but denying herself because it cost $5,000.

And no way could Meena afford—or justify spending—that much money on a bag.

And, all right, Shoshona had it in aquamarine, not the ruby red that would perfectly round out Meena's wardrobe.

But still.

Meena stared after her, grinding her teeth.

Now she was going to have no choice but to make an emergency run at lunch to CVS in order to restock her secret candy drawer.

Chapter Seven

Alaric Wulf didn't consider himself a snob. Far from it.

If anyone back at the office ever bothered to ask—and, with the exception of his partner, Martin, none of those ingrates ever had—Alaric would have pointed out that for the first fifteen of his thirty-five years, he'd lived in abject poverty, eating only when his various stepfathers won enough money at the track, and then only if there was enough cash left over for food after his drug-addicted mother was done scoring.

And so Alaric had chosen to live on the streets (and off his wits) in his native Zurich, until child services caught him and forced him go to a group home, where he'd been surprised to find himself much better cared for by strangers than he'd ever been by his own family.

It was in the group home that Alaric had been brought to the attention of, and eventually recruited by, the Palatine Guard, thanks to what turned out to be a strong sword arm, unerring aim, an innate aptitude for languages, and the fact that nothing—not his stepfathers, social workers, priests who claimed to have the voice of God whispering in their ear, or blood-sucking vampires—intimidated (or impressed) him.

Now Alaric slept on eight-hundred-thread-count Egyptian cotton sheets every night, drove an Audi R8, and routinely dined on favorite dishes like foie gras and duck confit. His suits were all Italian, and he wouldn't have dreamed of donning a shirt that hadn't been hand pressed. He enjoyed swimming a hundred laps, then sitting in the sauna every morning at the gym; had an active sex life with numerous attractive and cultured women who knew nothing of his background; collected *Betty and Veronica* comic books (which he had to have specially shipped to Rome from America at a not-unimpressive cost); and killed vampires for a living as part of a highly secretive military unit of the Vatican.

Life was good . . .

True, he had a life*style* upon which most of his coworkers frowned. The majority of them, for instance, preferred to stay in local convents or rectories while traveling, while Alaric always checked into the finest hotel he could find . . . which he paid for himself, of course. Why not? He didn't have any children or parents to support. Was it his fault that an early interest in investing (particularly in precious metals, specifically gold, which he couldn't help noticing there seemed to be a great deal of around the Vatican) had made him his Zurich banker's favorite client?

Still, in no way did Alaric Wulf consider himself a snob. He could "rough it" like anyone else. He was, in fact, "roughing it" now.

Sitting in his rental car outside a large discount retail establishment in Chattanooga—Chattanooga; what a name for a city!—Alaric watched as the lunchtime crowd flooded toward the store. A sketchy report from a pair of frantic parents had worked its way to his superiors at the Palatine Guard: A young woman who worked at this particular Walmart had been attacked by a vamp in this very parking lot on her way home from work one night. She still bore the telltale puncture wounds on her neck.

The problem was that she insisted to her parents that the marks were not from an "attack" at all but were the result of a "love bite."

In other words, she adored her attacker.

Of course, Alaric thought with his customary cynicism. *They all do.* Society had romanticized vampires to the point that many impressionable young women threw themselves at the actors who played vampires in movies and on television.

Not that it was their fault. Women were genetically programmed to be attracted to powerful and good-looking men, men with a high testosterone level who would make good providers for their children, which was how vampires—rich, tall, strong, and handsome—were usually portrayed on film.

Alaric wondered if women would feel quite the same about vampires if they could have seen his former partner Martin in the ICU after they'd tangled with the nest of vamps they'd found in that warehouse outside of Berlin. They'd torn half of Martin's face off. He was still sucking his dinner through a straw.

Fortunately, the demons had left him the use of his eyes, so he would still see the daughter he and his partner Karl had adopted—Alaric's goddaughter, Simone—celebrate her fourth birthday.

Thus Alaric's dedication to his work.

Of course, he'd been dedicated before that particular incident. How many other careers allowed you to use a sword? He could think of very few.

And Alaric was very fond of his sword, Señor Sticky. The blade, unlike humans, did not lie. It didn't cheat, and it didn't discriminate . . . even if vampires *were* stupid. Especially American vampires. They hung out in places Alaric himself would never have gone, especially if he were immortal. Such as high schools. And Walmart.

If Alaric were a vampire—and that was never going to happen, because if by some heinous accident of fate he were even bitten enough times for that to occur, Martin was under instructions to kill him instantly, no matter how much he fought—he'd step it up. Target, maybe.

Alaric supposed vampires avoided Target because of the parking lot security cameras. (It was a myth that vampires wouldn't show up in mirrors or on film. Certainly in the old days it had been true, when silver-backed mirrors and film had been the norm. But now that the world had gone digital—and mirrors were cheap—vampire reflections could be caught just like anyone else's.) Alaric actually liked Target. They didn't have Target in Rome. He'd bought a Goofy watch the last time he'd been in a Target. The other guards had made fun of him, but he liked his Goofy watch. It was old-fashioned and didn't do anything but tell time.

But sometimes all you needed was to know the time.

Alaric's cell phone buzzed, and he laid down his *Betty and Veronica* comic and fished the phone from his coat pocket, then read the text he'd received with interest.

Manhattan. Reports of completely exsanguinated bodies. At least three dead.

Alaric had to read the message twice to make sure he'd read it right.

Exsanguinated bodies? There hadn't been a vampire stupid enough actually to *drain* a body completely of blood in a century. At least not that Alaric knew of.

Because that—unlike what this vamp was doing in Chattanooga—was murder, and not simply assault with a pair of fangs.

And assault like that could never even be proven—not in a regular court of law—because the victim had given consent . . . due to mind control, of course.

But only the Palatine and the girl's parents would ever believe that.

If some vamp was stupid enough actually to be murdering his victims, that could only mean one thing:

The prince would be crawling out of whatever hole he'd been hiding in for the past century.

He'd have to. He'd never allow something like this to jeopardize the safety of his minions.

Alaric grinned. His week was looking a whole lot brighter.

Suddenly, through the crowds, Alaric saw a uniformed Walmart employee coming his way, toward the car the girl's parents had described as hers and that Alaric had carefully parked alongside.

Sarah didn't resemble the photo her parents had provided . . . at least, not anymore. Being a vamp's personal blood donor could do that to a woman. Her formerly round cheeks were thin, and her uniform was hanging on her wasted frame. Her curly red hair had lost its bounce, and she was wearing a kerchief of some kind around her neck to hide the "love bite" her new friend had left behind during his last visit.

She was so anemic, she didn't even notice when Alaric got out of his car and stood there in front of her, a massive figure in the noonday sun,

Señor Sticky carefully hidden—for now—in the folds of his trench coat. She just kept slurping on the large cup of soda she was holding.

She needed all that soda, he supposed. She had to keep building up new plasma if she was going to be someone's dinner tonight.

"Sarah," Alaric said quietly.

She stopped short and finally looked up at him, her blue-eyed gaze listless.

Now was the time to show her the sword. Sometimes it was the only thing that got through to them in their ardor-induced stupors.

Alaric pushed back the folds of his coat.

"Just tell me where he is, Sarah," he said gently. "And I'll let you live."

Chapter Eight

2:00 P.M. EST, Tuesday, April 13
ABN Building
520 Madison Avenue
New York, New York

> YOU ARE CORDIALLY INVITED....
> WHAT: *A fancy dinner at our place, 910 Park Avenue, Apt. 11A*
> WHEN: *Thursday, April 15, at 7:30 P.M.*
> WHY: *Emil's cousin, the prince, is in town!*
> DRESS: *Fancy! DRESS UP! This is your chance to meet real, old-fashioned royalty! Dig out your fanciest, sexiest, most expensive shoes and dresses and have fun! No need to feel down just because your husband won't let you take the platinum card out for a spin! Shop your closet and we'll see you on Thursday!*
>
> *xoxo Mary Lou*

Meena stared at her computer monitor.

She was supposed to be working on the dialogue for next week's explosive scene in which Tabby confronted her mother for sleeping with her riding instructor, Romero, on whom Tabby herself had a crush.

But all she could think about was Shoshona's promotion and her horrible vampire story line, which Fran and Stan had, of course, approved, agreeing with the network (who agreed with CDI) that it was going to make *Insatiable* more appealing to the all-important eighteen-to-forty-nine female demographic ... which would in turn bring in more advertising money. Which would in turn get them all raises (the *Insatiable* writing staff had been under a pay freeze for more than a year).

Then Mary Lou's e-mail had popped into her in-box.

And Meena lost all ability whatsoever to concentrate on anything else.

Appalled, Meena forwarded the e-mail to her best friend, Leisha.

"Who *is* this person?" Leisha called a few minutes later to ask.

"My next-door neighbor Mary Lou," Meena said, astonished that Leisha wouldn't remember. She only complained about something Mary Lou had said or done every other day.

"Oh, that's right," Leisha said. "The one you used to like until she started stalking you on the elevator every day—"

"—trying to fix me up with every single guy she knows," Meena finished for her, "after David and I broke up. Right. Plus, she keeps going on about how she traced her husband Emil's ancestry back to Romanian royalty. She figured out he's a count, which makes her a—"

"Countess," Leisha said. Meena could hear hair dryers buzzing in the background. Leisha worked as a stylist at a high-end salon in SoHo. "Wasn't she the one on the co-op board of your building who wouldn't let you and David buy the apartment at first because you weren't married? But then when she found out you write for *Insatiable,* she changed her mind because she's a big Victoria Worthington Stone fan?"

"Yeah," Meena said. She took a bite from the mini-Butterfinger she'd pulled from her secret snack drawer. "And she hates Jon but she pretends she doesn't."

"What's she hate your brother for?" Now Leisha sounded surprised.

"She thinks he's a mooch for moving in with me," Meena said. "The real question is, how am I going to get out of going to her party?"

"Uh," Leisha said, "no offense . . . but why wouldn't you go? Last I heard, your social calendar wasn't exactly jam-packed."

"Yeah, well," Meena said, "I don't have time to be hobnobbing with alleged Romanian princes when I need to be worrying about what's going to happen next to Victoria Worthington Stone and her vulnerable yet headstrong daughter, Tabitha." Meena took another bite of her mini-Butterfinger. The important thing was to make each one last as long as possible, which was difficult, because they were so small.

"Stupid of me," Leisha said. "Of course. So what *is* going to happen to Victoria Worthington Stone and her vulnerable yet headstrong daughter, Tabitha?"

Meena sighed. "One guess. It came down from on high today. Written on a stone tablet from Consumer Dynamics Inc. itself."

"What was it?"

"*Lust* started a vampire story arc, and they're killing us in the ratings. So . . ."

Leisha let out a little burble of laughter. "Oh, yeah. Gregory Bane. Guys have been asking me to do their hair like his for weeks. Like it's an actual *style* and not something accomplished with a razor blade and some mousse. People are psycho for that guy."

"Tell me about it." Meena spun around in her office chair so she could look away from her computer screen and out over the gray valley of skyscrapers that made up Fifty-third Street between Madison and Fifth. She knew that, somewhere out there, Yalena was finding out that her dreams of a new life in America weren't exactly turning out the way she'd expected them to. Meena wondered how long it would be before she'd call. Or if she'd ever call. "I don't get it. The guy looks like a toothpick. With hair."

Leisha bubbled with more laughter. Meena loved the sound of Leisha's laughter. It cheered her up and reminded her of the old days, before they'd both ended up with mortgages.

Still, Meena felt obligated to say, "It's not funny. You know how I feel about vampires."

"Yeah," Leisha said, sounding a little bored. "What is it you're always saying again? In the cult of monster misogyny, vampires are king?"

"Well," Meena said, "they do always seem to choose to prey on pretty female victims. And yet for some reason, women find this sexy."

"I don't," Leisha said. "I want to be killed by Frankenstein. I like 'em big. And stupid. Don't tell my husband."

"Even though these guys admit over and over to wanting to kill us," Meena went on, "the idea that they're nobly restraining themselves from doing so is supposed to be attractive? Excuse me, but how is knowing a guy wants to kill you hot?"

"The fact that he wants to but doesn't makes some girls feel special," Leisha said simply. "Plus, vampires are all rich. I could deal with having some rich guy who wants to kill me—but is nobly restraining himself—being super into me right now. Adam doesn't have a job, but he won't even help with the laundry."

"Vampires aren't real!" Meena shouted into the phone.

"Calm down. Look, I don't see what the big deal is," Leisha said. "If someone who can tell how everyone she meets is going to die can exist, why can't vampires?"

Meena took a deep breath. "Did I tell you Shoshona got the gig as head writer? Why don't you just twist the knife?"

"Oh, my God." Leisha sounded apologetic. "I'm so, so sorry, Meen. What are you going to do?"

"What *can* I do?" Meena asked. "Wait it out. She's going to screw up eventually. Hopefully when she does, the show and I will both still be here, and I can step in and save the day."

"Got it," Leisha said. "Hero complex."

Meena knit her brows. "*What?*"

"Vampires are monster misogynists," Leisha said. "And you have a hero complex. You always have. Of course you think you're going to save the show. And probably the world, while you're at it."

Meena snorted. "Right. Enough about me. How's Adam?"

"Hasn't gotten off the couch in three days," Leisha replied.

Meena nodded, forgetting that Leisha couldn't see her. "That's normal for the first month after a layoff."

"He just lies there in front of CNN, like a zombie. He's starting to freak out about this serial killer thing."

"What serial killer thing?" Then Meena remembered what Shoshona had been talking about in her meeting with Sy. "Oh, that thing with the dead girls, in the parks?"

"Exactly. You know, he actually grunted at me the other day when I asked him if he'd picked up the mail from the box downstairs."

Meena sighed. "Jon was the same way after he lost his job and had to move in with me. At least he does laundry now. Only because I have a washer-dryer unit in the apartment and you can't help tripping over the piles on the way to it."

"I asked Adam when he was going to get started with the baby's room," Leisha said. "Or the baby's alcove, I guess I should call it, since that room is so small, it's practically a closet. Still, he has to put a door on it, and the drywall, and paint it and everything. You know what he said? It's still too early and that there's plenty of time. Thomas is coming in two months! Sometimes I don't know if we're going to make it. I really don't."

"Yes, you will," Meena said soothingly. "We'll get through all of this. Really, we will."

Meena didn't believe this, of course. It had been months since her brother, Jon, had been laid off from the investment company where he'd worked as a systems analyst, and he was no closer to finding a job than he'd been the day of his firing . . . same as Leisha's husband, Adam, who'd been Jon's college roommate before Jon had introduced him to Leisha. The few jobs that were out there in their fields had hundreds, maybe thousands, of equally qualified applicants vying for them.

"Is that a prediction?" Leisha asked.

"It is," Meena said firmly.

"I'm holding you to that," Leisha said. "Well, good luck with the prince. I'd wear black. Black is always appropriate. Even for meeting royalty." She hung up.

Meena set the receiver down, chewing her lower lip. She hated lying to Leisha.

Because things *weren't* going to be fine.

Something was wrong. Leisha kept telling Meena that her due date was two months away.

And maybe that's what her doctor had said.

But the doctor was wrong. Every time Leisha said it—"Thomas is coming in two months"—Meena felt an uncomfortable twinge.

The baby—Meena was positive—was coming *next* month. Possibly even sooner than that.

And Thomas! Leisha and Adam wanted to name their baby *Thomas Weinberg*!

That kid was going to be a pretty funny-looking Thomas, considering that it was a girl and not a boy.

But how did you tell an expectant mother that everything her doctor was saying was wrong . . . when it was all just based on a *feeling*? Especially when all of your previous predictions had been about death, not a new life?

Easy. You didn't tell her at all. You kept your mouth zipped up tight.

Turning back to her computer monitor, Meena was confronted again with Mary Lou's e-mail. Sometimes she found it hard to believe there were still people who didn't have to work for a living . . . ladies with *princes* for relatives who did nothing but plan elaborate parties and use their husband's credit card to go shopping all day.

And then meanwhile there were girls like Yalena, being preyed upon by scumbags like her boyfriend, Gerald, about whom the cops could do exactly nothing. . . .

But these people existed.

And they lived right in her building. Right next door to her, in fact.

Meena resolutely hit Delete, then opened a new document and began to write.

Chapter Nine

L ucien Antonescu did not like to fly commercially, but not, perhaps, for the same reasons other people might dislike it. He had no control issues—other than his concerns about controlling his own rage—and of course no fear of death. The idea of a fiery or otherwise painful end did not trouble him in any way.

He was, however, disturbed by the way the airlines packed their customers into the metal tubes they were currently calling "planes," then expected them to sit in those impossibly small, cramped excuses for "seats" for so many hours on end, with no exercise or fresh air.

So it had been some time since Lucien Antonescu had been on an airplane he himself did not own (his personal Learjet was ideal for most trips but not powerful enough for nonstop transatlantic flight). When asked to speak at an overseas conference or tour for one of his books, Lucien tended simply to decline. He wasn't fond of publicity in any case . . .

But today Lucien was flying first class. The seats there were designed as individual compartments, so that other passengers seated in front of, behind, or beside him were not visible.

At a certain point during the flight, the attractive and very pleasant stewardess—they were called flight attendants now, he reminded himself—presented him with a menu from which he was asked to choose from a dizzying selection of food choices and wines, including some quite decent Italian Barolos. . . .

Later, after the pilot turned out the lights, the flight attendant asked him if he'd like her to make his bed for him. He accepted, purely out of curiosity. What bed? His wide and spacious seat, it transpired, automatically folded out into a reasonably sized (though not for him, being several inches over six feet tall) bed, all at the touch of a button.

The lovely flight attendant then produced a padded mattress from yet another hidden recess, real sheets that she "tucked in," a duvet, and a pillow, which she fluffed.

She then handed him a cloth bag containing a large pair of designer pajamas, a toothbrush and paste, and an eye mask.

Finally, she wished him good night with a smile. He smiled back, not because he had any intention of changing into the pajamas or of going to sleep, but because he found the entire procedure—and her—so utterly charming.

His smile made her blush. She was divorced from an unscrupulous man who had been cheating on her throughout their eight-year marriage and was supporting their toddler on her own. She wished only that her ex-husband would pay his child support on time and visit their daughter once in a while. She did not tell Lucien these things . . . but then, she did not have to. He knew them because he could not be around people without their secret thoughts intruding upon his own. It was something to which he'd grown accustomed over the years, something that he occasionally enjoyed. It made him feel human again.

Almost.

She excused herself to see to another passenger, a corpulent businessman seated across the spacious aisle, in 6J. The passenger in seat 6J could not seem to stop complaining: His pillow was not soft enough, his pajamas were not large enough, his toothbrush bristles were too stiff, and his champagne glass was not filled quickly enough.

Based on Lucien's observations, the man in 6J was pressing the call button approximately every four to five minutes, annoying both the flight attendant and the lady in the seat in front of him, who raised her sleeping mask and peeked out from her darkened compartment to see what all the commotion was about. She had an important meeting in the morning and needed to get her rest.

Lucien rose while the flight attendant slipped back to the galley to fetch the businessman another pillow. Then he stepped across the aisle to pay a visit to 6J.

"What do *you* want?" The man—whose mind was as shallow as a thimble—looked up to sneer at Lucien.

When the flight attendant came back, she was surprised to find the passenger in 6J appearing alarmingly pale and in such a deep sleep, he seemed almost to be comatose. She threw a quick, questioning glance around the cabin, meeting Lucien's gaze, for he was standing, reaching for a book he'd left in the overhead bin.

"Tired out from all that champagne, I expect," Lucien said to her. "Not used to so much alcohol at such a high altitude." He gave her a wink.

The flight attendant hesitated, then, as if transfixed by Lucien's grin, smiled shyly back and offered him the extra pillow.

"Why, thank you," he said.

Later, as he strolled along the darkened aisles while the jet hurtled through the night sky toward New York, listening to the breathing of the unconscious passengers and sampling their dreams, Lucien looked down at their bare, vulnerable throats as they dozed and thought that really, someone should do something to make airline travel more enjoyable for everyone, not just the privileged few in first class.

Chapter Ten

6:30 P.M. EST, Tuesday, April 13
910 Park Avenue
New York, New York

Meena stabbed the Up button, then looked around furtively. She was tired after her long day and hoped one thing—just this one little thing—would go her way.

And that was slipping onto the elevator of the building in which she lived without running into her neighbor Mary Lou, so that she could take the eleven-story ride to their floor in restful silence.

Meena's building—910 Park Avenue—was elegant, with a doorman guarding its shiny brass doors, a marble lobby, a crystal chandelier, and an underground garage with parking spaces for which residents could pay an additional $500 per month (though Meena would have preferred to put that money toward a certain Marc Jacobs jewel-encrusted dragon tote . . . if she could have afforded an extra $500 a month, which she couldn't).

But her apartment didn't exactly live up to the building's elegance: it needed repainting badly; the moldings along the ceilings were crumbling; the parquet floor needed sanding; the antique fireplaces didn't work; and the French doors leading to the minuscule balcony that looked out over her neighbor Mary Lou's terrace (which was practically the size of Meena's whole apartment) stuck. And she was running out of closet space.

The important thing was, it was hers—or at least it would be, when she finally paid David back for his share of the down payment. They'd been fortunate to have bought when the market was at rock bottom and the previous owners had been divorcing and desperate to sell . . . and just as a small inheritance from Meena's great-aunt Wilhelmina, for whom she'd been named (her mother had spelled it Meena for fear that her teachers and classmates might forever mispronounce her name "Myna"), finally came through.

Though David was long gone, Meena never pictured her apartment as a place to which she could bring back a date. But when she'd seen Shoshona leaving the office with a good-looking guy (whom she now realized had to have been the infamous Stefan Dominic; Meena had only managed to catch a glimpse of the back of his dark head before the two of them had disappeared onto the elevator for after-work drinks), she'd felt a twinge of envy.

Meena couldn't even remember the last time she'd been on a date . . . unless she counted the first—and last—time she'd let Mary Lou set her up with a guy, someone from her husband's office . . . the one whom Meena had felt compelled to inform over calamari when they'd met at a trendy restaurant downtown that he needed to have his cholesterol checked, or he was going to have a heart attack before the age of thirty-five.

Needless to say, he'd never called for a second date.

But hopefully he *had* called his doctor and gotten on Lipitor.

And yet she persevered in praying for the one thing that never, ever seemed to come true.

With the frequency of their encounters, Meena might as well have been dating her neighbor.

Every morning, poof! Mary Lou appeared, just as Meena pushed the Down button. Same thing each evening.

It was uncanny.

And every single time, any hope of having a civilized commute was shot.

Because then Meena was forced to listen to Mary Lou wax enthusiastic about whatever new guy she'd met whom she was convinced would be just perfect for Meena or whatever incredible story line idea she'd thought up the night before for *Insatiable*.

Oh, really? Meena would be forced to reply politely. *Thank you, Mary Lou. Actually, I'm seeing someone. Someone from my office.*

Or, *No, really, I'll definitely run your idea that Victoria Worthington Stone should become foreign ambassador to Brazil by Fran and Stan. I'm sure they'll love that.*

Except that there was no guy from Meena's office whom she was seeing (except Paul, platonically; he'd been happily married with three kids for twenty-five years), and the countess had never, not even once, come up with a single usable story line for her favorite character, Victoria Worthington Stone.

It was too bad, because Meena genuinely liked warm, if somewhat over-the-top Mary Lou and her unassuming, slightly harassed-looking husband, Emil.

It was just that Meena was beginning to feel a little how Ned must have felt the day of his nervous breakdown in the ABN dining room . . . especially since David had left, and Mary Lou had become obsessed with Meena's love life. How was Meena going to bring a date home if her older brother was always hanging around the apartment, making fettuccine Alfredo? Someone just needed to give Meena a little push in the right direction.

And Mary Lou had obviously appointed herself that person.

This became especially obvious that day, when Meena was once again unable to meet her goal of avoiding the countess at the elevator. . . .

Poof!

There she was.

"Meena!" the countess cried. "I'm so glad I ran into you! Did you get my e-mail? Emil's cousin, the prince, is coming to town. You're going to love him; he's a writer, just like you. Only he writes books, not for a soap opera. A professor of ancient Romanian history, actually. You got my e-mail about the dinner party I'm having in his honor this Thursday, right? Do you think you'll be able to make it?"

"Oh," Meena said. "I don't know. Things are crazy at work—"

"Oh, your *job*!" Meena realized she should have kept her mouth shut, since Mary Lou warmed to the subject immediately. "You work way too hard at that job of yours. Not that I don't love every minute of it. Last week when Victoria made out with Father Juan Carlos in the vestibule after she went to confession over her guilt about sleeping with her daughter's riding instructor, I had to stuff a napkin in my mouth to keep from screaming my head off and startling the maid while she was vacuuming, I was *that* excited. That was so brilliant! That story line was one of yours, wasn't it?"

Meena inclined her head modestly. She *was* proud of the Victoria-and-the-hot-priest story line. It was different when it was a *priest* who was nobly restraining himself from sleeping with a woman. Father Juan Carlos didn't also want to kill Victoria.

"Well, actually—" she started to say, but Mary Lou interrupted her.

"Still, you're going to drive yourself into early menopause slaving away for that show. Anyway, listen . . ."

With a ding the elevator doors opened, and Meena and the countess stepped inside to begin what would, for Meena, anyway, be the eons-long ride up.

Mary Lou then proceeded to give Meena a long description of the castle in which the prince spent his summers in Romania. Mary Lou was intimately acquainted with it, because it was near the castle where she and her husband summered for two months every year—two blissful months during which Meena was able to ride the elevator countess-free.

By floor five, Meena was wondering why she'd never gotten a feeling about Mary Lou's or her husband Emil's impending demises. It was odd, really.

On the other hand, it was possible her power to predict death, which had shown up when she'd reached her tweens, was starting to wane now that she was approaching thirty (a girl could dream).

More likely, however, given Meena's luck, it was morphing into something else . . . look at the strange feelings she got around Leisha and her baby.

By the tenth floor, Meena had heard all she could stand about Saxon architectural influences.

"Oh, would you look at that," Meena said when the elevator doors finally, and mercifully, opened at their floor.

"Oh, Meena," the countess said as the two of them strolled toward their respective doors. "I forgot to ask. How's your brother doing?"

And there it was. The Head Tilt.

The Head Tilt was accompanied, of course, by the Sympathetic Look. The countess was no stranger to Botox, as Meena well knew, since the countess had to be well over forty, but her face was as unlined as if she were Meena's age—perhaps because Mary Lou had such an extraordinary collection of picture hats, as well as gloves, which she wore with fierce resolution to keep out the sun. Today's was a gargantuan maroon concoction.

So it was all there, the Head Tilt, the "eleven" between the eyebrows (two crinkled lines of concern), the purse of the lips as if to say, *I care. Deeply. Tell me: How's your brother doing?*

"Jon's doing great," Meena said with as much enthusiasm as she could muster, given how many times a week she was forced to repeat this phrase. "Really great. Working out, doing a lot of reading, even cooking. He tried a new recipe last night for dinner. He made a great Chinese orange beef for me that he got out of the *Times.* It was delicious!"

This was an outright lie. It had actually been terrible and Meena had been furious with Jon for even attempting it. He was no great chef. Steaks on Meena's hibachi on the balcony were his forté, not something they could just as easily have ordered in. She'd had to throw it down the garbage chute. Meena hoped the countess and her husband Emil hadn't smelled it when they'd come home from whatever benefit they'd been attending. They were always going to—when they weren't hosting—charity events, all over the city, late into the night, and had their names mentioned on the society pages regularly, as much for their generous gifts as for their party-hopping.

"Oh!" Mary Lou flattened her hand against the front of her Chanel jacket. "That's great. I so admire what you're doing, letting him live with you until he gets back on his feet. So generous. The prince just loves generous people, and so he'll just love you. Of course . . ." Mary Lou brought her hand away, and the seven- or eight-carat diamond that she'd been wearing beneath the glove she'd stripped away flashed in the glow from the overhead light in the hallway. "Do bring Jon when you come over for dinner to meet the prince on Thursday night. He's always welcome as well. Such a sweet young man."

Meena kept a smile frozen on her face.

"Well, thanks," Meena said with forced cheer. "But I'm not sure about our plans. I'll let you know. Have a good night!"

"You, too," Mary Lou said. "*Au revoir!*"

One thing, Meena thought as she hurried toward her apartment. One good thing could still happen to her today. She was never going to give up hope. Without hope, what did you have?

Nothing. That's what.

She could still find the ruby dragon tote. Maybe online, used somewhere.

Except that, even used, it would still be more expensive than she could afford. It would be selfish and horrible of her to buy something so frivolous that she clearly didn't need, especially when so many people were out of work and could barely afford food and had horrible people like Yalena's boyfriend preying on them.

She was never going to buy the bag, of course. Not even used.

But it was important to have hope.

Chapter Eleven

HAVE WHAT IT TAKES TO JOIN THE NYPD?

In order to be considered for appointment in the NYPD, you must pass a series of medical, physical, and psychological examinations to determine your suitability. Want to learn more about our requirements?

Jon, staring at the computer screen, shrugged, took another sip of his Gatorade, and clicked *Learn more.*

Applicants must be at least 17½ years of age by the last day of filing of the exam they are applying for.

"Oh, yeah," Jon said. "That's what I'm talking about."

Meena's dog, Jack Bauer, hearing the sound of a human voice, jumped up from his dog bed and trotted curiously over to the couch to see what was happening. Jon tilted his bottle of Gatorade in the dog's direction in a toast and kept reading happily.

Applicants must not have reached their 35th birthday on or before the first day of filing of the exam they are applying for.

"Done," he said to Jack Bauer. "We are so joining the NYPD!"

Jack Bauer tilted his head questioningly, sat down on his haunches, and yipped.

"Yes." Jon put down his Gatorade, picked up the phone, and dialed. As soon as the person on the other end lifted the receiver, he said, "Dude. We're joining the NYPD."

"The hell we are," Adam said. "I'm about to be a father. I may need a job, but not one where I get my ass shot off. Did you know there's a serial killer on the loose out there?"

"I'm sure there are several," Jon said. He put his size-twelve feet on his sister's coffee table. Jack Bauer, inspired by this development, leapt onto the couch, where he was strictly forbidden by Meena from sitting. Jon moved over a little to make room for him. "And we're going to catch them. Because guess what? The New York City Police Department? Hiring. All you gotta be is over seventeen and a half years of age and under thirty-five. Bingo. That's us."

"Also crazy. Did you read that part? How somebody would have to be crazy to apply to be a cop in this freaking city?"

"Yes, in addition to a written and physical exam, there is a psych evaluation," Jon said, glancing at his laptop. "And you might have some problems passing that part, seeing as how you were a mortgage-backed-security trader."

"Are you done?" Adam asked. "Because I have to go now."

"Yeah," Jon said. "Okay, go to the NYPD website. I really think we should do this. We can do something to make a difference, Weinberg. We can arrest perps. We can help little abused children."

"Listen to you," Adam said. But Jon could hear clicking in the background and knew Weinberg was doing as he'd asked him to. "Perps. Like you know anything about perps. Have you been watching *The Wire* again?"

"I'm serious. Think about it. What did we do at our last jobs? Sure, we made a ton of cash, for other people and for ourselves. But did we really touch people's lives in a meaningful way? No."

"I beg to differ," Adam said. "I handled the Alaska Teachers' Union pension fund."

"And," Jon said, "what happened to it, Adam?"

Adam grumbled, "It wasn't my fault."

"Those teachers are gonna be fine," Jon said. "Okay, probably not. But maybe getting laid off is a blessing in disguise. This could be our chance to give back what we lost. By helping people who are really in need."

"And carry guns," Adam pointed out. "Admit it, Harper. The part you like is the part where we get guns."

"The thought that we would be issued firearms and permission to legally carry them did cross my mind," Jon said. "But it's really about helping people, Weinberg. Do you honestly just want to let this serial killer you're worried about roam around free?"

"No," Adam said. "I want to find a job doing what I'm trained to do. I would like to implement cash and derivatives strategies and execute trades while communicating market information and trends to other investment professionals within the firm."

"Really?" Jon couldn't hide his disappointment. "That's the line you're going with on the résumé?"

"That's what I told the HR rep at TransCarta," Adam said. "Which is the only place that seems to be hiring right now."

"When you could be saving lives."

"Let me ask you something," Adam said. "Have you run this one by your sister?"

"What do you mean?" Jon asked defensively.

"I think you know what I mean," Adam said. "I mean, have you told that bat-shit-crazy sister of yours that you're thinking of applying for a job with the NYPD?"

"I don't have to tell my sister everything I'm thinking about doing," Jon said stiffly.

"Oh, yeah?" Adam laughed in an evil way. "Well, I'm not applying for a job with the NYPD unless your sister says she sees the two of us retiring as lieutenants or whatever."

Jon said, with a spurt of irritation, "You should know by now it doesn't work that way with her."

"Yeah," Adam said. "I guess if it did, neither of us would be in this situation, would we?"

Jon sighed. His sister's gift had never exactly made life easier for him. Why couldn't she have been able to predict winning lottery numbers, or which girl in the bar was most likely to sleep with him, or something actually useful? Hearing the ways in which he might conceivably die was interesting, Jon supposed.

But he'd rather have gotten rich. Or laid.

Jon heard the scrape of Meena's key in the lock. Jack Bauer heard it too, and quickly leapt off the couch to return to his dog bed.

Jon said, "We'll talk about this later. I gotta go," to Adam, then hung up and took his feet off the coffee table.

Meena came in looking flustered and fresh faced, as she always did when she returned from anywhere. She asked, "Was Jack Bauer on the couch just now?"

"Of course not," Jon said, getting up. "How was your day, dear?"

"It sucked. I met a girl on the subway I think is going to end up sold into white slavery and then killed."

"Sweet," Jon said sarcastically.

"Tell me about it," Meena said. "And Shoshona got the head writer gig. And the network is mandating a crappy vampire story line, so my beautiful and totally awe-inspiring proposal about the bad boy with the police chief dad was completely dead on arrival."

"Shoshona got the head writer gig?" Jon asked. "That blows. You gave the subway girl your card, didn't you?"

"Yeah," Meena said, throwing her keys into the little tray on the kitchen counter, which she'd started keeping there for that purpose after Jon finally pointed out that her psychic power was useless at finding the things she kept losing. "Hopefully she'll call."

"What about Taylor?" Jon asked. He tried to keep his voice casual. He'd had a crush on Taylor Mackenzie—whom his sister had pointed out many times was way too young for him—since Meena had first started writing for the show.

"She's the one getting the new vampire boyfriend," Meena said. "They've got Gregory Bane's best friend coming in to read with her on Friday. He's hot, apparently. I think I saw him leaving the office with Shoshona tonight. But it was mostly only the back of his head."

Jon glanced at his reflection in the round antique mirror Meena had hanging above the dining table.

"*I'm* hot," he said, admiring his own reflection. "What do you think? Don't I look like vampire material to you?"

Meena snorted. "Right. Playing a chorus member in the musical *Mame* when you were in high school doesn't count as acting experience. Especially since you only did it for extra credit to keep from getting kicked off the baseball team thanks to your D in Spanish."

She shrugged out of her jacket and crossed the room to meet Jack Bauer, who'd run over to give her a welcome lick.

"And how's my little man?" she asked. "Did you save the world today? I think you did. I think you saved the world from nuclear annihilation, just like you do every single twenty-four hours. Look at you. Just look at you."

Jack Bauer was a Pomeranian-chow mix Meena had insisted on bringing home from the ASPCA the first time they'd ever set foot in it, "just to look," after David had walked out on her and she'd been pretty much comatose with depression. The tiny mutt had been sitting in a big empty cage by himself, his huge brown eyes so filled with anxiety that Meena had remarked that, with his blond fur, he resembled Kiefer Sutherland during a particularly dramatic moment on the television show *24*.

When the dog had fallen into her arms as soon as the cage door was opened, showering her face with grateful kisses, the inevitable adoption was sealed, and the name Jack Bauer stuck, because the anxious look in the mutt's eyes rarely vanished all the way, unless he was lounging in the apartment by Meena's side.

"He saved the world, all right," Jon said. "He tried to hump a maltipoo in the small dog run at Carl Schurz Park."

"My hero," Meena cried, scooping the dog up and hugging him. "Keep showing your male dominance, even though you've been fixed." She turned to Jon. "So, what did you do today?"

"I was totally going to make chicken," Jon said. "But when I got to the store none of the chickens looked any good."

"Really?" Meena said, going over to the couch and reaching for the remote.

"Yeah," Jon said. "They were all past their expiration dates. It was like the Perdue delivery didn't come in on time or something."

"Let's just order in," she said. She'd flipped on the news. "We haven't had Thai in a while."

He felt a surge of relief.

"Thai sounds great. Or Indian."

"Indian sounds good, too," she said. "Oh, my God, we got invited to the countess's on Thursday. If we keep the lights out," she added, like this was a perfectly reasonable way to deal with the problem, "we don't have to worry about them seeing that we're home under the crack in the door."

"Meena." Jon loved his sister.

But she was totally and completely insane.

And she always had been.

Meena shook her head. "Jon. You know I can't help but love her. But she's trying to fix me up with some Romanian prince her husband's related to. Come on."

"A prince?" Jon raised his eyebrows. "Seriously? Is he rich?"

"I don't want to meet a prince," Meena said. She sounded mad. She *looked* mad. "I'm already having the worst week of my life, and it's only Tuesday!"

Jon knew Meena well enough to know this wasn't about Shoshona getting the job, or the girl she'd met on the subway, or even the show, which she adored.

"What," he said flatly. "What did you see?"

"Nothing," she said, throwing him a confused look. "I don't know what you're talking about."

"You know something," Jon said. "You know what I'm talking about. Who is it about? Me? It's about me, isn't it? Just tell me. I can take it. When am I going? Is it this week?"

Meena looked away. "What? No. You're fine. I don't know what you're talking about."

Jon shook his head. He didn't think he was wrong. He'd lived with his kid sister long enough to recognize the signs.

She obviously knew something about somebody now . . . only who? And why wasn't she saying?

"Is it Mom and Dad?" he asked. "I thought you said they were fine. I mean, relatively speaking."

"They *are* fine." Meena glared at him. "For two people who continue to whoop it up at happy hour every night down in Boca like they think they're F. Scott and Zelda Fitzgerald."

"Then I don't get it," Jon said. "Your crazy-ass millionaire neighbor who thinks she's a countess invited you to a dinner party at her place to meet a real Romanian prince on Thursday night. And you're telling me you don't think you're going to get any story ideas out of that? Are you serious?"

Meena looked at him, her big dark eyes luminous in the light from the sun setting just outside her windows, turning the sky from rosy pink to a delicate lavender. Finally she smiled.

"You're right," she said. "How could I miss such a fantastic opportunity, so rich with the promise of pretentious buffoonery for me to mock later on *Insatiable*? I have a professional duty to be there."

"Absolutely," Jon said.

"I'll RSVP yes to the countess," Meena said.

"Way to go." Jon reached out to ruffle her short, boyishly cut dark hair. "I'll go order us some samosas."

Meena grinned and turned up the volume on the news, which was all about how they still hadn't been able to identify any of the victims of what they were now calling the Park Strangler. They were urging any members of the public who might recognize the women to come forward.

"After all," Meena said thoughtfully, clearly not paying attention to the information the grim-faced anchorwoman was doling out, "Victoria Worthington Stone's dated plenty of doctors, lawyers, millionaires, shipping magnates, gangsters, murderers, maniacs, cops, cowboys, priests, and once even her own half brother—until she found out who he really was. It's about time she dated a prince."

"That's the spirit," Jon said, and started dialing.

Chapter Twelve

Alaric Wulf wasn't surprised to find that Sarah, like most women—and men—in love with a vampire, was initially resistant to the idea of giving up the address of her lover.

"Just tell me where he is, and I'll let you live."

Sarah had hedged for a while. Like most victims, she didn't care anymore about her own life. Her brain was too nutrient deprived. She cared only about protecting her sire.

Until Alaric finally put his sword to her throat.

The Palatine Guard was listed in most encyclopedias and search engines as a now-defunct military unit of the Vatican, formed to defend Rome against attack from foreign invaders.

This was partly true: the Palatine Guard was a military unit of the Vatican.

But it was hardly defunct. And the invaders it had been formed to defend against weren't foreign.

They were demon.

And the Guards weren't defending just Rome from them, but the entire world.

Members of the Guard had different methods for getting victims of these demons, who were often besotted by their attackers, to talk.

Abraham Holtzman—currently the Guard's most senior officer, who'd trained both Alaric and Martin—had always preferred deception. He'd flash a fake card from a fancy (fictitious) legal firm, explaining that he'd been hired by the vampire's estranged family to deliver a large inheritance check.

Often the victim was so flustered by delighted surprise that she didn't notice Holtzman had never even mentioned the vamp's name.

That was because he didn't know it.

But that was Holtzman. Alaric had always suspected that Holtzman could get away with this because he was so scholarly looking. His Jewish parents had been appalled when he'd gone to work for the Vatican, though Holtzman hadn't converted. (Conversion was not a job requirement. It was difficult enough to find anyone able to keep his head while swinging a sword at a screaming succubus, let alone someone who was also a devoted Catholic. Palatine Guard members were of a wide mix of religions . . . even, like Alaric, complete nonbelievers.)

It helped Holtzman's ruse, Alaric supposed, that he *looked* like a lawyer.

Still, there was nothing wrong with looking like a muscle-bound demon-hunter . . . especially if that was what one was. Alaric didn't have degrees in anything, except chopping the heads off vampires and returning their victims to full humanity once more.

So Alaric didn't waste time on ruses the way Holtzman did. Especially not when it came to Sarah. He got straight to the point . . . by applying Señor Sticky to her throat.

When she finally stammered, "Felix . . . Felix lives in a loft over an antiques store on West Fourth . . . but please . . . ," he grabbed her by the back of the neck and stuffed her into the passenger seat of his rental car. He didn't need her texting her undead lover any warnings so Felix could call his vamp friends and set up a trap.

It wasn't the most uplifting drive over to Felix's place. Especially because Sarah sobbed most of the way and whispered, "Please, please . . . don't hurt him. You don't understand . . . he doesn't want to be the way he is. He hates what he is. He hates that he has to . . . hurt me."

"Yes?" Alaric glanced at her. He'd turned the car radio to the heavy metal station. He didn't particularly like heavy metal, but he needed something loud enough to drown out the sound of her sniffling. "So why do you let him do it, then?"

"Because," Sarah said, sniffling, "he'll die if I don't."

"You're wrong about that," Alaric said. "He can't die unless someone stabs him with a wooden stake through the heart or cuts off his head. Or, alternatively, if someone shoves him into some direct sunlight or completely immerses his body in holy water. But then," he added, throwing a glance her way, "you must know all this."

"None of that's true," Sarah said. "He told me all those things were myths. Also about how vampires can live on animal blood. He said if they do that, they'll die. That's why he has to drink my blood. To stay alive."

Alaric rolled his eyes. "Do you realize girls like you have been falling for that one for centuries? Vamps just don't *like* animal blood. It weakens them. And they don't look as nice after they've been drinking it for a while. And if they're anything, vamps are vain. Human blood's like filet mignon to them. So if he told you he'll die if you don't let him drink your blood, he's a damned liar, in addition to being a putrid stinking woman-abusing soulless abomination."

Sarah seemed to find his language objectionable, since this statement only made her weep harder.

Alaric felt a little bad about this. Holtzman was always telling him that he needed to work on his people skills more.

Accordingly, Alaric passed her a tissue from the little packet the rental car agency had left in the car.

"You're mean," Sarah said, blowing her nose into the tissue. "Felix isn't a soulless abomination. He's sensitive. He has feelings. He reads me poetry. Shakespeare."

Alaric wanted to pull the car over so he could throw up, but they didn't have time. The sooner they got this over with, the sooner he could go back to the hotel; order some room service; have a nice, relaxing bath (in the world's tiniest tub, which had those grainy strips attached to the bottom, so guests wouldn't slip in the shower—this was Alaric's number one pet peeve about less-than-five-star hotels; he was a grown man, he knew how to stand without falling in the tub); and go to bed.

Then, tomorrow morning, he'd fly to New York, check into the Peninsula, find the prince, and kill him.

This made him quite happy to think about.

"This," Alaric explained to Sarah in what he thought was a kindly voice, "isn't love you're feeling. Only dopamine. Because Felix isn't like anyone else you know. Being a creature of the night, he's new and exciting and activates a neurotransmitter in your brain that releases feelings of euphoria when you're around him . . . especially because you know you can never actually be together, and he seems complicated, and perhaps even sensitive and vulnerable at times. But I can assure you: he's anything but."

"How dare you?" Sarah demanded hotly. "It isn't dopa . . . whatever! It's love! *Love!*"

Alaric wanted to argue. Vampires were incapable of love—human love—because they didn't have hearts. Well, technically, he supposed they *possessed* hearts, since that's what he had to stab a stake into in order to kill them. But their hearts didn't pump blood or beat.

So how could they feel love, much less return it?

But arguing with a teenager over the semantics of vampire love didn't seem like a winning proposition to him.

"Oh, come on, then," Alaric couldn't help saying finally, noticing that his passenger continued to sob quietly to herself. "It's not all bad."

"How?" Sarah demanded, flashing an aggravated look at him. "How is this not all bad? You're going to try to kill my boyfriend!"

"True," Alaric said. They were nearly to the address she'd given him. "But look at it this way. He promised to turn you into a vampire, didn't he?"

"Yes," Sarah said, sounding a bit surprised. "He said he was going to turn me, just as soon as he got his strength up. Then I'll be beautiful, like him. And immortal."

"Right," Alaric said a little sarcastically. He knew this Felix had no intention whatsoever of turning her. Doing so would deprive him of his primary food source.

What Alaric was sure the vampire would do instead was string her along for a few more months; then, when she grew too sickly from anemia to be of any more use to him, he'd move on to some healthier host. He'd probably tell her it was him, not her . . . that he needed time to "think about things." Then he'd disappear.

Then, after her broken heart—and even more broken body—had healed, Felix would probably find his way back to Sarah—and to Chattanooga—and start the cycle all over again. Unless Sarah found the strength to put her foot down and tell him no, she would *not* be abused in this way.

But that wouldn't happen. The vamps were just too alluring. And their victims just never seemed to think they deserved better than the treatment they were given. It was almost as if they were afraid to put their foot down, because they thought they'd never get anything better. . . .

But that was what Alaric was for. He would be Sarah's foot, since she didn't have the strength, or willpower, to put her own down. He'd make sure she got something better and stop the cycle from continuing. Permanently.

Alaric found a parking space . . . except that it was beside a fire hydrant.

It didn't matter. They wouldn't be there that long.

"Supposing he did turn you into one of his kind," he said, switching off the engine and turning to look at her, "then me, or one of my fellow officers, would only have to kill you eventually, because that's what we do. We're demon killers. And trust me, you really wouldn't want any of us on your tail. We'd be your worst nightmare. It's much better this way. This way, you'll stay a human, and maybe you can go to college and get a degree and a fun job doing something you like. Or maybe you can find some nice guy back at the Walmart you can go out with, even marry. And, assuming you want them, you two can have a few babies, and grow old and watch *them* have babies, and be grandparents someday. Wouldn't you like that? You could never have babies with Felix."

"Vampires can have babies," Sarah informed him. "I read it in a book."

"Yes," Alaric said, feeling annoyed. "Well, in books, the vampires struggle nobly against themselves not to bite you, because they love you so much. But that didn't exactly happen, did it? So the books aren't really very accurate, are they?"

Sarah glared at him.

"I hate you," she said.

Alaric nodded. "I know," he said. He reached across her and opened the car door. "Get out."

She looked at him blankly. "What?"

"Go on," he said. "I know you're dying to run ahead and give lover boy the heads-up. I'm going to let you. Tell him I'll let him go, on one condition."

Her entire demeanor changed. Suddenly, she was all that was accommodating and pleasant.

"What condition?" she asked eagerly.

"Tell him that if he tells me where I can find the prince, I'll let you both go. Then you can run off and have vampire babies together."

Alaric couldn't say the last part without laughing, though he did try, remembering that he was supposed to be working on his people skills.

Sarah evidently didn't notice.

"Oh, thank you!" Sarah was smiling as she scrambled from the car. "Thank you so much!"

"Not a problem," Alaric said. He watched as she ran across the sidewalk and up to an unobtrusive-looking door beside the display window of an antiques shop inside an industrial-looking building. He gathered his things as she pressed an intercom. Then he calmly strode to the alley, where, as he'd suspected, there was a fire escape. He leapt for the rusted metal ladder as he heard Felix's voice asking through the intercom, "Who is it?"

Then the buzzer went off, letting Sarah inside the building.

It only took Alaric a moment or two to climb to the roof of the building, and less than that to secure a grappling hook to the side of the building, then fasten the end of the rope to his belt.

A few seconds later, Alaric jumped from the roof, crashing through Felix's plate-glass living room windows. . .

. . . just as the vampire was putting on a black cloak to shield himself from the sun, preparing to make a run for it. Sarah screamed as UV-protection glass went flying everywhere.

The vampire, desperate to get out of the sun's rays, which could be fatal to him, threw himself at the front door.

"Now, Felix," Alaric said calmly. "You can't go that way, either."

A second later, Felix was shrieking. This was because Alaric had hurled a glass vial filled with holy water at the door. It burst over the knob, singeing the vampire's fingers as he reached for it. He drew his hand away, hissing with pain and cradling his smoking fingers.

"I thought you said you'd let him go if he told!" Sarah shouted with outrage.

"And I will," Alaric said, smiling at her. He turned toward Felix. "So," he said. "Where can I find your prince?"

Felix, who looked like a handsome boy of eighteen or twenty—and appeared from his taste in wall posters to have a fondness for the band Belle and Sebastian—curled back his lips to reveal a set of extremely strong white teeth. His incisors were unnaturally long and, true to his species, not unpointy.

"I'll never tell, demon hunter," he growled.

Then he threw back his head and let out a hiss, his long tongue darting in and out of his mouth like a lizard's tail.

Sarah looked shocked. She'd apparently never heard her boyfriend use that tone of voice before. Or seen his eyes glow red.

"Felix," she cried. "Just tell him! He said he'd let you go if you told."

When Felix swung his glowing red eyes and twisting tongue toward her, she staggered back a step. "Why did you bring him here, you stupid whore?" Felix demanded.

Horrified, Sarah started crying all over again.

Alaric took her tears as his cue that it would be all right with her if he performed his duty. So he stepped forward, swinging Señor Sticky free of its scabbard.

It was over in a matter of seconds. To his credit, the vampire put up a good fight.

But cornered by sunlight on one side and holy water on the other, he had nowhere to go. There was no escape.

Alaric didn't give him a chance for any last words. In his experience, vampires didn't really have anything that interesting or insightful to say. It was all Shakespeare and emo.

When he was done, he looked at the girl. She was curled up in a ball over by the broken window, weeping softly to herself.

But—and Alaric knew he wasn't imagining it—her hair had already begun to recover its luster, and there was color in her cheeks that hadn't been there before.

She'd be fine in a few days, if her parents fed her enough protein.

He sheathed his sword.

"Get up now," he said in what he hoped was a soothing voice. He was so bad at this part. Martin was the one who always knew the right thing to say. "I will drive you home to your mother."

She uncurled a little and looked at him coldly. "You said you wouldn't kill him if he told," she said. Her voice sounded stronger than before, and her eyes had a shine to them that had nothing to do with tears. She was, he knew, her own person again and no longer a pawn to a vampire sire. His killing Felix had released her.

"And he didn't tell," Alaric pointed out.

"You didn't give him a chance!" she cried.

But she was getting up, carefully avoiding looking in the direction where the body was.

Except that there was no body. Only clothes lay where Felix had been. He had to have been over a hundred years old. His bones were dust.

"He would never have told," Alaric said. "If he had told, the prince, or his minions, would have killed him, and far less gently than I did. He chose to die by my sword because he knew it would be quicker." He looked down at her. "They'd have killed you, too, you know, if they'd have found you here with him. They'd have fed on you until there was nothing left."

Sarah blinked. "You mean . . . he died to protect me? Oh . . . that's so sweet!"

Alaric wanted to show her the photographs he always carried of what some of her now former boyfriend's friends had done to Martin. How they'd bitten and peeled strips of his flesh off, just for fun. Vampires were incapable of sweetness.

But Holtzman, he knew, wouldn't approve of this.

Besides, his job there was done. She was free now.

And that meant it was time for him to go back to the hotel and pack for New York, to go after a vampire who might really prove a challenge to his sword arm, unlike her silly boyfriend.

So he only said, "Let's take you home now."

And that's exactly what he did.

Chapter Thirteen

10:00 P.M. EST, Tuesday, April 13
910 Park Avenue, Apt. 11A
New York, New York

What is this?" Emil walked into the spacious master bedroom he shared with his vivacious and slender wife, holding a printout of the e-mail he'd found on his desktop.

"Oh, hon," Mary Lou said as she breezed by on her way to her dressing table. "That's just a little Evite I sent out to all my girlfriends for the dinner party I'm having in Prince Lucien's honor on Thursday."

Emil felt a small but persistent sensation in the center of his belly that was not unlike being poked over and over by someone with very long nails . . . a sensation with which, as it happened, Emil was not unfamiliar.

"You sent out an *e-mail* about the prince?" he said. "You do realize that if this message falls into the wrong hands, it could jeopardize everything?"

"Oh, don't be such a ninny," Mary Lou said. "I only sent it to my very best friends. Whose hands is it going to fall into?"

Emil fought for inner patience.

"The Dracul, for one?" he said drily when he could speak again. "The Palatine Guard, for another? Not to mention the humans? All the people who'd like to see us, not to mention the prince, destroyed?"

"Oh, pooh," Mary Lou said. She sat down in front of the large mirror behind her dressing table and began removing her makeup.

"You're being melodramatic. No one wants to destroy us anymore. The prince has the Dracul under control. The Palatine Guard don't know where we are, and the humans love us! Look at how popular we are in books and on the TV. Why, if everyone found out, I'm sure I'd be invited onto *Oprah* as a special guest."

"Mary Lou!" Emil stared at her reflection in astonishment. "Someone is killing women! All over town! No one is going to be inviting you onto *Oprah* while women are being killed by a member of our brethren. And the prince isn't going to want a dinner party in his honor. He's going to prefer to keep a low profile while he's in town, *trying to find that killer.*"

"I have so many beautiful, intelligent female friends," Mary Lou said, gazing thoughtfully at herself. "Why shouldn't I show them off? The prince has been alone too long."

"Lucien's not here," Emil said, feeling as if he were drowning, "to find a wife. He's here on *business.* The murders—"

"And if he should happen to meet a nice girl," Mary Lou said, interrupting, "while he's here, would that be so terrible? Apparently he hasn't had any luck in his own country. But you know we have the most amazing women in the world right here in the good old U.S. of A—"

"Mary Lou." Emil stared uncomfortably at his wife's bare shoulders. "You understand that you're putting me in a terribly awkward position. Lucien asked that I not mention his arrival to anyone, and here you are sending out e-mails to everyone on your cc list, an e-mail that could be traced back—"

"Not everyone," Mary Lou said indignantly. "Just my best single girlfriends, and a few of the married ones so as not to make it look obvious he's being set up. None of them is employed by the Vatican, for goodness sake, or members of the Dracul. I just asked Linda and Tom, and Faith and Frank, and Carol from your office, and Becca and Ashley, and Meena from across the hall."

"Meena?" Emil was confused. Many things about his wife confused him. He was certain that even if they spent an eternity together—and it already felt like they had—he'd never fully understand her. "The prince . . . and *Meena Harper*? But she's—"

"Why not?" Mary Lou gave her naturally curly—and still naturally blond—hair a flip. "At first glance she may not seem like his type, but I like her. She's got that cute little figure, and a pixie cut suits her. Most women can't pull it off, you know, but she works it. And if the prince likes her, just think how grateful he'll be to us. Besides," she added with a shrug, "all she does is work to keep her and that no-good brother of hers financially afloat. I think she needs a break."

"She likes her job," Emil said, thinking of all the times he'd seen his neighbor in her pajamas barefoot in their floor's trash room, disgruntledly stuffing heavily crossed-out script pages down the chute to the incinerator.

Well, maybe she didn't *always* like her job.

"Oh, sure," Mary Lou said. "The soap opera thing. But do you think she'd work if she didn't have to?"

Emil thought about this. "Yes," he said.

"Well, that shows what you know about women, which is nothing. Look at those ladies she writes about on *Insatiable,* Victoria Worthington Stone and her daughter, Tabby. Victoria's never had a job in her life, except for that time she was a model. Oh, and a fashion designer. Oh, and when she was a race car driver, but that was only for a week before she crashed and lost the baby and was in that coma. Those aren't even real jobs. They say you write about what you wish would happen to you. So, obviously Meena wishes she didn't have a job."

"Or," Emil said, "she wishes she were a race car driver."

"And Prince Lucien would be able to provide for her." Mary Lou went on, ignoring him. "And since the prince likes writing, the two of them already have something in common."

"It's a very different kind of writing," Emil said. "Lucien writes historical nonfiction. And anyway, he made it very clear when I spoke to him that he wanted to keep his visit under the radar. We're at a very critical time with the Dracul. These murders—"

"Oh, stop being such a worrywart," Mary Lou said. "No man wouldn't want to have dinner with a lot of pretty ladies." She laughed and turned to poke her husband in his belly, which stuck out ever so slightly over the waistband of his trousers. "Don't tell me you wouldn't enjoy being the center of attention of me and all my friends. Not that you aren't . . ."

"Well." Emil felt the pressure in his gut receding slightly. "Maybe he won't mind so much. A man has to eat, after all."

"Exactly," Mary Lou exclaimed. "And so why not do it in the company of a lot of lovely, accomplished ladies?"

"Why not?" Emil asked.

Maybe, he thought, his wife was right:

The man did have to eat, after all.

Chapter Fourteen

Meena stared at the bright red numbers on the digital clock in her bedroom. Three forty-five. She had five hours before she had to leave for the office. Four more to sleep before she had to get up to start getting ready.

Except that she couldn't sleep. She lay there, staring at the ceiling, grinding her teeth, and thinking about Yalena—all she could see was a picture of the girl's body, battered almost beyond recognition—and Cheryl and CDI and the job she hadn't gotten and Jon and her parents and David and the countess and Leisha and Adam and the baby.

Now she'd never get to sleep.

There was only one answer to Meena's problem, and it lay in a little orange prescription bottle in the medicine cabinet in the bathroom. She hated resorting to pills, but lately she'd been relying on them more and more.

She was just about to reach for her secret stash of pills in the medicine cabinet when she heard it:

The clickety-clack of Jack Bauer's claws on the hardwood floor behind her.

Seeing her up and around, Jack Bauer thought it was morning and time for his first walk of the day.

"Okay, Jack," Meena whispered to him. "*Okay*. We'll go."

She spat out her mouth guard, leaving it in the sink, then slipped as quietly as she could into her coat and a pair of sneakers and got Jack Bauer's leash from its hook.

She'd just take him on a short walk, she decided, then go back to bed. She'd be home in less than fifteen minutes. With half a pill, she could still get a full four hours of restorative sleep before work. Everything would be okay.

In the lobby of Meena's building, Pradip, the night doorman, had dozed off with his head resting on one of his textbooks. He was studying to be a masseur, which Meena thought was a fine career option for him, since people were having multiple careers nowadays well into their eighties, and his death didn't appear to be imminent.

Meena crept past him, careful not to disturb him—all the staff in her building worked so hard—and slipped out the automatic doors to the sidewalk, where Jack Bauer hurried to relieve himself against the potted palm just beside the red carpet by the building's entrance, as was his ritual. Meena waited beside him, inhaling the fresh morning air. Or was it still night? She wasn't sure. The sky above was a dark blue wash, a paler blue at the edges, where it disappeared behind the tall buildings.

Meena gave Jack Bauer's leash a tug, and he obediently began trotting beside her. They had a route they always took this time of night—down Park Avenue to Seventy-eighth; past St. George's Cathedral, currently closed for badly needed renovations; then back down Eightieth, and to the apartment.

But for some reason that night—or that morning—Jack was feeling jumpy. Meena could tell, because he ignored some of the places he usually liked to take an inordinately long time sniffing and just kept trotting forward, nervously snuffling the air, almost as if . . . well, as if he were anticipating something.

But because this was the way he often behaved—his name was, after all, Jack Bauer: he was a jumble of nerves, always expecting the worst, barking at their front door when it was only the countess and her husband coming home from a party—Meena thought nothing of it.

She let Jack Bauer pull her along, thinking idly about work. How was she going to fit a *prince* for Cheryl into Shoshona's vampire story line?

And Yalena—should Meena have followed her to her meeting with the boyfriend? She was wondering whether she could have said something to him, given him a look, done *something* to let him know she was onto him, when she noticed the first other person she'd seen on foot since leaving her building, coming toward her on the same side of the street, but from the opposite direction.

It was a man.

But he was a very tall man, dressed in a long black trench coat that flapped behind him almost like a cape.

Meena tightened her grip on Jack Bauer's leash, and not just because the dog had begun growling. She was alone on a dark street approaching a large man she didn't know. What on earth was he doing out at four in the morning without a dog if he wasn't drunk?

She didn't blame Jack Bauer for being suspicious. She was suspicious, too.

But as they approached the wide steps to St. George's Cathedral, surrounded by scaffolding, Meena saw from the security lights shining down from the church spires that the man was unusually good looking—maybe in his mid to late thirties—and was in no way giving off signs that he didn't belong in the ritzy neighborhood. His clothes were impeccably tailored and in good taste; his dark hair, brushed back from his temples without a hint of gray, immaculately groomed. Even his sideburns were the perfect length.

She was the one, she belatedly realized, who probably looked suspicious, given the fact that her short hair was doubtlessly pointing up in spikes (as it was wont to do when she'd just gotten up), she was without makeup, and her blue flannel pajama legs—with white puffy clouds on them—were sticking out of the bottom of her own trench coat, above her well-worn sneakers.

When she raised her gaze to meet his as he walked past her—Jack Bauer was practically snarling by this time—she was smiling apologetically, both for her appearance and for her dog's behavior.

He smiled back, his eyes dark and as full of mystery as the windows peering down around them.

And she relaxed.

She had no bad feelings about this man. Not a single twinge about how or when he was going to die. Amazingly enough she felt nothing . . .

. . . nothing at all about him.

"Shhh," Meena said to Jack Bauer, embarrassed over the dog's antics.

It was right then that the sky collapsed.

Chapter Fifteen

4:00 A.M. EST, *Wednesday, April 14*
St. George's Cathedral
180 East Seventy-eighth Street
New York, New York

The sky didn't really collapse, of course.

It only seemed that way, because a huge section of it came swooping down at Meena from one of the spires of the cathedral.

She screamed and ducked, covering Jack Bauer with her body and arms, trying to protect them both from what looked like an ink-dark swath of material that came hurtling down at her head.

Except that she could see glimpses of the misty yellow glare from the street and security lights between the objects that were propelling themselves toward her at such an unbelievably fast speed.

Which was when Meena realized this wasn't a single solid piece of St. George's Cathedral, crumbling at last.

It was, unbelievably, bats. Hundreds, maybe thousands of black, shrieking bats, all headed straight at her, their pink mouths open, razor-sharp claws extended, beady yellow eyes bulging as they swept down from the cathedral's spires, blocking out most of the night sky and available lamplight with their foot-wide wingspan, their only target Meena Harper and her Pomeranian-chow mix.

At first Meena froze. She wasn't paralyzed with fear so much as with shock. All she could think was, *this* was how she was going to die? Being chewed to death by rats with wings?

Meena had been envisioning other people's deaths for so long, it had never occurred to her that she might one day be experiencing her own.

And now, faced by her own imminent destruction, all she was able to think was that she'd never, not even for a second, seen it coming.

Then, her heart stuck in her throat, too terrified to let out a second scream as she stood at the bottom of the steps of the cathedral, she pulled Jack Bauer into her arms—those bats were nearly as big as he was—then dropped to the pavement to protect her dog, her face, and her eyes. Burying her nose in Jack's fur, she began frantically to pray, though she'd never been a particularly religious person before that moment. *Oh, please, oh, please, oh, please,* she prayed, to no deity in particular, as every second the bats' shrieks sounded more and more loudly in her ears.

And then, just as it seemed the first of those claws *had* to sink into her scalp, the back of her neck, her unprotected spine, she felt something—or rather some*one*—drop on top of her, envelop her, blocking out the light and sound almost completely.

And she realized, risking a brief upward glance, that it was the man who'd been standing next to her . . . the tall, good-looking man with the nice hair, in the expensive coat. The man about whose future she'd felt exactly nothing.

Except that that was impossible. Because he'd thrown himself over her, in order to protect her from the bats.

And now he, not she, was being torn apart by bat claws and pummeled by the impact of their careening bodies. She could feel the force of them as they struck him, one after another, reverberating all the way through his body to hers, as the two of them crouched on the cathedral steps, bombarded by keening winged missiles.

Why he wasn't crying out with the pain he had to feel as each talon struck him, Meena didn't know. He wasn't even trying to shield his face and neck from the bats as they continued to tear at him. Meena couldn't quite see his face beneath the dark protective folds of his coat, which had formed a sort of canopy over her, shielding her from the menacing attack.

But she thought she caught a glimpse of his eyes once as she glanced out, trying to see what was happening, and she could have sworn. . .

Well, she could have sworn they flashed as red as the brake lights she'd seen all up and down Park Avenue.

But that, of course, would have been impossible.

As impossible as the fact that she hadn't sensed he was going to die tonight the minute she'd seen him coming toward her.

And die protecting *her*.

But that had to be what was happening. Because no human being could go through an attack like this and live.

Meena couldn't believe any of this was happening. It was four in the morning, and she was on Seventy-eighth Street in front of a church she'd walked by a hundred—maybe even a thousand—times before, and she was being attacked by killer bats, while a man—a total stranger— had thrown himself over her, voluntarily giving his own life for hers.

And then, just when Meena was certain she couldn't take it a moment longer—when she was convinced the attack would never stop and that they would eat right through the man's body and down to hers—as suddenly as the bats had appeared, they were gone.

Just vanished into the night sky, disappearing as mysteriously as they'd come.

And the street was silent again, save for the distant sound of traffic over on Park Avenue. There wasn't a noise to be heard, except for Jack Bauer's whines and her own ragged breathing. She hadn't realized until then that she was crying.

She couldn't hear the man's breathing. Was he dead already? *How could he be dead without her having felt his death approaching?* Even though he was a stranger to her, she ought to have known. Her power to predict death—unwanted as it had always been—had never once failed her before.

"Oh!" She found that she couldn't catch her breath. She was trying to take in large gulps of air, but no oxygen seemed to be reaching her lungs. And it wasn't because her protector was dead weight on top of her, either. "Oh, my God."

That was when the man rolled off Meena and, in a deep voice tinged with an accent that sounded to her like a mixture of British and a hint of something else, asked, "Are you all right, miss?"

Chapter Sixteen

N one of it was the slightest bit possible, of course.

That he should be completely unhurt and conversing with her as politely as if she'd just tripped over Jack Bauer's leash and fallen across the sidewalk and he was a passerby who'd stooped to help her back up.

That she was looking into the eyes of the charming stranger kneeling beside her and saw that they weren't red at all, but a perfectly ordinary dark brown.

"I—I'm fine," Meena stammered in response to his inquiry after her health. She'd let Jack Bauer go because she could no longer hold on to his wildly wiggling body. He darted as far as the end of his leash would allow him to, then stood there growling, all the fur on his back raised. Meena couldn't believe how horribly behaved he was being.

"Are *you* all right?" she asked her rescuer in a trembling voice.

"I'm very well, thank you." The man had risen to his feet and now reached down to take Meena's hands in his, to help her up. "I'd heard, of course, that New York City was dangerous. But I'd no idea it was quite as dangerous as *that*."

Was he . . . ? He *was*.

He was making a little joke.

His grip on her hands was steady. Meena felt oddly reassured by it. And by the little joke.

"I-it's not," Meena stammered.

Meena needed, she decided, to sit down. His grip on her hands was the only thing keeping her on her feet.

"I think we should get you to a hospital," she heard herself say.

Or me, she thought. *For a full head CT.*

"Not at all," the man said, putting an arm around her shaking shoulders. His grip seemed to say, *I'm in control. There's no need to worry about anything. Everything is going to be all right now.* In a distant part of her brain, she hoped he would never, ever let go. "I'm fine. I think we should get you home, though. You seem done in. Where did you say you lived?"

"I didn't," Meena said. Her mind was awhirl, she knew. But whose wouldn't be after such an event? How could he be so calm? Bats, Meena remembered, sometimes carried rabies. "Did any of them bite you? You should go to the ER right away. They can stop rabies if they catch it early enough."

"None of them bit me," he said in an amused tone of voice. He had taken the leash from her and was now walking both her and Jack Bauer— though unlike Meena, Jack Bauer wasn't in the least bit unsteady on his feet and was fighting against his lead, wearing an expression not unlike the one Kiefer Sutherland wore when terrorists kidnapped the president on his show, like he was going to attack anyone and everyone who got in front of him. "But I'll go to the hospital and get myself checked out as soon as I've gotten you home safely."

"It's important," Meena said as they crossed the street. She was babbling. She knew she was babbling, but she couldn't help it. *What was going on?* Who was this man? How could he be uninjured? Why was Jack Bauer acting like such a maniac? "It's important you go. Victoria Worthington Stone got rabies once from a rabid bat when she was in a plane crash in South America, and in the ensuing brain fever, she slept with her half brother . . . although she didn't know he was her half brother at the time."

What was she talking about? *Victoria Worthington Stone?* Oh, God. Really?

The man hesitated. "Is this a friend of yours?" he asked.

Cringing with embarrassment, Meena said, "Well, I mean, Cheryl is. She plays Victoria Worthington Stone on *Insatiable*. I write her dialogue. But it's true about the bats and rabies. We may be just a soap opera, but we strive for authenticity in our plotlines. . . ."

Or at least we used to, before Shoshona made head writer and caved to the demands of the sponsor, she just managed to stop herself from adding.

"I understand," he said, gently leading her past the grocery store where Jon had said the chicken delivery hadn't been made. There was a delivery truck outside the store now, though, the motor running noisily. *Oh, so there'll be chicken today,* Meena thought disconnectedly. Yeah. She was losing it.

"So you're a writer."

"Dialogue writer." Meena felt the need to correct him. "I've never written a scene like *that*," meaning what had just happened outside St. George's.

She couldn't get it out of her head: the sound of all those wings flapping. And the smell of them—so foul, the way she'd always imagined death would smell, had she ever smelled death, which, thankfully, she hadn't. She'd known so many people for whom death had come so near, some of whom it had even touched, because she hadn't been able to save them. . . .

But death had never, ever come that close to her.

And the shrieking . . . that sound they'd made as they'd come tearing down from the sky, and then as their bodies had thudded into his . . .

And those eyes. Those red eyes.

Surely she'd only imagined those.

Meena had now come as near, personally, to death—to hell on earth—as she ever wanted to.

And she didn't understand how she'd escaped it. She didn't understand it at all.

"I'm sorry," she said, pulling to a stop in front of him and lifting her chin to look him in the face. She didn't care about the tears anymore, or the way she must have looked and sounded. She had to know. She *had* to know what was going on. "But I don't understand. How can you not be hurt? I *saw* them. There were hundreds of them, coming right at us.

I *felt* them hitting your body. You should be torn apart. But there's not a scratch on you."

He was so handsome, so . . . nice. How could she ever have thought anything about him, except that he was what he was? A tall, wonderful stranger who'd saved her life?

"D-don't get me wrong," she said, shaking her head. "I'm eternally grateful. What you did . . . that was so incredible. I'll never be able to thank you enough. But . . . *how* did you do that?"

"They were only a few little bats," he said with a smile.

Only a few little bats.

But . . . no. It had been more . . . much more than that. She was sure of it.

As sure as she could be of anything so late at night, after something so traumatic.

"You're home now," he said, and nodded toward the automatic brass doors a few feet away. "I'm sorry for what happened. I'm afraid it was my fault. But you should be quite safe for the night."

Meena's gaze focused, and she realized that, indeed, they'd arrived at 910 Park Avenue. The familiar green awning stretched over their heads. Through the glass of the doors, she could see Pradip, still dozing at the reception desk with his face on his textbook.

"But . . ." She looked back up at her rescuer, confused. "I didn't tell you where I live. I never even told you my na—"

Jack Bauer whined, tugging on his leash, anxious to get away from the man who had saved their lives.

"Of course you did. It was wonderful to meet you, Meena," the man said, letting go of her shoulders. "But it would be better for you if you forgot all about this and went inside now."

Jack Bauer pulled her toward the doors, which opened automatically with a quiet whooshing sound. Pradip, behind the desk, stirred and began to raise his head. Meena's feet, as if of their own accord, began to move toward 910 Park Avenue.

But at the threshold, she turned to look back.

"I don't even know your name," she said to the tall stranger, who stood waiting with his hands in his coat pockets, as if to be certain she made it safely inside before he went on his way.

"It's Lucien," he said.

"Lucien," she repeated, so she would remember it. Not that it was likely she'd forget anything about this night. "Well. Thank you so much, Lucien."

"Good night, Meena," he said.

And then Jack Bauer pulled her the rest of the way inside, and the automatic doors closed with a gentle whoosh behind her.

When she turned to see if she could catch one last glimpse of him, he was gone. She wasn't entirely certain he had ever been there at all.

Except for the fact that, when she got safely inside her apartment again, she saw that the knees of her pajamas were dirty from where she'd scraped them diving for the sidewalk.

Proof that what had happened hadn't been a dream—or a nightmare—after all.

Chapter Seventeen

It wasn't to be borne. They'd attacked him, and in the open, where anyone could have seen. Someone *had* seen. Granted, only the human girl, and she was in too much shock from the extreme violence of what had occurred and her own near brush with death ever to give anyone a rational account of it. . .

. . . in the unlikely event she were to remember it at all, which she wouldn't.

But that wasn't the point.

Someone was going to have to pay.

The question was, who?

Lucien stood in front of the cathedral, staring up at the spires. He had circled back after delivering the girl safely to her home. He hadn't missed the irony of *where* she lived. But that was probably only to be expected. In many ways, Manhattan was a collection of small villages, just like his home country. People rarely ventured out of their own neighborhoods, especially young women walking small, fluffy dogs at four o'clock in the morning.

St. George's. The irony of *that* wasn't lost on him either. For hadn't St. George slain the dragon?

And now the cathedral stood empty while undergoing renovation.

What better time for the children of Dracul—or "dragon," in his native Romanian—to desecrate it?

And what better time than now for the Dracul to convey their message to the only full-blooded son of the prince of darkness that they would no longer abide by his rule?

Sighing, Lucien climbed the steps where, just moments before, he'd fended off the attack from his own kind. They must have put out word of his arrival mere seconds after he'd set foot on American soil in order to have rallied so many to the cause of destroying him.

It was a bit disappointing to discover that he was so violently disliked among his own brethren.

On the other hand, he'd never asked to be liked. Only to be obeyed.

Glancing up and down the street to make sure he was alone—no more pretty, pajamaed dog walkers—he lifted away a section of the blue scaffolding that surrounded the cathedral, then slipped behind it. The church, badly in need of repair—and even more in need of cleaning—rose up before him, some of its ornate stained glass windows broken, even where they were covered in metal wire.

Not that this would keep him out, nor any like him.

They were all gone now, of course. How long they must have waited, knowing he would pass by eventually, going to or from Emil's. He could only imagine the bickering. Especially among the females. The Dracul women had always been venom tongued.

With only a quick adjustment, he was inside the chained doors of the church and striding down the trash-strewn center aisle. The pews were in disorder, some knocked completely over, some lying askew like drunken sailors after a night out.

Just as he'd suspected, the Dracul had been inside the church as well. There was a primitive spray-painted outline of a dragon on what had once been an ornately decorated marble altar.

Now it was completely ruined. However much the congregation had raised for their renovation, they would need that much more to have the altar sandblasted.

Lucien shook his head. So much needless destruction. So much disregard for beauty.

Behind him, he heard something and whirled, his lightning-fast reflexes a fraction slower than usual from all the energy he'd had to exert during the encounter outside the church.

But fortunately it was only a dove, fluttering up from between the riotously disturbed pews, that interrupted Lucien's solitude now. The Dracul had all gone, no doubt frustrated by their ineffectual attempt to assassinate him.

Relieved he would not be called again to defend himself so soon, he let his shoulders sag a little. It had taken every ounce of power he'd had left after the attack to heal himself from the wounds he'd received from the Dracul. It wouldn't have been right to have allowed the girl to see the gouging his face and body had undergone, and so he'd taken care to repair himself even as the wounds were being inflicted. There were those humans who could take in stride the sight of a man's face shredded by an attack of flesh-eating bats. . . .

And then there were those who could not.

The dog walker had definitely fallen into the category of *not*. She had seemed like a good sort of person—or someone who strived to do the right thing, anyway. Though her thoughts, for some reason, had been as difficult to penetrate as a rain forest.

Some humans were like that. Some had minds as dry and arid as a desert, and just as easily navigated. Others had psyches more like the dog walker's, only accessible with a machete.

It was strange that such a pretty, vivacious girl would have so much emotional baggage. He trusted, however, that whatever dark secrets she was harboring, they wouldn't get in the way of the memory wipe he'd conducted upon on her, which would guarantee that she'd remember none of the incident and go happily about her business as if the attack had never happened.

He wished he could be as fortunate.

Lucien stood in the ruins of the cathedral, contemplating his next move. The sun would be coming up soon. He needed to go to ground, then have a few words with his half brother, Dimitri.

And of course make out a generous check to the St. George's Cathedral Renovation Fund.

Chapter Eighteen

8:45 A.M. EST, Wednesday, April 14
The Tennessean Hotel
Chattanooga, TN

Alaric, just back from his morning swim, stared down at the message on his computer screen. It seemed entirely too good to be true.

> YOU ARE CORDIALLY INVITED. . . .
> WHAT: *A fancy dinner at our place, 910 Park Avenue, Apt. 11A*
> WHEN: *Thursday, April 15, at 7:30 P.M.*
> WHY: *Emil's cousin, the prince, is in town!*

"Where did you get this?" he asked Martin over his mobile phone.

"The IT department found it during their routine scanning and thought it might be something."

The Vatican had gone high-tech some time ago and now employed an entire fleet of full-time computer programmers and analysts for the Palatine, taking their battle against the forces of evil to the cyber as well as street level.

"And what makes them think," Alaric asked in Italian, "that this has anything to do with *our* prince?"

Martin sounded annoyed. And no wonder. It was nap time in Rome, at least for Martin's daughter, Simone. And probably for Martin, too. He'd been sleeping a lot while recovering from his wounds, thanks to all the painkillers he'd been prescribed by the Vatican surgeons.

"They're checking the passenger manifests of every incoming flight, private as well as commercial, to New York City, and there was a Lucien Antonescu, professor of ancient Romanian history, on a flight from Bucharest last night. First-class seat."

"So?" Alaric was bored already. His kill the day before hadn't been all that exciting—except for the part where Alaric had crashed through the window, which of course he'd enjoyed. And the breakfast buffet, which he'd checked out on his way back to the room from the pool, had been uninspiring, to say the least.

"They've looked into this Professor Antonescu," Martin said. "Rumor has it he's been teaching at this university—night classes only—for thirty years. But they got hold of a copy of his last author photo . . . the guy looks thirty-five, at the oldest."

Alaric snorted. "Oh," he said sarcastically. "His author photo. Well, that cinches it. No writer would *ever* use an outdated author photo."

"He has a summer place in Sighişoara," Martin went on. "A castle, people say."

"Who *doesn't* own a castle in Sighişoara these days?" Alaric asked. He picked up the remote from his hotel bed and began flipping through the channels. The Tennessean, which had promised to be a luxury hotel, offered only one premium cable channel, HBO, and there was nothing good on it, except, predictably, a show featuring vampires. Alaric watched the Hollywood vampires for a while, smirking at how attractive and self-restrained they were. If only people knew the real story.

"I think this one might be legitimate, Alaric," Martin said. "The woman who sent it, her last name is Antonescu. She's a Manhattan socialite. Her husband's a big real estate wheeler-dealer. We've never had any reason to suspect them before, except that the techno geeks got a hit with the names, the word *prince,* and the flight today. Anyway, it can't hurt to check out the party, is what they're saying from above. Everyone says this guy is a royal. He's got to be the prince from the e-mail. I mean, this woman claims her husband's descended from the Romanian royal family, and that she's a countess. They've got property in Sighişoara as well."

"Romanian royal family." Alaric's finger froze as he was flipping away from the Hollywood vampires.

"Exactly," Martin said. "That's why Johanna sent it my way. She thought you'd want to see it."

"Why didn't she just forward it straight to me?" Alaric asked, confused.

"Why do you think, dumbass?" Now Martin sounded not only annoyed but amused. "It's not your case. You're supposed to be finding the serial killer. Besides . . ."

Alaric leaned forward. "Besides what?" he asked. He hadn't slept well. The pillows of his hotel bed hadn't been very comfortable. He'd piled them all up against one another, and they still didn't equal the luxuriousness of his goose-down-filled pillows from home. Alaric hadn't even wanted to think about what he'd find if he ran a blue light over the bed's comforter. He'd wadded it up and stashed it in the closet anyway along with what had passed for the room's wall "art."

"Holtzman's ordered that you be kept on the Manhattan serial killer. Johanna says there's a feeling you might be too personally invested in all this to be allowed to go after the prince." Martin finished quickly. "Sorry, old bud."

Alaric nearly choked on the swallow he'd taken from the bottle of sparkling water he'd plucked from the minibar.

"I know," his former partner said soothingly as Alaric spurted out a few choice curses. "Look, I know how you feel. You think it's not killing me to be out of action while all this is going down?"

"This is bureaucratic *bullshit,*" Alaric declared, and hurled his empty water bottle at the place on the wall where the offensively bad art had once hung. Irritatingly, the bottle didn't even break. It was plastic.

"I know," Martin said into his ear. "But look at it from Holtzman's perspective. You can hardly be considered impartial anymore. And you don't exactly follow protocol when it comes to demon hunting, do you? Nor is impulse control one of your strong suits. What did you just throw?"

"Nothing," Alaric said, getting out of bed and going to pick up his sword. "And I resent the implication that in a one-on-one with the prince of darkness, I'd be anything but strictly professional." He pointed his sword at the pretty vampire boy on the television screen. "I'm eminently capable of keeping my emotions in check while severing that bastard's head from his body."

"I know," Martin said. "Why do you think I sent you that e-mail in the first place?"

Alaric shook his head. Damned bureaucrats. He loved his job, but one thing he could never understand was how the higher-ups couldn't see that they only made things more difficult with their damned red tape.

Take Martin, for instance. He still had to keep the fact that he was married to a man a secret from their superiors. Not from Holtzman, of course . . . Holtzman, like Alaric, couldn't have cared less who his fellow guards went home to at night, as long as they got the job they'd been trained to do done (although in Holtzman's case, he preferred them to do it under budget).

But times—and attitudes—were changing all over the world. One could only hope they'd change soon in the Papal Palace.

"Look, just remember," Martin said. "You didn't get that e-mail from me. Understand?"

"Yeah," Alaric said, sheathing his sword. "Thanks. How are you feeling, anyway?"

"Been better," Martin said. "Been worse. I gotta go. Simone wants her nap. What are you going to do today?"

Alaric grinned. "Oh, the usual. Check out. Fly to New York. Save the world."

Chapter Nineteen

2:00 P.M. EST, *Wednesday, April 14*
ABN Building
520 Madison Avenue
New York, New York

I already know." Cheryl's lower lip began to tremble. Just a little. "Shoshona told me last night."

"Don't cry," Meena said, plunging her hand into a nearby box of tissues and then passing a wad of them to *Insatiable*'s leading lady. "Seriously. You know how your makeup runs when you cry. And we're in high def now."

"It's fine," Cheryl said. But she took the tissues and dabbed at her eyes just the same. "They can spray it back on. I just can't believe after all these years, they're selling out by going with a *vampire*. For *Taylor*."

"It came down from the network," Meena said. Although she didn't know why she was defending Shoshona. "CDI wants it. I'm sure there's some kind of new tie-in product they want to market. . . ."

"That just makes it worse," Cheryl said with a sob.

"Look, don't tell anyone," Meena said, trying to sound encouraging. "But I think I've thought of something for you. Something fantastic."

She just wasn't willing to say it out loud. Not yet. She didn't know why, exactly.

Well, all right, she did know why: the network was going to hate it. And okay . . . maybe Leisha's reaction over the phone when Meena had called her earlier in the day to tell her what had happened outside St. George's had shaken her confidence a little.

"Bats?" Leisha had echoed.

"Yes," Meena had said emphatically. "Bats."

"In front of St. George's Cathedral," Leisha had said, as if requesting confirmation. "And this random guy just threw himself over you to protect you from them?"

"And Jack Bauer," Meena had said, reminding her.

Leisha ignored her. "And he didn't get a scratch on him, even though all of these bats attacked his face?"

"Yes," Meena had said. "And then he walked me back to my building. *Even though I never told him where I lived.* It was like he just knew."

"Okay, look," Leisha had said. The sound of hair dryers blowing in the background was loud, as usual. "There's a totally rational explanation for the whole thing: You took the sleeping pill, even though you don't think you did. And then you took the dog for a walk. And you had a waking nightmare."

"Except I didn't take the sleeping pill." Meena had insisted. "Leisha, I took it when I got home. I had to; I was shaking so badly from everything that happened. How else do you think I got to sleep after something like that? I was a wreck."

"Well," Leisha said, "there's no other explanation. Because none of what you're describing could have happened. Huge flocks of bats—or whatever it's called when it's bats and not birds—do not just go swooping down out of nowhere, attacking people in Manhattan. And how could he possibly have known where you lived—and your name, which you also said he knew—even though you didn't tell him? There's no such thing as mind readers, Meena. Except Sookie Stackhouse, and she's made up. All you can do is tell how people are going to die, which isn't nearly as useful or cool. You took the pill before you went out and just don't remember, and then dreamed the whole thing. You're working on a story line about vampires, remember? It's natural you'd dream about bats. Vampires, bats. I'm surprised the guy you dreamed up wasn't wearing a big black cape or sparkling or something."

"He was in Burberry," Meena said, knitting her brow. "But he definitely didn't sparkle. He was very polite, though. And strong. He kept his arm around my shoulders the whole way home. It's the only reason I didn't fall down. He was so in control."

Thinking about how strong and in control Lucien had been brought back feelings of warmth, even when Meena remembered it in the daytime. Except for one thing.

"But Jack Bauer hated him. Why would I dream that?"

"God, I'm just glad you're all right," Leisha had said, sounding concerned. "Whatever happened last night. You shouldn't be out so late, even with Jack Bauer. What if the guy hadn't been so polite or such a gentleman? Did you tell Jon about it?"

Meena had frowned as she'd sipped her morning soda. "No. I mean . . . sort of. I told him I saw some bats outside the church. That's all."

"You didn't tell him because the guy was hot." It was a statement.

"No! Leisha, come on. I barely talked to him." She didn't mention the feelings of warmth she got when she thought about how strong and in control he'd been.

"What? You're mumbling! Over some guy you met in a *dream*! I can't believe it. You *like* him."

"If it was a dream," Meena had said defensively, "parts of it were really vivid. And why shouldn't I like him? He saved my life. And Jack Bauer's," she'd added hastily.

Leisha had said, "I knew all this crazy soap opera writing would catch up with you someday, and now it has. *Meena, you're in love with a guy your subconscious made up for you.* A superman who saves you from bat attacks. God, it's so obvious. He saved you from having to write about vampires, which you hate! Especially now, with Shoshona being your new boss."

Meena had gotten up to throw her soda can away. She'd paused as she was about to toss it over the lip of her office recycling can.

"Well," she'd said, "I guess I never thought of it that way. But . . . now that you mention it, the bats *could* represent my deep and abiding loathing for vampires."

"Right," Leisha had said. "Of course. Doesn't that make more sense than any of it actually having happened?"

"Maybe," Meena had said. "But then how do you explain the knees of my pajamas? They were filthy when I got up this morning. Obviously I was on the ground at some point. . . ."

"You really did go out to walk Jack Bauer, and you knelt down to scoop up some of his poop?" Leisha had suggested. "And don't remember it?"

Meena had made a face. "You really know how to kill the romance in a story, don't you?" she'd said.

"That's what best friends are for, sweetie," Leisha'd said. "It's a dirty job, but somebody has to do it."

But now, sitting in Cheryl's dressing room, Meena wondered. . . .

Had it all been a dream? Her subconscious working out her frustration over having to write about something she hated, like Leisha said?

And if it was . . . well, why not let it work to her advantage?

"Look," Meena said. She glanced around the veteran actress's luxurious dressing room as if she was worried someone might be eavesdropping. But there was only Cheryl's vast doll collection—all dolls from the Madame Alexander Victoria Worthington Stone collection—watching. "Don't say anything to Shoshona, because I haven't written anything up yet—but I was thinking of having Victoria meet . . . well, a prince, actually."

"A *prince*?" Cheryl was so astonished, she actually stopped crying. "What kind of prince?"

"A . . . Romanian one," Meena said.

The truth was, ever since she'd gotten up that morning—still woozy from her ordeal the night before, even though Leisha was probably right and it had all been a dream brought on by her frustration over having lost out on the head writer job and having taken her sleep medication before, and not after, Jack Bauer's walk—she hadn't been able to get Lucien, and his ever so slightly European accent, out of her head.

And okay, so it was possible he *was* a figment of her overactive imagination, a manifestation of how she envisioned her creative self (weird that her creative self was a hot guy in a black trench coat, but whatever), who went around saving her from bats, also known as vampiric story lines thought up by Shoshona (who was wearing fishnets today, and they probably weren't even control-top).

But Meena had felt so secure and protected in his arms. She hadn't felt that way in so long. It always seemed lately as if the wolves—or bats—were bearing down on her. If it wasn't the bills coming due at the end of the month, it was Shoshona, getting all the promotions but doing none of the work at the office.

Meena suspected Cheryl probably felt the same, since she suddenly sighed, gazed at her reflection in her dressing room mirror, then tugged on her décolletage.

"I don't know, kiddo." Cheryl looked skeptical. "No offense. But you against the network? I don't think so. They let Gregory Bane kill off Beverly Rivington from *Lust* the other day. Twenty-five years she'd been on that show, and they had some scrawny kid with a funny haircut suck all the blood out of her. If that's not an analogy for the way my career is going, I don't know what is."

"I know," Meena said. She'd been hoping Cheryl hadn't heard about Beverly. But that was ridiculous in a business like this, where everyone carried an iPhone and was connected to E! Online twenty-four/seven. "But I'm not going to let that happen to you."

"Oh, really?" Cheryl raised an eyebrow. "How?"

"I'm going to write in a Romanian prince vampire slayer for Victoria to hire to kill off her daughter's vampire boyfriend," Meena said dramatically.

Meena knew she was treading on thin ice. Introducing a new character solely to kill off Shoshona's character? The vampire who was supposed to save *Insatiable* from the beating they were taking in the ratings from *Lust*? The vampire the *network* wanted?

Was she insane?

Except that she had never felt more sane in her life.

Cheryl evidently didn't agree.

"It's your funeral, hon," she said dubiously.

"It spells Daytime Emmy to me," Meena said.

Cheryl looked modest. "Oh, sweetheart. From your lips to the Emmy voters' ears. Well." She gave her highly stylized hair a pat. "I guess I better go out there and suck face with that priest."

Meena followed Cheryl out into the hallway. But instead of heading for the studio, she turned to go back upstairs to her own office. She needed to get started writing about Lucien, the Romanian prince who was going to kill off Shoshona's vampire, right away. Who knew almost being killed by a lot of bats could be so creatively inspirational?

But it wasn't, she knew, the bats that had gotten her creative juices flowing; it was Lucien's warm brown eyes. . . .

Maybe while she was at it, she thought, she should write a Craigslist Missed Connections ad. How else was she ever going to see Lucien again?

It was as she was trying to figure out how she'd describe those warm brown eyes in her ad that she almost smacked into Taylor, coming out of the elevator in full costume and makeup for a scene she was shooting in the riding stables with her character's current love interest, Romero, her riding instructor.

"Oh my God, Meena!" Taylor cried, flinging both her arms around Meena. "Thank you so much!"

Meena, feeling a little strangled, hugged Taylor back. "Of course. Any time." *Thank you for what?*

"You just don't know," Taylor said, finally releasing her and peering down at her with tears brimming her wide blue eyes, "how much it means to me to snag this fantastic story line. I've just been so jealous of Mallory Piers on *Lust* for getting all this press for those scenes she's been doing with Gregory Bane. And now I'm getting a vampire of my very own!"

"Oh," Meena said. "That. Yeah." Meena ran a hand through her short hair distractedly. She couldn't help but feel a little guilty about the fact that she'd just been heading upstairs with the intent of killing off Taylor's new love interest. "Well, that was more the network's idea. CDI's, actually . . ."

"I know," Taylor said. "Shoshona already stopped by and told me."

I bet she did, Meena thought. Shoshona seemed to have been all over the building, flapping her mouth.

"I think it's so great that the two of you are working together to put some young blood back into *Insatiable*," Taylor said, reaching out to squeeze Meena's hands.

"No problem," she said to Taylor. She didn't think now would be a good time to point out that she was planning on writing a romantic lead for Cheryl who was going to put a stake through the heart of Taylor's new on-screen boyfriend.

"Thanks again," Taylor said. "And thanks, too, for all the deli sandwiches you keep dropping by my dressing room. But you know, they really aren't part of my new diet. Let's do sashimi sometime!"

She ran off, her thighs so slim they looked like they belonged on a gazelle. Meena got into the elevator with a hint of a scowl on her face, only to find Shoshona already in the car.

Great.

"Hello, Meena," Shoshona said with a kittenish smile.

"Hello, Shoshona." Meena couldn't help noticing that Shoshona was carrying her Marc Jacobs dragon tote. Up close, Meena could see it had the perfect detachable messenger-bag strap, too, so no matter how much junk you stuffed into it, it wouldn't cut into your shoulder. "Going up?"

"Of course," Shoshona said. "Looking forward to meeting our new Maximillian Cabrera on Friday?"

"Who's Maximillian Cabrera?" Meena asked, bewildered.

"Taylor's vampire lover," Shoshona said, rolling her eyes as if Meena were stupid for not knowing. Except that Meena hadn't seen the breakdowns for the vampire story line. How could she, since in her usual fashion Shoshona hadn't even given them to Paul to write? "Stefan's coming in to read for the part on Friday. You were there when I told Sy about it. Remember?"

Meena, annoyed, kept her gaze on the numbers above their heads as they lit up. "Oh," she said. "Right."

"And Stefan told me that Gregory himself might come with him," Shoshona added.

"Oh, goody," Meena said. Maybe she *would* bring Jon to work with her on Friday. He couldn't do worse at the audition than some friend of Gregory Bane's.

And God knew Jon was better looking. Not that Meena would ever have admitted this in front of Jon.

"I'm really glad you've decided to be a team player about this, Meena," Shoshona said. "You scratch my back, and maybe someday, I'll scratch yours."

I bet you will, Meena thought cynically.

Chapter Twenty

The club was dark and the techno music pounding, louder even than in most discos in Bucharest.

Not that Lucien frequented such places . . . if he could help it. They were too smoky for his taste and tended to attract a rough crowd, lured by the promise of copious amounts of cheap liquor and scantily clad women. Those kinds of clubs were more for students. It made Lucien uncomfortable to be spotted in the same places as his students. It wasn't, he felt, appropriate.

Particularly when his female students threw their legs over his and began rubbing their groin over him, a dance move popularly referred to as "grinding."

Lucien had seen many dance styles come and go, usually with more amusement than alarm. But of all of them, he hoped "grinding" would be of shortest duration. There really wasn't anything attractive or sexually alluring about it.

However, as he stood surveying the crowded dance floor of Concubine, he saw that grinding was as popular in the States as it was in Bucharest. It was a bit difficult to tell because of the smoke from the dry ice machines. But it certainly seemed that way from all the bodies writhing up against one another.

When one body, garbed only in black leather pants and a metal bikini top, detached itself from the others and wriggled up against him, Lucien asked, "Where's Dimitri?"

The girl ran a black-nailed hand along his flat abs, pulling his white shirt from his trouser belt. She looked up at him through her spiky blond bangs as she began grinding against him in time to the music and said flirtatiously, "We don't need him. Unless you like it that way."

Lucien reached up and caught her wrist in an iron grip before she could dip her fingers into the waistband of his trousers.

"Where," he asked again, his eyes flaring red, "is Dimitri?"

The girl stopped grinding and said, her voice rising to a fearful whine, "He's over there. God! I was just trying to be friendly."

Lucien let go of her wrist and strode toward the VIP area, where she'd pointed with a shaking finger. He hadn't meant to frighten her.

On the other hand, she'd been high and hoping he had drugs on him to get her even higher. Beyond that, her mind had been empty as the Sahara. Lucien couldn't help being reminded of the dog walker from the night before, whose mind had been just the opposite—impenetrable as a jungle.

He wondered why he couldn't seem to stop thinking about her. He told himself it was only because she and the dancing girl were close in age and both attractive.

The resemblance ended there, however. He'd given up feeling sorry for addicts like the dancing girl. There were too many of them these days.

The VIP area where Dimitri was sitting was separated from the dance floor with black velvet ropes and featured a series of elegant, high-backed booths that formed a retreat from the loud music and gyrating bodies on the dance floor. On the soft black leather seats lounged a half dozen middle-aged men—much too middle-aged, and far too paunchy, for the extremely young and slender women who were draped all over them, their doe-eyed gazes as blank as that of the girl who'd just attempted to grind upon Lucien.

In a neighboring booth sat a few much younger men. One of them looked up and smiled as Lucien approached . . .

. . . just as two heavyset bodyguards attempted to block Lucien's path.

"Sorry, sir," said one of the men, who weighed nearly three hundred pounds and was wearing a gold chain around his thick neck with the name *Reginald* emblazoned on it. "This area is for VIPs only."

"I can see that, Reginald," Lucien said. "I'm here to see Mr. Dimitri. And you're going to let me pass."

"Of course I am," Reginald said, and he moved aside. "I'm very sorry, sir."

Reginald's partner, who weighed nearly as much as Reginald, all of it muscle, was appalled.

"Reggie!" he cried. "What are you doing?"

Reginald explained, as he unhooked the velvet rope for Lucien to pass, "You heard the man. He's here to see Mr. Dimitri."

Dimitri had risen from his booth and come to meet Lucien. A tall, dark-haired man in a business suit that fit as perfectly as any of Lucien's, he wore a white shirt that was open at the throat, revealing a leather cord from which hung a small iron dragon symbol.

"Brother," Dimitri said, stretching out a hand to take Lucien's in his. "This is a surprise. It's been too long. When did you get in?"

"Dimitri," Lucien answered coolly. He shook his half brother's hand, pointedly ignoring the question. "You're doing well, I see."

"Oh, this?" Dimitri's wide gesture with his left hand (in which he was holding an expensive Cuban cigar; he'd always, Lucien remembered, had a fondness for smoking, one that matched Lucien's own fondness for fine wines) encompassed Reginald and his partner, the VIP area, the whole of the club. "This is nothing. I have four more nationwide, and am opening another one in Rio de Janeiro next month."

"Rio," Lucien said, raising his eyebrows. "Still treading dangerously."

"What danger? It's a nightclub," Dimitri said, emphasizing the word *night*. "Only we call them lounges now. You would love Rio. The humidity! Very good for the skin. Come, you must meet my new friends from TransCarta. You must have heard of it, the private equity firm? They're brokering a rather large deal at the moment and are in need of some stress relief. So of course they've come here. Everyone who works in finance has such a bad reputation these days. Negative publicity. That's something you and I know a bit about, don't we, brother?"

Dimitri laughed at his own joke as he took Lucien's arm, attempting to steer him toward the booth of middle-aged men being nuzzled by the reed-thin young girls.

"Maybe later for that, Dimitri," Lucien said. "I'd rather speak privately to you for a moment first. We have much business to discuss, I think, you and I."

"Nonsense," Dimitri said. "Pleasure before business! I know what you're talking about . . . and why you're here." He slapped an arm around Lucien's shoulder and began steering him toward the booth he'd just vacated. "An unfortunate thing, about these young dead girls. And I've asked around—believe me, it's not good for the club, having a maniac like this loose—and I can assure you, no one knows a thing about it. If they did, don't you think I'd have taken care of it already? You know me, Lucien. Anything to improve the bottom line!"

Lucien tilted his head toward the girl who'd approached him as he'd come in, the one in the metal halter top. She was now gyrating by herself on the dance floor, off in her own little drug-induced stupor.

"And her? You aren't doing a very good job of keeping hard drugs out of the place," he remarked. "Surely that can't be helping to improve the bottom line."

Dimitri followed his half brother's gaze.

"Oh, drugs," he said, and rolled his eyes. "Well, what are you going to do? They're everywhere. The government should legalize them already, then tax them and use the money to pay off the deficit and get the addicts the help they need. But why are we talking about such a depressing topic? Come, you haven't seen Stefan in ages. And you have to meet my very latest project."

"Your latest project?" Lucien raised an eyebrow. "It isn't this . . . lounge?"

"Not at all!" Dimitri guided him toward a table at which sat a somewhat seedy-looking young man and his even seedier companion, both of whom were wearing extraordinarily tight trousers and shirts open to mid-chest beneath leather motorcycle jackets. They were flanked on either side by pencil-slim young women who did not appear to be wearing much in the way of clothing at all but had exceptionally flat chests and very straight hair.

"A new business venture," Dimitri announced enthusiastically. "Gregory Bane, meet my brother, visiting all the way from Romania, Lucien Antonescu."

"Hello, sir." The thinner of the two young men stood to shake Lucien's hand. Lucien knew why he was being so obsequious even before he felt Gregory Bane's skin . . . or saw the slim dragon tattoo that decorated the inside of his pale wrist.

"A pleasure," Lucien said unsmilingly.

"It's all mine," Gregory Bane said, his eyelids fluttering nervously.

Lucien wondered how long it had been since the boy had turned and who'd turned him. Not Dimitri, surely. His brother was many things . . . but not that. More than likely he'd seen an opportunity and had one of his many paramours do it. The boy was, Lucien supposed, good looking by the standard set by his current crop of female students, who tended to be slim and unwashed.

The other boy, who wore his dragon like Dimitri's, in the form of an iron symbol on a leather wristband, stood and extended his right hand. . . .

"Uncle Lucien," Stefan said a little diffidently.

But then again, the boy had never been all there, Lucien thought as he shook his nephew's hand.

Whether that was because he'd seen his father murder his mother before his very eyes—it had been a different time and place, when uxoricide hadn't been all that uncommon, but still, Lucien hadn't approved—or because he'd been turned too young, Lucien had never been sure.

The young man was a definite disappointment. Dimitri was forever formulating some scheme or another to give him some direction. But he'd never even allowed the boy to use his last name. How could he expect Stefan to exercise any sort of career initiative?

What game was Dimitri playing at now? Lucien wondered. And what did the paunchy financial analysts from TransCarta have to do with it, if anything? Was it all really just part of his half brother's new "business venture"?

Or something more insidious?

Oh, Dimitri acted the part of welcoming family, all open arms. . . . He even ordered bottles of Veuve for the table, though champagne was never Lucien's favorite. He'd never been fond of bubbles, which vanished immediately on the tongue. He preferred heavier, meatier wines that coated the mouth like . . . well, a meal.

But it all seemed a little like the champagne, or the young human women who'd draped themselves over Gregory Bane and the hapless Stefan—not to mention over the hedge fund managers in the booth next door—who said nothing but disappeared often to go to the ladies' room, then came back wiping their noses, their minds as empty as that of the girl who'd tried to get him to dance with her.

Too showy. Not enough substance. Just a lot of air.

After a while, Lucien felt he had seen enough. If there were answers at his half brother's club, he wasn't going to get them this way.

He excused himself, saying that he had to go.

Dimitri showed him out through a back exit, since the front was now too crowded with drug-addled partygoers for him to leave without having to push his way through.

"Where are you staying while you're here?" Dimitri asked—too casually—blowing smoke from his cigar toward the starry night sky, which was just visible from the dark alley in which they stood.

"Emil found me a place," Lucien said. The less said about where, Lucien figured, the better. He trusted his brother. . . .

But only to a point.

Dimitri gave a chuckle. "Emil," he said. "Is he still with that idiotic wife of his?"

"He is," Lucien said.

"Marriage," Dimitri said. "Now that is the one thing you and I do have in common. No need to get tangled up in *that*. Well. Again."

"It's never seemed prudent," Lucien carefully agreed.

Dimitri stared at him for a second or two before bursting into surprised laughter.

"Prudent," he cried. "Listen to you! You haven't changed, have you? Not in all this time."

Lucien shot him an appraising look.

"No," he said. "I don't suppose either of us has."

Dimitri stopped laughing abruptly and pointed at Lucien.

"I don't like the sound of that," he said in a deep voice. "I hope you didn't come here to stir up trouble, Lucien. Because we've been doing perfectly fine on this side of the Atlantic without even a hint of trouble from the Palatine . . . and without any *interference* from you."

His eyes, normally every bit as dark as his half brother's, glowed as red as his cigar as he said the word *interference*.

A second later, a layer of the trash, dirt, gravel, and broken glass lining the alley floor just in front of Lucien began to rise into the air, then swirl more and more rapidly together until it was a towering, violently destructive tornado headed straight at him.

Lucien threw an arm up to guard his face from the debris.

That was when Dimitri found himself thrown back against the side of a Dumpster, as if an unseen wind had lifted him and blown him there. His fall was broken by some empty liquor boxes someone had flattened and stacked before the Dumpster for recycling. Otherwise, he would have slammed against the steel receptacle with as much force as if he'd been shot from a nail gun.

As he lay there, stunned, the vortex Dimitri had created died as abruptly as he'd crumbled, all the pieces of glass and trash falling back to the alley floor.

Lucien strolled up to where his brother lay, pausing on his way to carefully stamp out the cigar Dimitri had dropped, then lift it and deposit it in the Dumpster behind him.

Lucien was furious . . . but even when furious, he was still conscientious about litter.

"I have no idea what kind of game you're playing here, Dimitri," Lucien said, leaning an elbow on the side of the Dumpster and speaking down to his brother in a voice that was almost eerie in its calmness after the violence that had erupted just seconds before. "Nightclubs filled with investment bankers and drug-addicted young women. That's your business, and I agreed long ago I'd stay out of Dracul business, so long as there weren't any human deaths from loss of blood. But now . . . it's not the Palatine you need to fear . . . it's me."

Dimitri, slumped against the side of the Dumpster like a piece of garbage waiting to be picked up, winced up at his brother.

"I know that," he said, rubbing the back of his neck. "I've always known that. You didn't have to hit me so hard, you know."

"These dead girls," Lucien said, ignoring his brother. "What do you know about them?"

"I told you," Dimitri said. "I don't know anything about them."

A stainless steel countertop that lay abandoned to one side of the Dumpster suddenly rose several feet into the air and dangled threateningly above Dimitri's head.

"Wait," Dimitri cried, throwing an arm over his face to protect his handsome features from destruction. "All right, all right. Yes, I've heard talk—"

Lucien let the countertop fall harmlessly to one side. The clatter it made was deafeningly loud, and the two men could hear rats squeak and scurry away. Dimitri, still seated in the muck on the alley floor, made a face.

"But you can't think I know who's doing it, Lucien," he said. "Obviously if I did, I'd put a stop to it. I don't even know why you'd think it's one of us. It's clearly some sick pervert."

"Who drinks human blood," Lucien said calmly.

"Well, lots of people do," Dimitri said. "It's quite stylish to be a vampire these days. Or act like one, anyway."

Lucien studied his younger brother. He would have liked to have believed Dimitri was as innocent as he claimed.

But Lucien had made the mistake of believing in his brother's innocence in times past.

And it had nearly cost him his life.

He wouldn't make that same mistake again, especially when it might now involve human lives.

"If I find out you know anything about these murders," Lucien said, "and you didn't tell me or do anything to stop the killer—or happen to be behind the killings yourself—I will destroy you, and everything and everyone you care about, Dimitri. Do you understand?"

Dimitri, trying to struggle to his feet and out of the garbage and slime, said, "Brother! We've obviously gotten off on the wrong foot again. I'm sorry about that little misunderstanding back there. Can't we—"

But Lucien wasn't done. He placed a hand on his half brother's shoulder and shoved him back down into the muck from which he'd just been attempting to climb.

Then Lucien leaned over him and whispered into his ear, "No. We can't. You know the agreement. Everyone can drink. But no one can—"

"For the love of God, Lucien!" Dimitri cried. "Do you think I don't know, after all these years? No one may kill a human, no matter how much he might thirst. To do so will bring swift and absolute retribution from the prince. The Dracul have lived under your orders for more than a century. Do you think we might have somehow forgotten them?"

"Yes," Lucien said grimly. "Because you have before. And you will again."

It was right then that the back door to the club opened and Reginald and his partner appeared.

"Mr. Dimitri?" Reginald asked in some alarm, seeing his boss lying on the alley floor.

Lucien straightened.

"Give him a hand, will you, Reginald?" Lucien asked over his shoulder as he turned to stride swiftly past him and into the dark night. "Mr. Dimitri is going to need all the help he can get."

Chapter Twenty-one

Meena stared at the cathedral. In the fading daylight, it looked beautiful, with its twin spires straining toward the spring sky and elegant stained glass, even if some of the windows were broken in places. Who would throw rocks at a church window, anyway?

Sure, it was surrounded with the familiar blue plywood that always went up around a building in Manhattan when construction was taking place.

But the plywood was nowhere near high enough to hide the large and lovely cathedral behind it.

A cathedral that, just two nights before, had been the scene of an inexplicable, brutal attack.

Or had it?

Meena stood with Jack Bauer on his leash at the bottom of the cathedral steps, exactly where they had been the night before last when the bats had come swooping down out of nowhere.

At first she'd been worried that Jack wouldn't want to go anywhere near the church because of what had happened last time they'd been there.

But he showed no sign of any reluctance, trotting right up and lifting a leg on a parked car in front of it.

He obviously didn't harbor any ill memories of the incident.

But though at first her own had been a bit fuzzy, she remembered it all now, as clearly as if it had just happened a few minutes, and not nearly forty-eight hours, ago. There was the place on the sidewalk where she'd crouched, her heart in her throat, for so long while the bats had flung themselves over and over at Lucien's face and body, trying—she'd been certain at the time—to rip him apart.

Except that he'd been fine, his face without a mark on it.

And true, there were no *actual* drops of blood or anything like that on the ground to show that there'd been any attack at all.

But she recognized the crack in the pavement; how could she forget it? Her face had been almost right up against it as Lucien had lain across her, keeping her safe.

It was strange, Meena thought as she stood gazing up at the church spires, wondering if the bats were in there now and when they might awaken—and attack—again. She didn't get a feeling of evil from the cathedral, even though the exact spot where she stood had very nearly been the site of a savage mauling.

Meena didn't flatter herself that as a dialogue writer for a show of *Insatiable*'s quality she was particularly gifted. She didn't put on airs that she was a creative genius.

Nor did she think of herself as any more creative than the artists she sometimes saw outside the Metropolitan Museum of Art, the ones who painted amateur sunsets and landscapes and then sold them to tourists who happened to be walking by.

Meena felt her scripts for *Insatiable* were much the same thing: a reflection of what was happening daily in front of the average American, just like a sunset . . . only maybe a little more dramatic, to keep people interested.

But she'd always been aware of being a tiny bit more sensitive to mood than other people, possibly because of her ability to tell when something horrible was going to happen to someone.

Maybe there just wasn't anything horrible about St. George's to sense. Because a tragedy at St. George's had been *averted* . . . thanks to Lucien, whoever he was. He'd saved her life. She didn't know how or why, but he had.

Did Lucien, Meena wondered, ever think about what had happened outside the church and how strange it had been? Perhaps he too had come to stand outside St. George's and asked himself the very same questions she was. Maybe he'd posted a Craigslist Missed Connections ad about *her* (she'd been too shy to post one about him). She'd better remember to check. . . .

"Meena?"

Meena jumped nearly out of her skin. She whirled around, half expecting to find Lucien himself staring down at her.

But it was only Jon, looking extremely surprised to find her standing in front of St. George's Cathedral on a Thursday evening, staring at nothing.

"What are you doing here?" Jon asked. "I thought you were taking Jack Bauer for a walk."

"I was," Meena said, tugging on Jack's leash. Jack Bauer was actually lying on the sidewalk, licking his hind leg, and ignored her. "I mean, I am. I was just . . . thinking about something."

"I can tell." Jon stood next to her and looked up at the church spires. He was dressed up in pressed khakis and a nice shirt, and was, for some reason, wearing a tie. In his right hand was a brown paper bag. "Are you still freaking out about that flock of bats?"

"It was a colony," Meena corrected him. "I looked it up on Wikipedia. Bats live in colonies. And I found out they don't normally attack something—or someone—as a group the way they did the other night. That had to have been a total fluke. They're really more solitary hunters. You know, because they use high-frequency sonar."

Jon looked down at her like she was crazy.

"Okay," he said. "Good to know. Are you going to come home and get ready? Because we have the Antonescus' dinner party in half an hour."

She blinked. "What?"

"The countess's dinner party," he said. "Remember? For her cousin, the prince. It's Thursday night. You said we'd go."

Meena rolled her eyes. "Oh," she said. "That. Yeah. We can't go. I didn't RSVP."

"Meena," Jon said, shaking his head. "We talked about this. We said we'd go."

"Well," Meena said, "I never told her we'd go. So, I guess we can't go. Too bad. Let's watch a marathon of *The Office* instead."

"No," Jon said. "Free food. Remember? Besides, I already saw Mary Lou in the elevator today and she asked if we were coming and I said yes. So we have to go. Look, I bought them a bottle of wine." He held up the paper bag. "It cost me six bucks. I'm not wasting it."

Meena's shoulders sagged. "Oh, my God," she said. "I don't think I can handle a party at the countess's tonight. It's been a really bad week."

"I know," Jon said, taking her by the elbow and turning her away from the church. "But you want to meet this prince guy, right? Isn't he the guy you want to use as a model for the vampire slayer in your spec script? The one for Cheryl?"

"Actually," Meena admitted as they started walking toward 910 Park, "I think I met someone who would be a better model for the prince."

"Really?" Jon said. "Who?"

"Oh, just a guy," Meena said, knowing what Jon would have to say about her adventure with Lucien outside the cathedral the night before last.

And if she told him, he'd only deliver a big-brotherly lecture about her leaving the apartment late at night, something she knew she ought not to have done. In their gender-unequal society, it still wasn't totally safe for American women to wander the streets of New York City unescorted late at night. (Although to be fair, it wasn't safe for *anyone* to do this, really. There were rampaging colonies of bats lurking everywhere.)

"Well, the guy we're meeting tonight is supposed to be a *prince*," Jon said. "Where else are you going to meet one of those?"

"Nowhere," Meena admitted, realizing Jon had actually been looking forward to this dinner party. He didn't get a chance to go out very often, since he was . . . well, broke and unemployed. And most of his friends were as well. Entertainment was the last thing on which any of them could afford to splurge. She ought to have known that to her brother, any chance to leave the apartment was a welcome one . . . even if it was just to go to the neighbors' place across the hall.

She glanced over her shoulder at the spires of the church shooting up toward the lavender evening sky, the clouds pink in the setting sun, as Jon steered her away from it. *Churches,* she thought idly. *What are they even for?*

To worship in, obviously. But to worship *what,* exactly? A god who gave you gifts you never even asked for, that were basically just a curse?

On the other hand, what else did people have, exactly?

Nothing.

Nothing but hope that things might get better someday.

The kind of hope that Meena, on her TV show, and the priests at St. George's tried to give people.

"You're right," Meena said with a sigh, turning around.

"We don't have to stay all night," Jon said as they rounded the corner. "If it's bogus, we'll leave."

"Sure," Meena said. "And who knows? It might even be fun."

Even though, of course, she didn't for one second actually believe this.

Chapter Twenty-two

L ucien was quite certain his cousin had lost his mind.

"A dinner party?" he echoed as he handed his overcoat to the maid, who took it to hang in the hall closet.

"It's just . . . ," Emil explained quietly, so that his wife, busy with the caterer in the dining room, couldn't overhear, "she seems to have this fantasy that you're in need of a bride and that New York is the place where you're going to find one. I can't tell you how sorry I am. If you want to smite me, my lord, I perfectly understand."

Lucien, instead of being furious—which he knew was the reaction Emil was expecting from him—felt only amusement. Although he'd made it clear he wanted no one to know of his arrival in New York, that, of course, was a moot point. The damage was done. Clearly, his enemies already knew where he was: an attempt had been made on his life. The information had simply traveled.

Much in the way Lucien expected that news of how he'd treated his own brother would get around. He didn't regret this. He *counted* on it. If everyone heard Dimitri had picked a battle with him and Lucien had won, they'd be even less inclined to stage a second attack of the sort that had occurred the other night, which he'd clearly survived.

The prince of darkness was in town and indomitable as ever.

But a dinner party? With humans?

The idea made Lucien smile.

"Your wife," he said to Emil, "is a bold woman."

"That's one way of putting it," Emil said with a queasy smile. "But, honestly, my lord, if you wish to go back to the penthouse—"

"It's all right, Emil," Lucien said soothingly. Sometimes he thought Emil would self-implode, he was wound so tightly. "I'm assuming you have some decent wines to serve."

Emil brightened considerably. "Of course, my lord," he said. "Some lovely amarones I purchased just for you. Come, let me open them."

Emil followed Lucien to his library, where he opened a fine Italian red. After a while, from the darkened, comfortable room, they could hear the first guests arriving and Mary Lou's vivacious voice as she greeted them.

"I suppose," Emil said reluctantly, "we should go out there."

"It will be fine," Lucien reassured his cousin. "I quite enjoy humans. I used to be one, remember? And I teach them."

The two men emerged into the living room, where Mary Lou shrieked with delight.

"Well, there they are!" she screamed. She had on a long turquoise dress with quite a lot of gold jewelry and matching gold shoes. Her eye shadow was the same color as the dress. Her long blond hair had been perfectly curled and coifed. "Where have you two been hiding? Prince Lucien, I want you to meet our friends Linda and Tom Bradford, and this is Faith and Frank Herrera, and Carol Priestley and Becca Evans and Ashley Menendez from Emil's office. Everyone, this is Prince Lucien Antonescu. . . ."

The women were attractive, the men jovial. Lucien shook hands with all of them, then joined in the small talk about New York City and the shows and restaurants he was to be sure not to miss while he was there.

It was a beautiful spring evening, and the Antonescus had opened all the French doors to their large wraparound terrace. The sun had already sunk into the west, and the sky was a lovely shade of pink and lavender. Lucien strolled out onto the terrace, joined by several of the women, all holding glasses of champagne and talking excitedly about an art opening they'd been to the week before.

Mary Lou had not chosen poorly. Her guests were beautiful, intelligent women.

When Lucien heard the doorbell to the apartment ring, he didn't look to see who was arriving next because he didn't want to seem rude. (And he could tell it wasn't a member of the Dracul or the Palatine Guard there to assassinate him. They would never bother using the bell.)

But then he did look, because something told him he needed to.

And the sound of the women's conversation around him died away. Not because they'd ceased speaking.

But because he was no longer listening.

It was the woman who'd been walking her dog the night of his attack, the one who'd nearly been killed herself. Meena Harper, her name had been.

He saw that Mary Lou was kissing her hello and taking a cheap bottle of wine from her tall, male companion.

Of course she was there at Emil's. Of course she was. What had he been expecting? Deep down, he must have known. Otherwise he'd have left, walked out an hour ago. He wasn't in New York to socialize with Emil's wife's human friends. He'd never wanted for female companionship when he needed it and was perfectly capable of finding it without Mary Lou's help.

And now the last woman in the world with whom he should have been consorting—because he could feel for himself the magnetic pull she had on him—had walked into the room. And he was just standing there, staring at her, in her inexpensive black dress and boyishly short hair.

And it was clear from the single glance she threw him that the memory wipe had *not* worked. No, she recognized him instantly. The way her large brown eyes widened and her jaw dropped, it was obvious she remembered their encounter with perfect clarity.

What's more, just the tiniest touch of her mind—which he threw across the room only to see if she was pleased to see him or repulsed;

it was pure vanity, and he supposed he deserved the shock he got in response to it—revealed something startling, something almost horrifying that Lucien couldn't, for the life of him, understand:

Vampire.

It was on the very tip of her brain. It was all she was thinking about. Vampires.

Also, almost as upsettingly, *death.*

He recoiled from her mind immediately . . . but not before he caught his own name.

Lucien.

She knew. She *knew.*

How, though? What had happened? What had gone wrong? Why hadn't the memory wipe succeeded? How could she possibly have put it all together?

Who was she? *What* was she? What was going on with this girl and her electrically charged, hyperactive brain?

He needed to figure it out before the evening—and his entire mission to New York—went swiftly and disastrously awry.

"Meena Harper," Mary Lou was crowing as he approached. He realized he'd left the women with whom he'd been chatting so amiably without a word. But the situation had turned dire. It had nothing, he told himself, to do with the darkness of Meena Harper's eyes and hair, or the slenderness of her waist in that cheap black cotton dress. Nothing at all. This was a matter of life and death, for all of vampire kind. "I want you to meet Emil's cousin Prince Lucien Antonescu."

"Oh," Meena said, smiling. Her two front teeth were slightly crooked. How had he missed this the other night? "I know. We've—"

"How charming to make your acquaintance," Lucien said, interrupting. He took Meena's hand even as her astonished expression was turning to one of confusion. *The prince!* her brain was crying. *It's* him*!*

What in God's name did this mean? Who *was* she?

"Right," was all she said out loud, though, in a voice that was considerably less excited than the circus-like atmosphere of her mind. "Nice to meet you, too."

Her hand was slim and warm. His, he knew, was anything but.

"And this is her brother, Jonathan Harper," Mary Lou said, her tone one of barely disguised disapproval.

"Jon." The dark-haired man standing beside Meena corrected Mary Lou, holding out his hand. "I'm Jon."

"Of course," Lucien said. He gave the brother's hand a quick shake, careful not to squeeze it too hard. Still, he saw the younger man wince.

He turned his attention back to the girl, who hadn't taken her gaze off him once since coming into the apartment. He tried reaching tentatively into her mind once again—

vampire death prince priest dragon

—then just as quickly withdrew.

No wonder he hadn't been able to wipe away the memory of him: She was clearly disturbed. It was complete bedlam in there.

"Jonathan," Mary Lou was saying to the brother, "I know you're good with electronics. My friend Becca just got an iPhone and she's having a dickens of a time downloading some of the, what do you call them? Oh, right, apps. Do you think you could help her?"

The brother looked at Becca, a large-bosomed young lady wearing a snug-fitting red sheath dress, and said, "Absolutely."

The girl watched her brother go without comment.

Vampire, Lucien couldn't help overhearing her mind screaming. *Lucien, prince, slayer, dragon, death.*

An image of a red tote bag with a jewel-encrusted dragon slithering down one side of it flashed into Lucien's mind, an image he could make no sense of whatsoever.

Not that he'd understood any of it.

"So it turns out," the girl spun around to say to him as soon as the brother was gone, "you're the prince I've been hearing so much about?"

He smiled at her politely—he was perfectly well aware of the devastating effect his smile had on human females—then took her by the arm and pulled her gently to an unoccupied corner of the terrace, saying something about what a shame it would be for her to miss the view.

He thought perhaps he could reason with her, even psychotic as she was.

"I haven't told my cousin's wife about what happened outside the church," he explained to her quickly in a low voice when they were well away from everyone else. "I didn't want to alarm her. No woman wants to hear about a colony of bats loose in the neighborhood. . . ."

Of course he wasn't going to mention the Dracul.

"I haven't told Jon, either," she said in a perfectly reasonable tone of voice, surprising him. "Well, at least . . . not the part about you."

"That was probably wise," he said. "We don't want to worry our loved ones."

She lowered her dusky gaze and appeared to be looking into the windows of the apartments below them instead of into his eyes. He had to admit he found her quite charming and had to warn himself to be careful. She was human and, judging by the cacophony in her mind, mad.

Which was a shame, since she was so lovely.

"Especially," she said, "since no one got hurt."

"Then we agree," Lucien said, "we won't mention it. To anyone."

"I told my best friend about it," she said, finally looking up at him. "She doesn't believe me. She thinks I dreamed it."

Maybe the situation, he thought, wasn't as dire as he'd initially supposed.

"Who can blame her?" he said. "The whole thing is a little hard to believe, don't you think? Bats on the Upper East Side. Absurd."

"Not as hard to believe as the only explanation I've been able to come up with for why you weren't hurt," she said, leaning on the brick wall of the terrace. "Since I know I didn't dream it."

Vampires, he knew she was going to say. He wasn't certain how he was going to proceed when she did say it. It had been so long since a human had found them out . . . a human who wished them harm. Other than the Palatine, of course.

That this disturbingly pretty, but unfortunately insane, girl should have done so was a little upsetting.

Even more upsetting was what he was going to have to do to her, by his own decree, if it was true that she knew.

"And what's that?" he asked, trying to sound casual.

"I think you're an angel," she said, smiling up at him sunnily. "And there was a miracle outside of St. George's that night."

Chapter Twenty-three

Prince Lucien Antonescu didn't like being called an angel.

But then, Meena realized belatedly, not many men would.

"There was no miracle," he kept saying insistently. "And I'm no angel. Of that I can assure you."

"That's not true," Meena said. She was teasing him. He struck her as a man who hadn't been teased often in his life. He seemed extraordinarily serious. "You risked your life to save my own, and then you disappeared without even letting me give you proper thanks. That's pretty angelic."

"I think your friend is right," he said to her as one of the caterers brought them flutes of champagne on a little silver tray, "and you're confabulating your dreams with reality. They were only a few little bats—"

"You said that the night it happened," she reminded him with mock indignation. "It wasn't true then and it's still not true. It was possibly the most horrifying thing I've ever been through in my life, and I still say it was a miracle you got by without a scratch. But if you want to keep minimizing it, go ahead. We can just talk about banalities like everybody else. How long are you going to be in the city, and have you been to see any good shows yet?"

He stared at her, his expression surprised. Then he burst into laughter. "I haven't, actually," he admitted. "I'd only just arrived the night we met, so I haven't been here long. What do you recommend?"

Meena sipped her champagne. She felt as if her mind was going a thousand miles a minute. What were the chances of Lucien—*her* Lucien, the one she'd met outside St. George's Cathedral—and the countess's prince being one and the same person? This was going to be so perfect! She needed to find out everything she could about him so she could write up the perfect character description with which to hit Sy.

Not, of course, that her prince was going to be an exact replica of Prince Lucien. For one thing he was too young for Victoria Worthington Stone. They'd need to find someone a little older to play a suitable romantic match.

Not that Cheryl wouldn't have gone for Lucien in real life, of course. She would have, in a New York second. Any woman would. Look at him! He was perfect . . . that profile, those impressive shoulders.

But whoever played him would definitely need to be more gray around the temples and have . . . glasses. Yes! That was it! A vampire slayer, or whatever it was they were called, should definitely be wearing glasses.

"I beg your pardon?" the prince said, looking down at her rather intently with those gorgeous dark brown eyes of his. "Did you say something?"

"No," Meena said. The directness of his stare unnerved her. It was almost as if he could read her thoughts. Or see through her dress.

Still, he was the sexiest man she'd met in a long time . . . whom she hadn't had to urge to give up his motorcycle.

"I mean, I was just wondering what you do," she said. "I know that's a rude, New Yorky thing to ask. We're all obsessed with what other people do for a living. But I'm really curious. I mean, what does a prince *do* all day? Do you make a habit out of rescuing damsels in distress, or was I just in the right place at the right time? Do you have a castle? Do you joust?"

He continued to look bemused. He seemed to find her very bewildering. Meena wondered what women usually talked to him about. It seemed natural to her to ask a prince about jousting.

"I do have a castle, actually," he said. "A family estate, really. Emil and Mary Lou come to visit in the summers. I'm certain she's told you about it—"

Meena held up a hand. She realized belatedly she'd heard way too much about the castle already.

"Never mind. I already know. In Romania."

"Outside Sighişoara," he said with a smile. "And in answer to your other question, no, I've never jousted. I teach."

"You teach?" If he'd told her he Twittered, she could not have been more surprised. "You teach what? Bat-attack evasion?"

"Eastern European history," he said, still looking amused. "At the University of Bucharest. Evening classes, mostly."

Meena raised an eyebrow. "Really?" She got the feeling, not just from the fact that he owned a castle but from the look of the expensive watch he was wearing and the way he carried himself in general, that Prince Lucien didn't exactly need the teaching job to support himself.

His next statement confirmed her suspicions.

"It's important to me," he said, "that my country's rich heritage not be forgotten by the next generation. You know how caught up the youth of today is in video games and text messaging. I try to make history compelling for my students, to awaken in them the kind of love I've always had for it. Whether I succeed . . ." He shrugged modestly.

Meena wanted to applaud. If he turned out to have a pair of bifocals in his jacket pocket, she thought she might actually jump up and kiss him on the mouth. "And you're here on spring break?" she asked.

"No, I'm not, actually," Prince Lucien said, removing a pair of silver-rimmed reading glasses from the inside pocket of his cashmere blazer and putting them on. "I'm here for a lecture series a colleague is giving at the Metropolitan on Vlad Tepes."

At the sight of the reading glasses, Meena swayed on her spindly high heels and almost fell down.

"Are you all right?" he asked with genuine concern in his deep voice. "Here, let me help you."

She felt his strong arm, so familiar from that night in front of the cathedral, go around her bare shoulders. A second later, he was steering her gently and expertly toward one of the countess's white, cast-iron garden chairs.

She sank gratefully onto the green-and-white-striped cushion, capable of thinking only, *The glasses! The glasses!*

He took the glasses off and tucked them hastily back into his pocket, bending over her with concern. "Shall I get you some water?"

"No," Meena said, draining the contents of her champagne glass and setting it down on the wrought iron table beside her. She hurried to say something to change the subject. "W-what's Vlad Tepes?"

"He was the most powerful prince of Wallachia, what is present-day Romania, in the fourteen hundreds," he explained. "He's considered a great hero in Eastern Europe. Are you sure you're all right? You really don't look well."

She laid a hand over his where it rested on the arm of the chair beside her. She couldn't help it. There was something about him that made her want to touch him. She didn't think it was only the fact that he'd saved her life, either.

"I'm fine," she said, thinking that his fingers felt a little cold. But then, it wasn't exactly summer outside. She wished she'd brought a cardigan. But they'd already been so late for the party, she hadn't had time to look through her closet for one nice enough to go with her dress. "I've just been having a really bad week at work."

"I'm so sorry to hear that," he said, slipping off his jacket and placing it gently over her shoulders . . . like this was the most natural gesture in the world.

Meena felt as if she'd been punched in the chest by a fellow shopper at a Marc Jacobs sample sale.

Calm down, she told herself. *He's a prince. This is what princes do. They're trained from birth to act this way.*

I mean, look at him. He's so cool, his jacket isn't even warm!

"Is that better?" he asked with what sounded like real concern.

Oh, Meena thought. *Shoshona. If you could only see me now. How you would cry into your dressing-free salad.*

"Thank you so much," she said. "It's a lot better, Lucien. Oh . . . may I call you Lucien? Or would you prefer Professor Antonescu? Or Dr. Antonescu? Or Your Royal Highness?"

"Lucien is fine," he said, smiling some more. He looked almost unbearably handsome when he smiled, with all that dark hair and those sad eyes. Meena couldn't help thinking to herself that Lucien Antonescu was a man who needed a *lot* of teasing. Maybe a lifetime of it, to make up for whatever had happened to him to put all that hurt into those brown eyes. "And what's caused you to have such a bad week?"

"Oh," Meena said. "Well, you've heard about the vampire war, haven't you?"

"I beg your pardon?"

For a split second, she could almost have sworn those sad brown eyes flashed red, like she thought they had that night outside the cathedral. The look he gave her was one of incredulity mixed almost with . . . well, anger. His hand slipped out from beneath hers as quickly as if her skin had singed his.

"Dinner is served," called the caterer in the blond ponytail and white shirt and black trousers, smiling at them from the nearby French doors.

Meena had no idea what she'd done to insult the prince. But he definitely seemed offended. He reached for the champagne glass in which he'd shown not the slightest interest before that moment and downed its entire contents.

What have I done? Meena wondered. What had she said? What had happened to make the prince go from tenderly loaning her his jacket to keep her warm to gulping down alcohol like a junkie reaching for his next fix?

"I-I'm sorry," Meena stammered. "I just—"

But when he swiveled his head to look at her again, she was relieved to see that his eyes had gone back to their normal shade of brown.

Of course. She must have imagined the red thing. She did have a pretty overactive imagination. It's what had gotten her her job.

"No, *I'm* sorry," he said, sounding more like his cordial self. She couldn't help but feel like he was controlling himself with an effort, however. The hand holding the champagne flute was white knuckled. In a second, she thought he might break the glass in half with his grip alone. "But I don't think I could have heard you correctly. Did you say *vampire war?*"

"Ye-e-es," Meena said slowly. She noticed the countess coming toward them from inside the apartment and felt a little relieved. Maybe Mary Lou could help her explain. "I write for *Insatiable*. It's on ABN. We're getting slaughtered in the ratings by *Lust*. They have this story line with a vampire. . . . I know, it's ridiculous, really. But this week my bosses announced they want *us* to do a vampire story line. . . ."

"Oh," he said. "*That* vampire war."

"Of course," she said, laughing a little incredulously. This guy was really intense! She hadn't been wrong about his needing to be teased a little. He needed to be teased a *lot.* "What other kind is there? Did you think I meant a *real* vampire war?"

She saw him throw a look in the countess's direction . . . a look Meena couldn't read at all. She wasn't sure what was going on between the two of them, but Mary Lou, reaching out to pry the champagne flute out of the prince's fingers, apparently before he could break it, said, "Now, what all are you two still doing out here? Dinner's on the table and everyone's waiting. What could you be talking about that you didn't even hear the announcement?"

"Oh, not much," Prince Lucien said, still looking as if he was holding his jaw very tightly. "Just the vampire war."

The countess glanced at him quickly, then tossed back her golden head and laughed.

"Oh, my stars," she said. Her southern accent always seemed to get more pronounced when she'd been drinking. "Meena must have been telling you about the vampire war between the television show she works for, *Insatiable,* and their archrival, *Lust.* No offense, Meena, you know I'm an *Insatiable* fan to the end. But I just can't get enough of that sexy Gregory Bane."

"Well," Meena said, scowling as she always did when she heard Gregory Bane's name, "I understand *our* vampire is going to be just as sexy."

Lucien, meanwhile, looked visibly relieved. "Television," he said. "Of course."

Meena still didn't understand anything that was happening. Like why the tightness had finally gone out of the prince's face . . . or why the smile he gave Meena when he turned around was so dazzling, it made her knees feel weak again, so that she wasn't sure she was going to be able to walk all the way to the Antonescus' dining room on her high heels. At least, not without wobbling.

But that was all right, because Mary Lou said with a laugh, "Of course that's what she meant, silly. What other vampire war is there? Well, far be it from me to interrupt your conversation. I've saved you two places at the end of the dining table. Prince Lucien, be a dear and escort Meena in."

Prince Lucien *was* a dear. He rose, gallantly presenting Meena his arm. She looked at it with a little astonishment at first.

And no wonder: no man had ever offered Meena his arm before. David hadn't exactly been the most gentlemanly of suitors, being more interested in his dental textbooks and Toastmasters meetings than manners.

Meena wasn't certain if she was supposed to slip her hand through the crook of the prince's arm or lay her fingers over it, the way she'd seen Jane Austen heroines do in BBC productions.

She actually felt just the slightest bit light-headed . . . but whether it was from the prince's proximity or the champagne, Meena wasn't sure. She wondered what was wrong with her. It wasn't as if she had never been around a handsome man before. She worked with some of the hottest actors in television, for heaven's sake.

Maybe it was just that none of them had ever shown any particular interest in her.

Or maybe . . . just maybe . . . it was because for the first time since David had left, she'd actually met a man to whom she felt attracted who wasn't already married, wasn't gay, and didn't have certain death looming over him.

She slipped her hand through the crook of his arm—in case she had to lean on him for support if the light-headedness got worse—and smiled up at him.

"So," she said. "Where were we?"

Chapter Twenty-four

W hat are you doing here?" the blue-haired old woman asked as
her Pekingese lifted a leg not far from where Alaric Wulf was
standing. "And don't try to lie to me, young man. I've been watching
you from my window. You've been standing out here for an hour."

"Just waiting for my wife, ma'am," he said. "She has an appointment
with Dr. Rabinowitz." He nodded toward the brass plate on the building he was leaning against that said *Dr. Rubin Rabinowitz, Obstetrics.*

The Blue Hair followed his gaze, then turned back toward him. She
wasn't, he saw from her expression, having any of it.

"This late?" the old woman demanded. "And why aren't you in the
waiting room?"

"Claustrophobia," Alaric said. He glared at the Pekingese. Its little
face was scrunched up in a look of disgust that seemed to echo its mistress's. "And Dr. Rabinowitz is very accommodating of my wife's busy
schedule as a jet-setting supermodel."

"Hmph," said the old woman, and she hurried on her way.

Alaric, standing next door to 910 Park Avenue—but out of sight,
leaning against the side of the building where he wouldn't be noticed
by anyone but elderly women passing by as they walked their impossibly
small dogs and cast disapproving looks at him—felt that he approved.

Not of Blue Hair, although he'd liked her. He liked women with spirit. They reminded him of Betty and Veronica.

What he approved of was 910 Park Avenue itself, and its tenants.

The living ones, anyway.

It was an elegant brick structure, built on a corner and obviously well maintained. The potted plants on either side of the electronic doors looked healthy and lush. There was a spotless red carpet beneath the green awning above the doors, and the doorman standing under it was young and eager to do his job well. Alaric saw him corner and cuff a Chinese food deliveryman before he'd managed to slink by him, determined to slip menus under unsuspecting tenants' doors.

The doorman also stopped to carefully check the name of each guest arriving to attend the Antonescus' party off a list they'd given him before allowing them up.

That was how Alaric had discovered that there was no way he could simply crash the party uninvited . . . unless of course he used force.

And he wasn't willing to play that card. Yet.

And because the building was twenty stories high, and the Antonescus lived on the eleventh floor with no fire escape, his "feet first through the window from the roof" trick wouldn't work, either.

Until he figured out a way to sneak inside through the parking garage in the basement—or possibly using the service entrance—he was going to get to know the parked cars outside of 910 Park Avenue pretty well, he suspected.

But that was all right. He had time. All the time in the world to plan his next move.

Alaric had checked into the Peninsula the night before and was very much enjoying the upgrade from his hotel in Chattanooga. There were several premium cable channels for him to enjoy—on a flat-screen TV, no less, while soaking in a big, deep tub with no rubber slide strips in the bathroom—and Frette sheets, not to mention an indoor pool in a glass atrium on the top floor so he could keep up his workouts; a vast and varied room service menu to explore; and several lounges where attractive women of all nationalities could be found after a day of shopping sipping tea and texting their friends. No, Alaric was in no rush to leave Manhattan.

Except for one small, unpleasant fact.

The reason he was there in the first place.

But then, if the e-mail Martin had forwarded him was genuine, the prince was in town for the very same reason: to make sure no more young girls had their life's blood sucked out of them.

The file containing all their photos had been waiting for Alaric when he'd checked in.

What that file contained had horrified him.

And it took a lot to horrify Alaric, who was convinced he'd seen everything in his twenty years with the Palatine.

There were no names attached to the victims' photos. The coroner's office suspected—due to the girls' dental work—that they were of Eastern European or even Russian birth and in the country illegally . . . which would explain why not a single person had come forward to identify them.

Alaric had given them American names to go with the American dreams with which he felt sure each of them had traveled to this country:

First was long-haired Aimee, found early one morning just ten days ago in the Ramble at Central Park.

Then red-haired Jennifer, found a few days later by a park employee in Bryant Park.

The final victim he called Hayley. Her photo was perhaps most disturbing of all to Alaric, because she bore more than a passing resemblance to Martin's daughter, Simone. Both were dark skinned, with black hair that spiraled around their faces in similar tight corkscrew curls.

She had been found just last weekend in Central Park, like Aimee. . . .

Alaric, studying the photos in his hotel room, had seen what the general public—and few members of law enforcement, beyond the coroner's office—had not. There was no question of cause of death and no question, once the photos had been e-mailed to the Vatican, who—or rather *what*—was responsible for those deaths.

The only question was, would the Palatine be able to exterminate him—or them, because Alaric, upon seeing the photos, became convinced there'd been more than just one attacker—before the prince could?

It still seemed mind-boggling to Alaric that a vampire could actually be in New York on a mission similar to his own. Not just any vampire, but the prince of darkness.

But, Alaric supposed, the prince didn't care about the dead girls. To him, the murders of those three girls only meant possible exposure to the public of his kind. Discovery by the rest of humankind that vampires were not some invention of Bram Stoker's feverish imagination—something that, if Alaric was honest, he had to admit the Vatican was at just as great pains to prevent as the vamps. They didn't need another panic like the one that spread through Eastern Europe during the 1700s, when ignorant villagers, goaded by charlatan "vampire exterminators," were led to believe their own family members were actually undead and, after being coerced into buying expensive "vampire weapons," dug them up from their resting places and decapitated them.

It made a certain kind of sense, Alaric supposed, that the prince would be there, trying to stop the killer—or killers—same as the Palatine. He had to be as worried as the Vatican that word could get out about the truth of his species' existence.

Still. It made Alaric feel livid, the fact that he might have the same goal as the prince.

Of course, Alaric had another goal, in addition to finding, and stopping, whoever or whatever was doing this: he intended to destroy the prince, as well. Whether his bosses at the Palatine approved or not.

He'd spent a lot of time working out his frustrations over his assignment in the hotel pool but had followed it with an excellent lunch at Per Se.

So while he wasn't happy with his current circumstances, he was at least eating well.

And he certainly wouldn't starve to death while he stood around staring at the entrance to 910 Park Avenue, waiting to see if the prince actually showed up.

He was even beginning to think he might—grudgingly, of course—approve of the people he'd assigned himself to watch. The Antonescus were rich—stinking, filthy rich. Like him, they seemed to find no shame in enjoying the finer things in life. They had the summer place in Romania—not too shabby, judging by the photos—and appeared to enjoy going to upscale restaurants. Last night they'd dined at the Four Seasons.

Well, "dined" was a relative term. Of course they hadn't eaten much, being the foul breathless beasts of Satan that they were.

The wife was the head of 910 Park Avenue's cooperative—some kind of board that chose who would be allowed to live in the building—undoubtedly so that she could keep out the "riffraff" (people like himself, Alaric supposed).

Still, no one to whom Alaric had spoken had anything negative to say about her . . . and none whatsoever picked up on his hints that she might possibly be a member of the undead. (Not that she'd have needed to sleep in her own coffin or have the earth from her grave near her. These were other old myths Stoker had gotten wrong in his book.) Either she wasn't a vampire, or she and her husband had assimilated better than any demons he'd ever seen. She even served on several charitable boards, one that helped pay for children with cancer to go to summer camp in the countryside.

Children with cancer. Nice cover, for a bloodsucker.

The husband owned and managed numerous real estate holdings throughout the city and often escorted the wife to benefits, like ones for the cancer camp.

Vampires who attended benefits to raise money for summer camps for children . . . with cancer! Hilarious. Even more hilarious than *Betty and Veronica*.

Now, he'd told Martin, he'd seen everything.

Simone had grabbed the phone while Alaric had still been chuckling with her father over the benefit-attending vampires and said, "Uncle Alaric?"

"Yes, sweetheart?"

"Are you going to get the people who ate my daddy's face?"

"Yes," he'd said, sobering instantly. "Yes, I am."

Just like he was going to get whatever had killed Aimee, Jennifer, and Hayley . . . or whatever the victims' real names were.

Because that was what it was all about. If these Antonescus really were related to this Lucien Antonescu, and he really was the prince of darkness, Alaric was going to destroy them. All of them. He didn't care what his superiors at the Vatican wanted or how much money the Antonescus had donated so that children with cancer could go to camp. They were still parasites—like ticks—that had to be exterminated for what they'd done to Martin. To that girl, Sarah, from the Chattanooga Walmart. To those unidentified dead women, lying in the morgue.

And to countless others like them whom Alaric had seen abused and victimized over his years with the Palatine. They had to be destroyed like the vermin that they were. Because they would only create more creatures like themselves, who would in turn victimize more people like Martin and Sarah and those girls.

Vampires were filth. And they spread their filth—and disease—to everything and everyone they touched.

They all had to be eradicated.

There wasn't much more to it than that.

In the meantime, Alaric would stand there outside of 910 Park Avenue and wait. He didn't care how many little old ladies walked by him and asked what he thought he was doing. He'd show them the pictures of Aimee, Jennifer, and Hayley if he had to.

And maybe, while he was at it, a photo of where Martin's face used to be.

That would shut them up.

Chapter Twenty-five

Mary Lou and her husband did an admirable job of making sure Meena's wineglass was never lower than half full throughout the evening.

But Meena was careful to drink from it only sparingly. The last thing she wanted was to get plastered in front of people she had to see in the elevator every day. . . .

Not to mention in front of the prince.

It wasn't until Mary Lou was asking if anyone cared for coffee that she realized it was past midnight. Meena noticed her brother, Jon, looking surreptitiously at his watch. Apparently his dinner companion, Becca, hadn't been able to take his mind off his celebrity crush, Taylor Mackenzie, which was no surprise. Few could.

"Oh," Meena said with genuine regret. "I'm so sorry. I have to go. I have work in the morning. And I still have to get home and walk my dog."

"I'll do it." Jon volunteered, hopping up from his place on the couch with a speed that Meena found a little embarrassing.

"I'll join you, Meena, if you don't mind some company," Lucien said, setting down his wineglass. "I'd enjoy stretching my legs a bit after that delicious meal."

Meena felt her cheeks turning red. She couldn't believe she was blushing. That was something she hadn't done in ages.

Until tonight, that is.

"I'd be delighted," she said. She didn't point out that Lucien had hardly touched a bit of that "delicious meal." He'd said he still had a little jet lag.

Jon sank back down into his place. "Oh," he said, struggling to hide his disappointment. "I guess you guys have it under control, then."

Becca had taken out her cell phone and was scrolling through her applications, looking everywhere but in Jon's direction.

"What a great idea," Mary Lou said enthusiastically. "You two go out for a walk. It's such a lovely night. Isn't it a lovely night, Emil?"

"It's a lovely night," Emil said.

But Meena couldn't help noticing he looked a little worried as he sent the maid to collect the prince's overcoat.

"We'll just go up the street," Lucien was saying.

"Let me run and get Jack," Meena said.

She slipped across the hall, aware that Jon had hastily made his good-byes and followed her, not seeming to care that his escape had been so awkward.

"What are you doing?" he asked when she'd unlocked the door and let them both into her apartment, then closed the door again behind them. "Are you actually into that guy or something?"

"Um, let me see," Meena said. She plucked her coat off the rack by the door and slipped it on, cinching it tightly around her waist, while Jack Bauer, over the moon at seeing her, danced around her feet excitedly. "What's not to like, exactly? His old-world manners, his dark good looks, or the fact that he's way into me and is probably going to be the father of my children someday?"

Jon had slunk over to the couch and collapsed onto it. Now he lifted his head off one of Meena's Pottery Barn throw pillows and stared at her. "I thought you didn't want kids," he said, " 'cause you don't want to be the worst, most smothering mother in the world, always following them around with Bubble Wrap and needles filled with adrenaline."

"Fine," Meena said with a sniff. "That was a figure of speech. I don't really want to have his children. Seriously, though. What do you think of him?"

"He's all right, I guess," Jon said, leaning his head back down and picking up the remote. "If you like the brooding, mysterious type."

"Honestly." Meena took Jack Bauer's leash off the hook on the wall and clipped it to his collar as he jumped around. "You have to get off that couch more, Jon. Lucien Antonescu is the perfect guy."

"I'm just saying," Jon said, flicking on the TV. "Don't blame me if he tries to ravish you in a dark doorway."

"I should be so lucky," Meena said. "And you could have been a little nicer to Becca. She seemed really sweet."

Jon looked confused. "I thought her name was Becky."

Meena rolled her eyes. "If I'm not back in an hour, *don't* wait up," she said.

"Practice safe sex," Jon called after her.

Meena threw him a disgusted look over her shoulder.

"Remember our conversation approximately five seconds ago regarding my not wanting to ruin the lives of any future progeny with my constant harping on their impending deaths? I never have anything *but* safe sex."

"Good," Jon said, and turned up the volume of *Top Gear*. "Because I'm too young to be an uncle."

Meena turned away with another eye roll . . . although at the last minute she grabbed her *other* purse—the big one that had the stash of condoms in it left over from her ill-fated date with the high-cholesterol guy, which had of course been wishful thinking on her part—and left the apartment.

It never hurt, she supposed, to be extra careful. And prepared. Even though nothing was going to happen, of course. He was a prince! Princes didn't do things like that. Not on the first date.

Lucien was waiting alone for her in the hallway, looking exactly as Jon had described him . . . brooding and mysterious. Meena's heart skipped a beat at the sight of him.

"Hi," she said, feeling suddenly shy. Okay. What was she *doing*?

"Hello," he said.

His gaze seemed to penetrate straight through her. Those dark eyes didn't seem so sad anymore. She was convinced now that he knew not only that she'd grabbed her purse that had condoms in it, but that he knew exactly what she looked like without her dress on.

The strange thing was that she didn't mind.

It was too bad that Jack Bauer did. Or at least she thought he did, judging from the way he carried on, tugging at his leash and growling.

"Sorry," she said, embarrassed by her dog.

"It's all right," he said, smiling. He pushed the Down button. "He seems a bit high-strung."

"That's putting it mildly," she said. "That's why we call him Jack Bauer."

"Jack Bauer," he said, gazing down at the dog, who continued to growl up at him. "Oh, I see. After the character on the television program."

"Right," Meena said, pleased that he finally got an American popular culture reference. "You've seen it?"

"Enough of it," he said. There was a world of condemnation in his tone. He did *not* like the show. "I don't tend to watch programs with torture in them."

"Oh," Meena said. She felt mortified. His tone implied he had personal reasons to dislike these kinds of story lines. Had he himself been tortured while serving in the military or something?

It was entirely possible. Meena knew next to nothing about the history of Romania, much less its military.

But she thought she remembered something about . . . oh, something awful. Why hadn't she Googled Romania really fast when she was in the apartment? Then at least she could have been informed.

"Well," she said uncomfortably. "I can understand that. I don't like to watch things where people die." That touched a little too close to home for comfort. "But, anyway, Jack Bauer only tortures bad guys."

"But can you be as certain as Jack Bauer is, Meena," Lucien asked as the elevator doors slid open and he smiled down at her while politely holding them, "that you always know the good guys from the bad guys?"

This caused Meena to hesitate before stepping into the car. Jack Bauer, on the end of his leash, was backing away, growling, reluctant to leave the hallway. For some reason, Jon's remark about dark doorways slipped into her mind, as did her flippant reply.

Did she know the difference between good guys and bad guys? Leisha insisted that David, whom Meena had always thought was a good guy, had been a bad guy . . . although Meena had never really been able to agree with her. In the end, hadn't he just been following his own heart?

And truthfully, Meena was much better off without him. If she'd stayed with David, she'd now be a housewife in New Jersey, where David had moved to start his new practice, with his new wife and his new house. And his baby on the way.

Meena loved her job and her life in New York City, even if they weren't perfect.

Given all of that, things with her and David had turned out all right in the end, hadn't they?

And here was Lucien, who had saved her life. That made him a good guy, didn't it? He was *definitely* a good guy.

All right, Jack Bauer might not have liked him.

But Jack Bauer had never liked Mary Lou or Emil, either . . . not since the day Meena had brought him home from the animal shelter.

And they'd always been lovely—except for making incredibly boring conversation on the elevator. But look at all the money they'd raised for charity.

Smiling back up at Lucien, Meena stepped carefully over the gap between the elevator car and the hallway floor, conscious of her high heels.

"I think you're a good guy," she said deliberately as Lucien joined her in the car. "And Jack Bauer does, too. He just may need a little more convincing than I do, because his brain is the size of a walnut."

Unfortunately, the dog illustrated this fact by not quite making it all the way into the car before the elevator doors started to close. Meena had to turn and give his leash a tug. The dog let out a startled yelp and careened into Meena's legs, which sent her lurching forward, right into Lucien's arms.

"Oh," Meena said, mortified. "Excuse me."

"No need to apologize," Lucien said. "Are you all right?"

"I'm fine," Meena said, suddenly unable to tear her gaze from his.

Neither of them, it seemed, was able to let the other go.

Instead, they stood looking into each other's eyes for a good five seconds. Meena's breathing felt a little shallow. She wondered if he felt the electrical charge that seemed to be pulsing between them . . . or if it was just her overactive imagination again. Her heartbeat was definitely quicker than usual and a little unsteady. The only sound, besides Jack Bauer's panting, was that of the elevator dinging off the floors as they descended.

She didn't want to break the silence between them, because it was the type of silence during which anything might happen.

He might, she felt, even tilt his head down and kiss her . . . if she kept her mouth shut long enough to let this happen.

But she couldn't, of course.

"What happened to you that you can't watch things where characters get tortured?" she asked in a voice that had gone a little hoarse.

She watched his face carefully to gauge his reaction.

But there was no discernible reaction in his features. Instead, he countered her question with one of his own.

"What happened to you," he asked, "that you can't watch things where characters die?"

She dropped her arms from his at once and turned toward the elevator door just as the letter L lit up and the door slid open to reveal the lobby.

"Oh," she said with an airy laugh as she dragged a badly misbehaving Jack Bauer out into the lobby. "I just love happy endings. That's all."

"So do I," Lucien said, following her with a smile. "Tomorrow I'm going to start watching this television show of yours."

"Oh," Meena said, delighted. "That'll be a good episode. Cheryl is making out again with Father Juan Carlos, and the town gossip sees them, and all hell breaks loose. Definitely not to be missed."

Lucien laughed. "Then I'll be glued to the screen."

They breezed past Pradip, who waved to them cheerfully with a "Good evening, Miss Harper!"

Then they strolled out into the evening air, which had a briskness to it now that night had fallen. Meena, feeling happier than she could remember being in ages, started in the direction she and Jack Bauer usually walked.

But Lucien took her by the arm and gently steered her in another direction.

"This way," he said. "I have something I want to show you."

Surprised, she smiled. "Really?"

Then she realized he was walking her away from two men who appeared to be having something of an argument in front of 912 Park . . . and also in the opposite direction from St. George's Cathedral.

And her heart swelled. He was protecting her!

It had been ages since a man (aside from her doormen, who didn't count, because she gave them generous tips at Christmas) had cared anything about her physical protection. Jon seemed to think she could more than adequately take care of herself (and besides, he didn't count either; he was her brother). Her father had pretty much given up speaking to her about more than perfunctory matters once she'd developed her ability to envision people's future deaths (including his own). Both her parents seemed to view her as some sort of biological freak. Whenever she visited them in Florida now, Meena overheard them arguing in hushed whispers over which side of the family she'd inherited her ability from (there'd been more than a hint that Great-Aunt Wilhelmina might be responsible).

And while it was true that she *could* take care of herself—the odd bat attack aside—it was terribly gallant of Lucien to try to protect her. It made her feel warm and feminine.

Who said chivalry was dead?

"What sort of surprise?" Meena asked, containing her glee with effort.

"One I think you'll like," he said. They were headed up Seventy-ninth Street, toward Fifth Avenue. That part of town was devoted exclusively to deluxe apartment buildings, hotels, and Central Park. . . .

And one other building, located at Eighty-second and Fifth, which they were fast approaching.

"The Met?" Meena looked up at Lucien curiously. He'd reached for her hand as they crossed Fifth Avenue and started toward the enormous building, sitting so imposingly lit up against the night sky. A few people sat along the steps, chatting, smoking, even reading books in the glow from the illuminated columns. Trying to ignore the tingle of excitement that shot up her arm at the touch of his skin to hers, Meena stammered, "But . . . but the Met . . . it's closed this time of night."

She wasn't certain that as a foreigner—even one who taught at a university and read the classics for fun—he fully understood.

"To most people," Lucien said with a mysterious smile. "Follow me."

And, still holding her hand in his own, he guided her up the long steps that led to the front doors of the Metropolitan Museum of Art. Meena, distracted by Lucien's touch, forgot to hold on to Jack Bauer's leash as tightly as she should have, and just as they got to an unobtrusive side door, he managed to dart off.

"Oh!" she cried. "Jack!"

She dropped Lucien's hand to chase after her dog. Jack ran only as far as a group of students who were sitting a few yards away, listening to one another's iPods and sharing a pizza, in which Jack was extremely interested. By the time she'd caught the dog up in her arms and apologized to the students, who smiled warmly at her, she turned back and found Lucien standing with the door open, waiting for her to join him inside the darkened museum.

"Oh," she said, glancing behind her. No one on the steps appeared to have noticed that her date had just broken into a New York City landmark.

Or so she supposed. Surely the prince didn't have a key to the Metropolitan Museum of Art.

Or did he? Maybe all Romanian princes-slash-professors did.

"You can't just . . . How did you . . . ?" She broke off, laughing. "Lucien, how did you get in there?"

He held up a black card with a magnetic strip on the back. "I told you," he said. "A friend of mine is giving a lecture here this week. I thought you might want to see what he's talking about. Come in. It's quite all right."

She still hesitated, glancing around her. "But . . . aren't there security guards?"

"Don't worry about them. I'll take care of them."

Meena raised her eyebrows. He would *take care* of them? What did that mean?

Oh . . . that he would bribe them. Of course.

Lucien was a prince. He was rich. He was used to getting his way. With everyone. Especially staff.

She supposed he had dozens of staff. Maids. Butlers, even. Staff for his summer palace. Pilots for his private jet.

Meena had staff—a housekeeper who came once every other week and refused to do laundry.

"But," she murmured lamely, "I've got the dog."

"No one cares about a little dog." He looked incredibly handsome, standing there with the darkness behind him, one hand stretched out to her, the other keeping the door open for her. "Trust me, Meena."

The incredible part was that she did. She hardly knew him at all.

But she *did* trust him.

Why wouldn't she? He'd already saved her life, and had done so by risking his own.

What was a little breaking and entering, compared to that?

But Meena had never been a risk taker . . . not on her own behalf. Leisha had nailed it on the head when she'd accused Meena of having a hero complex. Meena would do anything to help save the life of someone else (if only they'd allow her to).

But when it came to herself? Though she could look into the future of complete strangers, she'd never been able to see what fate had in store for her.

And so too many times she'd done what was easiest—stay with a boyfriend who didn't really love her; not complain about a coworker who was taking advantage of her—instead of what she knew, deep down, was right.

And now?

She knew if she slipped her hand into Lucien Antonescu's, she wouldn't just be risking possible arrest by the New York City Police Department.

She'd be risking her heart.

Was she really going to do this?

But what other choice did she have? Was she just going to sit on the couch like Jon for the rest of her life, waiting for the perfect person, the perfect job, the perfect life to come along?

How did she know that perfect person wasn't standing in front of her right now? How did anyone know?

Easy. They didn't. They took a risk.

She slipped her fingers into his.

Maybe she couldn't see into her own future.

But that didn't mean she didn't have one.

"All right," she said with a smile. "Show me. Show me everything."

Chapter Twenty-six

12:45 A.M. EST, Friday, April 16
910 Park Avenue
New York, New York

Alaric saw them come out of the building together—the tall, dark-haired man and the petite brunette with the short hair and the tightly cinched trench coat. She was walking a Pomeranian mix. The dog looked like it was foaming at the mouth in its desire to attack the dark-haired man . . .

. . . who looked exactly like the author photo of Lucien Antonescu that Martin had e-mailed him earlier.

Alaric dropped the Archie comic into his pocket and straightened. He wasn't going to go for his scabbard. Not yet. He'd follow them and see where they went, if the guy tried anything.

Then when he did—and he would; Alaric knew he would, knew it as surely as he knew that his sword arm would never fail him—Alaric would slice off his head and have the pleasure of watching the prince of darkness finally turn to dust.

The only problem was, when Alaric took a single step toward the couple, a heavy hand fell upon his shoulder. Startled—it wasn't often Alaric was taken by surprise—he spun around, his sword half out of its sheath. . . .

Only to come face-to-face with his boss.

"Goddamnit, Holtzman," Alaric said, lowering his blade. "What are you trying to do, get yourself filleted?"

"You're in violation of orders, Wulf." Abraham Holtzman was a balding man who'd dressed for the assignment of shadowing the ruler of all that was unholy in jeans and sandals. With socks. At least he had the sense to wear a Star of David at his neck. "You're not supposed to be here."

"Nice socks," Alaric said. "Very unobtrusive. No one in Manhattan will notice you or think you're from out of town. Now, if you'll excuse me, I'm going to go kill the prince of darkness before he gets away."

"Stop!" Holtzman threw out a hand to halt Alaric just as Lucien Antonescu put out his own hand and, his gaze falling on Alaric and Holtzman, steered the dark-haired young woman in the opposite direction, away from them.

Had the prince seen the two of them? Alaric didn't know.

But he had felt a sort of chill just as that dark-eyed gaze had rested, however briefly, on him.

Had the prince known who, or what, he and Holtzman represented? Did he know that the Palatine Guard was watching him?

Alaric would never know. Because Holtzman was reaching into his suit coat and pulling out the only thing in the universe Alaric dreaded more than a pack of vampires whipped into a frenzy by the smell of fresh human blood.

The Palatine Guard Human Resources Handbook.

"No," Alaric said, a spurt of irritation coursing through him. "For God's sake, Holtzman. We don't have ti—"

"Look here, Wulf," Holtzman was already saying. "It says right here on page fourteen of the handbook, 'If an officer should witness his partner wounded in the line of duty, he will be *required* to take a minimum of *no less than* two weeks' leave for psychological R and R *as well as* undergo mandatory counseling,' which we both know you've dodged, as usual. And it says that he will not be allowed back on duty until he's completed both of these. Now, we all know what a workaholic you are. You haven't had a vacation in years. And God knows what Martin went through in Berlin was horrific. You stalked that entire nest by yourself afterward . . . don't deny it, I saw the report. It's not your fault they went underground and were never found . . . undoubtedly because they didn't relish the idea of being stalked by you. So we've been willing to turn a blind eye to your refusal to follow the rules. But when it comes to the prince of darkness, you're going to have to stand back and let us— Alaric! I say, Alaric!"

But Alaric had already heard more than he could stand and had sprinted off after the couple who had just disappeared around the corner.

Except of course by that time he'd lost them.

Which shouldn't even have been possible. The man was over six feet tall and the woman a diminutive five-four in heels, at the *most*. They made a striking couple and certainly stood out in a crowd. She'd been toting along a golden-brown walking fuzzball of a dog.

How could they just have vanished?

"They're gone," Alaric cried when Holtzman came rushing up beside him. "They're gone. And it's your fault, you bureaucratic buffoon. If you hadn't stood there quoting the HR handbook at me—"

"They aren't gone." Holtzman scanned the street. "He's playing with us."

"What?" Alaric shook his head. He'd always have some respect for the training his boss had given him during his early days as a vampire hunter. But the man's refusal to do things any way but by the book had always made Alaric's blood boil.

"He saw us," Holtzman said. "And he's thrown up a glamour to protect himself."

Alaric was taken aback. "Of course. Why didn't I think of that?"

Holtzman shook his head sadly. "Because you're too personally involved in this, Alaric. Why do you think I asked you to concentrate on the case to which you've been assigned—finding the killer of the dead girls—and not the prince? Your desire to wipe out the entire vampire race for what they did to your partner . . . it's made you ineffective at your work. Now go back to your hotel. Which, I've heard, is the most expensive one in the city . . . as usual. I hope you don't think Accounts Payable will accept receipts from a place like that. There's no earthly reason why you couldn't have stayed downtown at the rectory at St. Clare's, like me."

Alaric set his jaw. He didn't like being told what to do, not even by his oldest mentor.

Or that he ought to stay in a barren church rectory on his employer's dime instead of the luxurious hotel he was paying for himself.

Nor did he like being told that his personal feelings were making him ineffective at his job . . . even if there was a *slight* possibility that it was true.

But most especially, he didn't like the fact that he'd encountered a vamp with the kind of casual power Lucien Antonescu seemed to possess. The ability simply to turn invisible on a less-than-crowded sidewalk? And to make the woman he was with—and her *dog*— invisible too?

Alaric had battled some pretty powerful vampires in the past—the South American ones, he remembered, had always been particularly awe-inspiring—but none with those kinds of abilities.

"We don't even know if he'll come back," Holtzman complained irritably, staring off toward Fifth Avenue. "He's seen us now. He'll know we know about the Antonescus. We've lost him."

Holtzman didn't come out and add, *And it's your fault, Wulf.* But Alaric could tell he was thinking it.

"We've still got them," Alaric said. "Mary Lou and Emil Antonescu. We can use them to find him."

"They'll never talk." Holtzman sounded sorrowful. "Especially not if I leave you in charge. You'll whack off their heads before I even get a chance to ask them anything. I know you."

Alaric shook his head. He squared his shoulders and turned around to head back to 910 Park Avenue.

"Wulf?" Holtzman seemed startled by his protégé's sudden activity. He hurried after him. "Wulf. I was kidding about whacking off the Antonescus' heads. They could still prove to be vital sources of information to us. Let's not do anything to tip our hand. They don't know yet that we've discovered them. Lucien might not really have seen us or figured out who we are. Don't do anything rash—"

Alaric strode up to the red carpet in front of 910 Park. As soon as he stood in front of the double brass-framed doors, they opened with a whoosh, and the doorman in the dark green livery, reading a textbook entitled *The Art of Sensuous Massage,* looked up from it and smiled.

"How can I help you, sir?"

"Yes," Alaric said, grinning broadly. "I could have sworn I just saw my best friend from college come out of this building—the tall, dark-haired guy—but he jumped into a cab before I could get his attention. Was that him, Lucien Antonescu, or am I crazy?"

"Lucien Antonescu?" The doorman kept right on smiling. "Lucien Antonescu? I'm afraid we don't . . . Oh, you must mean the tall gentleman who was visiting Mr. and Mrs. Antonescu tonight! Yes, yes. There was a Mr. Antonescu on the list."

"I knew it," Alaric said, just as Holtzman came hurrying in behind him. "I knew that was Lucien!"

The doorman, whose nameplate said *Pradip,* looked down at a list on his desk. "That's right," he said. "There was a Lucien Antonescu at Mr. and Mrs. Antonescu's party tonight."

"See, Dad," Alaric said, turning to Holtzman. "I told you it was him."

"Dad?" Holtzman said. Now it was his turn to be taken aback.

"And that beautiful young lady, the one with the dog, who was with him," Alaric said, turning back to the doorman, "must have been his wife. I can't believe it. He never told me he got married!"

"Oh," Pradip said, laughing. "No, that was Miss Harper. She lives here in the building. Oh, no. No, Miss Harper's not married."

Alaric let his face fall. "Are you serious?" he asked. "That wasn't Lucien's wife?"

"No, no," Pradip said. He was having a grand old laugh now, as if the thought of Miss Harper marrying Mr. Antonescu was the funniest thing he'd ever heard in the world. "No, Miss Meena Harper lives here with her brother, Mr. Harper. She and your friend just met tonight, at the Antonescus' party, I think."

Alaric's estimation of 910 Park Avenue went up another notch. Pradip the doorman was observant, indeed, but a little too forthcoming with total strangers about the personal lives of his tenants. . . . Alaric now knew that the woman accompanying Lucien Antonescu tonight was named Meena Harper, that she lived in the building, and that she lived with her brother. No small amount of information considering that all he'd volunteered about himself was the lie that he'd been Lucien Antonescu's college roommate.

"Well, I'm sorry I missed him," Alaric said. "You know what? I'm going to see if I can look him up on Facebook."

"Oh, that's a great idea," Pradip said. "You know, you can get in touch with practically anyone on Facebook these days. I was on there the other day, and I managed to get in touch with an old friend of mine I hadn't seen since kindergarten. Can you believe that?"

"You see, Dad?" Alaric grinned at Holtzman. "Facebook. That's how it's done."

Holtzman looked dazed. "Facebook?" he echoed.

Alaric winked at the doorman. "Thanks, Pradip," he said. "You wouldn't have any idea where Lucien is staying while he's here in the city, would you?"

"Oh, no. But if you'd like to buzz up to the Antonescus," Pradip said as he lifted the receiver to the intercom, "I'm sure they'd be happy to—"

"Not necessary," Alaric said, stretching his hand out in the internationally recognized sign for *stop*. "I wouldn't want to trouble them this late. Maybe I'll drop by again some other day, thanks."

And he turned and left the building, Holtzman following closely behind him.

"Impressive," his superior said to him. "Nice to see you using one of the techniques I taught you for a change, instead of simply swinging that sword of yours around."

"I try to avoid killing the civilian population whenever possible," Alaric said, shooting his boss an irritated look. "You taught me that as well, remember?"

"I remember," Holtzman said. "But what exactly did you accomplish there, aside from very likely alerting the Antonescus that we're aware of them? You know that doorman is going to tell them we were there. And we're no closer to finding him."

"No," Alaric agreed. "But we have the name of the girl."

"And what earthly good will that do us?"

"Oh," Alaric said, "quite a lot of good, I imagine. Because she's going to lead us straight to him."

Then he added thoughtfully, "If she lives through the night, that is."

Chapter Twenty-seven

1:00 A.M. EST, Friday, April 16
Metropolitan Museum of Art
1000 Fifth Avenue
New York, New York

Meena had spent quite a lot of time in the Metropolitan Museum of Art, back when she'd first moved to the city. She'd been especially drawn to a portrait of Joan of Arc by an artist called Jules Bastien-Lepage, which hung in the nineteenth-century wing.

The painting showed Joan standing in the yard of her parents' cottage, staring off into space, apparently listening to the voices of saints. Ethereal, haloed figures floated behind Joan's back, seemingly whispering to her.

The painting wasn't anything that special. Compared to other treasures the museum held, it was considered one of the collection's lesser works.

Still, Meena always made the canvas her primary destination upon entering the museum and would, when she was feeling especially disheartened or hopeless, stand for nearly an hour looking at it, in the company of similarly downtrodden souls.

But Prince Lucien didn't lead Meena toward the nineteenth-century wing when he pulled her into the Metropolitan Museum that night.

Instead, he guided her toward the medieval art exhibit on the main floor, through the darkened, hushed Great Hall.

It was strange being in the museum after it was closed. Meena had never seen the halls so empty . . . or so quiet.

She could actually hear her own heart thumping steadily with the excitement of what they were doing—despite Lucien's insistence that it was fine, she felt that there was something illicit about their being there. Of course there was!

And now Lucien was holding her hand again.

His grip wasn't exactly warm—his fingers always seemed a bit cool to the touch—but it was oddly reassuring, the way it had been that night outside of St. George's Cathedral.

And yet there was an almost boyish excitement about him, too, an eagerness with which he seemed to want to show her the treasures the museum held. He playfully held a finger to his lips as he guided her along.

"Are we going to set off any alarms?" Meena asked nervously, holding a squirming Jack Bauer in one arm.

"Only if you try to steal something," the prince jokingly replied.

"Oh, well, I guess I'll have to restrain myself then," Meena said, teasing him back. She was pleased to see that a lively side to him was coming out. He may not have watched much television, but he knew how to have fun.

Soon they were surrounded by hauntingly beautiful triptychs of the Madonna and child, and bejeweled golden crucifixes that seemed to glow with the otherworldly light that came from their display cases. Lucien steered her away from these and toward a collection of fifteenth-century portraits and woodcuts. Meena couldn't read the cards on the display cases attached to the portraits because it was too dark, but Lucien explained, "These are of Prince Vlad Tepes of Wallachia—you know, the man I was telling you about, the one who's such a hero in my country. He lived in the age of the first printing presses, so there's a great deal of historical documentation about him. His father, Vlad the Second, was a member of the Order of the Dragon—established by the king of Hungary in order to unite neighboring kingdoms against the Ottoman Empire. So Vlad Tepes was indoctrinated in the order as well . . . at the age of five, right before his father handed him and his little brother over as hostages to the sultan of the Ottoman Empire as a personal guarantee he wouldn't attack the sultan while the boys were under his roof."

"Oh, dear," Meena said, feeling slightly deflated. This story was a bit of a downer.

She supposed she wasn't surprised to hear of Vlad's father's cruelty, giving his sons over to a sultan in order to preserve peace, considering his image in the portrait. If Vlad Tepes looked anything like his dad, he couldn't have been very nice. He had a long, sinister-looking black mustache and beady eyes.

Or maybe they just didn't know how to draw very well back then. Meena had always avoided this part of the museum. Her tastes tended to run more toward the Romantics. . . .

Lucien didn't seem to notice Meena's dislike for the subject matter, however. As a history professor, he was obviously very enthusiastic on the topic of his country's greatest forefather.

Lucien went on. "Although his brother was a great favorite of the sultan, the Ottomans didn't treat Vlad Tepes very well, I'm afraid. And when he finally did inherit the throne from his father and return home to Wallachia, he was still quite bitter about the whole thing . . . and things didn't improve much for him after that, I'm afraid. He had an unfortunate life, filled with much sorrow. His first wife, whom he dearly loved, was a beautiful and innocent young woman. Some people even whispered that . . . well, that she was like an angel on earth."

Meena raised her eyebrows upon hearing this, and she saw Lucien give her a quick smile.

"Yes," he said. "I thought you'd like that part of the story."

He took her hand and led her toward a primitive black-and-white woodcut depicting a turreted castle with a river running beneath it.

"Unfortunately," he said in a voice that seemed carefully devoid of emotion to Meena, "it doesn't have the kind of ending you like. Vlad and his wife lived in warlike times. Upon hearing their castle was under siege by the Turks—who were rumored to be unspeakably cruel to royal female prisoners back in those days—his young bride threw herself out an upper-story window, preferring death to what she thought she'd face at their hands."

Meena sucked in her breath, her gaze flying to one of the high turrets pictured in the woodcut.

"She fell into the river beneath the palace window and drowned," Lucien continued in the same emotionless tone. "That river is still referred to today as the Princess's River."

"Oh," Meena said unhappily. She was liking this story less and less. "How sad!"

"It *was* sad," Lucien said in agreement. "And it gets sadder still. Her husband had married her for love . . . a rarity in those days. He was never the same after her death. Some say he went mad. He began to treat his enemies—and even his own subjects, his own *sons*—in a . . . well, in a very regrettable manner."

Meena looked up sharply when she heard him say the words *a very regrettable manner*.

Because while his tone had still been as distantly academic as ever, and probably no one else would have noticed the slightest difference in his voice, Meena knew: the prince was thinking about his own childhood. Lucien's father had treated *him* in "a very regrettable manner." She was certain of it . . . even more so as she watched the way his gaze seemed to burn as he stared down at the woodcut of the Princess's River.

And Meena's heart twisted with pity for him. Yes, he was a prince, and handsome and rich and worldly.

But she knew what it was like to have problems. *Real* problems. The kind that kept you up nights, stumbling around in the dark, reaching for amber prescription sleeping-pill bottles.

It was at that moment that Meena was gripped by an urge, as sudden as it was fierce, to save him . . . the same urge she felt with everyone she met and knew was going to die soon.

Only in this case, she wanted to rescue Lucien from the sadness she could see in those dark brown eyes, not from certain death . . . the same way he'd saved her that night from the bats that had come shrieking down from the spires of St. George's Cathedral.

Only she didn't know how. She knew how to save people only from their futures (and even that she didn't do very well).

How did you save someone from his past?

Then, Lucien seemed to shake himself and gave her hand a squeeze and said with a smile, "I'm sorry, Meena. You said you like stories with happy endings, and I tell you this one, which is most decidedly *not* happy. I don't know why I felt such a strong desire to share it with you. It's an important story—to me. To my people. But . . . it's not for a woman like you, who is so filled with life and joy."

Meena raised her eyebrows. Boy, did he ever have *her* wrong.

"But the point is," Lucien said, still smiling, "Vlad Tepes is Romania's greatest hero . . . like your General Washington. We wouldn't exist as a country if it weren't for him."

"Oh," Meena said. "Well, in that case, good for him."

But she wasn't sure she believed him. Not about this Vlad person, whoever he was, but about the smile he'd given her. She knew it was fake. She could still sense the secret sorrow in him. . . .

And because she knew what it was like to feel so alone, she felt that it was up to her to find a balm for his despair.

Her gaze wandered, searching for something that might help.

And a second later, she was guiding *him* toward an icon that glowed gold in the light from its display case.

"Look," she said triumphantly, thinking to herself, *Oh, good. This will do the trick.* "This is appropriate, considering the way we met."

Meena smiled at the cheerful painting, on wood, of a knight on his valiant steed, his lance piercing the heart of a slithering serpent writhing beneath his mount's hooves.

"Ah, yes," Lucien said in the same academic tone that he'd used when discussing Vlad Tepes. "St. George. There's the spring, guarded by the fearsome dragon, who for so long has not allowed the villagers to draw the water they so badly need . . . not unless they first sacrifice a maiden. But on this day, there is no maiden left in the village, save the king's daughter. She's bravely gone to the water's edge, despite her father's protests, expecting to die. But look who's appeared . . . a knight called George who will slay the dragon and save her and her people. They'll be so grateful to him, they will abandon paganism forever."

Meena stood with her hand in his, gazing down at the icon.

Okay, she thought to herself. *So, that didn't work. He looks as depressed as ever.*

And now I feel depressed, too. Thanks, St. George. Who knew you were also the patron saint of downers?

And then, just like that . . .

She knew.

It was crazy. It was revealing far too much of herself to him . . . far more than she'd ever wanted to.

But it was something, she realized, she had to do.

"Do you want to see my favorite painting in the whole world?" Meena turned to ask him.

He looked surprised . . . and amused. "I would love to," he said.

This time Meena was the one to lead him . . . out of the medieval art exhibit and up the stairs to the nineteenth-century wing.

She was a little nervous when they approached the painting she'd loved for so long that it might not be everything that she'd remembered.

Then again, what was she worried about? This was Joan of Arc, beloved by everyone. . . .

As they approached, she saw that she had nothing to worry about. No, the painting, as ever, was amazing . . . at least it was to Meena. The picture light above the elaborate gold frame was turned on and glowed down on the face of the boyish-looking peasant girl as she gazed off into the distance, while behind her, the archangel Michael beckoned. Meena was so transfixed, she actually forgot to be concerned over whether or not Lucien would like the painting.

She put Jack Bauer down on the floor and went right up to the painting, standing closer to it than she'd ever dared during museum visiting hours.

"Isn't she beautiful?" she breathed, marveling at the painting's details.

"She is," Lucien agreed somberly.

With a turn of her head, Meena was unnerved to discover that Lucien was standing much closer than she'd realized . . .

. . . less than two feet away from her. He hadn't even been looking at the painting when he'd agreed that it was beautiful.

His dark-eyed gaze had been riveted on her face.

Blushing, Meena realized she might actually have found a rival for the painting's beauty in Lucien's tall frame and perfect features.

He also, Meena had to admit, smelled good. She couldn't quite put her finger on what, precisely, it was that he smelled like. Jon had been through a succession of men's colognes in his lifetime, most of them cloying and obnoxious.

But Lucien's was light and clean smelling.

Meena wanted to pour whatever it was all over herself.

"And what is it about St. Joan," Lucien asked, smiling down at her, "that appeals to you so much?"

"Oh," Meena said. She realized with a pang of regret that she'd set herself up for this one.

Still. He'd asked her to trust him when she stood outside the museum.

She couldn't tell him the truth, of course. She knew what would happen. The same thing that had happened with David. Lucien would think she was a flake. Worse than a flake, even.

He'd think she was a freak.

She wouldn't let that happen. She was going to hide the truth from him as long as possible.

Forever, if she had to.

But she could tell him a *version* of the truth, she supposed, without giving too much of herself away.

"I guess," she said, choosing her words with care, "it's that she managed to make such a difference in so many people's lives, despite being poor and a girl . . . huge handicaps for the age in which she lived. She made predictions, you know . . . remarkably accurate predictions that at first no one believed. But eventually she convinced enough people that she was telling the truth that she was given an audience with the king. Who believed her." Meena squinted some more at the painting, trying to imagine what it must have been like for Joan, so determined, yet with so many strikes against her. "Of course people said she was insane. Today some people say that the 'voices from God' she heard were adolescent-onset schizophrenia. And as a teenager, I guess she'd have been the right age for it. . . ."

"But you don't want to believe that," Lucien said when her voice trailed off.

Feeling herself blushing again, Meena looked down at her feet.

She didn't kid herself that part of the reason she loved the painting they were standing in front of was that she, like Joan, had her own inner voices to contend with. Not that she believed that her inner voices—the feelings she had that told her how people were going to die—came from God.

But she knew she wasn't schizophrenic, either.

"A lot of people didn't believe Joan, either. At least at first," Meena said finally, raising her gaze to meet his. "But eventually, she persuaded enough people of her sanity that she was brought before the king . . . and *he* believed her. How could a crazy woman trick a king whose own father had psychosis? He would have recognized the signs. No," Meena said, looking back up at the painting and shaking her head. "She wasn't schizophrenic. She knew things. She was the greatest military strategist the French army ever had . . . a teenage girl who listened to the voices inside her head and guided her men to victory again and again. . . ."

When Meena looked back up at Lucien, she was embarrassed by the tears that had sprung spontaneously into her eyes.

"Until," she went on, a catch in her voice, "she was captured by the enemy, abandoned by her king, and burned to death at the stake for being a witch."

Lucien's smile had been amused . . . until her tears came.

Then his mouth gave a twist, and he reached for her.

Suddenly Meena found herself pulled against him, his arms wrapped around her, her face pressed against his chest. . . .

"You look like her," he said into her short dark hair.

Meena, ashamed of her tears and mortified at finding herself in his arms because she was crying—and over a long-dead saint—felt herself turning redder than ever.

"No, I don't," she said hastily against his shirtfront. "I have nothing in common with her at all. Really, I don't. I—"

"Yes," he said, holding her away from him by her arms so that he could look down into her eyes. "You do. I noticed it the minute we walked up. Your hair is shorter and darker. But you have the same intensity about you. Tell me something: do you hear voices, too, Meena Harper?"

She didn't know what to do. She wanted to burst out sobbing. She wanted to burst out laughing. She wanted to cry, *Yes. Yes, I do.*

Only not about you.

Which could mean only one thing. Either her "talent" was finally going away, or . . .

He wasn't going to die. Unlike every other man she'd ever met before to whom she'd been attracted, Lucien Antonescu wasn't going to die.

Not for a good, long time, anyway.

And then, before she could think of anything at all to say in response to his question, he'd slipped one hand beneath her chin and was tilting her face up toward his, forcing her to look him in the eyes.

"Meena," he said. His voice was a gruff whisper in the darkened gallery. "What are you hiding from me?"

Her voice was as throaty as his. "Nothing," she lied. "I swear."

And then the incredible happened. His mouth came down over hers.

Meena was so shocked that at first she froze, uncertain what to do. It had been so long since a man had kissed her, she couldn't believe it was happening at all.

And yet, there was the incontrovertible proof that she was in his arms . . . they were holding her very firmly to him. She could feel his lips against hers, strangely cool, like his fingers had been around hers, but so sweet, so patient, as if he'd be more than willing to wait all night for her to catch up with what was happening. . . .

And suddenly, Meena *did* catch up. Her heart gave an explosive double thump, and she realized, *Why, he's kissing me.*

And she rose up on tiptoe and slipped her arms around his neck, kissing him back, sinking into him, exulting in the fact that his arms were tightening around her, inhaling the crisp clean scent of him. She closed her eyes against the beauty of the painting behind him as he lifted her off her feet and pressed her closer and closer to his heart, which she couldn't feel due to the frenetic beating of her own.

And then it was as if the ceiling overhead suddenly evaporated and the cold white glow from the stars and the moon above combined into one brilliant shaft and went shooting down toward Meena.

She'd had no idea that being kissed could feel this way.

But Lucien's kisses made her feel . . . *cherished*. His hands cradled her as gingerly as if she were one of the precious objects around them . . . a vase from the Met's Chinese art collection he was afraid might crack if he exerted too much pressure on it. His lips explored hers, gently at first, then, when he seemed to realize that she wasn't going to shatter beneath his touch, with growing urgency.

She couldn't help letting her mouth fall open beneath his. . . .

And suddenly, it seemed as if something inside him burst. Something that appeared to have been pent-up for far too long, and which let loose at the touch of her tongue to his. All his polite civility was gone.

And Meena didn't mind at all. His need for her matched hers for him. It was as if he'd asked a question.

And she'd said yes.

The only problem was, the more passionately he kissed her, the louder Jack Bauer's growls grew. Finally, Meena had no choice but to draw her head away, and, glancing over at her dog, she said with some irritation, "Jack. Shut up!"

Jack Bauer let out a startled yip, stared at Meena with his ears tilted forward . . . then sneezed.

Meena couldn't help but burst out laughing. She glanced at Lucien to see if he was smiling as well. . . .

Only he wasn't. He was staring down at her with an intensity she could only have described as . . . *fiery*.

Judging from his expression, she saw that he didn't appear to find the situation the least bit amusing. Still holding Meena so that her feet dangled a few inches above the ground, he was looking deeply into her eyes.

"Spend the night with me," he said in a passion-roughened voice.

Meena wasn't shocked.

It wasn't as if she hadn't known he was going to ask. She'd felt the way their bodies had fit together. It was as if they'd been made for each other. She'd sensed the hunger in his kiss after the initial gentleness . . . it had matched her own. He wanted her every bit as much as she wanted him.

Still, the last thing she needed—the *very* last thing—was to fall in love.

And she was falling in love with Lucien Antonescu . . . and his kisses, which seemed to burn through her skin, down to her very soul.

She could feel herself slipping over the edge . . . that deliciously narrow precipice between admiration and friendship, and love.

It was silly—it was foolish. But it was true. She was falling head over heels, crazy in love with a man she'd only just met.

It didn't make any sense. She barely knew him.

But how could she *not* fall in love with him, after what they'd been through together, after what he'd done for her?

And now she was helpless in the face of his kisses. They turned her to ash.

But what good was sleeping with Lucien Antonescu going to do her? He was just going to leave. He was in town for only a short time. She'd never had a chance to try one out, but Meena very much doubted she'd be any good at a long-distance relationship. He wasn't going to move to New York.

And she certainly wasn't going to move to Romania.

Or, to put it another way: she was going to try *very* hard not to follow him back to Romania.

So, the sensible thing was to say no to his invitation to spend the night with him. No. Two little letters. N. O.

She wasn't a risk taker. Remember?

"Okay," she heard herself whispering.

What? What was *wrong* with her? Was she *crazy*?

Lucien, smiling, held her even closer—something she hadn't thought possible—then swung her around in a circle until Meena, laughing, begged him to stop, while Jack Bauer barked. Lucien, laughing as well, put Meena down on her feet, his expression seeming almost triumphant.

"You won't regret it," he said sincerely.

Meena was by then kneeling down to calm Jack Bauer. She looked up quizzically at Lucien's words.

She wouldn't regret it? Of course she wouldn't regret it.

Why would she?

Chapter Twenty-eight

L ucien knew what he was doing was wrong.

But that didn't mean he could stop himself.

She let him take her coat, then stood admiring the apartment Emil had found for him, a sleek, starkly decorated corporate penthouse with the most sophisticated security system available and a terrace that made Emil's, on which twenty or so people could mingle comfortably, look like a postage stamp. The view, through U V-blocked windows—sliding glass doors to the wraparound terrace made up most of the walls—was of downtown Manhattan to one side, the Hudson River to another, Union Square Park to a third, and then the skyscrapers uptown, stretching out before them like brilliantly lit Christmas trees. In the distance, past the East River, one could see the red lights of planes flying low over Queens, landing at the various airports there.

"It's amazing," Meena Harper breathed, going to one of the glass doors and gazing out across the darkness at the bright lights and clear, moonlit sky. Her long slender neck, rising up from the back of her plain black dress, looked particularly vulnerable with her close-shorn hair.

She obviously hadn't the slightest clue of the emotional maelstrom in which he found himself.

He'd known his behavior was reprehensible—quite possibly downright evil—from the moment he'd opened his mouth at Emil's and asked the girl if he could come with her while she walked the dog.

Even the dog, who smelled what he was, knew what Lucien was doing was wrong.

He'd been berating himself for speaking the words even as they came out of his mouth.

And then when she'd slipped into her apartment, followed by the brother—whom Lucien had thought for a moment had gone to try to dissuade her from leaving with him—he'd thought, *Good. Good for him. He'll stop me. As a brother should.*

But no. The brother, it turned out, was too self-centered to see what was actually happening. (Though Lucien supposed that was harsh. He'd been what he was for over half a millennium. The brother had been alive for only a little over thirty years. Lucien supposed he shouldn't think so unkindly of him.)

Lucien had actually stood in the hallway telling himself to just go. Take the stairs, let her be. She was a good person, a better person than he was . . . someone who obviously tried to do the right thing. She didn't deserve to have her life ruined by his kind. What was Mary Lou up to even getting her involved in the mess that was their lives?

Let Mary Lou make up some story about where he'd disappeared to. Allow Meena Harper to have her happy little life.

But he couldn't do it. He was too intrigued. He couldn't remember the last time he'd been as curious about a woman, let alone a human woman.

Or as attracted to one.

But that didn't mean he deserved to have her. Especially since everything he touched, he defiled.

That was the way of his kind.

He didn't take his own advice. Even when he reminded himself that he couldn't afford the distraction. There were too many other things that needed his attention at the moment: the fact that someone was draining young women of their blood and then leaving their nude corpses scattered across Manhattan like used tissues.

The fact that someone was trying to kill him.

The fact that possibly these two people were one and the same.

In any case, he needed to keep his head.

He'd been turning toward the stairs, determined to let her go, when her apartment door opened, and she came back out into the hallway.

And he knew he was waging a hopeless battle with himself. He wasn't going anywhere. She looked as fresh as a newly wrapped gift.

And he wanted to be the one to open that gift.

The worst part was that it wasn't merely a sexual attraction. There was also the puzzle of her mind. The cacophony he heard in Meena Harper's head wasn't, he'd figured out, due to the fact that she was insane. No. She was hiding something. Something she didn't like to think about, something she'd become expert, over the years, at hiding from everyone . . . even from herself.

It was something, he could tell, that haunted not only her dreams but her waking hours, as well. He could barely read the mental pictures that streamed through her consciousness because she'd buried certain painful memories so deeply within it. And so her thoughts came to him only in fits and starts, like a radio station, fading in and out.

He had never made a habit of using his powers to discover the true feelings of a woman in whom he was romantically interested. That was neither gentlemanly nor sporting.

But in Meena's case, he couldn't help it. Her lively interior mono-logue—what he could understand of it—shone like the lights over on the Empire State Building, too bright to ignore.

And yet the view was obstructed.

This made her all the more fascinating. It was hard to imagine that beneath her vivacious personality—her flirtatious teasing and her love of happy endings—lurked something so dark that she could hardly stand to allow herself to think of it.

Yet it seemed to be the truth.

And he knew this very darkness was what drew him so inexorably to her.

Was it possible he had met a woman who could understand the monster within him . . . because she was hiding a monster of her own?

And if this was so, why did he also get the feeling that there was a sweetness about her in which he could somehow find his own redemption?

It wasn't possible. Man could find redemption only through God.

But God had forsaken his kind centuries ago.

And yet Lucien couldn't deny what he'd been feeling all night as he'd gazed into her dark eyes . . . the growing conviction that Meena Harper might be his salvation.

Or was he asking too much of one person . . . and a human being, at that?

He didn't know.

But he was desperate to find out.

It had taken all of his self-control at the museum to keep his hands off her. He realized now that he'd been trying, in his own clumsy way, to give her fair warning, showing her the portrait, trying to make sure she knew what she was getting herself into. Stupid.

But true.

And for a split second, he'd been certain she'd known . . . something. Not everything, of course, or even as sympathetic as she was, she would have fled in terror.

And there'd been other times, as well, like by the painting of St. Joan. . . .

Lucien had lived long enough to know there were no such things as angels or saints—despite what Meena evidently wanted to believe regarding Joan of Arc. Or if there were, he'd never encountered any. Obviously, or he and his kind would have been wiped out long ago.

But how else could he explain Meena Harper . . . and the aching need he felt to make her his own?

On the other hand, he *was* a vampire—something her own dog had been at great pains throughout most of the night to warn her about, though she seemed perfectly unaware of the fact. Even now, as she was walking slowly around the penthouse, taking in the view, she had no idea of the danger she was in.

Lucien felt he had to say something. It was only fair to give her a fighting chance.

It was the gentlemanly thing to do.

"You mentioned the vampire war earlier," he said. He'd switched on the sound system when they'd come in; a string quartet played softly overhead. Now he went to the glass and chrome wine refrigerator and selected a bottle. Something light, he thought, like her. She wouldn't like anything too heavy, too dark.

"Oh," she said with a laugh. "That. Yeah. Work." She gave a shudder. "Let's not talk about work. Kind of a mood killer, you know?"

He found a pinot noir Emil had stocked. Perfect. "I'm sorry," he said with a smile. "Is it that bad?"

"It's pretty bad," Meena said, coming over to where he was standing by the bar and slipping onto one of the chrome and black-leather stools beside him. "I lost a promotion I really wanted, *and* channel four is killing us in the ratings, all because they have this horrible monster misogynist story line that people seem to love."

Lucien paused midpour. "Monster misogynist?" he asked, one eyebrow raised quizzically.

Meena held up both hands like they were claws. "You know. Vampires." She bared her teeth and hissed like a vampire in a movie.

Lucien nearly dropped the glass of wine he was holding out to her, just as her dog, standing a few feet away from them, barked with impressive ferociousness for such a small animal.

"Jack Bauer!" Meena dropped her hands and turned on her stool. "You have to relax!" To Lucien she asked, "Do you have any hamburger or something in the fridge?"

Lucien froze. If she opened the refrigerator, she would find his latest black market delivery from the New York Blood Center. "I don't think I—"

"Oh, never mind," she said, interrupting. Fortunately, she'd begun looking through the purse she'd hung on the back of the stool. "I might have something in my bag. Oh, here. Some dog treats. I'll just lure him into the bathroom and lock him in there, and then maybe we'll have some peace."

Meena slipped off the stool and held out her cupped hand to the dog, who continued to bark . . . until he caught the scent of the treats.

Then his foxlike ears tipped forward and he trotted toward her until he reached the room that Lucien had indicated was the bathroom. After rinsing a soap dish she found there, filling it with water, and leaving it on the floor for him to drink from, Meena piled the treats alongside it, and as soon as Jack Bauer was too busy wolfing them down to notice what she was doing, she shut the door behind her.

Lucien tried not to show his relief over the narrow escape he'd had. Normally he didn't do things as stupid as put his blood supply in the kitchen refrigerator, where any woman he brought home might discover it while casually looking for a snack for her little dog.

But he certainly hadn't expected to be sleeping with anyone while in New York. He was there on business. It was only because Meena Harper was so completely unlike any other woman he'd ever met that he'd violated his own personal—and long-held—code of conduct.

And nearly ruined everything in doing so.

"There," she said, resuming her position on the barstool. "Sorry about that. I don't know what's come over him. He's usually really good with people. Except your cousin for some reason. And Mary Lou. Maybe it's anyone who owns a summer castle. Jack Bauer obviously has Marxist leanings." She laughed and raised her glass. "So."

"To Jack Bauer, budding Marxist," Lucien said, clinking the side of her glass with his own.

She laughed again, her large dark eyes bright over the wide rim of her wineglass. He hadn't been flattering her when he'd made the observation that she looked a little like the girl in the painting with which she obviously felt such a connection in the museum. The actual truth was, she was much prettier.

Much prettier, and much more vulnerable looking.

"So I take it you don't like vampires?" he asked carefully.

Meena laughed. "Considering they're basically ruining my life right now? Not much."

"And monster misogynists are . . . ?"

"You know," Meena said, "how in horror movies and books and TV shows, the monster or the serial killer with the chain saw always goes after the helpless pretty girl. It's so sexist." She went on. "And vampires are the worst of all. That's because, as Van Helsing points out in *Dracula,* vampires know the girl's family is going to be all squeamish about cutting off her head—even if they know she's a vampire now. I guess because it's supposed to be easier to cut off your son's head than it is your daughter's."

She gave a shudder, then added, "And what's with vampires always wanting to make the pretty girl their undead girlfriend? Or worse, *not* wanting to make her his undead girlfriend. And then she talks him into it, to the thrill of the audience. Because being dead and with someone is apparently a happier ending than being alive and alone. Only how is being dead a happy ending?" Her eyes flashed. "Believe me. Being dead is *never* a happy ending."

He studied her. There'd been a great deal of passion behind that last statement. He wondered where it came from and if that odd obstruction in her mind had something to do with it.

"But," he said carefully, "you don't *believe* in vampires."

She choked on her wine. "W-what?" she stammered. "Did you just ask me if I *believe* in vampires?"

Lucien returned his hand to the stem of his wineglass, staring at the ruby liquid within it. He knew it was important to look everywhere but into her eyes. He was afraid of how much he might give away if he looked into those eyes that seemed to see so much . . . and yet so little.

"Forgive me," he said. "I just thought, the other night, at the church . . ."

"Oh," Meena said. She took another sip of her wine. Her glass was almost empty. "That? Aren't you the one who keeps saying it was only a few little bats?"

His own words, thrown back at him. He supposed he deserved that. "But you believe St. Joan heard voices," he said. "Voices telling her the future. How can an educated woman like yourself believe this and not in creatures of the night? Or"—he smiled—"do you prefer only to believe in happy things, like your preference for happy endings?"

The look she gave him was so sharp, it could have cut glass. "Joan's story didn't end happily," she said, reminding him. "And I like a good horror story as much as the next person, so long as they kill off some men, too, and not just girls. But the voices Joan heard were *real*. There's clear and substantiated proof they were real. She won battles that would otherwise have been lost because of what those voices told her in advance of them, allowing the French generals to strategize in ways completely different than they did before Joan came along. People's lives were saved because of what those voices told her."

"And," Lucien said, his gaze still on his glass, "there's no such proof that vampires are real."

"There's plenty of proof that some corporations are making a fortune off audiences who like to think they're real," she said. "Including *Lust*'s advertisers. Why do you think our sponsor is so adamant that we get in on the action? The money's very, very real. But soulless undead who walk around biting people on the neck and drinking their blood, who can't go out during the day or they'll burn to a crisp and who have to sleep in coffins? Please."

"Some of the mythology has been exaggerated over the years," Lucien said with a slight quirk to his mouth. "Some authors—including your Mr. Stoker—may have taken liberties."

"And who can turn into bats?" Meena added.

"And some haven't," Lucien said a little stiffly. He refilled her wineglass, which she'd finished off. "So, just to be sure. Even though you've never met one—because they don't exist, of course—you want nothing to do with vampires?"

Meena bit her lower lip. Lucien couldn't help noticing the way the blood rushed into it, making it even lusher and redder than before. "That does sound a little prejudiced," Meena said. "Would you think ill of me if I admitted that I don't like werewolves—or hobbits—either?"

Lucien reached out and laid his hand over hers where it rested on the bar. Her skin looked temptingly smooth and soft. It felt as good as it looked. "I could never think ill of you," he said.

"Oh," she said, raising her glass to her lips with her free hand and taking a fairly large sip of her wine. "Trust me. You could. You don't know everything about me. Yet."

Her voice sounded a little sorrowful.

"And if I told you I was a vampire?" Lucien asked, tracing a little circle on the back of her hand. "Would you hate me?"

"Ha," Meena said, laughing. "You'd make a terrible vampire."

He raised his eyebrows. "I would?"

"Of course you would," she said, still laughing. She put down the wineglass, then slipped her hand out from under his to take hold of his tie instead, swinging toward him on the barstool until her knees were between his thighs. "You had plenty of opportunity to bite me that night with the bats—and then again in that big, dark, deserted museum—and you didn't. Don't think I didn't notice."

She placed her other hand on his barstool, directly between his legs, so she could balance herself as she leaned forward and, using his tie to gently tug his head down so it was just inches from hers, she said, in a voice so throaty from the wine that it was almost a growl, "The thing is, I've already been with a boy who bites . . . figuratively speaking, of course. I was kind of hoping to avoid guys like that in the future."

Lucien wondered just who, exactly, was in danger here. Her eyes were twin pools, dark as midnight.

He felt as if he were drowning.

And he didn't think he minded.

"I'll never bite you," he whispered. "Unless you give me permission to, of course."

Then he was pressing his lips against hers.

And Lucien wasn't certain if he'd failed . . . or succeeded more spectacularly than he could have hoped. He'd told her what he'd felt honor-bound to share.

Was it his fault she didn't believe him?

Yes. It was. Because he hadn't offered her the proof she'd said she needed.

But Lucien wasn't about to do that now . . . not when her hand was resting so dangerously close to his inner thigh. The part of him that was a man may have longed to be redeemed by her.

But the part of him that was a monster wanted something else entirely.

The man would have to wait.

His arms went around her waist, dragging her to him with a possessiveness that seemed to surprise her, if the little gasp she let out against his mouth was any indication.

But he'd gone past the point of civility. He pulled her from her stool and onto his lap, crushing her against him, draining with his lips and tongue what he couldn't drain with his teeth . . . the essence of her, what he hoped—what he'd dreamed for so long—might save him.

He knew from the soft sound Meena made—whether of protest or pleasure he didn't know, and the signals he was getting from her mind were cloudy, as usual—when his lips came down over hers that this kiss was even more proprietary than the one inside the museum had been, as if he were claiming ownership of her.

But he couldn't help it. There he'd kissed her reverently, as if he were afraid she might break.

This was a different kind of kiss . . . a demanding kiss, a kiss that, he knew, was laying his soul bare in front of hers. . . .

And yet at the same time laying claim to hers.

And Meena didn't seem to mind. She hadn't flinched or tried to push him away when he'd pulled her toward him. The opposite, in fact. She'd parted her legs to straddle him beneath the wide skirt of her dress, only the black lace of her panties and his suit trousers separating their skin, her arms going around his neck. She clung to him, the heat emanating from her mouth and slim body seeming to consume him. He could feel her heart pounding against him through the thin material of her dress, a rhythmic pulse coming from her body that raced in his temples and drove him to kiss her harder than ever . . .

. . . then slide his mouth over her lips, down her chin, toward her throat. He reached up to lay a hand over the curve of one of her breasts and felt her heart beating beneath his fingers, racing like a greyhound's, before lowering his head down to where his hand lay, replacing his fingers with his lips, pressing his mouth against the silken flesh he revealed by pushing away the neckline of her dress, then the lacy cup of her bra.

Meena reacted by threading her fingers through his hair, straining to bring his mouth closer to her. Her appreciative gasp at the touch of his tongue, delicately tasting her skin, caused him to tighten his grip on her hips. . . .

And this pressed those black lace panties more firmly against the front of his suit trousers.

Lucien jerked his lips from her breast. He could take it no more. He abruptly pulled her from him, slipped one arm beneath her waist and the other beneath her knees, and then rose, lifting her with him.

Meena let out a delighted laugh and tightened her grip around his neck.

"Don't tell me," she said. "You're taking me to the bedroom to ravish me."

"Yes," he ground out.

And turned resolutely toward the darkened bedroom door.

He would be damned for what he was about to do.

But then, he was damned anyway.

Chapter Twenty-nine

9:15 A.M. EST, Friday, April 16
15 Union Square West, Penthouse
New York, New York

Meena woke to the smell of frying bacon.

For a few seconds, she thought she was back home in the house in which she'd grown up in New Jersey. That was the last time she could remember waking to the smell of real bacon.

But when Meena opened her eyes, she found herself not in the purple and white bedroom of her youth, surrounded by her childhood Beanie Baby collection, but in Lucien Antonescu's ultrachic urban penthouse, all soothing tones of gray and brown, with her dog, Jack Bauer, standing on the mattress beside her head, panting anxiously into her face.

"Jack," Meena said woozily. What had *happened* last night? "Get down."

What had happened last night began to return in bits and pieces as Meena lifted the dog and plopped him onto the black tile floor, on which his claws made a hectic skittering sound as he turned and then made a running leap to bound back up onto the bed.

The countess. She had gone to the countess's apartment with Jon—because he'd made her—and *he*'d been there. . . .

Lucien, the man from St. George's Cathedral, the man who'd saved her life. They'd talked and laughed, and afterward, he'd asked if he could join her while she walked Jack Bauer.

And then he'd broken into the Metropolitan Museum of Art. And they'd kissed in front of the portrait of St. Joan. And he'd invited her back to his place. And she'd gone with him.

And then they'd . . .

They'd . . .

Oh, God, they'd . . .

Meena bolted upright in bed, then seized her temples—head rush!—and collapsed back against the pillows.

Had she really made love with Lucien Antonescu all night long?

And was he really—if what she was smelling was any indication—making her breakfast?

A huge smile broke out across Meena's face. At least until her dog launched himself strategically against her midsection.

"Oof!" Meena said. "Jack! That's not funny."

But Jack didn't seem to be trying to be funny. He was whining and pawing at her—not a pleasant sensation, since Meena was completely naked beneath Lucien's dark gray sheets—while attempting to shower her face with anxious licks.

Why, out of all the dogs at the New York City ASPCA, had Meena had to bring home the most maladjusted one?

"All right, all right," she said. "I'm getting up."

A glance out the wall of floor-to-ceiling windows that led to Lucien's massive terrace showed her that it was a beautiful spring day. The glass seemed to be slightly tinted, but Meena could tell it was already late morning.

And a glance at her cell phone, which she dug out of her bag, sitting at the floor of the bed, confirmed it. She was late to work. Great.

She also, she saw, had seven messages, four of them from Leisha, two from her mother, and one from Jon (probably warning her that their mother had called the apartment looking for her). Meena didn't really go missing all that often (all right . . . ever).

But when she did, she did it in a big way.

Meena sat on the edge of the bed and texted *I'm fine* back to Leisha, whose messages had gotten consecutively more and more frantic as Meena neglected to respond. *More than fine. I'll call you later.*

To Jon, all she wrote was, *U didn't tell Mom anything, did u? PS I <3 Romania*

She wrote nothing back to her mother. She'd have to call her later. Her mother didn't know how to text.

She wondered what to do about work. What day was it? She couldn't even remember. . . . Oh, right. Friday. What was happening today? Something about someone reading for something . . .

"I thought you were up," a deep voice said from the doorway, startling her. Jumping, Meena turned and saw the most delectable sight she could remember seeing in a long time:

Lucien Antonescu wearing only a pair of gray silk pajama bottoms, holding a crystal champagne flute filled with what appeared to be orange juice.

"Mimosa?" he asked.

Meena would have thought she was still dreaming if Jack Bauer hadn't chosen that moment to hurl a paw into her kidney.

"Ow," she said, giving the dog a gentle shove off the bed while holding the gray sheet to her chest. Jack let out a little yelp as he fell onto a tangled pile of Meena's and Lucien's clothes. "How thoughtful of you, Lucien. I'd love one."

Lucien came toward her with a loving—there was no other way to describe it—smile on his face, and Meena was able to observe his half-naked body in the daytime. It was perfect . . . as perfect as it had seemed the night before, large but without a hint of fat, athletic without seeming muscle-bound, thrillingly masculine. Meena remembered running her fingers down that broad back and circling her arms around that lean waist, trying to hold him more closely. She even recalled—and now the blush grew distinctly deeper—kissing the trail of dark hair along that firm belly.

Her blush deepened.

"Good morning," he said, leaning down to kiss her as he handed her the champagne.

"Is that bacon I smell?" Meena asked, trying to change the subject . . . of her own sinful thoughts.

"It is indeed," he said. "You're not a vegetarian, are you?"

"I should be," Meena said, sipping the drink he'd brought her. The oranges had been freshly squeezed. "Being an animal lover and all. But I'm just a hypocrite, instead."

"I like a girl who eats," he said, running a finger along her cheekbone. "I'm making eggs, too. How do you like yours?"

Meena could not recall any man ever asking her this in her entire life, including her own father.

"Um," she said, "scrambled?" She smiled up at him, relishing his touch and trying to ignore her dog, who was growling from the opposite side of the bed.

"Then they'll be ready when you are," Lucien said. "I thought maybe you'd like a hot bath. I've run one for you in there." He pointed toward a doorway opposite the one through which he'd just entered. Meena noticed for the first time that white curls of steam were wafting from it.

"Oh," she said, stunned. "You did? That's so sweet. Really, you didn't have to do all this."

"No," Lucien said. "Really. I did."

He cupped her face, leaned down, and kissed her deeply. Meena was reminded of how much kissing they'd done the night before. Her lips felt a little bruised by it all. In fact, all of her felt a little bruised. In a good way.

Jack Bauer, from the pile of clothes he'd fallen into, gave a low growl.

"Oh," Lucien said, breaking the kiss and throwing the dog an inscrutable look. "And I've walked your dog."

Meena raised both eyebrows. This was too good to be true. "You *have*?"

"Well," Lucien said, "perhaps I should have said I've *had* him walked. He seemed to want to go out, and the doorman was happy to take him. In any case, you needn't worry about him. Now go." He pointed a little imperiously at the bathroom door. "Before you distract me even more than you have already."

Meena laughed. It was kind of fun to be bossed around by a handsome man in a pair of gray silk pajama bottoms.

Especially one who had done the things to her last night that Lucien had done.

So, gathering the sheet to herself, she popped off the bed and headed into the large, brown marble bathroom, Jack Bauer trotting at her heels. What she saw in the vast mirrors there reassured her. She didn't look like a total train wreck. She actually looked sort of . . . good. Maybe because for the first time in a long time she'd had a good night's sleep? Well, what little sleep she'd gotten had been good.

And for once, Meena had actually woken up happy. She hadn't even missed her night guard. She didn't think she'd ground her teeth once during the night.

The huge Jacuzzi tub was half filled with steaming hot water. She wondered what Romanians considered a comfortable bathing temperature and turned on some cold water to even it out, then sank into the deep water when it felt just right.

Bliss. Except for Jack Bauer, nervously sitting beside the tub. She could see the tips of his ears, just over the side, tilted toward her alertly. She tried to ignore him and bathe in peace.

But his anxious, foxlike little face peering up at her when she stepped out and reached for one of the thick fluffy white robes she'd found hanging on the back of the bathroom door made her feel guilty. Where had Jack Bauer spent the night? Had she really locked him into this bathroom? At least the bath mat was as thick and fluffy as the robes and had probably served as a comfy bed.

That was it, though. She'd been a horrible pet owner. She was going to have to give him a good, long walk to make up for her bad behavior. . . .

She slipped into the robe—it was so big on her, she had to roll up the sleeves to keep her hands from being lost inside them—then rinsed with some mouthwash she found. She had some makeup in her purse. She put some on, but her cheeks and mouth were so red from the chafing they'd endured at the assault of Lucien's lips that she needed only a little mascara and eyeliner.

She discovered her dress slung over a black leather ottoman and her underthings strewn across the floor. She pulled them on, thinking about how later, after work, she'd have to do the walk of shame in front of her doorman. Would whoever was on duty realize she was wearing the same clothes she'd left in the night before? She prayed Pradip wouldn't be there when she got home. Not that she cared what her doormen thought of her.

But what if she ran into Mary Lou in the elevator? Not what if. She *would* run into Mary Lou in the elevator.

But maybe, given what had happened last night, her luck was finally starting to change.

She refused to think about whether or not Lucien was going to ask her out for tonight. Friday night. She wouldn't mention it, either. No game playing. They were both too old for that. He was in town on business. She wasn't going to seem needy. . . .

"Are you free tonight?" Lucien called from the kitchen, where the smell of bacon, now joined by coffee, was stronger than ever.

She called, "Uh, I think so," and followed the sound of his voice.

Lucien had set the glass and steel dining-room table with one place. One dark gray cloth napkin, one set of silverware, one cup of coffee, one glass of orange juice, one everything.

Lucien, noticing her curious gaze from the other side of the pass-through, said, "I hope you don't mind, but I had mine earlier. I went for a run and I was famished after. I didn't want to wake you . . . you were sleeping so sweetly. Like an angel." He winked at her.

Meena said, "Oh, no. That's fine."

That's just weird, she thought.

She slipped onto the chair behind the table setting just as he came out of the kitchen holding a plate. He presented it to her with a flour-ish. On it sat three curls of perfectly cooked bacon, two eggs scrambled to a golden yellow, a slice of delicately toasted whole wheat toast with apricot jam, a few paper-thin slices of orange, and a plump, perfectly ripe strawberry.

Meena stared down at it with her mouth hanging open.

Lucien pulled out the chair beside hers. "I wasn't sure how you take your coffee. There's sugar and cream on the table."

"Thanks," Meena murmured when the ability of speech finally re-turned.

He's a prince, she told herself. *This isn't so unusual. All princes probably do this to impress their girlfriends the first time they spend the night.*

Maybe, she thought, lifting her fork and idly admiring how his biceps looked in the daytime, *the thing about his going running already isn't so weird either. He has to work out to stay looking so nice. I should start working out, too. We could work out together. Before he goes back to Romania, I mean.*

"I thought tonight we could go to the symphony," he said. "If you're free. I have tickets for the Philharmonic. Masur is conducting Beethoven. I don't think you'll hate it too much."

Meena looked at him primly over a forkful of eggs. "I won't hate it at all. I happen to like Beethoven." She wondered how long it would take for him to catch on that she had no idea who Masur was. She supposed she could use the time during the concert to think up some good dialogue for the new vampire-hunter proposal she was going to pitch to Sy.

"Excellent," he said. "Unfortunately I have an early dinner engagement with a colleague. Shall I meet you by the fountain at Lincoln Center at seven thirty?"

"I'll be there," Meena said. "And without him." She shot Jack Bauer a meaningful look since he was sitting beneath the table, alternately growling at Lucien and looking up at her beseechingly for any crumbs of food she might spill.

"He's a very loyal companion," Lucien observed mildly.

"Yeah," Meena said, taking a sip of coffee. "Something like that. How long do symphonies usually last?"

"If you're asking because you want to know how long it will be before I once again rend off all your clothing and perform the kind of indecent sexual acts upon your body that I performed last night and that would horrify your mother were she ever to find out, we could do that right now," Lucien offered.

Meena, who'd been staring at him with cheeks growing ever more deeply crimson as he went on, said, as she pushed herself away from the table, "I can't. I mean, I-I'd like to. But I'm already late for work. So I . . . I better go. I'll see you at seven thirty."

Lucien laughed and, rising from the table as well, caught her up in his arms. "Did I mention how much I enjoy seeing you blush?"

"Well, that's good," Meena said to the center of his chest, since she couldn't seem to raise her gaze any higher than that. "Since it's all I seem to be able to do around you. See you tonight?"

"Don't forget your coat."

He got it for her from the closet, helped her into it, then walked her to the elevator—it was the kind that came straight up into the apartment. When it arrived, he caught her up around the waist again and pulled her against him, then kissed her deeply, not seeming to mind that she must have tasted of toast and coffee.

"Seven thirty," he said when he released her. "Don't be late."

He smiled as she wandered onto the elevator like a woman in a daze. Jack Bauer, however, strutted stiff-legged onto it, clearly delighted at seeing what he thought to be the last of Lucien Antonescu. The dog turned and gave him a parting warning yip.

"And the same to you, my friend," Lucien said just as the doors shut.

Meena, alone in the elevator, watched as the numbers above her sank lower and lower. With each one, she felt, sanity returned. When the doors finally opened to the lobby and she and Jack Bauer stepped out of the luxury building's entrance and into the sunshine of the bright spring day, reality finally sank in.

And with it, the full impact of what she had just done.

Chapter Thirty

Alaric swam a hundred laps every morning, freestyle, before breakfast. He might switch to the backstroke if there was anyone of the attractive female variety lounging at the side of the pool.

But with the Peninsula hosting a national conference for designers and salespeople of dental implants, that was most decidedly not the case.

Alaric was on his one hundred and eighty-eighth lap (the pool at the Peninsula was smaller than Alaric was used to, so he'd had to increase his number of laps) when a hand erupted through the crystal-blue water and seized his head.

Alaric's usual lightning-fast reaction would have sent the person who'd accosted him plummeting over his shoulder and into the pool if he hadn't looked up at the last minute and realized it was his boss.

"Goddamnit, Wulf!" Holtzman thundered as he strode away, looking for a towel with which to dry his now-soaking-wet arm and shoulder. "Did you have to try to drown me? I was only trying to get your attention. We've got a crisis here, in case you're too busy enjoying your luxury accommodations to notice."

Panting, Alaric clung to the side of the pool. He tried not to show his delight at the fact that he'd managed to ruin his boss's incredibly ugly suit jacket.

"What crisis?" he asked. His voice echoed satisfyingly in the glass-enclosed pool atrium.

"Shhh," Holtzman said. He'd gotten a towel from one of the pool attendants and was rubbing vigorously at himself. "Not so loud. Someone will hear you."

Alaric shrugged. There were two or three conference attendees around, but they were hardly a threat to Palatine Guard business.

"None of them speaks German," Alaric said in German. "They're American dentists."

"Nevertheless," Holtzman said. He came to the side of the pool where Alaric waited for him. "There's been another dead girl found in a park this morning."

Alaric perked up. "Meena Harper?"

"No, it wasn't Meena Harper," Holtzman said. "How could Meena Harper have been found dead? She was with the prince last night, and the prince is here to stop the murders, not commit them."

Alaric, disappointed, shrugged. Not that he would have liked to have seen Meena Harper dead, of course. She was their only lead to finding the prince, and she was, if he remembered rightly, quite pretty, in her way.

But her death would have connected his case to the prince.

And then the head office might have let him go after the prince, after all.

"They haven't identified the dead girl yet," Holtzman said. He had knelt down by the side of the pool, careful to avoid any wet spots on the deck, and was speaking out of the side of his mouth. As if anyone in the pool area might not already realize that Holtzman and Alaric knew one another. "Just like all the others."

"Then it might be Meena Harper after all," Alaric said, thinking a little regretfully of Meena Harper's shapely legs and dark hair.

"It isn't her," Holtzman said angrily. "I saw a picture of her. The dead girl has long hair. Meena Harper had short hair. Would you stop with this obsession with Meena Harper?"

"I'm not obsessed with her," Alaric said. "It's just that if we're going to catch the prince—"

"*We're* not going to do anything," Holtzman said. "*I'm* going to catch him. You're going after this killer. I want you to get dressed and go look at passport photos of recent émigrés fitting this girl's general age and description to see if you can get a match. They think because of her dental work that she might be of Eastern European descent, too, like the others."

"Right," Alaric said. *Waste of time*, he thought. "But if I were you, what I would do this morning is go pay a visit to Meena Harper."

"Oh, you would, would you?"

"Well, what do you think she and Lucien Antonescu did last night? They didn't go back to her place. She knows where the bat is roosting. Find out where that is, and we'll have him."

"I have a better idea," Holtzman said. "I thought I would just pay a visit to Emil and Mary Lou Antonescu."

Alaric splashed an enormous wave of water on his boss.

"Stop that!" Holtzman cried, leaping back. "What do you think you're doing?"

Some of the dental implant salesmen, lounging on nearby chaises, laughed.

"Say one word to the Antonescus, and you'll have the entire Dracul population of Manhattan on our heads," Alaric declared. He was angry now, really angry. First Holtzman had ruined his swim. And now he was making even more sweeping bureaucratic decisions that were going to make his job more difficult.

"I don't know how the prince didn't see us last night," Alaric said, "but evidently he didn't. I know that because the two of us are still alive, and the Antonescus haven't moved out of 910 Park Avenue. You know how I know that, Holtzman? Because I'm still breathing and I called the building this morning pretending to be the cable repairman asking about a connection in their apartment. And they're *still there*."

Holtzman stared down at Alaric, his brown-eyed gaze troubled.

"I knew I should have put you on psychological leave," he said. "You aren't fit for duty. You—"

"I'm the best you've got, Holtzman," Alaric said, hauling himself out of the pool. He reached for the towel his boss had dropped. "I'll bring your killer in. But more important, I'll bring the prince in, too.

Just let me do my job without telling me *how,* for once. No manuals. No rules. Just dead vampires."

His boss stared at him. Alaric was not unaware that Holtzman's gaze had gone to his lean, well-muscled torso.

And why wouldn't it? Alaric took good care of himself, working out regularly with weights besides swimming laps. He cut quite an intimidating figure. Even the dental implant salesmen couldn't help looking.

Then he noticed Holtzman's gaze seemed particularly riveted to a rather ugly, raised scar just beneath Alaric's rib cage, where one of the vamps in Berlin had managed to worry open a section of his flesh— using just its razor-sharp fangs—while Alaric had been trying to pry Martin from the jaws of some of its brethren.

Alaric sighed. He knew why Holtzman was staring.

The Vatican doctors had advised plastic surgery.

But Alaric had refused. He didn't like hospitals, let alone unnecessary medical procedures.

Holtzman, Alaric supposed, was assuming Alaric had refused to rid himself of the scar for the same reason he'd refused counseling after the Berlin incident.

But the scar served an important purpose: it reminded him every time he saw it just how very much he hated the undead.

And how important it was that he rid the world of them all.

"If you want to find a vampire," Alaric said, ignoring Holtzman's stare and the fact that the older man was obviously trying to think of something to say about the scar, "you ask his latest meal. In the prince's case, that's Meena Harper, 910 Park Avenue, apartment 11B."

This seemed to distract Holtzman from the scar. "Quite right," he said. "That's why I'm going to her apartment this evening, pretending I'm a—"

"Abraham," Alaric said, interrupting him. "The bit with the inheritance check from the long-lost relative isn't going to work. She isn't going to believe you. Who'd leave an inheritance check for a *prince*? The guy is richer than Midas."

"Oh." Holtzman looked crestfallen. "Right. I hadn't thought of that."

"That's why *I'm* going to her apartment tonight," Alaric said. "And I'm going to do the interview my way."

"I don't think that's at all wise," Holtzman said. "In fact, I forbid you to go. I will not allow it."

Surprised, Alaric stared at him. "Why not?"

"Because you're only going to do that thing where you go bursting in with your sword drawn. You know we've had quite a few complaints about that, Alaric. People really don't seem to like it."

"She just spent the night with the prince of darkness," Alaric said indignantly. "You really think *I'm* so scary in comparison?"

Alaric found it disappointing that Holtzman only glanced at his scar again and said nothing. His scar wasn't so scary. What was really scary, in Alaric's opinion, was Holtzman's suit.

Chapter Thirty-one

10:30 A.M. EST, Friday, April 16
BAO
155 Avenue of the Americas
New York, New York

"Well, look at this," Leisha said when Meena appeared before her styling station that morning at BAO (By Appointment Only). "Someone's been a bad, bad girl."

Leisha was stretched with her long, bare legs crossed at the ankles like a Nubian queen in her own styling chair, balancing a large grilled-chicken salad in a plastic carry-out container over her bulging stomach, even though the salon's owner, Jimmy, had a strict no-eating-at-your-station rule.

But Jimmy's rules didn't apply to Leisha since she was his most popular hairstylist and seven months pregnant, besides. It would be a disaster for Jimmy—and BAO—if Leisha quit.

Meena pointed wordlessly to the empty chair at the station next to Leisha's.

"Take it," Leisha said, waving a hand, her many bracelets jangling, her nails, Meena noticed, recently French tipped. Someone in the salon had been using her fingers for practice. "Ramone took a personal day because he found out his boyfriend hasn't deleted himself from Grindr. So." Leisha shot her an aggravated look. "I'm totally pissed at you. Jon said you went on a walk with some guy after the countess's party, and then you never came back. And then this morning on the news, they said they found another dead girl. Obviously, I've been sitting here all morning thinking it was you. At least until you finally texted me back. I was worried sick. You can ask anyone here. *Sick.*"

Meena looked pointedly at the chicken salad. "Not so sick that you couldn't order an early lunch without me."

"This isn't me," Leisha said, pointing at her belly. "It's him! *He* doesn't care what happens to you. He's starving. And kicking me. Oh, my God. You wouldn't believe how he's been kicking me all morning. And it's all your fault."

"How is it *my* fault?" Meena asked, leaning down and picking up Jack Bauer and putting him on her lap. He snuggled against her, needing a little TLC. Now that Lucien wasn't around, he was back to his normal, nongrowling self.

"For putting me through all that!" Leisha declared. "You think Thomas can't feel how scared I was for you? What were you thinking? You *never* hook up with strange men. What was going through your head, Harper?"

Meena gave Jack Bauer a good scratching beneath his neck, and he threw back his throat in ecstasy.

"He wasn't a strange guy, Leish," she said instead of pointing out that Leisha's doctor had gotten her baby's sex wrong, which didn't seem like it would be helpful. "He was the guy from the other night. With the bats."

Leisha stared at her. "But that's impossible."

Meena was scratching the dog so hard that his hind leg began to thump. She toned it down.

"No," she said. "Not impossible. Fact. Lucien Antonescu—the guy the countess was trying to fix me up with?—is the same guy who saved me from the bats outside of the cathedral. I know it sounds crazy. But it's true. And, Leish, I like him. *More than* like him."

Leisha shook her head. "No wonder you came straight here instead of going home before work. You're having a mental breakdown."

Meena frowned. "How am I having a mental breakdown? Do you think I'm making this up?"

"No. Because that's so messed up!"

"Because I slept with him?"

"Because it's so weird that it should be the same guy!" Leisha declared. "Of *course* you slept with him. And I should hope you like him. Seeing as how you scared us all half to death disappearing into the night with him." She set her chicken salad down on the rolling hair dryer stand between their two chairs and tried to get as comfortable as a seven-months-pregnant woman could. "So. How was it?"

"It was—" Meena looked up toward the ceiling, which Jimmy had left open, though he'd had all the ductwork painted silver and black and the ceiling behind it painted a deep purple. "Amazing," she said, sighing. "Really. I don't know any other way to describe it."

"Adjectives, please," Leisha said. "I've been having sex with the same man for almost seven years now, and I'm over it. I want details. Did he sink your battleship?"

"Leish!" Meena cried, laughing.

"Seriously," Leisha said. "I don't care about anything else. Oh, wait, I do. What's his expiration date?"

Meena regarded her friend with a face wreathed in smiles. "That's the best part. He doesn't have one. Or maybe it's just . . ."

Meena let her voice trail off. She'd been going to say, maybe it was just that her ability to foretell people's deaths was fading.

But she knew that wasn't true. What about baby Weinberg and the weird feeling she had about her?

She had to tell Leisha. She had to.

But how could she do it without scaring the wits out of her?

"Maybe it's just what?" Leisha gave her an exasperated look. "What is with you? You look so weird. Are you sure you're all right? I think you might have a fever or something. Let me feel your head."

Leisha's fingers felt cool against Meena's forehead. Meena wished she'd keep them pressed there forever. Maybe she *did* have a fever.

"Hmmm," Leisha said. "You're definitely running a little hot. What'd this guy *do* to you, exactly? Is that the flush of a new love affair? Or did he give you swine flu?"

"Oh, Leish," Meena said. "He was so great." She knew she was gushing, but she couldn't help it. She could still smell Lucien on her skin from where he'd kissed her good-bye. "He's just so . . . different than other guys I've met lately, you know? I mean, he doesn't even know what *Call of Duty* is. And he made me breakfast. *He asked how I like my eggs.* And he ran a bath for me. And he was nice to Jack, even though Jack behaved like a total lunatic and did nothing but growl at him all night long. And . . ."

"So it was perfect," Leisha said, finishing for her.

"It was perfect," Meena said. Then something occurred to her, and she chewed her lower lip. "Except . . ."

"What?" Leisha's dark brows slanted downward. "Don't tell me. He's married. He's got a wife back in Estonia."

"Romania," Meena said, correcting her. "And no, of course not. That's not it. There's just something . . . okay, don't laugh. But there's something . . . *sad* about him."

"*Sad?*" Leisha shook her head so that her long black hair, which she'd straightened with a hot comb and then curled into a sassy retro flip, skimmed her shoulders. "What do you mean, sad? Like a loser? Haven't you had enough of losers after David?"

"No," Meena said. "Not loser sad. More like something really sad happened to him once. And he never got it over it."

"Maybe his wife died in childbirth," Leisha said. Leisha, unlike Meena, loved movies with unhappy endings; the sadder the better. Leisha was a huge Nicholas Sparks fan. "Or died in a tragic car crash just hours before they were supposed to get married! Or was smothered to death in a Peruvian mudslide while inoculating orphans."

Meena gave her a sarcastic look.

"Coming back to reality," Meena said, "I think he had a crappy childhood. He didn't seem to want to talk about it. Afterward—you know—I asked him about his family, and he said both his parents were dead. He said he has a half brother, but they're not close."

"Well, so there you go," Leisha said, looking a little disappointed there wasn't a dead wife who could be played by Rachel McAdams in the movie version of the story. "He just needs the love of a good woman to perk him up. A woman like you . . . the woman he saved from a bat attack! It's so romantic. Except for the part where you boned him on the first date. That is totally so out of character for you. Let me feel your head again. I want to see if your fever's gotten any worse."

Leisha was reaching out to feel Meena's forehead again when a young man, his skin almost as dark as Leisha's and his black hair clipped into a light fade—a creation of Leisha's, Meena didn't doubt, since it suited his face shape perfectly—appeared in front of Leisha's station.

"Oh my God, Meena!" he cried with a huge smile. "And Jack Bauer the Second! I'm so glad to see you both!" He walked right over to her, lifted Jack Bauer from her lap, and began coddling him. Jack lapped his face excitedly. "Leisha told me the good news!"

Meena recognized him as Roberto, one of BAO's stylists-in-training.

But she had no idea what he was talking about.

"Good news?" she echoed as she leaned back in her chair.

"About *Insatiable*," Roberto said as he rubbed Jack Bauer's ears. "Finally getting some vampires on it. I'm so excited! It's about time. I just love that Gregory Bane. I'm glued to the screen every time he comes on. Him and that other guy, from those vampire movies based on those books? Oh my God, they're so hot. I want them to make a vampire sandwich out of me."

Meena threw an aggrieved look at Leisha.

"Oh," she said. "Right."

"Oh, and I took your advice, remember, last time you were in here? I told Felipe no way was I going to Morocco for our anniversary, like he wanted." Roberto went on, giving Jack more ear rubs. "Like you told me to. I said we should go to the Bahamas instead. So we did. And the weirdest thing happened: The hotel Felipe made a reservation at, the one in Morocco? The same week we were supposed to be there, some suicide bomber blew it up! Can you believe that? It was like you *knew* or something! Felipe can't get over how lucky we were not to have been there. We could have been sitting there in the lobby having our breakfast and freaking *died*!"

Meena gave Roberto a watery smile. All she could think of, of course, were the people who *had* been there having their breakfast and who *had* freaking died . . . the ones she *hadn't* saved. Just like Angie Harwood.

"I'm glad you had a nice time in the Bahamas," Meena said as Leisha mugged at her owlishly behind Roberto's back.

"Oh, are you kidding me?" Roberto beamed. "It was the best. Listen, so who's going to hook up with the vampire on *Insatiable*? Is it going to be Victoria Worthington Stone or Tabby? Because I really think you guys should let Tabby get some. She's like the oldest teen virgin on television—"

"Roberto," Leisha said, interrupting him. Her patience for her fellow employees had never been high, but since her pregnancy it had been ebbing lower and lower. "I'm thirsty. Why don't you run on back and get Meena and me a couple of seltzers? And a bowl of water for Jack Bauer."

"Oh, no problem, sweetie," Roberto said. With obvious reluctance, he put Jack Bauer back down on Meena's lap. "You want some fruit or something?"

"Mango?" Leisha smiled. When Leisha smiled, no one could deny her anything. It had been that way since she and Meena were kids. "Cut it into the little squares; you know, how you did last time. That was so good."

"No problem," Roberto said. He scurried off to fulfill Leisha's wish.

Leisha turned her dark, thick-lashed gaze on Meena.

"Okay," she said. "He's gone. Sorry about that. Thanks for saving his ass with the Morocco thing, by the way. I actually would have missed him if he'd have been blown to smithereens with all those other people. And not just because he brings me freshly sliced mango. Anyway, back to Lucien. So . . . irresistibly drawn to the stunningly good-looking foreign guy with the deep dark secret. Not that you would know anything about having a deep dark secret. What exactly did he do to you to get you into bed with him in the first place? You're so repressed you wouldn't even shower in the locker room with the rest of us after gym class, remember? That's why Angie Harwood used to call you Steenka Meena."

Meena blushed again.

"Well, for one thing, he took me on a private after-hours tour of the Met," she said. "That's where I first saw him looking so sad . . . and I don't know . . . it just . . . it felt right. I *really* like this guy, Leish."

Leisha stared at her. "Uh-oh," she said. "I do *not* like that look in your eye, Meena. You don't just like this guy. You love him. Even worse . . . you want to *save* him. Admit it!"

"So what if I do?" Meena looked down at the top of Jack Bauer's head and sighed. "It doesn't matter. He's going back to Romania."

"When?" Leisha asked.

"I don't know," Meena said with a shrug. "I didn't ask. I didn't want to be that girl, you know?"

"You mean you didn't want to be yourself?" Leisha asked.

"Shut up." Then Meena brightened. "He asked me to the symphony tonight."

Leisha made a face. "Oh, ugh! Does he even know the real you *at all*?"

"I love the symphony," Meena said in protest. "I happen to be extremely cultured. I played the clarinet in sixth grade."

"Um, badly, if I remember," Leisha said. "You were like twentieth chair. Out of twenty-one."

"Says the person who sat in the twenty-first chair," Meena retorted wryly.

"So he doesn't know about this"—Leisha tapped her head—"either?"

Meena made a face. "Why would I tell him about that? I'm not going to mess this up like I've messed up every other relationship with a guy I've ever had."

Leisha frowned. "Meena. Seriously. If you want this to go anywhere, you've got to be honest with him. You can't play games. Your ability is a huge part of who you are—"

"But not the *only* part," Meena cried.

"You mean like the part where you don't ever want to have kids?" Leisha asked pointedly.

Meena's eyes widened. She was speechless.

"I'm not trying to be hurtful," Leisha insisted. She wasn't teasing anymore. "I think you're amazing. Why else would I have picked you to be my best friend, instead of Lori Delorenzo? She had way better hair than you did. I think you're generous—so much so that it gets you in trouble sometimes. You care about total strangers—again, to the point that you go out of your way to help them, which I think is a little above and beyond. And you're funny and smart and pretty and sweet. But the truth is, Meena, if this guy sticks around, he's going to find out who you really are. Like he's going to find out you don't really like the symphony. Maybe you should just be straight up with him from the beginning and see what happens. You might be surprised."

"Like with David?" Meena gave a sarcastic laugh. "I don't think so. Maybe I'll just ease him into getting to know the real Meena Harper a little bit at a time."

"Yeah, well, it sounds like he got to know at least a pretty good part of Meena Harper last night," Leisha said with a sarcastic laugh of her own. Then she sobered. "Seriously, though, Meena. I know I bitch about Adam, but the reason we've lasted this long is because he's the first guy I've ever been with who I've been able to just be myself around, no holds barred. If you can't be who you really are with this guy, you might as well just keep being alone."

Meena looked at her friend thoughtfully. Leisha had a point . . . a good one.

The scary part was that she didn't know how much Meena was holding back from *her*. . . . Meena was just going to have to tell her.

And judging from the size of her belly and the level of alarm bells that went off in Meena's head every time Leisha mentioned *the baby,* it was going to have to be soon.

"Hey," Leisha said, glancing at her watch. "Shouldn't you be at work or something?"

"Yeah," Meena said slowly. "That's kind of what I wanted to talk to you about. . . . Can I leave Jack here until after work, then come pick him up? You know how everyone loves him—"

Roberto, coming back with a bowl of water for Meena's dog and a plate of perfectly cubed mango for Leisha, overheard this last part and gasped. "Yes, please!" he cried. "We'll babysit the puppy!"

Meena, suppressing an urge to laugh, glanced at Leisha. "It's just, I don't want to go all the way back uptown to my apartment to drop him off, then have to come all the way back downtown to go to work—"

"We love the puppy!" Roberto cried. "We'll give him a puppy pedicure!"

"You," Leisha said, glaring at Meena as she popped a mango cube into her mouth, "owe me one."

"I really do." Meena agreed.

"You're going to watch my kid for me when he's born," Leisha said. "For free."

"Believe me," Meena said under her breath as she surrendered a wiggling Jack Bauer to Roberto's waiting arms. "I already am."

Chapter Thirty-two

"This is the latest victim," Emil said, producing a red file folder and placing it solemnly on the black-granite-topped table.

Lucien stared down at the photo.

She'd probably been pretty once . . . the kind of girl who would have had difficulty keeping herself from smiling when a camera was pointing in her direction.

Except . . . how had he known that?

But violent death had robbed her of any beauty. Now her face was a dour gray mask, dark purple shadows beneath her eyes.

And below her neck . . .

Lucien turned the photo over. He'd seen this kind of ravaging before.

But not in the past two centuries.

"They estimate that her time of death was around three this morning," Emil said.

What had he been doing at three in the morning while this girl's blood was being drained from her body?

He knew perfectly well. If he'd been doing what he'd come here to the city to do, she might have been alive right now.

"The killings are happening closer together," Emil observed.

"Whoever is behind them, he seems to be getting more desperate. Or greedy. He tried killing once and found that he liked it. He wants it all the time now. He doesn't want to stop. Perhaps he *can't* stop."

"Perhaps," Lucien said. He wasn't sure what to believe anymore about these killings. "It can be addictive. Which is why it can't be allowed. But these bite marks aren't from a single individual."

"It's still going to get us all staked when the humans finally realize what's going on," Emil said mournfully, "and decide to eradicate us the way the Palatine wants to . . . the way they did your father."

Emil shuddered, perhaps remembering how Lucien's father had met his ignominious fate. Then he raised his suddenly guilt-ridden gaze to Lucien's and blurted, "It's my fault, my lord. This latest girl's death. Mine, and mine alone. I should never have allowed my wife to invite . . . er . . . *her* to our home last evening."

There was no mistaking whom Emil meant by *her*. The name seemed to linger in the air of the penthouse the way the scent of her humanness did. . . .

Meena Harper. Meena Harper. Meena Harper.

Emil went on. "I realize in doing so, I was very wrong. Of course you were distracted from your duties. I would understand it if you chose to kill me, my lord, for my gross negligence."

Lucien looked down at the smaller man, who was bowing his head, humbly waiting for his body to be lifted and hurled through one of the UV-blocked windows and into the daylight, where he would instantly fry in the sun like a potato crisp.

But Lucien could no more blame his cousin for what had happened the night before than he could explain it. He didn't yet know why he was so convinced that the dark-eyed girl in pajamas he'd rescued that night outside St. George's Cathedral would turn out to be the source of his spiritual and emotional redemption.

He certainly hadn't treated her the way one would treat a redeemer. He had spent the night doing things to her that, in the light of day, he wasn't sure she remembered . . . but it had to be admitted that at the time, she'd seemed to fully enjoy them.

God knew he had.

Now Meena Harper's essence seemed to have entered his long-empty veins. They thrummed with her life force and energy, giving them a kind of electric vitality.

But that wasn't all. He seemed to . . . know things.

He couldn't explain it. It didn't make any sense. It was almost a sort of . . . madness. *Her* madness, the exact same flickering images that he'd seen coming and going inside her head every time he'd entered it. How had he known, for instance, that the girl in the photo had difficulty keeping herself from smiling when there was a camera around?

The girl in the photo was dead. And he had never met her.

What did it mean?

He didn't yet know.

But he knew it meant something different.

And different, after five centuries, was good.

Very, very good.

"It's all right, Emil," he said. He felt kindly toward his cousin. Which was ridiculous. Merely a week ago, he'd have been raging over this colossal cock-up. Was it Meena Harper who was making him feel so mellow?

Or something else?

Emil raised his head, confused.

"Then . . ." He looked around the room, as if expecting to see another of Lucien's minions appear, stake in hand. "You don't want to kill me, my lord? Or my wife?"

"I think there's been enough death lately," Lucien said mildly. "Why don't we concentrate instead on finding this killer and stopping him—or them. Are you telling me that no one," Lucien asked, getting up from the table and going to stand by the plate-glass windows, "was able to give the police any kind of description of any sort of suspect? No one at all was seen dumping the body or anywhere around it?"

Emil, looking immensely relieved to have been given a reprieve, grabbed his files, then leafed quickly through them.

"Oh, plenty," he said. "So many possible suspects the police are still interviewing them all. Everyone thinks they saw something. Which means, of course, that no one saw anything. Because whoever did this had sense enough to wipe the memory of anyone who might have seen anything useful."

Lucien frowned, staring out over the city. He could see the red warning lights of the airport towers across the East River in the distance.

The lights reminded him of the glow he'd seen the other night in his brother's eyes. Dimitri had always been power hungry, forever looking for new ways to expand his business, his dominance, his control. It had nearly killed him when their father had left all his immense fortune to his eldest son . . . even though Lucien had been more than willing to share it.

Did Dimitri's hunger for wealth and power extend to other things, as well? Lucien wasn't certain he knew for sure.

Which was a sad thing for a man to have to admit about his own brother.

Lucien turned away from the window with a start. Emil had been speaking to him all this time, and he hadn't been paying the slightest bit of attention.

"Of course," he said. Whatever it was, Lucien was certain Emil would handle it admirably, as he did all of his endeavors on the prince's behalf. "Emil."

"Sire?"

"I'm going to have to cancel my previous plans for this evening."

Emil looked uncertain. "My lord?"

Lucien ignored the pulsing in his veins—a new sensation . . . or at least one he hadn't felt in half a millennium—and said, "I'd made plans to go to the symphony tonight with Ms. Harper. But in light of . . . this"—he indicated the file on the table—"I obviously have more pressing affairs to see to."

"Oh," Emil said, his eyes reflecting true disappointment. "I see. Of course. I'll take care of it. But are you certain? Surely there's time for pleasure as well as—"

"Later." The skyscrapers of midtown Manhattan stretched out beneath him. Somewhere down there, he knew, lurked a killer. More than one. He needed to find and stop them.

But would it be before they killed again?

"Four women have already died," Lucien said. "I can't afford to be so negligent again."

But even as he said it, he knew it would be a matter of only hours before he began craving her again. He talked of the killers being addicts.

Yet who, precisely, was the true addict?

Chapter Thirty-three

2:00 P.M. EST, Friday, April 16
ABN Building
520 Madison Avenue
New York, New York

I know who you are," Tabitha Worthington Stone said in a breathless voice. "Or I guess I should say *what* you are."

"Do you?" The tall, dark-haired young man looked down at her with a gaze that smoldered, a faint smile playing on his perfectly formed lips. "What am I?"

"You're a . . . a . . ." Taylor glanced away, biting her luscious lower lip and throwing an arm dramatically over her forehead. "No! I can't say it. It's just not possible!"

"Say it." Maximillian Cabrera grabbed her by both shoulders. "Just say it!"

"Oh, hey." Paul, one of the breakdown writers, nodded at Jon. "Here to see Meena?"

Jon tore his gaze from the incredibly passionate scene being acted out on the empty soundstage in front of him. Taylor Mackenzie still somehow managed to look sexy in leggings and a large gray cardigan, which she wore open over a belly-revealing black T-shirt.

Too bad Jon didn't have anything as good to say about her costar-to-be, Stefan Dominic. He thought Dominic looked terrible, all black skinny jeans, greasy hair, and a two-day growth of razor stubble.

No way they were going to give him the part, Jon thought. They'd be way smarter to give it to someone cleaner-cut looking. Like Jon, for instance. Dominic was just so . . . *obvious*. For someone supposed to be playing a vampire, that is.

"Yeah," Jon said to Paul. "I mean, Meena knows I'm here, anyway. I had to phone up in order for security to let me sign in." He pointed to his visitor pass, clipped to the collar of his jean jacket. "But I haven't seen her anywhere."

"She's in her office," Paul said. "Under the pile of breakdowns I just handed her. You better look out. She's in a foul mood."

Jon frowned. "Really? Why?"

"If I had to guess, that's why," Paul said, nodding toward the sound-stage.

Fran and Stan, Meena's bosses, had stepped out in front of the cameras and were giving Taylor and Stefan some feedback.

"That was fantastic," Fran, a middle-aged lady with a lot of pendant necklaces and wildly curling gray hair, was saying. "Stefan, you gave me goose bumps."

"Thanks," Stefan said laconically, standing around with his hip bones poking out.

Jon wanted to punch him in the kidneys.

"Right, Aunt Fran?" A skinny girl with very straight black hair and wearing a pencil skirt stepped out from behind a heavyset man. Shoshona, Jon realized. And the heavyset man was Meena's other boss, Sy. "He's just brilliant."

Brilliant. About as brilliant as Jack Bauer. The dog, not the one played by Kiefer Sutherland.

"Thanks," Stefan said again, pushing some of his dirty-looking hair from his eyes.

"I get a really good feeling from him," Taylor said in her tinkly little voice. "I think we've got good chemistry. It works for me."

Oh, God, Jon thought with an inward groan. Why had he even bothered showing up? This was just torture. To see—actually see, in real life, not on a television screen—his beloved Taylor in the arms of another? It was too much.

And then the next thing Jon knew, Taylor was coming toward him in her little white tennis shoes. He sucked in his breath—and his gut, although he didn't have much of one, because he'd really been working out this time, not just saying he was going to, since he was serious about this police exam thing—and said, "Hey, Taylor," as she walked by, leaving a faint scent of grapefruit in her wake.

She turned her head and saw him, her heavily glossed lips parting in surprise . . . then curling upward in a smile of recognition.

"Oh, hey . . ." She clearly couldn't remember his name.

"Jon," he said quickly. "Jon Harper. Meena Harper's older brother?"

"Oh, right," she said, giggling. "I'm so bad with names. How's it going?"

"Great," he said. His heart was thumping like a basketball. "I just caught the last bit of that scene with you and . . . what's-his-name. That was some fantastic work."

"Oh, thanks," Taylor said, her eyes shining. "His name is Stefan. He's going to play the new vampire on the show. I'm so psyched 'cause it's really going to pull in a younger demo for the show. Isn't Stefan fabulous?"

No, Jon thought. You're *fabulous. Not Stefan. That guy sucks.*

"So they're definitely going to cast that guy, huh?" Jon asked. "Because, you know, I did some acting in high school—"

"Oh, I think so," Taylor said. "The network wants him. And he's got the same manager as Gregory Bane, you know, from *Lust*? That guy over there. Dimitri something-or-other."

She pointed to a man who was standing in one corner, talking to Stan and Fran and Sy and Shoshona. Dimitri Something-or-Other was huge—physically, just really tall and broad-shouldered, a little like Meena's prince—and in an impeccably tailored suit that had probably set him back a cool three grand or so. He seemed to have a couple of bodyguards with him.

So he was rich, too.

Another guy Jon was going to have to punch in the kidneys.

"Interesting," Jon said, pretending not to care. "Hey, what are you doing now? Wanna go grab a drink?"

"Oh," Taylor said. "I would, but I have to go meet my trainer. Maybe next time, okay?"

Then she actually stood up on tiptoe, placed a hand on his wrist to balance herself, and gave him a little kiss—light as the brush of a butterfly wing—on his cheek.

And then she was gone, skipping away to go work off some imaginary fat.

Jon stood there staring after her for a minute or two before he was able to rouse himself enough from the spell she'd cast over him to go look for his sister. He eventually found her exactly where Paul had said she'd be, in her office—which, strictly speaking, was actually more of a cubicle than an office, although it did have a narrow window with a view.

She was typing furiously, pages spread all across her desk and every other available flat surface in a seemingly random fashion, though Jon knew from experience that if anyone dared to touch them, she'd scream bloody murder, because there was some kind of order to them; only his sister knew what it was, however.

"Hey, Meen," Jon said. Since there weren't many seats for him to choose from, he settled onto a stack of scripts piled perilously high on a chair in front of her desk.

"Go away," she said. She didn't take her eyes off the screen in front of her.

"What's wrong?" he asked.

"Everything," she said. "Nothing. Just go away. This place is imploding. Like my life. You wouldn't *believe* the lines Fran and Stan—no way Shoshona was smart enough to write this—gave me to feed poor Taylor. Not to mention Cheryl. There's product placement *everywhere*. I've never even heard of any of this stuff. I don't think they're CDI products. Revenant Wrinkle Cream? Strigoi Sunglasses? There's even some kind of spa where Victoria goes to get a total rejuvenating makeover—have you ever heard of the Regenerative Spa for Youthful Awakening?"

Jon shrugged. "No. But, Meena, what did you expect? They've got this new vampire story line, and CDI thinks the show has a chance of getting some younger viewers. Why wouldn't they throw in some product placement? They're trying to make some money."

She sighed. "I don't know. I thought that they'd show some integrity. Respect for the devoted audience this show has had for thirty years.

But *I'm* the idiot, I guess. What are you doing here, anyway?"

"Oh," he said. "I'm here for the audition."

"What audition?" Meena looked at him bewilderedly.

"For the part of the vampire," Jon said. God, she really *was* out of it.

"There's no audition," she said. "Stefan has the part. They're just making sure he and Taylor have chemistry—which basically means that he isn't shorter than she is."

"Yeah," Jon said a little bitterly. "I sort of get that now."

"Look," she said, turning back to her computer screen. "I'm really busy. You'd better go."

Paul had been right. She really was in a foul mood.

"What is *with* you?" he asked. "I mean, I get that you're upset about the new vampire plot, but you could try being a little nicer to people."

He thought he heard her mutter something like "I *am* trying" and something else about a baby. He had no idea what she was talking about. "What baby?" he asked bewilderedly.

"Just forget it," she said to the monitor.

But there was no hiding the expression on her face, which he recognized only too well.

And like a bolt from the blue, he knew.

"*That's* why you've been acting like such a psycho lately?" he demanded. "You had a vision about Adam and Leisha's baby?"

"No," she said with a laugh. "Of course not. Don't be stupid."

"That was the fakest laugh I ever heard," Jon said, shaking his head. "What did you see?"

She hesitated, then abruptly gave up.

"Fine," she said. "Whatever. And I didn't *see* anything. It's just a feeling. And it isn't even a bad feeling, necessarily. I just don't want Leisha to worry. Worrying that something bad is going to happen could be what actually causes something bad to happen. So we're not telling her, all right? Or Adam. Because there's nothing to tell."

Jon shook his head. He had never really understood his sister's gift, but he'd learned to respect it over the years. Except when girls had refused to go out with him because he was the You're Gonna Die Girl's brother.

"You're sure about this?" he asked.

"Positive," she said firmly.

"Okay," he said. "So then what are you stressing over?"

She widened her eyes at him and he realized belatedly that he'd asked exactly the wrong thing.

"Wait," he said, holding up a hand while she sucked in her breath. "Let me put that another way. What can I do to make things a little easier on you?"

She considered this. "Can you go downtown to pick up Jack and take him home? I dropped him off at Leisha's salon on my way here from Lucien's this morning. I'll owe you so, so big-time. After selling my soul to corporate all day like this, I just want to go home and—"

"Start working diligently on the great American novel?"

"—get ready for my big date tonight," she finished with a grin.

"Jesus," Jon said, getting up from the towering pile of paper on which he'd been perched. "You're seeing him again tonight? You've really got it bad for this guy."

Meena's grin widened. "You said I should start being nicer to people."

"I meant me, but fine, I'll go pick up your dog. And don't worry," he added. "I won't say anything to Leisha about your weird non-vision concerning her unborn kid."

"You better not," Meena said. "Considering there's nothing to tell. Come on, I'll walk you to the elevators."

As they approached the elevator bank, he heard Meena curse beneath her breath. He looked up, then saw why. Fran and Stan were standing there, along with Meena's arch-nemesis, Shoshona; Stefan Dominic; Stefan's manager; and the bodyguards. Quite a crowd.

"Hi, Meena," Shoshona said in a voice dripping with honey.

"Hi, Shoshona," Meena said. She looked like she wanted to be anywhere but there.

"I'm not sure you've met our newest cast member, Stefan Dominic," Shoshona said, turning to the skinny, dark-haired guy Jon had been longing to sucker-punch just a half hour or so earlier.

"No, I haven't had the pleasure," Meena said politely, and she shook hands with the man who would soon be getting the pleasure of sticking his tongue in the mouth of Taylor Mackenzie on a daily basis.

"Nice to meet you," Stefan Dominic said, looking down at Meena.

Meena, shaking Stefan Dominic's hand, kind of froze, staring up at him. Jon knew she was having another one of her visions.

"Have we met before?" she asked curiously.

Which wasn't what she usually said. Usually she said something like *Don't take the freeway* or *I'd switch to wheat from white flour, if I were you.*

"I don't think so," Dominic said.

"You look so familiar." She was still holding on to his hand. "I could swear I've seen you before."

"Well, Meena," Shoshona said with a little sneer, "Stefan's my boyfriend. You probably *have* seen him before. Around the office here, with me."

"Oh," Meena said. She let out an embarrassed little laugh and dropped his hand. "Sorry. Of course."

With that, the elevator came, and Jon got on it, along with Dominic and his manager, who'd said good-bye to Shoshona and her aunt and uncle.

The last face Jon saw before the elevator doors closed and he rode down with them in silence was Meena's. She looked confused.

But no wonder: she had a lot to feel confused about. Jon didn't give Meena's confusion a second thought.

Instead, he thought about how Taylor Mackenzie had kissed him. It seemed a much more pleasant thing to ruminate on during the elevator ride down to the lobby than the conversation he'd just had with Meena.

What Jon didn't realize was that his thinking about Taylor Mackenzie instead of his sister actually saved his life during that elevator ride.

Chapter Thirty-four

5:00 P.M. EST, Friday, April 16
910 Park Avenue
New York, New York

Meena, after carefully scoping out the lobby of her building, realized it was countess-free and made a dash for the elevator.

She couldn't believe it. She had actually made it past the doorman—*not* Pradip, thankfully, as he wasn't on duty—and to the elevator without running into her neighbor. This week had been such a roller coaster—plummeting from best to worst to best again—that she wasn't quite sure what to expect from moment to moment. Right now, she appeared to be on another upswing.

Except that, just as the elevator doors were about to shut, a too-familiar, heavily diamond-ringed hand appeared to keep them from closing all the way.

And then Meena heard Mary Lou's southern-accented voice cry, "Yoo-hoo! Meena?"

The door opened to reveal the countess standing there, looking as if butter wouldn't melt in her mouth, wearing a peach-colored suit with a matching picture hat and holding several armfuls of shopping bags from Bergdorf Goodman.

"Oh," Meena said. She could hardly hide her disappointment. She was glad she'd cinched her trench coat so tightly. Maybe Mary Lou wouldn't notice she was still wearing last night's little black dress. "Hi, Mary Lou."

"Well, look at you," Mary Lou cried. "Aren't you looking rosy cheeked and pretty as a picture? You know, I was just thinking about you. I saw your brother Jon leaving earlier and asked how you were and he said he didn't know, that he hadn't seen you yet today."

Meena made a mental note to kill Jon when he got home from BAO with Jack Bauer. "Oh, uh . . . ," she said intelligently. She wished the elevator floor would drop open and allow both of them to plummet to their deaths.

No such luck, however. The door closed, and they began the long ascent to the eleventh floor.

"So you liked the prince?" Mary Lou asked completely unnecessarily.

Meena would have thought it was obvious she liked him since she'd clearly spent the night with him. "Oh," she said, giving up. What was the point? She was in love with Lucien Antonescu. The whole world was going to find out soon enough if they kept seeing each other. "I liked him, all right." *Did that sound too needy?*

"I'm so glad," Mary Lou said, beaming. "I knew you would. Isn't he good looking? And nice. I just think he's so *nice.*"

Then Mary Lou, of all people, looked worried that *she'd* said the wrong thing. "But not too nice, you know?" Mary Lou added. "I mean, he's no pushover. I've seen him do things—well, they'd make your hair curl, let me tell you."

Meena raised her eyebrows. She had no idea what the countess could be talking about.

"Oh, never mind me. Emil says I have a tendency to run my mouth. I just meant Lucien is a real man's man, if you know what I mean."

Meena knew exactly what she meant. She had the chafing to prove it.

Meena realized this little girl-talk might be a good opportunity to learn a thing or two about the prince. They had only six floors left though, so she figured she'd better hurry it up.

"I thought there was a little something . . . melancholic about him," Meena said.

"Melancholic?" Mary Lou looked as if she wasn't sure what the word meant.

"Yeah," Meena said. She knew she had to tread carefully. She didn't want to say anything that might send the countess yapping to Lucien, saying Meena had been talking about him behind his back. She needed to be subtle. But not too subtle. God, she'd forgotten how hard it was to be in love! "Like something might have happened to him . . . maybe in his childhood . . . that might have made him sad?"

"Oh," Mary Lou said, rising to the bait like a champ. "You bet. His dad was a real monster. But his mother! Couldn't have asked for a lovelier woman. A living saint. I never met them, mind you; they passed away before my time. This is just what Emil told me. But anyway, yes, his father—"

"Did he used to beat him?" Meena asked, dropping her voice even though they were alone on the elevator.

"Yes," Mary Lou whispered back. "From what I hear."

Meena's heart wrenched for Lucien as she recalled his expression in the museum as they'd stood looking at the portrait of Vlad Tepes. What did it mean, she wondered, that he was so interested in a national hero who'd treated his sons the way Lucien's own father had apparently treated him?

And no wonder he hated the show 24. It must have brought back horrible childhood memories.

The poor man! It was amazing how far he'd come in the world since his obviously traumatic beginnings.

"So what do you two have planned for tonight?" Mary Lou wanted to know. "Don't tell me he hasn't asked you. It's Friday night!"

Meena felt herself blushing. She really was going to have to get over this blushing thing where the prince was concerned if they were going to be an item, at least for however long he was in town. "We're going to the symphony," she said.

"The Philharmonic?" Mary Lou shrieked. "Oh, how great! I got him those seats, you know. I mean, they've been sold out for months. But I know someone who knows someone. I'm so glad you're going with him; it will be good for you both. You two have so much in common, you don't even know. You both work way too hard. And you both need to *relax* a little, take some time off to actually enjoy life. That's why I thought you'd be such a good couple. Now," Mary Lou said as the elevator reached the eleventh floor and the doors opened, "you have to borrow this vintage Givenchy of mine for tonight; it will look like a knockout on you. I know I'm a little bit bigger than you, but I didn't used to be, believe it or not."

Meena opened her mouth to protest that she didn't need to borrow anything to wear, but Mary Lou wouldn't hear of it. There was no putting her off. She dragged Meena into her apartment and then her walk-in closet (which was as large as Meena's bedroom) and dithered around in there until she found the dress she was looking for—an admittedly gorgeous vintage Givenchy cocktail dress, covered all over in hand-sewn ebony crystals that caught the light and shimmered like black diamonds.

"You'll need to wear a slip with it," Mary Lou said critically, holding the dress up to the lights that shone above the mirror of her built-in dressing table. "I forgot how sheer it is. Do you have a slip?"

At the sight of the gorgeous dress, Meena forgot all her protests. She was going to look fantastic in it. Even if she knew Lucien was going to be more interested in how she looked out of it.

"I do," she said. She had a black slip she'd bought to wear beneath the dress she'd worn as Leisha's maid of honor.

She didn't know what was happening to her. She was turning as girly as a teenager getting ready for her junior prom. She had never spent this much time discussing clothes.

Love. It had to be love.

"Don't worry about hurrying to return it," Mary Lou said, walking Meena to the front door. "Keep it as long as you want. I'm glad someone's finally getting to enjoy it after all these years. You know, I don't think I've worn that thing since the sixties."

Meena laughed. "You mean when you were a fetus?"

"Wait, did I say since the sixties?" Mary Lou laid a beringed hand on her chest and laughed. "I meant it was *made* in the sixties. I don't know what I was thinking."

"Thanks, Mary Lou," Meena said. She really did feel grateful to the older woman. Some of the antipathy she'd harbored lately toward her was starting to ebb away. "And thanks for introducing me to Lucien. He really is . . . well, what you said. Very nice."

This was the understatement of the decade.

"Oh, hon," Mary Lou said, leaning down to kiss Meena on the cheek. Meena caught a strong whiff of the countess's perfume. "I'm so happy for you. You don't even know. I just knew it would all work out between you two the minute I saw your eyes meet across the room last night. It was almost like you'd met before or something."

Meena swallowed back her almost instinctual *Oh, but we had.* "Thank you, Mary Lou," she said again, the dress tucked over her arm. "I . . . just thanks."

She had to flee across the hallway before the sudden pricking of tears she felt at the corners of her eyes overflowed. What was the matter with her? She was never this emotional about anything. Well, except what was going on with Leisha and the baby. And her job, of course.

Oh, God, her job. She had to sit down and get to work on her proposal for the Romanian vampire-hunting prince who was going to kill Shoshona's vampire and end up as Cheryl's love interest. If she didn't finish it by Monday, she knew there'd be no hope of the story line ever being accepted. Once Maximillian Cabrera won over viewers' hearts, she'd never be able to convince Fran and Stan—let alone the network and CDI, which was obviously investing a lot into this whole vampire thing—to kill him off.

What was it about Stefan Dominic that rubbed her the wrong way? The moment she'd seen him standing there by the elevators Meena had known—just known—that she'd seen him before.

And not, as Shoshona had suggested, out with Shoshona.

No, Meena knew Stefan Dominic from somewhere else.

And not somewhere good.

Unlocking her door, Meena let herself into her apartment, which was mercifully empty. Jon was still out fetching Jack Bauer. Meena almost sagged with relief to be alone, at least for a little while. Hanging her bag and coat on the hooks by the door and throwing her keys into the tray she kept on the table, she went to place Mary Lou's dress carefully in her closet.

Then she changed into her "writing clothes" (a pair of leggings and one of Jon's old sweatshirts), grabbed her laptop, pushed up her sleeves, and curled up in her favorite comfy armchair to work.

And just sat there, staring at the empty screen.

How was she supposed to work when all she could think about was Lucien?

She'd have thought this would have helped her creative process, since she was writing about him. At least in theory.

But instead of writing, she could only sit there and remember the possessiveness with which Lucien had snatched her up and kissed her the night before . . . the way he'd seemed almost to devour her, even his dark-eyed gaze consuming her every time he'd looked down at her before kissing her, again and again . . . the taste of wine on his lips.

And then she'd recall the paths those strangely cool lips had traced across her skin as he'd dragged his mouth from her high round breasts, to her rib cage, to the soft curve of her belly; the way his hands had molded and pressed and squeezed her skin, silently demanding things she was more than willing to give because he, in turn, was so giving; the way he'd cradled her against him afterward, as if he'd been afraid she might slip away from him in the night.

How could she think about anything else? Her skin still felt singed in all the places he'd touched it.

She was kidding herself if she thought she was going to get any writing done. She Googled him instead and read about the books he'd written (she'd have ordered the books, but they were all in Romanian). She was still reading about him when she noticed the time, swore, and jumped up, rushing to the bedroom. She had to start getting ready if she was going to look absolutely stunning and still get to the Upper West Side in time to meet him.

She was adding a last layer of lipstick when the door opened and Jon came in with Jack Bauer.

"Why are you so dressed up?" he asked, leaning down to let the dog off his leash.

"My date with Lucien," she said. "Remember?"

"Oh, right," he said.

The dog ran up to Meena excitedly, ready to throw himself against her knees. She jumped up onto the couch, not wanting her pantyhose ruined.

"No," she said, firmly. "*Down.*"

Jack Bauer looked confused and disappointed.

"Jon, can you feed him or something?" she asked him. "He's—"

It was right then that the buzzer to the apartment's intercom sounded, startling Meena half out of her skin. She leapt off the couch and reached for the receiver.

"Yes?" she asked.

"Hey, Miss Harper," Roger, the day doorman, said. Pradip still hadn't come on duty. "Delivery for you."

Meena, bewildered, said, "I didn't order anything." She looked at Jon. "Did you order something?"

He shrugged. "Like what? I just got here."

"We didn't order anything," Meena said into the receiver.

"You didn't?" Roger sounded as bewildered as she did. "It's a messenger. With a big box from Bergdorf Goodman."

"Oh," Meena said. Maybe something Mary Lou had ordered, mistakenly addressed to her apartment instead. "Well, send him up, I guess."

"Will do, Miss Harper," Roger said, and hung up.

"What did you order from Bergdorf Goodman?" Jon asked after Meena, too, had hung up. "I thought we were broke."

"*We* are," Meena said, going to her purse for a tip for the delivery guy. "And I didn't order anything."

"Then where'd you get that dress?" Jon asked. "I never saw it before."

"Mary Lou lent it to me," Meena muttered.

"What was that?"

"Mary Lou loaned it to me," Meena said more loudly.

Jon hooted. "Wow," he said. "Aren't you two chummy? What are you gals going to be doing next? Going for mani-pedis together? Tea at the Plaza?"

"Shut up," Meena said. "She's not so bad."

"Well, this is a change of pace," Jon said. "Lately you've been going out of your way to avoid her. I guess a roll in the sack with a prince gives you a whole different outlook on life, huh? Suddenly your snooty neighbors with the summer castle aren't so bad after all."

"Seriously," Meena said, going to the door to unlock it. "Shut up."

"How much you think that thing set her back? Three grand?"

"No," Meena said. "It's vintage. From the sixties."

"Well," Jon said, "it does look good on you. I'm not kidding. Lucien is going to pass out when he sees you. You look like a princess."

Meena beamed. Her brother rarely paid her compliments on her looks, so this one meant a lot.

Especially since she'd been having such a strange week.

"Aw, Jon," she said, her eyes filling with tears. "Thanks so much." She moved toward him to give him a hug.

"Whoa," Jon said, hugging her back. "What's going on? I just said you looked nice, that's all. What's with the waterworks?"

Fortunately at that moment there was a knock at the door, and Meena, hastily releasing him and wiping her eyes—worried her mascara was running—went to open it as Jack Bauer barked at her heels, excited that there was a visitor.

A man in a beige windbreaker and a baseball cap, holding a huge black box with a gold ribbon around it, asked, "Meena Harper?"

"That's me," she said, and took the box, slipping him the five-dollar bill she was holding.

"Thanks," he said, and headed back to the elevator.

"Um," Meena said as he stood there, waiting for the car.

"Yeah?" He looked back at her inquiringly.

"Nothing," Meena said, and started to close the door. Then she had second thoughts, opened it again, and said, "Just . . . look out for pepperoni pizza, okay?"

The deliveryman stared at her, uncomprehending. "Okay."

Meena smiled and closed the door. Then she brought the package inside the apartment, Jack Bauer tripping after her.

"What?" Jon said. "Cholesterol?"

"Choking," Meena said. She set the box down on the dining room table. "But maybe he won't now, if he's careful. Who could this be from?" It definitely had her name on it, not the countess's.

She untied the gold ribbon and lifted the lid off the box. It was filled with white tissue paper. She parted the folds, then caught her breath. . . .

The leather tote with the jewel-encrusted dragon slinking down the side.

In ruby red.

"It's the bag," Meena breathed, holding it in one hand and reaching out to stroke each individual crystal with the other.

"What bag?" Jon asked.

"*The* bag," Meena said, feeling as if all the wind had been knocked from her. "The bag I've always wanted. In exactly the right color. Shoshona has it in aquamarine. But the aquamarine is ugly. The ruby is perfect. Just perfect. Oh, Jon. It's so beautiful."

She wanted to cry all over again. She had never seen anything as gorgeous.

"Well, *I* didn't get it for you," Jon said. He began to paw through the tissue in the box. "Who did? Is there a note or something?"

"*He* got it for me," Meena said, not looking away from the bag. "I know he did."

Only how had he known? She'd never told him. They'd never discussed anything as ridiculous as Meena's inappropriate lust for a Marc Jacobs bag with a crystal dragon slinking down the front, that she could—by the way—never have afforded.

"Who's he?" Jon wanted to know, pawing harder. "Lucien? Prince Charming? Is that the cutting edge in morning-after gifts these days? Purses?"

"It's a tote," Meena said, opening it to see that the messenger bag strap could be exchanged for an elegant gold chain for evening wear or, alternately, a slim leather strap for more formal business events. "Not a purse."

"Oh, of course it is," Jon said, pulling a silver envelope from the depths of the box. "Here's a note."

The envelope had the word *Meena* written across it in elegant, slightly old-fashioned handwriting that she instantly recognized as Lucien's, although she'd never actually seen his writing.

"What's Mr. Big Pants got to say for himself?" Jon asked crabbily. Meena supposed he was jealous because he'd never gotten anything as tasteful and elegant for any of his ex-girlfriends. She thought she recalled his having bought one of them a bracelet at Tiffany once, only to have her break up with him when she found out he'd bought the exact same bracelet for their mother for Christmas.

Meena put the bag down and ran a nail beneath the fold of the envelope. She pulled out a piece of ivory stationery.

My darling Meena, he'd written.

She smiled. She'd never been called *my darling* by anyone before.

> *Every moment away from you feels like time spent in a sort of cell. I can think of nothing, dream of nothing, but you. Unfortunately, I will have to remain in my self-inflicted prison a bit longer, since work will keep me from meeting you tonight. I can't seem to find a way to avoid this . . . however, I hope this gift will make up for my unforgivable behavior. I saw this and thought of you, and St. George. You have slain the dragon.*
>
> *Until we meet again, I am your Lucien*

Meena read the note once and then another time.

Then her eyes filled, once more, with tears.

"He's not coming," she said to no one in particular.

Jon stared at her. "Wait . . . you mean to the concert tonight?"

She nodded, not looking at him. She let the note flutter to the floor.

"He's not coming," she said again.

Then she turned and walked over to the armchair where she'd been curled up a little while earlier, not writing, and collapsed into it, the tulle skirt of Mary Lou's Givenchy dress puffing up all around her.

Jon bent to pick up the note.

"Wait," he said. "Are you *crying*?"

"I don't know what's wrong with me," Meena said miserably, lifting her knees and hugging them to her chest.

"Well, don't cry all over the countess's dress," Jon advised her. "She'll probably make you pay for the dry cleaning." He read the note. "'*You have slain the dragon*'? What the hell does that mean? How big is this guy's dick, anyway?"

Meena dropped her forehead down onto her knees and started to cry. "Don't be coarse," she said.

"Holy crap," she heard her brother say in some alarm. "Don't *cry*, Meen. I know you've had a bad week, but he's not breaking up with you. He's just got to work. He'll probably see you tomorrow. I mean, for Christ's sake. He sent you a really nice note. And a purse."

"It's not a purse, it's a tote. And that's just it," Meena said, lifting her tear-stained face. "I never told him."

"You never told him what?" Jon asked, coming to sit on the arm of the chair after he'd pushed some of the tulle out of the way.

"I never told him about it," Meena said. "I've been wanting that purse—I mean tote—forever. But we can't afford it. And I never told him. It's like . . ." Her voice dropped to a whisper. "It's like he read my mind."

Jon raised his eyebrows. "Well," he said drily. "I could see how that would be upsetting for someone who's been doing just that to people for fifteen years or so herself."

"Shut up," Meena said, unable to keep from laughing a little.

"No," Jon said. "Really. It must be a real blow to your ego to have to admit there might be someone else out there who can do what you do. Oh, wait . . . no, never mind. The prince can't tell when people are going to die. He just has the psychic ability to know what handbag his girlfriend secretly lusts after."

Meena reached up to wipe her eyes. "You're not funny," she said.

"Then why are you laughing?" he asked.

"Okay," Meena said with a sigh. "Maybe I overreacted. But it's pretty weird. You have to admit."

"I think the fact that you spent the night having sex with a prince is pretty weird," Jon said. "But who am I to judge? So, since you're going to be home tonight . . . Chinese food and a DVD?"

Meena smiled. She still felt shaken.

Shaken to her core, actually.

But it was good to have Jon around to ground her.

"Sounds good," she said.

"Great." Jon gave her knee a pat through some of the tulle. "I'll walk over to the video store and pick something out. As a compromise, I'll get something with a romance where stuff also gets blown up. Moo shu sound good? I'll get garlic chicken, too, for a change. Come on, Jack." He slapped his thigh, and Jack Bauer, delighted, scrambled after him as he walked toward the wall for the dog's leash. "We'll be back in a bit."

Meena, smiling—though still a little shakily—got up from the armchair and, after Jon and her dog had gone, unzipped Mary Lou's dress, stepped out of it, and hung it carefully back on the hanger in her closet. She would, she supposed, get some other chance to wear it. It wasn't such a terrible thing.

She picked up the note Lucien had written to her and read it again. It made her smile and made her heart beat a little faster.

You have slain the dragon. She didn't understand what it meant either.

But she liked it.

She decided to take another shower and wash off all the makeup she'd put on—not to mention the perfume. No sense wasting it on Jon. She'd wiggled out of her pantyhose and was padding barefoot over to the bathroom to turn the water on and take off her sexy black slip and panties—she *definitely* wasn't suffering through those all night if she didn't have to—when the buzzer on the intercom rang again.

What was this? Grand Central?

She picked up the receiver. "Hello?"

"Hello, Miss Harper," Roger said. "Delivery."

"*Again?*" Meena said. "I didn't order anything, Roger."

"I know, Miss Harper," Roger said. "These are flowers. From Mr. Antonescu, the deliveryman says. Not Mr. Antonescu in 11A, but your friend Mr. Antonescu. You know, from the party last night."

Meena smiled. So much for keeping the doormen in the building from knowing everything about her personal life. "Send him up, Roger," she said, and put down the receiver.

Flowers *and* the bag? Lucien already had her heart. He didn't have to keep trying to win it.

She went to her purse and looked in her wallet for a tip for the flower deliveryman. She didn't have any small bills left. She'd have to see if the flower guy had any change.

You have slain the dragon.

What did it mean?

Before she had a chance to slip on a robe, Meena heard a sound outside her door. She looked out the peephole. There they were. Red roses. A huge bouquet of them.

Her heart swelled. He was crazy. And too extravagant.

Yes, he was a prince.

But this was too much.

Meena unlocked the door and opened it a crack.

"Thanks so much," she said to the flower deliveryman. "Do you have change for a ten?"

That was when he lowered the roses away from his face.

And Meena, for the first time in her life, knew that she was the one about to die.

Chapter Thirty-five

7:00 P.M. EST, Friday, April 16
910 Park Avenue, Apt. 11B
New York, New York

The most amazing thing—to Meena, anyway—was that she never would have guessed he was a killer. Not at first glance, anyway. He was dressed so nicely, in dark form-fitting jeans, a cashmere sweater, and a long, black leather trench. The scarf around his neck looked as if it were made from cashmere, too—at least from where Meena was standing—and brought out the blue in his eyes . . . the kind of bright blue eyes that wouldn't have been out of place on some hunky blond heartthrob making his way down a red carpet or paddling a surfboard off a sandy white Australian beach.

They hardly looked like the eyes of a killer.

Except that Meena had known that's what he was from the moment she'd opened the door and he'd brought the big bouquet of red roses down from in front of his face.

Why had she fallen for that old trick? That bouquet-in-front-of-the-peephole trick? She deserved to get killed just for falling for a trick she'd used a million times herself in her own scripts.

And now here she was, facing down death in nothing but her bra and a black silk slip. She was furious with herself for not having grabbed a robe first, or something she could at least have employed as a weapon . . . a can of hair spray and a lighter to use as an impromptu flamethrower . . . even a shoe, for God's sake, to throw at the guy.

But she hadn't realized how close she was to death until now, when it was too late. All she'd reached for was her BlackBerry, which in almost any scenario was pretty much useless.

And in this case it was just plain pitiful, unless she wanted to call some cops to come over and be killed along with her.

Because no way was this guy going to let himself be arrested without a fight. She could tell that just by looking at his handsome, pitiless face.

And of course, like any proper assassin, he already had a foot wedged firmly inside the jamb, so she couldn't slam the door shut in his face. It would just bounce harmlessly off the edge of his steel-toed boot.

The fingers of his right hand rested on a you-know-what. Yeah. It seemed unbelievable, but given everything else that had gone on this past week, Meena realized she shouldn't have been surprised. It was an honest-to-God *sword hilt*.

She held her breath as that blue-eyed gaze drifted toward her.

"I am not here for you, Meena," he said, in a German-accented voice so deep, it seemed to reverberate through her chest.

How could he know her name? She had no idea who he was. She'd never seen him before in her life.

And yet . . . she felt as if somehow she'd known him forever.

Maybe that's how everyone felt when they met their killer.

Or maybe it was just Meena.

He unsheathed the sword. The blade made a ringing sound in the stillness of the hallway, clear as a bell, as it came out of its scabbard.

Meena swallowed hard.

It's amazing what you think right before you die. All Meena could think, for instance, was, *Wow. No foreplay for this guy.*

Then, *Wait, that's not even funny.*

Then, *Although actually, that would make a good line for Victoria on the show.*

Then, *But I'm not going to live long enough to write another episode for the show. This is so unfair.*

She knew just by looking at her killer's rock-hard, chiseled profile that there wasn't the slightest flicker of hope.

But it's incredible what we'll do to try to survive.

Meena pried her lips apart. Forced her tongue to moisten them.

"I know you're lying," she said. "You're holding a *sword*. You're here to kill me."

"I'm not lying," he said. "Just tell me where he is, and I'll let you live."

Meena had no idea who—or what—he was talking about. She pointed at her purse where it hung on the hook she'd slung it onto after coming home. "Look," she said. "There's plenty of money in there. I just went to the cash machine. Take what you want and go. Otherwise, there's some costume jewelry my great-aunt Wilhelmina left me, but it's all fake, I swear to you. . . ."

He looked annoyed. Meena felt her heart rate speed up. *Way to go, Meen. Antagonize your killer. That's smart.*

"I already told you, Meena," he said, his dark blond eyebrows raised a little sarcastically. "I have no interest in killing you. Only him. But if you are going to be difficult . . ."

Difficult. He had no idea how *difficult* Meena could be. Especially since she already knew she was as good as dead.

Meena knew then that she had absolutely nothing to lose.

Which was why she chose that moment to hurl her BlackBerry at him with all her might.

Hey. It was all she had. That and her life.

Then she turned around and made a run for it.

Chapter Thirty-six

Meena couldn't exactly escape out the front door, since the sword-wielding maniac in a trench coat standing in front of it had shut and locked it behind him.

But she figured if she could throw open the French doors to the balcony in the back bedroom, then scream for help, someone would definitely hear her.

Mary Lou. Mary Lou would hear her.

If she was home. Which was unlikely, it being a Friday night.

But no sooner had Meena whirled around to make her escape than something impossibly hard—and amazingly strong—locked around her bare ankle and flipped her to the floor. She went sprawling down amid all the fallen roses, her right foot pulled out from under her before she knew what was happening, her palms skidding on the parquet as she tried to break her fall.

She craned her neck to look down the length of her body in astonishment and saw the man with the sword standing above her.

Wow. He was *really* fast. Meena had only just hurled her BlackBerry at him—and hadn't waited around long enough to see if it had hit him, though she'd thought she heard a dull thud, then the smack of plastic parts hitting wood floor—and already he'd yanked her foot out from under her?

What was he, bionic?

"Meena," he said in the same calm, slightly bored voice, still gripping her foot. "You've got nowhere to run to. I think you know that."

The sad thing was, he was absolutely right. Even with the breath knocked entirely out of her body from the force of her fall, Meena did know that.

She'd always wondered what it would be like when it was finally her turn to meet death face-to-face.

But now that it was actually happening, she knew something else: that she wasn't going to go without a fight.

"I'm not going to die tonight," she said from between gritted teeth. "Sorry."

And she twisted around so that instead of lying on her stomach, she was on her back . . .

. . . and in a better position to grind her free foot into his groin.

The only problem was, he seemed to anticipate the move, since he let go of her ankle, and—so quickly Meena barely had time to register what was happening—was on top of her . . . his full body weight stretched over her, heavy as a steel beam and just as strong.

"I told you, Meena, I'm not here to kill you," he said. His face was just inches from hers now.

So was the sword blade. He held it propped casually against Meena's throat as he peered at her, like she was some kind of interesting species of butterfly he'd managed to capture and pin to his collection.

This was not really how Meena had anticipated her amazing kick-to-the-groin move going.

"Oh, really?" she grunted, trying to sound like she didn't care. This wasn't easy, considering the fact that her heart was hammering so hard, she wondered if he could see her pulse in her throat.

Also, he wasn't light. She was finding it difficult to draw a breath with him on top of her like this.

Still, she tried to sound casual. Like she didn't care that he was stretched across her body like a lead blanket. Like she wasn't conscious of the fact that she was a slight young woman wearing nothing but a black bra and silk slip and he was a man roughly her own age weighing at least eighty pounds more than her and holding a knife—sorry, a *sword*—to her throat.

She was beginning to reconsider the whole not-afraid-to-die thing.

"No," he said in the same disturbingly deep and much too calm voice, with that slight accent. "I already told you." Was it Meena's imagination, or did he sound a little insulted? "I'm not interested in you."

Meena had to laugh at that. Even though she was about to die. Or worse. Maybe she was hysterical.

Still, she had to admit, it *was* kind of funny, a guy tackling you while you were half naked, holding a sword to your throat, then intimating that he wasn't interested in you. Especially when he was on top of you.

"You could have fooled me," she said. "You seem *really* interested in me at the moment."

He raised a blond eyebrow. "That?" He shifted a little. "That's just my scabbard." Then, apparently fearing that he might appear ungentlemanly, he added, "Not that you're unattractive. But you're not really my type."

Meena glared at him. Really, this was just too much. To kill—well, come here with the intention of killing her, then insult her, too?

"Well, you're not my type either," she said angrily.

"Oh, I know that." He grinned down at her. His teeth were white but not quite even. One or two of them were just crooked enough to prove they were all real, not veneers. "I'm alive."

Meena stared up at him. Since he was obviously a foreigner, she thought maybe he'd misunderstood her.

"What are you talking about?" she asked. "I meant that I don't happen to like men who come barging uninvited into women's apartments, waving swords."

Now he was running his fingertips—from the hand that wasn't clutching the sword—along the length of her arm. He was doing it seemingly absently, as if he couldn't resist the feel of her skin.

But he evidently had understood her.

"I know," he said. "I meant I know your type. Lucien Antonescu is your type. That's why I'm here. All I want is for you to tell me where he is. Then I'll go."

Meena would have frozen if she hadn't already been rendered immobile by his body weight. Lucien? This was about Lucien?

She supposed it made a crazy sort of sense. Men with swords had certainly never come bursting into her apartment *before* Lucien had come into her life.

And Roger *had* said the flowers were from Lucien.

"You know Lucien?" she demanded.

She should have known. It had all been going so well. Too well. The amazing night they'd passed together. The note, saying he was hers. The bag.

She should have known it was too good to be true.

It ought to have been as obvious to her as the sword in front of her face. Leisha had even suggested it:

Lucien was married.

Of course he was. No single man his age was as perfect as he was. They were all gay, completely baggage ridden, or taken.

Obviously, Lucien's crazy wife had hired this man to scare the living daylights out of her.

Well, it had worked.

"Actually," the man said—he was still absently stroking her skin, like he didn't even realize he was doing it—"we've never met personally, the prince and I." She realized he was still answering her question about whether or not he knew Lucien. "But I'm certainly acquainted with his work."

"His work?" Meena was more confused than ever. She tried to picture this man attending a course in Eastern European history and failed. He obviously wasn't a scholar. A homicidal maniac, maybe. But hardly an academic. "You mean his books?"

The man laughed shortly. "No. I was referring to his extracurricular activities."

Meena had no idea what he was talking about.

But she didn't miss the insinuation in his tone. He meant that he knew that she and Lucien . . .

Well. What they'd done together, last night.

God. Had he taken pictures? Wasn't that what private detectives hired by wives did?

She wanted to die.

Clearly, the Lucien she knew and the Lucien this man knew were two different people. She'd known Lucien had secrets—which was all right. She was keeping secrets from him, too.

But she was furious that Lucien's secret was that he was married. He just hadn't seemed the type. She'd even asked him straight out if he had a wife, and he'd said no. If she ever saw him again—and she certainly would, because as soon as she got rid of this blond-haired mammoth on top of her, she was packing up the Marc Jacobs bag and heading straight over to Lucien's apartment to return it, preferably with some of Jack Bauer's excrement smeared all over it—she was going to tell him exactly what she thought about men who cheated on their wives with innocent dialogue writers.

"Look," she said in what she hoped sounded like a strong, firm voice. Irritated by the man's laughter, Meena twitched her shoulder away from his hand.

For the first time, he seemed to realize he'd been touching her skin. He looked almost surprised and instantly drew his hand away.

"I don't know who you think you are," she said. "But you can't come bursting in here with . . . with . . . *medieval armaments* and boss me around. You can tell Lucien's wife from me that it's over. I don't want anything more to do with him. Okay? So her little attempt to scare me away from him, or whatever this was, has had its desired effect. She can have Lucien back. I don't even want him anymore."

He was frowning now. He seemed displeased.

But he wasn't looking at her. He was looking down at his hand.

"Did you hear me?" Meena demanded. She was conscious that the sword blade was still very close to her throat. Very close, and very sharp.

On the other hand, he seemed a little distracted, looking down at his hand, then back at her skin. *Now,* she thought, *might be a perfect moment to knee him in the nads.* Then, while he was curled up in excruciating pain, she'd grab that Pottery Barn lamp over there and smash it over his head. . . .

"Did he even bite you?" the man demanded, swinging his blue-eyed gaze back at her.

Meena, who'd been formulating the third part of her plan—the part where she went for her Wüsthof knife set in the kitchen—froze. "What? Bite me? What are you *talking* about?"

The man did something then that totally astonished her (not that anything he'd done since she'd opened the door hadn't thoroughly astonished her). He grasped her chin with the hand that wasn't holding on to the sword and turned her head first one way, then the other, examining her neck the way her general practitioner checked for swollen lymph nodes.

"What are you *doing*?" Meena demanded. It would have been one thing if he'd been going to kill her.

But with every passing moment, Meena felt less and less that this was actually what was going to happen.

Especially when he threw the sword aside entirely—it fell to the hardwood floor with a musical clang—sat up, and, still straddling her, pulled down the front of her slip, along with a sizable portion of her bra.

"Hey!" Meena yelled, bucking beneath him.

"Shut up," he said. "Lie still."

"I will *not*," Meena raged, punching him in the chest.

"He bit you," the man said, laying a hand upon her clavicle and shoving her back down to the floor. "He *had* to have bitten you. He couldn't not have. Look at you. Your skin is like silk. *I* want to bite it. The question is, where did he do it? Not the carotid artery, obviously. You don't have any bruising. Sometimes they go for the heart. Have you looked?"

Meena, her bra and slip straps dangling around her shoulders, just lay where she was, staring up at him.

She could never even have written a scene like this. And even if she had, Fran and Stan would never have let it air.

Because no one would believe it. It was just too bizarre.

"Who *are* you?" Meena asked.

"I am Alaric Wulf," the man said patiently. He didn't actually sound like a lunatic. Or look like one . . . sword aside. He was good looking, if you liked tall blond muscular types who dressed well and spoke with a slight Germanic accent.

Which ordinarily Meena supposed she would have. If he wasn't sitting on top of her, calmly checking out her chest for some kind of mystical bite.

"And I work for an organization that's very interested in finding Lucien Antonescu. So if you would kindly just tell me where he is, I'll gladly leave you alone, Miss Harper."

He looked like he meant it. He looked like he really didn't like her very much at all.

Which was fine with Meena, since the feeling was 100 percent mutual.

"I'd like the name of this organization," Meena said, "so I can report you to your superiors. Does your employer know this is how you treat women, terrifying them to death and then sitting on them? Get off me—" She twisted under him, punching him in the chest some more.

And then, as he was warding off her blows with open palms, there came the sound of a key being turned in the lock to the front door.

In a blur of motion, Alaric Wulf leapt to his feet, simultaneously yanking Meena to hers by the wrist with one hand and grasping his sword in the other.

By the time Jon had the door unlocked and was standing in the entranceway, Alaric had Meena thrust behind him and his blade pointed just inches from Jon's throat.

"Shit!" Jon said, and dropped the bag of Chinese food he'd been holding, along with a DVD.

Jack Bauer immediately darted forward and began eagerly to lick up the spilled liquid from the bag, completely oblivious to the fact that there was an armed man threatening his mistress a few feet away.

But Lucien Antonescu, Meena thought cynically, he'd barked at all night. Great guard dog she'd selected. Just great.

Alaric lowered the sword when he saw who it was that had come in.

"Jonathan Harper," he said, his broad shoulders losing some of their tension. "Age thirty-two. Former systems analyst for Webber and Stern. Unemployed for the past seven months. Arrested once for public intoxication and indecent exposure for urinating against a parking meter in Miami Beach, Florida, while visiting his parents four years ago."

Meena's jaw draw dropped. "*Jonathan!*" she cried.

She'd always thought it was strange Jon had kept having to go back to Miami "for business." He'd said he'd been thinking about investing his share of the inheritance from Great-Aunt Wilhelmina in a vacation condo near their parents' in Boca, which was weird in and of itself.

But then nothing had ever come of it.

"Shit," Jon said again in a different tone, quickly closing, then locking, the front door behind him, as if he was afraid the Antonescus might overhear. "It was four o'clock in the morning! Outside of a Subway. That was closed. No one was around! I really had to go."

Meena shook her head. "Still . . ."

"And I paid all that money to those lawyers to get my record expunged," Jon said mournfully.

"Lawyers," Alaric said, shrugging. He turned back to Meena. She didn't like the glint in his ice-blue eyes. "We need to talk," he said, and pulled her, not very gently, over to the sage green couch. "Sit down," he said, and pushed her down onto the cushions with a single large, commanding paw.

Meena, her anger having reached a boiling point, popped right back up to her bare feet.

"No," she said. She didn't have to put up with his manhandling. "I will *not* sit down. I still don't know who you are or what you're doing here. I'm calling the police. Jon." She turned toward her brother. "Please call the police. This man forced his way in here against my will, and then he—"

"Sit *down*," Alaric said again, and shoved her back onto the couch, this time by spreading his mammoth fingers across her *face* and pushing down.

Meena, completely stunned by this barbaric treatment, just sat there, staring at the kitchen pass-through in astonishment. Who even *did* that?

"What exactly is going on here?" Jon asked, looking down at the destroyed bouquet of roses and the broken pieces of Meena's BlackBerry scattered across the floor. Jack Bauer, in the middle of it all, was still licking up liquid from the overturned Chinese food cartons. When he glanced up at Alaric, his tail wagged happily in greeting. Her dog. Her own *dog*!

"Your sister did that," Alaric Wulf said to Jon about the mess. "She's being very uncooperative."

Meena made a noise that was half whimper, half protest. What? *She* was the one who was being uncooperative?

"Meena Harper," Alaric went on in a completely deadpan voice, ignoring her, "is in grave danger. Lucien Antonescu is a soulless monster. It is imperative that I find and destroy him and that you do exactly what I say if you want her to live."

Jon stared at the man with the sword standing in the middle of Meena's living room. Then he looked down at Meena, who mimed dialing a cell phone. Then she mouthed, *Call the police.*

"Uh," Jon said to Alaric. "Sure. Right."

"Meena Harper," Alaric said, even though he wasn't looking in her direction. "I see what you're doing. If you don't stop, I will have no problem handcuffing you to something. In fact, I will enjoy it."

Meena, furious, said, "Lucien isn't a monster! Okay, he might have tricked me and said he wasn't married, but I assure you, no one is in any danger from—"

"He isn't married," Alaric said. "He has never been married. No one knows why. Some say it is because he witnessed his own mother's suicide and never got over it. Others say it is because he has never met his soul mate. I have the feeling that might have changed recently." He threw Meena a piercing glance, then went on. "That's why it is vital for your survival that you tell me where he is. Also, you need to stop talking, because I find your voice very annoying."

"Uh"—Jon raised his hand—"sorry. I know I came in late, but no one's answered my question. What the hell is going on here?"

"It is simple, really," Alaric Wulf said. "Lucien Antonescu is the prince of darkness."

Jon nodded. "Yeah," he said. "We know. He's got a castle and stuff."

"No," Alaric said again, shaking his head. "The prince of *darkness*."

Jon glanced at Meena, then back at Alaric, then back at Meena again. "The prince of . . . did he say what I think he said?"

Meena rolled her eyes. "Sorry to be *annoying*," she said, as sweetly as possible, to Alaric. "But Lucien's not the devil."

"I did not say he was the devil," Alaric said. He shrugged out of his trench coat, then brushed it carefully with his hand before going to hang it neatly on one of the decorative hooks by the door. Then he unbuckled his sword and leaned that, too, by the door. Then, after stepping over the scattered roses and pieces of BlackBerry, not to mention the Chinese food containers, leaned down to pat an appreciative Jack Bauer on the head, before saying, "He is the dark prince. The all-powerful one. The leader of the creatures of the night."

Meena and Jon exchanged glances. Then Meena said, again trying to keep her tone devoid of waspishness—since he apparently found her voice so annoying—"I'm confused then. I thought the prince of darkness was the devil."

"The devil is the personification of evil and the enemy of God and humankind," Alaric said. He crossed the room and sat in the armchair Meena had spent an hour or so not writing in, after first giving it a disparaging glance—he didn't seem to much appreciate Meena's taste in home furnishings. "The prince of darkness is the anointed one, who performs the devil's work on this, the mortal side of hell."

"Wait," Meena said, blinking. "Are you saying . . ."

"Yes," Alaric said. "That is exactly what I'm saying."

Jon looked blank. "I don't understand. Is he the devil or not?"

"Lucien Antonescu," Alaric said, "is a vampire. Not just any vampire, but ruler of all the vampires."

Chapter Thirty-seven

Alaric Wulf was staring at her. His eyes really were very blue. Alarmingly blue. If he'd been anybody else—if Meena had met him anywhere else—she'd have said, "What a nice-looking man."

But since he'd attacked her in her own apartment with a sword and was now accusing her boyfriend of being a vampire, she was just going to have to say it was a shame such good looks were wasted on someone so . . . whatever he was.

"Brother Jon," he said. His gaze was so intense, it seemed to pierce her to the couch, much in the way his body weight had pierced her to the floor. "Get your sister something to drink now. Something sugary. She doesn't know it yet. But she's going to need it in a few minutes."

"Uh," Jon said, "okay." And he got up to go to the kitchen.

"Excuse me," Meena said. What was wrong with this guy? "But I can actually get my own drinks."

"No," Alaric said. "You stay where you are. You are not to be trusted."

Meena held up both palms in protest. "What?" she said. She couldn't help bursting out laughing, even though it was all so . . . sad. "Why? Because I date an alleged vampire?"

"He is not alleged," Alaric said. "And, yes. You are his minion now."

"A minion!" Now Meena had heard everything. "What? I'm *infected* because I went out with Lucien?"

"You can put it like that, yes," Alaric said. "It is certainly a form of infection. Are you getting that soda or not, Brother Jon?"

"Soda on its way," he called from the kitchen.

"Jon," Meena called from the sofa. "While you're in there, put a little—"

"Do not listen to her," Alaric said. "She is going to tell you in some kind of code only the two of you will understand, because you are siblings, to call the police on your cell phone. But if you do that, I will kill you and dispose of your body in a place where no one will find it. The river, I think. Your doorman is so stupid, he won't notice if I leave this building carrying a body in a rolled-up carpet."

Jon poked his head out of the pass-through to look at Meena.

"Yeah," he said. "I'm just going to get a couple of Cokes and avoid the whole being-rolled-up-in-a-carpet thing, 'kay, Meen?"

She glared at him. "Yeah, real great, Jon." She looked at Alaric. She could handle this. It was no different than one of Taylor's I'm-so-fat tantrums. Well, maybe a *little* different. "Look, Mr., uh, Wulf. I appreciate your trying to warn me about this. I really do. *But there's no such thing as vampires.* They're made-up. We writers made them up. I'm sorry we did such a good job that we made the whole world paranoid, but it's true. They're fictional. Blame Bram Stoker. He started it."

"No, he did not, actually," Alaric said. "They existed long before Stoker was ever even born, in almost every culture and on almost every continent on this planet. They are like mosquitoes . . . they feed off the blood of others. They cannot exist without a host."

"And how do you," Meena asked, playing along, "know so much about them?"

"I battle vampires almost daily in my profession," he said in a bored voice. "They are loathsome and brutal creatures. A group of them almost killed my partner some months ago."

"Oh, really," Meena said. She'd crossed her legs and was now jiggling one bare foot up and down. *Vampires! Seriously?*

Get over it, Harper, Shoshona had said. *They're everywhere. You can't escape them.*

It wasn't fair. Why couldn't she escape stupid vampires? Work, TV, Leisha's salon, and now here, at home.

They really *were* everywhere. Even handsome—but obviously deranged—strangers who broke into her apartment, trying to kill her, were raving about them.

"They cornered us in a warehouse outside of Berlin," he went on, looking far away. "It was partly my fault. I got cocky. I thought there were not so many of them and that we could take them. But there were more than I thought, and they caught us by surprise. Here." He reached into the inside pocket of the dark, close-fitting sports coat he wore. "This is a picture of how my partner looks now. His name is Martin."

What Meena saw when he handed her the photo sent a physical shock wave through her. She wasn't expecting . . . *that*. It was a picture of a man with half a face. Where his features should have been on the lower half was only skull. It had clearly been shredded by fangs.

Meena could only stare.

Alaric took the photo from her limp fingers and said, putting it away, "But a photo, I know, doesn't prove anything. Next you will say what happened to his face could have happened in a car accident."

Meena stammered, "I . . . I wasn't going to say that."

She didn't know what she was going to say. She looked over at Jon. He was still busy in the kitchen with the sodas. She wished he would hurry up. She was feeling less and less certain that Alaric Wulf was actually deranged with every passing second.

Why that should be more unnerving to her than the alternative, Meena wasn't sure.

"Here," Alaric said. "These are photos of the four girls who've been recently murdered in your city, their bodies found in city parks the next morning, naked and drained of all their blood."

He scattered four photos onto the coffee table in front of Meena. They were pictures of the women, taken from the chest up. The one thing they all had in common was the multiple bite marks they had not just on their throats, surrounded by ugly purple and green bruising, but all over, as if they'd been savagely attacked by someone. . . .

Or something.

Meena gazed down at the photos. Jon, coming back from the kitchen holding three glasses of soda, joined her on the couch and stared down at the photos as well.

"These are the girls they've been reporting about on the news?" he asked.

"Yes," Alaric said.

"But it didn't say anything about them having died from being bitten," Jon said. "It said they died from being strangled."

"Because the mayor's office doesn't want to start a panic," Alaric said.

"But you're not saying Lucien did this," Meena said in a faint voice, still unable to tear her gaze away from the photos. She worked in a world where photos like these were faked every day . . . a world where duping viewers into believing something this incredible could happen was what she and her fellow writers strived for. She was trying desperately to find some sign that these photos had been faked, that they'd been an invention of someone like herself or Shoshona.

But the images looked heartbreakingly real. She recognized the girls' faces from photos she'd seen on the news. Photos that had carefully shown nothing below the chin.

"No," Alaric said, taking a sip of his soda. "The prince is not behind these murders . . . insofar as he himself did not commit them. But one of his kind did. One of his minions."

"Minions?" She stared at him. "You said *I'm* a minion."

He shrugged his broad shoulders. "Different kind of minion. To become a vampire, one must be bitten three times, then drink the blood of one's host. I take it that you didn't do that last night, did you?"

Meena's eyes widened with horror. Jon, sitting back on the ottoman, raised his eyebrows to their limits.

"Whoa," he said. "I've heard of some kinky stuff, but that's—"

Meena interrupted him.

Because, really, she'd heard about as much as she could.

"Excuse me," she said, knowing she was lashing out because suddenly, she was frightened . . . frightened of the photos she'd just seen but had no rational way to explain. But more than that, frightened of some things she'd suddenly begun to piece together in her mind. "But you can't just come in here and expect us to believe that there's this gigantic vampire conspiracy out there that the rest of humanity knows nothing about but that my boyfriend is the head of, and that you, somehow, have been privy to. I mean, what are you, anyway? Some kind of vampire hunter?"

"Yes," Alaric said simply.

Meena sagged against the back of the couch. "Oh," she said. "Right. Of course you are."

Because after the week she'd had, what else was he going to be?

"Seriously?" Jon asked. He looked excited. "How do you get a job like that? Are there benefits?"

"You have to begin training very young," Alaric said, not taking his gaze off Meena. "And there's a hiring freeze right now."

"Yeah," said Jon. "Of course. There are hiring freezes everywhere. But the thing is, I think I would be exemplary in a position like that. Because you know, I'm very good with my hands, and I've always really, really hated vampires. I mean, *Dracula* was like my favorite movie when I was a kid. Tell him, Meen. The part where they stake him—"

"Decapitation is more effective," Alaric said, still not taking his gaze off Meena.

"Now, see," Jon said, "I'd be even better at that. I was on my high school baseball team. I could really swing a bat. Meena, seriously. Tell him."

Meena didn't say anything. She was watching Alaric. He'd reached into his inside pocket again. This time he pulled out a small gold medal, which he flung down onto the center of the coffee table as casually as if it were a coin. Jon snatched it up and held it toward the light from the lamp beside the couch.

"Cool," he said, squinting at it. "What is this? I recognize this. On one side . . . isn't this . . . ?"

"The papal seal," Alaric said in the same bored voice he seemed to use habitually.

"The Pope?" Jon glanced at him. "No way."

"That is my employer." Alaric continued to stare at Meena. She stared right back at him. She noticed in a detached part of her brain that his mouth was too small for the rest of his face.

The rest of her brain was screaming that it couldn't be true. It *wasn't* true. She and Lucien had had that whole long conversation about vampires, back at his apartment. . . .

Oh. *God*.

"And what's this on the back?" Jon asked. "Meena, here, you look at it."

Meena took the medallion from him. She could clearly see the image on the back.

It was of a mounted knight. Slaying a dragon.

She caught her breath.

"St. George?" Her heart twisted.

"The patron saint of the Palatine Guard," Alaric said. "My order. St. George and St. Joan are the patron saints of soldiers. St. George slayed the dragon—"

"I know," Meena said quickly. Suddenly, it was hard to breathe.

"Hey," Jon said excitedly. "Didn't Lucien say something about dragons in that note he wrote to you, Meena? That you'd slain the dragon?"

"Yes," Meena said. Why wouldn't Jon just *shut up* for once? Her heart was pounding so hard, she could barely breathe.

Alaric, she noticed, had raised a single light brown eyebrow. "He wrote to you?" he asked.

"Yeah," Jon said, getting up and crossing over to the dining table where Lucien's letter rested alongside the bag he had sent her. "The note's right over—"

"*No*," Meena said, her heart pounding even harder as she darted up from the couch. "Jon, don't give it to—"

But Alaric was, as usual, too quick for her. He was up from his chair and throwing a rock-hard arm around her waist, swinging her off her feet before she'd gone more than a single step.

"Give me the note," he said, still holding a struggling Meena as Jon, taken aback by this turn of events, stood there in the space between the living and dining rooms, staring at them, Lucien's letter in his hand.

"Don't give him the note, Jon!" Meena yelled hoarsely, lashing at Alaric's legs with her bare feet.

Which of course he didn't feel at all.

She didn't even know why she felt so determined to keep the note from him. It was simply imperative he not see it.

But it was too late. Jon handed the silver envelope over to Alaric, who let go of Meena, opened the note, and scanned the contents. Meena looked unhappily at her brother.

"It's just a note, Meen," Jon said with a shrug. "It doesn't even have his address on it or anything. It's all right."

But it wasn't all right.

Especially when Alaric looked up and said, "*Dragon* in Romanian is *dracul*."

"What?" Meena said. She didn't understand.

"Dragon," Alaric said casually. "When he tells you in his note that you slayed the dragon, he means himself. The Romanian word for *dragon* is *dracul*. Dracula."

Meena inhaled sharply. The room had started to sway a little.

"Wait," Jon said. "So St. George wasn't really slaying dragons? He was slaying *vampires*? Are the dragons in all the pictures supposed to be metaphors for vampires or something?"

But on this day, she remembered Lucien saying in the museum, *there is no maiden left in the village, save the king's daughter. She's bravely gone to the water's edge, despite her father's protests, expecting to die. But look who's appeared . . . a knight called George who will slay the dragon. . . .*

No wonder Lucien hadn't looked very happy when she'd steered him toward that particular picture.

"I think I'm going to be sick," Meena said. Suddenly, her head was pounding. She thought she might pass out.

"Sit," Alaric said, pushing her back down onto the couch again. Only this time, even she had to admit, he did it gently.

"No, really," she said. The room was tilting in front of her. "I have to—"

"Drink the soda," he said. "The sugar will help." His hand on her shoulder was warm. It reminded her—with another stomach lurch—

that Lucien's hands had never been warm. They'd always felt cool. Strangely cool.

Even his lips, as they'd slid over her body, had been cool. . . .

"Oh, God," she said. She gulped some of the soda, then dropped her head between her knees. If she didn't get some blood back into her temples, she felt certain she was going to pass out.

"But there's no such thing as vampires," she said to her bare feet. "There's no such thing. *There's no such thing*. . . ."

It seemed to Meena as if the more she repeated it, the more likely it was to come true.

But so many things from the night before—including the memory of Lucien's own voice—came flooding back to her.

But you believe St. Joan heard voices, he'd said.

How can an educated woman like yourself believe this and not in creatures of the night?

Creatures of the night.

Oh, my God.

It was true. It was *true*.

"Drink your soda." She heard Alaric's voice urging her gently. "In the meantime, I want to tell you about a man named Vlad Tepes."

Meena, her head still between her knees, groaned as soon as she heard the name.

"Oh," Alaric said, sounding pleasantly surprised. "You've heard of this man? Well, I will tell your brother about him, then. Vlad Tepes was a prince from a part of Romania called Wallachia . . . what is today better known as Transylvania—"

Meena moaned more loudly. Not Transylvania. *Anything* but Transylvania.

"He was a brutal and cruel man who ruthlessly employed a method of torture you might have heard of called impaling—"

"Wait," Jon said. "Are you talking about Vlad the *Impaler*?"

"I am," Alaric said, brightening some more. "I see you've heard of him."

"Everyone's heard of Vlad the Impaler," Jon said. "Impaling was where, as a method of torture, a long stake, usually not particularly sharp, would be driven through the victim's various orifices—"

"I need something stronger than just a Coke," Meena sat up and said suddenly. "Whiskey. I need whiskey. Oh, God—"

The room swayed dangerously, and she quickly put her head back down between her knees.

"No whiskey," Alaric said firmly.

"Why can't she have whiskey?" Jon asked.

"Then she will drunk-dial the vampire," Alaric said. "And warn him about me, and I will lose the element of surprise. It's happened before. Vlad the Impaler," he went on, "ruled what is now modern Romania from 1456 to 1462. He was known for his exceptionally cruel punishments, both of his enemies and even his own servants, although it is impossible to say how many people he actually killed. He may have impaled a hundred thousand people or more, leaving them to die slowly in excruciating pain, sometimes for days, on long stakes along the road leading to his palace as a way to intimidate visitors to his native land."

Meena closed her eyes, wishing she could shut out his words.

But she couldn't, any more than she could wish herself back in time, to the point where the doorman had buzzed, saying she had a delivery.

Alaric Wulf was not a delivery anyone could ever have wanted.

Now she knew how everyone must have felt when she'd given them her news about their impending death.

"Vlad himself was said to have been killed in battle against the Turks in 1476. He was decapitated and his head was taken on a pike to the sultan in Istanbul to prove that he was dead."

Jon sounded disappointed. "So. Not a vampire."

Meena lifted her head hopefully.

"Maybe. Or maybe it wasn't Vlad Tepes. He was reportedly buried at an island monastery near Bucharest," Alaric said, continuing, "but when his tomb was recently excavated, it was . . ."

"What?" Jon asked eagerly.

" . . . found to be empty," Alaric said.

Jon looked confused. "So where is he?"

Alaric regarded him and Meena both patiently.

"Vlad Tepes is more commonly known in his native country by his given name, Vlad the Dragon, for his service to the Hungarian Order of the Dragon," he went on. "Or, if you employ the Romanian for dragon,

Vlad Dracul." He looked at Meena, his blue-eyed gaze unwavering. "Best known to the English-speaking world as the inspiration for Bram Stoker's *Dracula*."

Meena sucked in her breath. She both knew and dreaded what was coming next. Knew it as well as she'd ever known anything in her life.

She just dreaded it more than she remembered ever dreading any words she'd ever heard.

"Lucien Antonescu," Alaric said, "is Vlad Dracula's son."

Chapter Thirty-eight

Meena could only stare wordlessly at Alaric as he went on. "Lucien—that wasn't his name back then—and his half brother went into hiding after Vlad, for reasons unknown but likely related to his ambitions to conquer the world, bragged to Stoker about what he was. That was how one of our officers managed to track him down and stake him."

Alaric had settled back into the armchair and was regarding both Meena and Jon, but mostly Meena, with a grimly serious expression.

"Then Stoker's novel came out and the name Dracula became infamous and synonymous with evil. His sons have been hiding in the general population ever since, frequently changing their names and professions, trying to stay one step ahead of us. But I can assure you, Vlad Dracula's death at the hands of the Palatine a hundred years ago made his eldest son, now calling himself Lucien Antonescu, the new prince of darkness. He has to be exterminated."

Alaric's blue-eyed gaze was so direct as it met Meena's, it again riveted her to her seat.

"And you're going to help us do that, Meena Harper, by telling me where you spent last night with him, so that we can find him and put him—and then all the members of his clan, the Dracul, whom we believe are the vampires responsible for killing those girls, as well as almost killing my partner—down."

Meena stared up at him with wide, disbelieving eyes. She couldn't stop remembering Lucien's face as he'd told her the story of the woman who'd plunged to her death in the Princess's River rather than be taken prisoner by the Turks.

If what Alaric was telling her was true, that woman had been Lucien's mother, whom he'd watched commit suicide before his very eyes.

Those dark eyes that Meena had found so filled with sadness.

And no wonder!

But that was impossible. Because if he'd actually seen Vlad the Impaler's wife kill herself, that would make Lucien *five hundred years old*.

On the other hand, if she hadn't been his mother, why else had Lucien made such a special point of showing her Vlad Tepes's portrait? It had to have some special, personal meaning to him.

Except . . .

There was no such thing as vampires.

Was she really supposed to think Lucien Antonescu was a *vampire* who'd magically transported himself into the museum, knocked out all the guards, and turned off the alarms . . . just to impress a date?

Except . . .

What *had* happened to all the guards?

And what about the bats? The bats that had attacked them outside of St. George's Cathedral?

"It can't be true," she said faintly, shaking her head. "He never . . . I mean, he seemed so . . . *normal*."

Except for the part where he'd been absolutely perfect.

Even to the point that she never got a sense that he was going to die someday. Of course not.

Because he was already dead.

What had Leisha said that day on the phone when Meena had told her about Shoshona getting the head writer gig? *If someone who can tell how everyone she meets is going to die can exist, why can't vampires?*

Suddenly cold, Meena reached for the blanket lying on the end of the couch, the one Jonathan often napped all day underneath.

But her arm fell short, and she didn't seem to have the strength to stretch for it.

He was already dead.

Oh, God.

Vampires were real.

And she'd slept with one.

"They've learned to blend over the centuries," Alaric said with a shrug. "They've had to, in order to survive. Look at your neighbors, the Antonescus."

Jon's jaw dropped. "*What?*" he cried. "You're not trying to tell me that—"

"It's never struck you as odd," Alaric said, "that you've never seen them outside in the daylight?"

Meena and Jon exchanged glances.

"I've seen Mary Lou outside in the daylight," she said. "All the time."

"Where?" Alaric demanded. "Tell me one place you have seen her."

Meena opened her mouth to say that she'd seen Mary Lou on the street plenty of times . . . outside the building . . . in the grocery store . . . at the deli counter. . . .

But then she realized she'd never seen her in any of those places. Never once.

"I've seen her in the lobby," Meena murmured. The chill she felt seemed worse, suddenly.

"Maybe," Alaric said. "Coming up from the garage where she and her husband keep their car, with its specially tinted windows."

"Well . . . yes. I've seen her there. She seems to always be there." In her wide picture hats. And gloves.

"Wait," Jon said. "They have that huge terrace. They just had us over for cocktails on it." Then he added, "Although it was *after* sunset."

"But they're huge donors to cancer research!" Meena cried.

"Jack Bauer can't stand them," Jon said.

"The dog doesn't like them?" Alaric asked Jon, ignoring Meena.

"Hates them," Jon said. "Has a fit every time he sees either of them in the elevator. Always has, since the day we got him." He looked over at Meena. "Come to think of it, he wasn't particularly fond of Lucien, either, was he, if the growling I heard in the hallway last night was any indication."

Meena looked uncomfortable. Jon was right, of course. Still. "Jack Bauer is nervous. He always has been. That's why his name is Jack Bauer. He has a lot on his mind."

"He appears that way," Alaric observed.

They looked at Jack Bauer. He was sprawled on his back in his dog bed, all four legs splayed, his belly and genitalia on full display, his tongue lolling as he dozed.

"Well," Meena said. "Not *all* the time, of course."

"I think," Alaric said, "that the reason your dog is so nervous in the elevator and hallway, and not when he's at home, is because he's a vampire dog."

"Now my *dog* is a vampire?" Meena cried indignantly. "Who next? Me?"

"I didn't say your dog was a vampire," Alaric said calmly. He had an infuriating habit of never losing his cool . . . even when he was threatening someone with a deadly weapon. "I said he was a vampire *dog*. Some animals, particularly dogs, are more sensitive to the smell of vampiric decay than others, and because of this they have been used since the very early days of man to help track and control the vampire population. Some have even been bred for tracking and capturing vampires. It appears your dog may have some ancient instinct for sensing and alerting at them." Alaric shrugged. "I suppose you scolded him for it," he added, "but he was only trying to warn you about an evil that you yourself failed to sense."

Meena, feeling ashamed—because she *had* scolded Jack Bauer for his behavior and even locked him in a bathroom overnight—was relieved when Jon changed the subject.

"If the Antonescus are vampires," Jon asked, "why haven't they bitten us, then, like someone did these girls?" He gestured toward the photos on the coffee table. "It's not like they haven't had plenty of opportunity."

"Because then we would have caught them," Alaric said. "Exactly the way we're going to catch whoever did this to these girls. Since your boyfriend has become prince, vampires have been under orders to go underground, taking care *not* to draw attention to themselves by murdering their victims. Instead, they just find weak-willed 'donors' they can use as human feed bags, draining them slowly, a little bit at a time. Only instead of the word *donor,* try using the word *slave*."

Meena let out a bitter laugh. "And you think Lucien is using me as one of these slaves? Well, think again, Mr. Wulf."

"Yeah," Jon said, looking skeptical. "I don't know if you've noticed, but there's nothing really weak-willed about my sister. I don't think anyone could make her their slave. Except a love slave, maybe."

The minute Jon said the words *love slave,* Alaric got a strange look on his face.

He rose to his feet.

"Lift up your skirt," he said to Meena.

She craned her neck to look up at him from where she sat on the couch. "I beg your pardon?" she said with a disbelieving laugh.

"Lift up your skirt," he said again in a commanding voice.

So she hadn't misheard him. "Uh," she said. She glanced over at Jon, who gave her an uncomprehending shrug. "No. I'm not going to do that."

Then, more suddenly than she would have thought possible, he'd grabbed her by the arm and yanked her to her feet. Jack Bauer, woken by the shriek she let out, looked up at this sudden burst of violence. Jon jumped to his own feet, his expression alarmed.

"Hey, now!" he cried.

"Stop that!" Meena yelled as Alaric Wulf reached down and began tugging up the skirt of her slip. "What do you think you're doing?"

"The femoral artery," Alaric was saying. He was practically dangling her in the air by one arm as he pulled up her slip with the other. "I forgot. The sexual ones always go for the femoral artery."

"Hey," Jon said, looking uncomfortable. "I don't think my sister likes you doing that—"

"I'm not doing this because I like it, you fool. I have to see if she's been bitten." Alaric threw Meena back down on the couch, where she landed with her legs spread slightly apart, the slip hiked up so high above midthigh that he was able to point and say triumphantly, "There!" while holding her down with his free hand.

Meena, furious, looked down her torso to see what he was raving about. At the most, she expected to see a love bite. She was willing to admit that, if she considered it objectively, things *might* have gotten a little out of hand with Lucien last night, it was true. A lot of what had happened in his bed, if she was completely truthful, was a blur.

But she never expected to see *that*.

It was a bite. There was no denying it. It wasn't at all unlike the ones she'd seen on the dead girls in the photos Alaric had left on the coffee table. In fact, it was *exactly* like those. Except not as big or as bruised.

"Oh, my God," Meena said with a gasp.

Meena quickly closed her legs, mortified, pulling down the skirt to her slip. Now both her brother and this rude stranger had seen her in her sexiest black panties.

"No wonder he sent you a tote," Jon said in a stunned voice.

"The inside of the upper thigh," Alaric said. He'd let go of her. "I should have looked there from the start. The femoral artery is often used for catheters and stents in hospitals, due to its easy access to the heart. But bites there generally go undetected." The look Alaric gave her was inscrutable, halfway between curiosity and disbelief. "Don't you remember him biting you?"

"I . . . I . . . ," Meena stammered. "I remember him saying he'd only bite me if I gave him permission," she said, feeling confused. And very cold.

"And?" Jon was still on his feet, towering over both Meena and the man who'd lowered himself onto the cushions beside her. "Did you?"

Meena blinked up at him. This couldn't be happening to her. Lucien had bitten her? The man who'd protected her from the bats outside St. George's Cathedral? The man who'd given her his coat at Mary Lou's? He'd bitten her?

And what's more . . . she was under the distinct impression she'd liked it.

"I said yes," she murmured to her lap. She could feel her cheeks turning scarlet. "Oh, my God. I think I said yes."

In the silence that followed, Jack Bauer gave a sneeze. He jumped to his feet, yawned, then stretched delicately. Then he walked over to the couch, leapt up onto it, gave Alaric Wulf a cursory sniff, then curled up into Meena's lap, rolling over onto his back to have his belly scratched.

"I don't understand this," Jon said, beginning to pace the room. "If these . . . these vampires are roaming around all over the place, just hiding in the general populace, feeding off innocent women like my sister, why do people like you keep it such a big secret? Shouldn't there be public service announcements so girls like Meena don't get themselves into this situation? Huh?"

Meena stared at her brother. Jon had always been slow to anger.

But once he got there, he was almost impossible to calm again.

"You think it would be better if things were like they were back in the seventeen and eighteen hundreds," Alaric Wulf asked mildly, "when thousands of innocent human beings were falsely accused of vampirism and murdered by their neighbors because people like you, who were upset because their sister had been bitten, pointed fingers at the wrong people? No. I don't think so. Better for them to think such things don't exist and for professionals like myself quietly to take care of the problem."

"Okay," Jon said, still pacing. "Fine. Then how do we do this? Holy water? Wooden stakes? You got any extra? Because I am totally coming with you. I want to pound a stake into this guy's chest. Let's go. I'm ready. Come on."

Alaric stayed where he was, sitting beside Meena. "No," he said calmly.

"I mean it," Jon said. "I'm not scared. Prince of darkness? Doesn't scare me. Nobody bites my sister and then sends her a tote and gets away with it. Come on. Let's go. Meena, tell us where the guy is staying. We're wasting time here."

Meena, rubbing Jack's stomach, glanced from Jon to Alaric and back again. She wasn't quite sure what she was going to do. There was a sudden roaring sound in her ears. It felt as if the bottom of her stomach had dropped out.

No. Not her stomach.

Her soul.

"He already said you're not going, Jon," she said, reminding her brother.

"I'm totally going," Jon said. "Just tell us where he is."

"No," Meena said, her fingers tightening on Jack Bauer's silky fur.

Alaric, taking up so much space on her couch, turned toward her. "Meena," he said. "I know that this man, the prince, told you things that maybe made you feel . . . things for him. Feelings of love or even pity. But despite what he might have told you, he's a bad man who does bad things."

"I don't believe that," Meena said. "You just told me yourself Lucien didn't murder those girls."

A muscle in Alaric's jaw twitched. His already small mouth seemed to shrink even smaller in frustration.

"What is he even doing here if he didn't kill them?" she demanded. "Tell me. He's here to find the person who did it, isn't he?"

"Ye-es," Alaric said slowly. "But that doesn't make him a good man. He's not even a man. He's a monster. Look what he did to you. And you did not even know it. What he is . . . it's a dead thing. It's not natural. And he's created others like himself . . . That's what the Dracul are. His minions. And they've gone on to create their own minions. You see how it never ends? And it is one of those others that's killing those girls. That's why my colleagues and I have to stop him. Before things get even worse. So, please, just tell me where he is, and I will leave here. You will never have to see me again."

Meena shook her head. Her grip on Jack Bauer's ear was hard enough that he jerked his head, annoyed. Her fingers felt like ice.

But she still didn't let go.

"I . . . can't," she said.

"You can't?" Alaric asked her, raising both his eyebrows. "Or you won't?"

"I won't," she said. Even her voice had begun to shake.

But what, exactly, was she supposed to do? She'd never liked vampires.

And now *he* had brought them to her door.

Well, she supposed *he* hadn't been the one to do it. That, she supposed, she'd brought upon herself, that night she'd put the leash on Jack and gone on that walk outside St. George's. . . .

"Come on, Meena!" Jon shouted at her. "What are you doing? You aren't that girl! Protecting your abusive boyfriend? Are you kidding me?"

"I'm not protecting him," she said through frozen lips. She was visibly trembling now. She couldn't help it. She had never felt this cold, not even during the most brutal of New York's winters, when the wind whipped down Madison Avenue in front of the ABN building. "I'm p-protecting the two of you," she said quietly, fighting back tears. "You d-don't understand. He's going to kill you. For trying to keep me from him. He's going to kill you both."

Alaric had turned toward her, one arm draped along the back of the couch. "What," he asked Jon, "is she saying?"

Jon's face had gone a little green. "She knows," was all he said in a faint voice.

"She knows *what*?" Alaric demanded.

"How everyone is going to die." Jon flung him a dazed look. "She's always known. It's what she does. She just knows. If Meena says he's going to kill us . . . we're going to die."

Chapter Thirty-nine

Alaric knew he might have overreacted just a little. Especially when the girl had thrown the phone at him. A phone!

But Meena Harper had shown a great deal more spirit than he had expected.

Of *course* he'd leapt on her. To immobilize her. That was all. What other choice had he had?

He didn't know why he'd been unable to keep his hands off her. *That* had been a surprise.

It was just that she had such nice skin. So soft and smooth . . . like the wax he used to polish his skis when he went to Kitzbühel every year between Christmas and New Year's.

It had been virtually impossible for him not to touch her . . . and to keep on touching her, even though it clearly annoyed her.

Well, *she* annoyed *him.* He didn't want to touch her. He wanted to find out where the prince was, go there, destroy him, then go back to his hotel room and have a nice hot bath.

What Alaric did *not* want was to be stuck in a New York City apartment crammed with cheap—albeit fairly comfortable—Ikea furniture with the big-eyed, silky-skinned current lover of the prince of darkness, who apparently had the psychic ability to predict how people were going to die.

"She knows all this?" Alaric asked the brother skeptically.

"She's never wrong," Jon said to Alaric. "She knows. She just . . . knows. Since she was a kid."

Alaric stared at Meena Harper. He had encountered a lot of things in his time since joining the Palatine: a succubus that had detached itself from the body of its evening's plaything with a discontented shriek because Alaric had hurled holy water at it.

Chupacabras—often mistaken for mangy coyotes but actually a vampiric species all their own, sucking the life from grazing sheep in Texas.

But when they couldn't find sheep, they'd suck the life from sleeping children happily enough, when they could get at them through an open window.

Demons, flying at him with mouths agape, as a local priest attempted to exorcise them from possessed villagers in the mountains of Colombia.

And of course more vampires than he cared to recall, all with blood streaming down their chins and scarlet-stained shirtfronts, rushing at him from the darkness, screaming obscenities.

Vampires, while romanticized on film and in literature, were generally quite foulmouthed in reality. Only the Dracul made any pretense at civility.

But Alaric could not recall ever once encountering a psychic—not one who actually had anything valuable to say. Why all psychics, if their powers were bona fide, did not immediately go and predict the winning numbers for the lottery, then take their earnings and move to Antigua, Alaric could never understand.

The Vatican didn't believe in them either—probably for the same reasons as Alaric—and didn't have a single one on its payroll.

But Alaric could tell by the frightened—yet resolute—look on Meena Harper's brother's face that he believed in his sister's abilities.

And he could tell by the misery on Meena Harper's face that she, too, believed.

Meena had shooed the dog off her lap and now sat with her elbows on her knees and her face hidden in her hands. With her petite build, short dark hair, and slender limbs and neck, dressed in nothing but the black silk slip, she looked like a ballet dancer.

A ballet dancer having a nervous breakdown.

In another place, in another lifetime, Alaric thought they might have had quite a pleasant time together, because she was not unattractive.

But this was not going to happen now. Because she quite clearly hated him.

Alaric knew what he had to do, of course: call for backup. Let Holtzman deal with these two. He just wanted the address. Señor Sticky would take care of the rest.

He would dispatch Emil and Mary Lou Antonescu, too, on his way out. It was going to be a very satisfactory evening, it turned out.

"Look," Meena said, lifting her tear-stained face from her hands and glaring at him. Her eyes were very large and dark in her face. "I know you don't believe me. No one ever does. But I'm not making this up. I didn't believe it myself until . . . well, until you said you were going to kill him and showed me that bite mark. And then I knew. And the fact . . . well, that he's already dead. Which is why I could never tell—never mind. But *he's* going to kill *you*. Both of you. You've got to believe me."

Her voice, which had irritated him before, had taken on a throaty sweetness now that she was worried. One that he found irresistibly sexy.

What was wrong with him? He was *not* going to fall for the charms of this . . . whatever she was. No way. He had some vampires to kill. Then some delicious room service waiting.

"Hold that thought, will you?" he said, and took out his cell phone, pressing Holtzman's number. "I just have to make a quick call. It will only take a second. Do you want another Coke? You're shivering. Maybe some tea. Your brother can make you some tea."

"He's going to find you first," she said, a single tear trickling down one of her smooth, gently rounded cheeks. Her eyes were closed, like she was observing something on the back of her eyelids. "Somewhere . . . a room made out of glass. An atrium. There's water everywhere. Like a pool. Yes. A hotel pool. But in the air. That makes no sense. . . . Maybe . . . on a roof. Are you staying in a hotel with an enclosed rooftop pool?"

Alaric's thumb froze as he was about to hit Send.

"Because that's where he's going to find you," she said. Was she actually seeing this vision, behind her closed eyelids? "Do you like to swim or something?"

Alaric stared down at her. "How in the hell would you know that?" he demanded before he could stop himself.

It took a lot to spook Alaric Wulf.

And that included the creepy way those chupacabras had lifted their heads from the sheep they'd been gorging on when he'd accidentally stepped on a twig while approaching them.

And the way the sheep's blood had dripped from their pointy little teeth as they'd cocked their heads at him questioningly.

She wasn't crying anymore.

"I just know things," she said with a shrug. "Believe me, I never asked for this . . . gift. And if I could, I'd give it back in a second. Do you think I *like* knowing my boyfriend is going to reach down into the water and grab you by your hair while you're swimming laps tomorrow, then lift you out of the water and gouge out your—"

"He's not," Alaric said quickly, putting his cell phone away and coming back toward the couch to sit down beside her. "He's not. Because now that you've told me this, that changes everything. Right? Is that how it works?"

Alaric Wulf wasn't a praying man.

But he was spooked. He was genuinely spooked.

And he was praying that was how it worked.

Because just as he knew he had made a believer out of her about the vampires, she had made a believer out of him about her powers.

"Your warning me that he's going to be there, that will cause me to change my plans," he said. "Doesn't it work that way? Now I'll be looking out for him. Maybe I won't even go swimming."

Alaric's heart was beating quickly.

And it took a lot these days to get his pulse jumping.

But the image she'd described of the prince of darkness grabbing him by the hair from the water and gouging something out while he was innocently swimming his laps at the Peninsula?

That had done it, all right.

Because there was no way this girl could have known that was where he was staying.

So she couldn't possibly have been making this up.

"Look again," he said to her. He was still speaking gently, because there was something about Meena Harper's body language—the way she'd curled in on herself ever since he'd shown her that bite mark on her thigh—that told him that she was a little bit broken and needed careful handling if she was going to heal.

But it was difficult for him to keep the urgency from his tone.

"What do you see?" he asked. He reached for a blanket on the end of the couch and wrapped it around her slender shoulders. "When you look now?"

Meena shook her head. "It's no good," she said. "He's still going to kill you both."

"Why me?" the brother whined. "What'd I do?"

"But where?" Alaric asked, ignoring Jon. "Where now?"

Meena was still going on. "Not the pool . . . Somewhere dark. But . . . something is on fire." Her eyelids flew open, and she stared at Alaric accusingly. Her voice had some of its old asperity back. "You can't blame him. He's only trying to defend himself. You tried to kill him first. You're the one who started it."

"Me?" Alaric jabbed a thumb at himself. "Oh, right, I'm the prince of darkness, anointer of all that is unholy, guardian of the infernal. Right. It's my fault."

"He didn't pick who his father is," Meena said hotly, "any more than you did."

Alaric reflected briefly to himself that it would have been nice to know who his own father was, if only so he could give the old man a well-deserved kick in the pants for deserting him.

"Meena," Jon said. "Don't you think you should just tell us where he is, so we can kill him before he finds and kills us? That's the way they always do it in the movies. They kill Dracula in his coffin during the day while he's defenseless sleeping."

"Vampires don't actually do the coffin thing," Alaric remarked.

"Really?" Jon looked stunned. "But—"

"Stoker just added that to amp up the drama," Alaric said. "Or who knows. Maybe Dracula told him it was true as some kind of sick joke. The guy was pretty twisted. It would make it a lot easier if it were true."

"You." Meena glared at Alaric. "You've delivered your horrible news. Okay. My boyfriend's the son of Dracula. Thanks. You can go now."

"Uh," Alaric said, "I'm afraid I can't do that. I've got a job to do. Slay the dragon and all of that. I thought I'd made that clear."

"Oh," Meena said, nodding. "Like your little medal."

"Right," he said with a wink. "Just like St. George."

"I see the resemblance," Meena said sarcastically. "Well, good luck with all of that. Now get out of my home before I call the police."

Alaric looked around the room. Then, spying the telephone sitting on a small table at the end of the couch, he lifted the receiver from its cradle, dropped it on the floor, then stomped on it with one of his massive steel-toed boots.

When he lifted his foot, the receiver lay in many individual parts beneath it.

Meena's eyes widened to their limits.

"I believe your cell is out of order as well," Alaric said, looking pointedly at the bits and pieces of her BlackBerry on the floor.

"You can't hold me a prisoner in my own home," Meena said . . . with considerable spirit, he felt, for one who had so recently served as a human blood bank for the son of the dark lord.

"If you want me to go," Alaric said politely, "I'll be more than happy to. Just tell me where I can find Lucien Antonescu, and I'll leave. And as an added bonus, you'll never have to see me again."

"But you'll give me your e-mail, right?" Jon asked Alaric. "Because I'm serious about trying out for this Palatine thing. I know about the hiring freeze, but I think I'd be awesome at—"

"Oh, never mind," Meena said, interrupting. "You're both giving me a headache. Go ahead, stay. Stay all night, for all I care. I'm going to bed."

And with that, she turned and stomped barefoot down the hall, the blanket trailing behind her. She slammed her bedroom door, directly in the face of Jack Bauer, who'd trotted after her.

"There's no phone in that room, is there?" Alaric asked the brother.

"Of course there is," Jon replied.

Moving with lightning speed, Alaric leapt across the coffee table and the debris littering the foyer, then flung open the door to Meena's tastefully decorated—Pottery Barn this time, Alaric had time to observe critically—bedroom just as she was lifting the phone to dial. He snatched the receiver from her hand with a stern, "Tsk tsk tsk. What did we say about using the phone?"

"I wasn't calling Lucien," Meena said. "I'm not stupid. I don't want to get you two killed. I was calling my friend Leisha. I need to talk to someone who isn't male."

But Alaric was already walking over to the French doors that led to a small balcony and throwing them open. The night air had become much cooler than it had been when he'd entered the building. Storm clouds, he saw, were moving in, rumbling toward the city across the river like an advancing army.

"Stop," Meena said, rushing out after him just as he stretched an arm over the ornate wrought iron railing.

"You can't tell *anyone* what's happening here," he explained. "Not your friend Leisha. Not your mother. Not the police. Not if you want them to live. Do you understand me, Meena? These monsters will kill everyone you love in the blink of an eye if they think it will benefit them in some way."

"I understand," Meena said. "But do *you* understand that there are people down there? If you drop that phone over that railing, you could hit someone."

Alaric looked over the side of Meena's balcony railing. "Got any premonitions of anyone's imminent demise?" he asked.

Meena chewed her lower lip. "Well," she said. "No. But—"

"Bombs away," he said, and let go of the phone. The wind whipped it quickly from his hand.

"—it doesn't work that way," Meena said, continuing. "I actually have to *meet* the person. But nice job. You probably just killed someone yourself."

Down below, a car alarm went off.

"Shame on me," Alaric said, shaking his head. "I killed a car."

"You think this is all a joke?" Meena glared up at him in what moonlight peeked out from between the fast-moving storm clouds. "Because it's not."

Alaric felt a twinge of disappointment. Meena Harper had done nothing but surprise him, from her resistance—no victim had ever put up as much of a physical fight as she had—to the discovery about her psychic ability.

It would have been nice if she'd proved to be unpredictable in this way as well. But he knew what she was about to say. He'd heard it hundreds of times before.

That was the problem with vampires . . . and why they needed to be universally eradicated. They worked their way under the skin of even the most sensible, intelligent people and turned them into junkies just as surely as black tar heroin did.

"I know," Alaric said flatly. "You love him. You can't live without him. But you see, I can cure that. If you just tell me where he is, I'll kill him, and then—"

"No," Meena said, interrupting him. "That wasn't what I was talking about. Do you ever stop to *listen* to people? Or do you just go rushing in waving that big sword of yours and ask questions later? He's *going* to kill you. And my brother, too. You know I can't let that happen, Alaric."

It was the first time she'd said his name. He didn't know why, but the sound of his name on her lips did something strange to the hair on the back of his neck.

Or maybe that was just the lightning over the Hudson River.

"I can't be responsible for what happens to your brother," Alaric said, fighting for calm. And not just because he was starting to realize his attraction to her was more than just physical. "Anyway . . . from what I understand, he's been collecting unemployment for some time. You should be happy he's showing some initiative—"

"Because he wants kill vampires?" Meena's voice rose above a far-off rumble of thunder. "All I wanted was for him to get a job and maybe install some drywall in the baby's room in Leisha's apartment. I never wanted him to get himself killed going after the undead!"

"Well, you should have thought about that before you had your little one-night stand with Lucien Dracula," Alaric said, folding his arms. Down below, the owner of the car had finally turned off the alarm. They were low enough that traffic sounds could still be heard, but they were faint. He thought she must be chilled in her slip, but she showed no signs of it, even though she'd abandoned the blanket from the couch. Her temper was keeping her warm, he supposed.

And her blushing cheeks. She didn't like him referring to her tryst with Antonescu as a one-night stand.

"But since you didn't," he went on brutally, "you're going to have to deal with the consequences. One of which is me. And I'm not going anywhere until you tell me where the prince of darkness is. It's your choice, really. *Him*. Or me."

She just glared at him. Then, without a word, she turned on her heel and strode, barefoot, from the balcony back into the bedroom.

Her decision was pretty obvious.

It was, Alaric realized, going to be a long night.

Chapter Forty

It was easy for Lucien to find his brother, Dimitri.

He was the prince of darkness, after all. He could find anyone he wanted.

Except, of course, whoever was killing girls and dumping their bodies in parks all around Manhattan. The person—or people—doing that seemed to want to keep it a secret from him, for an obvious reason. . . .

They valued their lives.

His brother was said to be entertaining another group of financial analysts at a burlesque club downtown. Lucien did not frequent such places—frankly, if he wanted to see a woman disrobe in front of him, he didn't have to pay for the privilege.

This particular club was more crowded than any he'd ever seen, and not just with men. There were women there, as well—all ages—waiting for the show to begin, most without seats. The club was standing-room only. Tables were said to be going for a "bottle fee" of a thousand dollars.

That meant patrons would be seated at a table only if they purchased a bottle of champagne or vodka . . . for a thousand dollars.

It was absurd.

But it was how the club made its money.

Lucien didn't have time to stop to listen to the grousing of the crowd, though. He was making his way through it and up the stairs to the red plush velvet box seats where his brother was sitting with the investment bankers with whom he was palling around for whatever reason.

Still, it was hard to keep the buzzing out of his head. Not the buzzing of the conversations around him, either, but the buzzing he'd felt ever since he'd left Meena's side that morning and that seemed to occur now whenever he was around humans.

It was the strangest sensation. He couldn't really equate it with anything he'd ever felt before. It was like having a tiny bee inside his brain. The sensation faded whenever there wasn't anyone living around.

But as soon as anyone with a heartbeat was nearby, the vibration started up again.

It wasn't just buzzing, either. He knew things. Just by looking into the faces of the people he brushed past. Like the waitress holding the tray of empty glasses, wiggling by him in her black satin bustier and lace garter belt. She needed to be careful on this narrow staircase in her precariously high platform heels, or she was going to trip and fall and break her neck.

This wasn't something he could tell by reading her mind. It was just something he knew, simply by looking into her heavily made-up eyes.

"Watch your step," he said to her as she sidled past him on the stairs.

"Thanks," she said, grinning up at him suggestively with her red lacquered lips. "I'd rather watch yours, though."

And not just her. The boy shouting into his cell phone at the top of the stairs, too.

"You're not going to believe this place," he was telling a friend on the other end of the phone. "One of the women onstage smokes! Not with her mouth, either, with her—"

"Son," Lucien said to him.

"Dude." The boy turned to him. "I'm not your son. And I don't know where the bathroom is. . . ." His voice trailed off as he looked into Lucien's eyes. He swallowed. "I'm sorry," he said. "Can I help you, sir?"

"Yes," Lucien said, holding out his hand. "Give me your car keys."

The boy, who couldn't have been more than nineteen—he'd obviously used a fake ID to enter the club—reached a trembling hand into his coat pocket and withdrew a set of car keys. He placed them in Lucien's outstretched palm.

Lucien placed the keys in his coat pocket.

"Take a cab home," he said to the boy, patting him on the shoulder. "I think you've had a few too many drinks to drive home safely."

"But . . ." The boy looked after him as Lucien moved away, toward the deep-red velvet curtains that closed off the box seats from the standing area on the second-floor mezzanine overlooking the stage. "I came in from Long Island City."

"Take the train," Lucien said with a wink. "You'll thank me one day."

He found Dimitri in a dark private box with six or seven business-suited corporate types, all lounging on couches and sumptuously decorative pillows around a drink-laden table. There were no women to be seen. They, Lucien knew, would be appearing on the stage below, in various states of undress, doing things with miscellaneous props that would have surprised even his father, who was raised by fifteenth-century Turks.

"Lucien!" Dimitri cried upon spying him. "What a surprise! Gentlemen, meet my brother, Lucien. Lucien, these are some friends of mine from TransCarta."

Lucien flicked a glance downward at the men beneath him, all of whom were middle-aged, running ever-so-slightly to fat due to sitting too long in front of a computer all day, and all of whom were going to die . . .

. . . within the week.

Wait. *All of them?*

How?

And why? Some kind of corporate plane crash?

But all Lucien could see in the fuzzy snapshot of his mind's eye was a room . . . a very dark room. A basement, maybe.

And blood. Quite a lot of blood.

A car crash in an underground parking garage?

That was the only thing that made sense.

Poor bastards.

What was happening to him? How did he know how all these people were going to die?

And *why* did he know it?

"How do you do?" Lucien said politely to the soon-to-be-dead men. There was no use warning them, of course. What was there to warn them of? "I'm sorry to disturb your . . . evening out. But I was wondering if I might have a word with my brother alone."

A look of annoyance passed over Dimitri's face. Lucien saw it. He was certain he saw it.

But it was gone almost as soon as it appeared.

"Of course," Dimitri said. "I'll just be a moment, gentlemen."

"Take your time," one of the soon-to-be-dead men said jovially. "Next act's not for ten more minutes. You should join us, Lucien. Girl apparently smokes out of her—"

"I've seen it," Lucien said quickly. "In Turkey once. But thank you for the invitation."

Dimitri rose and ducked through the curtain Lucien was holding open for him. "What is this?" he asked grouchily, following Lucien down the side of the balcony, toward a sign marked *Exit*. "I'm actually here on business, you know. I don't have time to keep having these not-so-brotherly reunions of yours."

A bald man with huge biceps, dressed in a black T-shirt and pants, who'd planted himself in front of the door marked *Exit* said, "Emergency exit only. Take the stairs."

"That won't be necessary, Marvin," Lucien said gently.

"No," Marvin said, looking confused. Then he stepped aside and pushed the door open for them. "I'm sorry, sir. I don't know what I was saying. Have a nice evening."

"We will," Lucien said.

They stepped out onto a fire escape over a back alley. The evening air was cool. It was much quieter outside than it had been inside the club, where pounding rock music had played. Though Lucien could hear the sound of distant thunder as a storm was brewing over New Jersey.

The bouncer closed the exit door behind them.

"Well?" Dimitri asked irritably, taking out a cigar and lighting it. "What is it? I thought we'd pretty much said all we had to say the last time we met."

"No," Lucien said. "Not everything. I've been thinking about you."

"Have you?" Dimitri looked suspicious. "What about me?"

"I was wondering what that little"—Lucien made a twirling motion in the air with his index finger—"was about before, actually."

Dimitri looked skyward. "I should have known. You think too much, you know. You always did. With you, it was always about books. And the past. Never the future."

"Have you ever considered that it's only by studying the mistakes of the past," Lucien said mildly, "that we can even have a future?"

Dimitri rolled his eyes. "Right. What you're doing now is so noble, molding little human minds. It's probably never occurred to you, has it, that *our* kind is beginning to say you've gotten soft. . . ."

Lucien raised an eyebrow. "Really. Do *you* think I've gotten soft, Dimitri?"

"I didn't say *me*," he said. "But I was giving you an opportunity to show them how wrong they are." He rubbed the back of his neck, as if remembering his hard landing at Lucien's hands. "You should be thanking me, actually. I think I did an exemplary job of illustrating that you're still at the top of your game."

"Interesting," Lucien said. "Since I was attacked earlier this week as well."

Dimitri looked up, surprised. Lucien couldn't tell if his surprise was genuine. Dimitri had always had a flair for the dramatic.

"Here?" he asked. "In the city?"

"Yes," Lucien said. "And in front of a human." He wasn't going to say a word about Meena. Nothing more than what he'd just said. He knew better than to let on that he had a special interest in a woman—particularly a human woman—in front of his half brother. "You wouldn't happen to know anything about that, would you?"

"For God's sake, Lucien," Dimitri said. He flicked some ash off the side of the fire escape railing. "Of course not. What do you take me for?"

Lucien reached for the dragon symbol that hung around his half brother's neck. "Someone who's tried to kill me in the past so that he could take over the throne himself. I see you're still wearing this," he said, letting the iron image dangle between his fingers, the very closeness of his hand to Dimitri's throat an unspoken threat. "So was your son, and that other boy you were sitting with in your club. Are you telling me that doesn't mean anything?"

"Of course it means something." Dimitri spat over the side of the fire escape, into the alleyway fifty feet below. "We're related to Dracula, for the love of God! Why wouldn't I use that, and the family coat of arms, to promote my image as a businessman? You know I've never understood your reluctance to do the same."

Lucien's expression twisted into one of disgust. "Perhaps because I want nothing to do with the Dracul," he said. "Nor do I see anything admirable about being a direct descendant of someone who killed tens of thousands of innocent women and children in his lifetime, and who was, quite rightly, eventually put to death for it."

Dimitri looked bored. "Well," he said, "I suppose if you're going to put it *that* way."

"And you're telling me that neither you nor your son had anything to do with the Dracul's attempt on my life in front of St. George's Cathedral?" Lucien demanded.

"Brother." Dimitri shook his head, his expression crestfallen. "What did I ever do to you to make you distrust me so?"

"I believe it was when you tried to have me buried alive at Târgovişte," Lucien remarked.

"Ancient history," Dimitri said. "You always did hold on to grudges for far too long. Father thought so, too."

"Strangely, I don't put much stock into anything Father said," Lucien remarked. "If he hadn't been so loose with his lips, the truth about our existence would never have been leaked to that fool Stoker, and we wouldn't have the Palatine after us and have had to change the family name."

Dimitri's brows lowered in an expression Lucien recognized. "There are ways around the Palatine," Dimitri said. "They aren't as almighty as they like to think."

Lucien reached out and, taking hold of his half brother by the throat, lifted him into the air. Not just off his feet, but until he was holding him over the side of the fire escape, fifty feet from the pavement below. Dimitri, panicking, grabbed at Lucien's sleeves, looking down desperately and gasping. He'd dropped the cigar, which tumbled to the ground and exploded with a shower of red sparks when it hit the cement.

"Father used to brag that the Palatine would never catch him either," Lucien said. "And look what they did to him. Is that what you want to happen to you?"

"I-I didn't mean it," Dimitri gargled. He wasn't in the most comfortable position, dangling by his neck so many feet above the ground. "Stop fooling around, Lucien. P-put me down."

Lucien tightened his grip. "You may actually have something to worry about, Dimitri, besides the Palatine . . . because just this morning I woke up with the strangest feeling that all of this—the dead girls, the attack on my life—somehow points back to . . . you."

Dimitri made a gagging noise. He appeared to be saying, *No. No, it's not me. . . .*

But Lucien only grinned.

"Oh, yes," he said. "I'm really quite sure of it, in fact. I can't prove it . . . yet. But I will. And when I do, I will do worse than decapitate you, I can assure you . . . as well as anyone I discover who may have helped you. I've turned a blind eye to your instigating rebellion against me in the past because you're my brother, Dimitri, and family is . . . well, family. But things have changed now. You don't need to know how, just that I won't do it anymore. Not when human lives are being lost and others are at stake. Do you understand me?"

Dimitri nodded. He didn't look happy about the situation. "Of course," he said, choking. "*My prince.*"

"That's a good boy," Lucien said.

Then abruptly he opened his hands and let his brother fall.

Dimitri, as Lucien had known he would, tumbled only a few feet before turning into something black and sleek, all wings and teeth and claws, that swooped in a graceful spiral before finally landing on the ground beside the abandoned cigar . . .

. . . then turned back into the shape of the brother he knew so well.

"Damn you, Lucien," Dimitri said, rising to his feet while brushing off his suit. He looked furious. "You know how I hate it when you do that!"

Lucien smiled to himself. Now who had gotten soft?

He turned and knocked on the emergency exit. Marvin, ever accommodating, opened the door to let him back in. While his brother's method of egress had been quicker, Lucien generally preferred to take the stairs.

Chapter Forty-one

1:00 A.M. EST, Saturday, April 17
910 Park Avenue, Apt. 11B
New York, New York

Meena lay in the dark of her bedroom, blinking up at the ceiling, Jack Bauer resting his head on her shoulder.

She was trying hard not to think about anything, because every time she remembered what was actually going on—why, for instance, she could hear the faint sounds of two men talking in her living room, along with *The Fast and the Furious* DVD Jon was playing—she wanted to start crying.

The muffled sounds from the other room seemed harmless enough: two grown men enjoying a film about cars and guns. They'd somehow managed to scrape together the Chinese food that hadn't spilled out of its cartons and were enjoying it, so she could smell that, too, the mingled odors of moo shu and fried dumplings. Just a typical Friday night at her place, while outside a thunderstorm was brewing. She could hear the wind stirring in the treetops below and the far-off rumble of thunder, and see the occasional flash of lightning against her wall through the slits in the shades over her window and the gauze curtains that covered the panes in the French doors to her balcony.

But she knew perfectly well what was really going on. Alaric Wulf was guarding her front door to keep her from sneaking out to go see Lucien. He was doing it for the same reason he'd smashed all her phones.

(She hoped he hadn't thought of e-mail. If he smashed her laptop, she'd find a way to sue. She didn't care if his boss *was* the Pope.)

But Alaric needn't have worried about her trying to sneak out. She wasn't particularly anxious to have a confrontation with Lucien. She'd even taken a weapon into bed with her: a single wooden knitting needle left over from a brief and ill-fated attempt at crafting she and Leisha had once embarked upon.

She held the knitting needle tight in one hand while with the other, she absently stroked Jack Bauer's head, watching the shadows dance against her ceiling, as the occasional slice of moonlight shone through the clouds.

What exactly she planned on doing with the knitting needle, she wasn't sure.

But stabbing it through the heart of any man who came into her bedroom—human or vampire—seemed to be a good plan. Meena wasn't feeling too warmly toward any members of the opposite sex at that moment.

She still hadn't exactly come to terms with everything that she had discovered during the course of the evening. She wasn't sure she'd ever really be able to understand—much less believe—it all.

All she knew for sure was that, after everything she'd seen and all she'd been through that night, she was feeling quite tired, and she wanted to rest.

But—even after changing into her softest white nightgown—the minute she'd lain down and pulled her comforter up to her chin, sleep became impossible. She felt wide awake, and not because of the thunder or the muted noises she could hear coming from the living room.

All she could think about was the fact that the man of her dreams—the guy she'd thought was so perfect . . . the guy whom, if she were really being totally honest with herself, she'd been idly considering moving to Romania for—was a vampire.

A vampire! Those creatures of fiction that she despised so much!

Only not. Because real-life vampires were nothing like the vampires of fiction. Real-life vampires did things—way more horrible things than vampires on film, the images of which Meena was convinced would forever be burned into the backs of her retinas—to people that no script-writer could ever in a million years have imagined.

Not only that, but Lucien was the *supreme ruler of the vampires*.

And he was the son of Vlad the Impaler. Of *Dracula*.

After locking herself into her bedroom, Meena dug out her old, bat-tered copy of the novel—which she'd bought during her death-obsessed goth stage in high school—and made the mistake of trying to read it again.

Then it all came flooding back to her. Not just the gory details about the creatures against whom Alaric Wulf had pledged to fight, but Mina! There was actually a character in the book named Mina! This was a character who, Meena remembered right away, fell in love with Dracula and actually drank some of his blood . . . then had, like so many women in horror novels and films, to be rescued.

And all right, in the book the name was spelled differently than hers. But still.

How did these kinds of things keep happening to her? Like it wasn't bad enough she had to know how everyone she met was going to die and then feel morally obligated to warn them about it.

Then she had to go and fall in love with—and *get bitten by*—the son of the most despised character in all of gothic literature? Who turned out actually to be real?

When she got through all this (and she would, indeed, get through all this—she had to; what other choice did she have?), she was going to write a book.

Of course she was. Someone had to get the word out there. It was the only way to save other women from what she was going through now.

Women Are from Venus, Vampires Are from Hell.

Meena lay there thinking about her book, watching as the shadows on her ceiling danced. She was so deeply engrossed in what she was going to say when Oprah asked why Meena had let Lucien do the things he had done to her, she didn't even notice when Jack Bauer lifted his head and, his gaze on the French doors, tilted his ears forward.

The Palatine, Meena was certain, would try to stop her from going on *Oprah*. Alaric Wulf had been adamant that word of the existence of vampires could not get out to the public.

But why, when they caused so much pain and heartache?

And those were just the ones who *weren't* murdering young girls.

And all right, she had pretty much given Lucien her full consent to do what he'd done. And she'd certainly enjoyed it.

But that didn't make it all right—

Beside her, Jack Bauer's body started to vibrate. He was growling, his foxlike face pointed toward the French doors. Meena looked at him, then glanced at the doors. She thought she saw something black flutter past the curtained windows.

A pigeon, more than likely. Or a plastic bag, tossed around by the growing storm.

"What is it, little man?" Meena whispered. "A bird? Are you going to go kill that bird?"

Jack Bauer rose onto his four paws, and standing in the middle of the bed with the fur on his back fully extended, he growled more loudly. All his attention was focused on the French doors, his small body quivering like a wire.

Meena felt her own skin prickle at his reaction to whatever he sensed outside her balcony doors.

This was no bird.

Who—or, more accurately, *what*—was out there?

"Okay, boy," Meena said quietly, swinging her legs from the bed. She clutched the knitting needle tightly in one hand. "Stay."

She should, she knew, go and get Alaric Wulf. This was what he was there for. To protect her.

Except that he wasn't. He was there to try to wrest from her the address of her lover.

So that he could kill him.

And, in turn, be killed *by* him. Along with Jon.

Meena couldn't let that happen, any more than she could let Lucien be killed, whatever he might be, whatever he might have done to her . . . however much he might have lied.

Lightning flashed. Thunder rumbled a second or two later, sounding much closer now than it had before. The storm had crossed the river. It would be upon them in a few minutes.

She couldn't run for Alaric. If she did, he'd die at Lucien's hands, and Jon would quickly follow . . . if she wasn't losing her mind and Lucien was, in fact, beyond those glass doors. Not, of course, that that was even possible, because she lived eleven stories up and there wasn't a fire escape he could have climbed (she refused to think about bats, or the way Count Dracula, in Bram Stoker's book, had been able to climb buildings like a lizard).

Raising the knitting needle shoulder-high in her fist, she moved cautiously toward the French doors, the gauzy white curtains obscuring her view of what was on the balcony. Behind her, Jack Bauer jumped off the bed and followed along, still growling, even though Meena hissed, "Jack! Bad dog! Stay!"

Jack, as usual, paid absolutely no attention to her whatsoever.

Laying a hand on the door handle, Meena took a deep breath and pulled.

A sudden gust of wind helped push the door toward her, and Jack, excited, ran out onto the balcony. Meena, her heart in her throat, whispered, "Jack! No!" and tore out onto the terrace to stop him before he got hurt.

Except that there was no one—*nothing*—there.

Meena, shivering, stood in the rising wind. Above her head, the sky was a wildly patterned mosaic of dark clouds, behind which lightning continued to flash every few seconds. She could barely see the moon anymore. Thunder sounded, so loudly she seemed to feel it reverberating inside her chest.

Maybe that's why she didn't hear her name at first. The voice calling it was as wild and as deep as the thunder.

But then she noticed that Jack was growling again, his head turned in the direction of the Antonescus' terrace, his nose poking through the wrought iron rails as he bared his teeth.

And when Meena turned, she saw it.

Chapter Forty-two

Lucien.

He was there, standing on his cousin Emil's terrace, his long black trench coat whipping around him in the wind like a cape. . . .

What was he *doing* standing there, staring at her like that?

It was the middle of the night. The clouds overhead fairly throbbed with rain.

She laid a hand to her thumping heart.

"Meena."

His voice was like liquid silk. She could almost feel it, licking her skin like the smooth white cotton of her nightgown.

He was calling to her. Calling to her the way the lightning was calling to the thunder.

What was she going to do? What was she going to say to him?

Meena moved to the terrace wall and, leaning against it, said, across the eight-foot-wide plunge that separated them, "I can't really talk right now, Lucien."

Her voice was shaking as much as her fingers, but she still managed to clutch her wooden knitting needle. She hoped he didn't notice.

"Why not, Meena?" Lucien asked, the concern in his voice a caress. "Are you upset because I had to cancel our evening together? Didn't you get my note?"

His voice curled and coiled along her heartstrings, the way his trench coat was wrapping against his legs every time the wind blew.

"I got your note," she said. "Thank you very much for the bag. But now just isn't a very good time."

"Perhaps I could come over," he said. "I tried calling earlier, but you didn't seem to be picking up the phone."

"I know," Meena said, swallowing hard. If he truly was the prince of darkness, he was going to find out sometime. So she might as well tell the truth. "I couldn't pick up my phone. There's a Palatine Guard in my living room. He destroyed all my phones."

Lucien grew very still. In fact, it seemed to Meena as if *everything* grew still. The sky above their heads froze. The lightning, the thunder, her heartbeat . . . even the wind died down. The clouds, which had been moving so swiftly overhead just seconds before, seemed to pile up on top of one another. The thick black storm clouds shut out the glow from the moon, concealing Lucien's expression.

"Meena," she heard him say.

The word—just those two syllables—told her everything she needed to know, as if the sudden meteorological display hadn't been enough to convince her. They held a world of pathos.

And danger.

Some small part of her—the romantic in her, she supposed—had been holding out hope that Lucien would deny it. A vampire? Of course not! How ridiculous. Everyone knew there was no such thing as vampires.

But she'd heard the truth of it just now in his voice.

"I tried to tell you," he said. His voice sounded as broken as her heart. "In the museum . . ."

"Go away." She was whispering so that they wouldn't be overheard by anyone in her living room. But it was as hard to keep the horror from her tone as it was the pain. "Go away, Lucien. And never come back."

"Meena." The moon was still lost behind the skidding clouds.

But now she could hear that he sounded less wounded and more impatient. Like he had any right to be impatient with *her*.

"I can't believe what an idiot I was." Meena felt as if she were choking. She was clutching the knitting needle to her chest like some kind of talisman to ward off evil. "Here I thought we had this incredible bond. Don't ask me why. Maybe it was the part where you saved my life in front of that cathedral. Except I didn't know it was *you* those bats were attacking! I didn't know you were a . . . a . . ."

She couldn't even say the word.

"Meena," he said. "I can explain."

Was he serious? He could *explain*? "Who were they, Lucien?" she demanded. "You knew them, didn't you?"

Lucien's tone was rueful. "In a way . . ."

"And the whole time"—Meena's voice sounded ragged, even to her own ears—"you were just reading my mind, weren't you? That's how you knew where I lived! And that purse!" She shook her head. "That stupid purse! I should have told him to throw *it* out the window instead of my phone. *You have slain the dragon.* God, I can't believe I ever fell for that! Have you ever considered writing dialogue for an American soap opera, Lucien? Because I could get you a job where I work."

"Meena," Lucien said. Now his tone was sharp . . . as sharp as his teeth, she thought, which she'd never even felt sinking into her skin. "Is he still there? The guard from the Palatine?"

"Oh, what's wrong?" She knew she probably sounded more hysterical than sarcastic. "Can't you read my mind to find out?"

An extremely strong gust of wind that seemed to appear from nowhere suddenly swept across her terrace and would have knocked her off her feet if she hadn't dropped the knitting needle and reached out to grab the balcony railing with one hand while shielding her eyes with the other.

For a few seconds she couldn't see, there was so much dust and debris—some of it was the dried petals from the dead geraniums on her balcony, swirling in a sudden springtime tornado, from out of nowhere.

But she was quite sure she saw the blurry outline of a large, bat-like object hovering between her terrace and the Antonescus', blocking out what little light still shone from the night sky and the windows of the apartments around hers. It was like the time the bats had swooped down to attack her and Jack Bauer. . . .

Except that now she knew they hadn't been coming after her at all. It had been Lucien they'd wanted.

And the reason they'd had no effect on him whatsoever was that he wasn't human. Their teeth and claws couldn't harm him because nothing could. Nothing except chopping off his head with a sword—at least according to Alaric Wulf—or stabbing a pointed piece of wood into his heart.

And she had foolishly just dropped the single piece of pointed wood she owned.

When the wind died down and Meena was able to open her eyes, she saw Lucien standing in front of her, on her own balcony, just a foot or two away from her.

Meena, her heart now feeling as if it might slam out of her chest, tilted her chin to look into his face—that incredibly sensitive, handsome face—and saw that he was wearing an expression of extreme displeasure.

For the first time, she recognized the surging of her pulse for what it really was: fear.

And not just for Jon and that Palatine Guard inside her apartment: fear for her own life.

"Frankly," Lucien said calmly, "I've never been able to read your mind, Meena. Your thoughts have always been a bit . . . jumbled."

Meena, her fingers shaking convulsively, tightened her grip on the balcony railing. What had she done? What was happening? What was he doing there? Was he going to kill her?

"I thought vampires c-couldn't enter a home unless invited," she stammered through teeth that had begun to chatter. Was it her imagination, or did his dark eyes have a flicker of red in them, deep inside the pupils?

"That used to be true," he said. The thunder had started up again, so loud it shook the metal railing beneath her fingers. The storm over their heads was beginning to crest. "At least in the days when people cared enough about their homes to have them blessed by their priests or rabbis. These days, when no one seems to bother anymore? It's not really such a problem for us."

"Oh," Meena said. "Right." Her gaze was fixed on his, though she fumbled surreptitiously with her bare foot along the balcony floor, searching for the knitting needle she'd dropped. If she found it, would she really have the courage—and the strength—to plunge it into his heart (or the place where his heart had once been)?

Maybe she should just jump. Death had to be preferable to this.

"But when we do encounter a sacred threshold," Lucien said, continuing in the same detached, almost conversational tone, "we can find ways around it. We can use mind control to get the less . . . strong-willed to invite us inside. Some of us can even turn into mist and go through a keyhole, if we don't care to be seen by others afterwards."

"You can turn to mist?" she asked faintly.

His red-eyed gaze focused on her. "Yes," he said. "I can turn to mist. I can turn into a wolf, too. And you're not going to kill me, Meena. Not with a knitting needle. You're not going to jump, and you're not even going to scream for that Palatine Guard to come out here, even disgusting as you find me." Now his dark eyebrows knit. "Why *is* that?"

He *could* read her thoughts. He could.

Almost, anyway.

Suddenly the world seemed to tilt crazily in front of her.

Lucien reached out and grabbed her around the waist, pulling her body against his. The feel of his hard muscles through the thin material of her nightgown caused her swaying universe to right itself.

But only a little.

Now his voice was a soothing tether. "I can understand why you're upset. . . ."

"No." She craned her neck to look up at him. She was ashamed of the tears that were swimming in her eyes, but there wasn't anything she could do to stop them. "I don't think you can. A few hours ago I thought you were the best thing that ever happened to me. And now I just found out I never knew you at all." Her conscience pricked her. "And all right, you don't really know me at all, either . . . but you aren't even *human*."

The sky lit up with a single brilliant streak of lightning and then gave a heaving shudder of thunder.

Then it began to rain. Fat, stinging drops that struck her head and shoulders.

Lucien said, "Meena." He didn't sound detached anymore. Now his voice, like the thunder, sounded angry and desperate. "I *was* human . . . once." He'd turned so that his body blocked Meena's from the rain, holding her in what dubious shelter the doorway to her bedroom offered from the downpour while the world continued to pitch sickeningly around her. Her dog, seeing them so close together, flew into a frenzy of snarls but didn't seem to dare approach.

"Don't you think I long to feel those things again?" Lucien asked her.

His voice was raw. He knew what he was—and clearly hated it.

But he had come to accept it . . . the exact same way, Meena knew in a moment of clarity, that she had come to accept what she was.

"Do you think I *like* what my father made me?" he asked her desperately. "No. But do you think I had any *choice*? I don't know what unholy pact he made or who it was with . . . demons, witches, or the devil himself. All I know is that one night I died and woke to find myself . . . like this. He did the same to my brother Dimitri. He told us not to worry, because now we'd live forever. Unlike my mother . . . her death was what drove him to seek this grotesque half life for all of us."

Meena stared up at him in horror from the shelter of his arms as behind him, the rain streamed down in a heavy curtain and thunder rolled relentlessly. She didn't want to hear this. She didn't want to hear any of it.

"Of course," Lucien said with a wry smile, "it wasn't as simple as that. There were . . . urges. I tried not to give in to them. But they were so strong. Father did nothing but encourage us, bring us . . . gifts. Dimitri, who had always been weak willed, didn't care about letting the fever take over and allowing his baser instincts to rule him, slaughtering innocents and becoming more monster than man. But I . . . I don't know. Maybe because I had the benefit of having been born of my mother, who, as you know, was rumored to have been part angel—"

"Lucien."

She pitied him. She did. She raised a hand . . . she didn't know why. Maybe to stroke his cheek.

She knew what he was. And she hated it.

But he was suffering.

He flinched before she could touch him and looked away, toward the rain.

"I'm not saying I'm a better man than my brother," he said. "Or that my mother was a better woman than his. And I'm not saying that I couldn't have done more to try to stop him and my father. I could have. I should have. Eventually I . . . did."

He looked back at her, and his eyes were burning coals. Meena lowered her hand as hastily as if it had been burned.

"When my father was finally destroyed, and I became prince," he said, "I told them all the killing had to stop."

Meena didn't want to hear it. The photos Alaric Wulf had shown her were fresh in her mind.

But she couldn't just stand there while he broke down in shame in front of her, either. Especially as the storm lashed at his back, pelting them with a hurricane-like downpour.

Like he'd said—he might be a vampire now.

But he'd been human once.

"Come inside," she whispered. "You're getting soaked."

He looked down at her, as if startled to see he was still holding her in his arms. Then his gaze focused with a laserlike intensity that she wasn't sure she liked at all.

Was he seeing her finally as Meena, the woman he loved . . . or as his next meal?

She knew it might be the worst mistake she'd ever made in her life.

But she still opened the door to her bedroom.

Lucien followed her into the darkness.

"You think I'm a monster," he said.

She couldn't deny it.

So she feigned hospitality.

"I have a towel here somewhere," she said as she lifted Jack Bauer, who'd followed them, still snarling, into the room. She deposited him inside the closet, grabbing a towel from there as well. Jack Bauer looked around confusedly at all of Meena's shoes, then yipped, just once, as she closed the door. He'd be all right, she knew, in there. Safer than she was.

More important, no one would hear him, especially over the sound of the storm outside and the movie she could still hear blaring away in the living room.

"You did something to me." Lucien accused her in a choked voice as she handed him the towel, then helped him shed his wet coat.

"What? *I* did something to *you*? *I'm* not the one who did anything," Meena whispered incredulously, sinking to face him on the bed. "All I did was make the really big mistake of falling in love with you. Which, believe me, I am putting up there with my deepest, darkest regrets, like that perm I got in the eighth grade because I didn't listen to Leisha, and going to the senior prom with Peter Delmonico. Okay? So just let's chalk this whole thing up to one really bad decision and end it now. When it stops raining, you have to go. Trust me, I'm doing you a really big favor. Because one scream, and that guard in my living room will be in here like a shot to stake you."

She saw that red-eyed gaze flick past her and toward her bedroom door.

She shook her head and, reaching up to grab twin handfuls of his white shirtfront, pulled him down beside her onto the bed.

"You know I can't go," Lucien said, still looking toward the bedroom door.

"Yes, you can," Meena said, shaking her head. She continued to cling to his shirtfront. "Why can't you?"

His gaze turned back toward her, the red dying down a little, thankfully. "You know why, Meena."

What was he *talking* about? He couldn't possibly mean . . . there wasn't any way he could—

"I can't go because I'm in love with you, Meena," he said in his deep voice. He reached up to curl his hands around hers. "I told you. You have slain the dragon."

He was *in love* with her? Lucien Antonescu was *in love* with her?

Just a few hours earlier, this news would have made her the happiest girl in the world.

But now . . .

Now she knew he wasn't just Lucien Antonescu, professor of Eastern European history.

He was the prince of darkness.

He went on in the same deep, ragged voice, still holding her hands. "But you're hiding something from me, Meena. And it's not just a Palatine guard in your living room. I've known since the moment I met you. Something that you hide from everyone—"

"*I'm* hiding something?" She knew exactly what he was talking about, of course. But she lied automatically. Because she always did.

"Yes, you," he said. Now his hands moved to grip her shoulders. "I know. I should never have thought I could deceive you, of all people. But you know I was as honest with you as I could be without . . . terrifying you. But you . . . you weren't honest with me, either. There's something about you. Ever since we . . . were together—I . . . I . . ."

"You what?" Meena asked. Her heart was thumping. She knew she was taking an enormous risk letting him into her room—let alone into her heart. At any moment, Alaric might come bursting in, bringing Jon running after him. After that, if the worst happened, it would all be her fault. . . .

By letting him into her room, she was essentially doing what he'd just confessed to doing, all those years with his father and brother . . . committing murder.

What was she *doing*?

"Ever since I left you this morning," Lucien said, "I've had the oddest sensation that I know how almost every human I've come into contact with is . . . is going to die. And not, whatever you might think of me, by my own hands."

Meena stared up at him. For the first time in as long as she could remember, she couldn't think of anything to say.

"I'm sure the man in your living room told you some very colorful things about me." Lucien went on. "A good many of them might even be true. I've been what I am for a very long time." He was obviously choosing his words with care. "But I've never, ever experienced anything like this. Not until . . . well, being with you. Would you care to tell me what, exactly, is going on? I think it has something to do with this secret of yours. The thing that you're hiding. What makes it impossible for me to read your mind fully. And what makes you identify so strongly with Joan of Arc, who heard voices. Because that's what I feel like I'm doing. Hearing voices."

In the next room, she heard a stereophonic car crash. *The Fast and the Furious* was pounding its way to a metal-crunching crescendo.

"It's me," she said. She heaved a tearful sigh.

His grip on her tightened.

Not very gently, either.

"What are you talking about?" he rasped.

"You drank my blood," she reminded him. "Not a lot, so it'll probably go away after your next feeding. This should teach you to be more careful. You are what you eat, you know."

Chapter Forty-three

2:00 A.M. EST, *Saturday, April 17*
910 Park Avenue, Apt. 11B
New York, New York

Lucien stared down at her. Her face was a pale, resolute moon beneath his.

How must his own look to her? he wondered. A mask of shock.

"You can tell," he murmured, trying to make sure he understood her correctly, "how everyone is going to die?"

"Well, not everyone," Meena said. "Obviously not you. Since you're already dead."

He had hold of both her arms, and he didn't let go or loosen his grip on her. He just kept staring down at her.

"That's why you have to go," Meena said in her husky voice. "I know you're going to kill the guard. The one from the Vatican. And also Jon."

On the word *Jon*, her voice broke.

Lucien felt as if the roll of thunder that sounded just then had come from somewhere deep within him. He shook his head, trying to shake the truth of her words from his mind, like the tiny rain droplets that were still clinging to the ends of his hair.

"No," he said. "Meena, I wouldn't. I haven't killed a human in centuries, and you have to know, I would *never* kill your brother or anyone you loved."

Despite the darkness in her bedroom, he saw the tears at the corners of her eyes, shining like diamonds. "Except that you're going to," she said simply.

"Meena," he said. His heart, which for so many years he'd suspected had died within him, along with his soul, was finally coming back to life. "What you see . . . your visions . . . they don't *always* come true. Do they?" He thought of the boy whose keys he'd taken away earlier in the evening.

"No." Meena lifted a wrist and scrubbed at her streaming eyes. "Not if I warn people. And they do something about it. But you're a *vampire,* Lucien. You're not just any vampire. Apparently, you're the ruler of all vampires, the *prince of darkness.* I'm really supposed to just . . . trust that you're not going to do anything to this guy? Or to my brother? Not even in self-defense? Because they both really want to kill you. Alaric Wulf's got a really big sword, and—"

Lucien released his hold on her shoulders then. But only to pull her close and rest his cheek against her hair.

"Shhh . . . ," he said. "Then what you saw is just one possible future."

"Unless something changes," Meena said, pushing him away. "And what needs to change is your being here. And you should probably tell Mary Lou and Emil to go, as well. Because the Palatine is onto them, too. And I'm really not trying to be prejudiced against . . . well, what you are. Because God knows I have my own problems with people thinking I'm this awful person just because I have this sort of . . . obsession with death. But they do call you the prince of darkness. And that tends to suggest that you're evil and so not very trustwor—"

"I'm *not* evil," he ground out. Then he reconsidered. "Well, not anymore."

"I believe the words *anointer of all that is unholy* were used in reference to you," Meena said. "Maybe I'm wrong, but to me, that doesn't suggest anything good."

"The Palatine are hardly unbiased where I'm concerned," Lucien said wryly. "But I've worked hard since rising to my position to bring about a new, enlightened age to my people, to protect both their interests and those of humanity."

"I saw a photo," Meena said, "of a Palatine guard with half his face eaten off. Alaric"—she nodded her head toward the bedroom wall—"said it was from a vampire attack."

Lucien nodded, his shoulders drooping. Alaric. Alaric Wulf.

"Yes. I know of this man. And," he added, unable to keep his shock that all of this was happening from showing, "his partner. That was the Dracul who attacked them."

"Was it the . . . Dracul"—she said the word like it was distasteful to her—"who attacked us outside St. George's the other night?"

"Yes," he replied. "Not us, though. Me. They were after me. You were never in any danger."

Meena let out a small, mirthless laugh.

"Well, you weren't in any danger while I was there," Lucien said, amending his statement.

"And is it the Dracul who are murdering those girls?" Meena asked.

He looked down at her. How could such a forceful personality be wrapped into such an impossibly small body? "Yes," he admitted. "I'm fairly certain so."

"So . . . the new enlightened age isn't really working out, is it?" Meena asked.

He had never felt such despair. Why was all of this happening now, when he had finally come so close to grasping a little happiness?

The bargain his father had sealed had achieved immortality for himself and his family.

But what was the point of eternal life if one was destined to spend it alone?

"It's complicated," he said. "Blood-lust is strong, especially in the newly turned, so they long to feed . . . but I won't allow them to kill. They know there will be repercussions if they disobey. But there are so many more of them now than there used to be. I can't manage them all. I've tried delegating, but . . . I think my brother is the one behind the rise against me. He's done it before. He always wanted the throne."

Meena reached for the towel he'd abandoned, lifting it to wipe his hair and the back of his neck. "Like dialogue writers," she murmured, gently kissing the places where she'd pressed the towel just seconds before, "always wanting to be head writer."

He glanced at her in surprise. The touch of her warm mouth against his skin had sent an electric shock through him. He didn't know how to react. He wasn't sure if the kiss had meant anything. . . .

Or everything.

"I'm sorry?" he asked, stunned.

Her eyes were wide. She looked as surprised by what she'd just done as he was.

"The fact remains, you're still going to kill my brother," she said.

"I'm not," he insisted, taking her hand and pulling her toward him, then dropping his face into the warm curve where her neck met her collarbone. He was careful not to kiss her there, though. He'd seen the copy of *Dracula* on the floor in one corner of her room, as if flung there with some violence. "Meena, I told you, I love you. I would never—"

"I know you wouldn't want to," she whispered into his crisply damp hair. Her voice was unsteady with unshed tears. "But I also know my brother doesn't know you like I do. And he's going to try to kill you. He wants to join them."

"Join who?" Lucien's mind felt woolly. Was this the result of her nearness or the remnants of her blood still fizzing through his veins?

"The Palatine," she said.

Lucien barely heard her. Somehow his shirt had come open, and she was kissing his shoulders as if she couldn't stop herself, her lips soft as flower petals. All he could think about was the smoothness of her skin—like a newly poured Montrachet—and the fact that he could hear her pulse racing in her veins, in *his* veins, an echo of the heartbeat he once used to have.

So he said only, "I don't think we need to worry about that happening. Any more than we need to worry about my killing Jon."

While he spoke, he lifted her snowy white nightgown over her head, not entirely certain whether she was even aware of what he was doing.

Now she knelt beside him, fully unclothed, her dark-eyed gaze searching his face. Even shadowy as the room was, he could see one tip-tilted breast trembling with every throb of her heart.

The wave of desire that slammed into him was stronger than anything he could ever remember feeling in his lifetime. Which had been half a millennium long.

"Meena," he said. His voice was an open wound, his need was so great. He stretched out a callused hand to capture that quivering breast.

Then, his final reserves of control broken by the feel of her satiny skin under his fingers, he found himself dragging her toward him, marveling at the quick hot litheness of her body, and lowering his mouth over hers, overwhelmed with an urge to consume her . . . devour her . . . engulf her.

She let out a small sound—whether of protest or desire, he couldn't determine—and flung both hands up against his chest.

He reluctantly tore his mouth away from hers and asked, his eyes half lidded, "What is it?"

"No biting," she whispered. "I really, really mean it this time."

Chapter Forty-four

Jon looked down at the pancake sizzling away in the skillet in front of him. Perfection. Really.

He was on a roll this morning. A dozen flapjacks, each more golden than the next.

This was going to be a breakfast no one would ever forget.

When he was sure it had cooked all the way through, he added the pancake to the stack on the plate next to the stove, humming a little under his breath.

He knew he probably shouldn't feel so cheerful, since his sister was going through such a hard time.

But could there be anything cooler about the fact that there was a vampire hunter from the Vatican staying in their apartment?

He looked out of the pass-through to check the dining room table. Oh, yeah. This was good. Table set. OJ poured into glasses. Napkins folded. Place looked like Sarabeth's for brunch. Only no strollers or yuppies or screaming toddlers.

He wished he could call Weinberg and invite him over to have some of his excellent pancakes. Also tell him what was going on. Vampires, in Manhattan? He'd never believe it.

A secret society of vampire *hunters*?

He, like Jon, would want to join up. No doubt about it. Kick a little undead ass!

On the other hand, Weinberg had shown marked reluctance about joining the NYPD. Maybe he wouldn't want to join. Maybe he'd just want to stay home and keep watching CNN and complaining about that serial killer that was—

Jon paused, the pitcher of pancake batter still raised in his hand. The serial killer. The serial killer Weinberg was always going on about these days.

Of *course*. It was the same vampire Alaric Wulf was hunting.

Well, not the same one who'd bitten his sister, if Jon understood what was going on—and Jon still wasn't sure he understood *exactly* what was going on.

But *a* vampire, anyway.

Oh, now he *had* to tell Weinberg.

Jon put down the pancake batter and grabbed the nearest cell phone and started dialing.

"Is that *my* phone?" Meena asked, coming into the kitchen fully dressed in jeans, a T-shirt, and a little red scarf and matching flats, her short hair curling damply on the back of her neck from her morning shower.

Jon looked down in surprise at the cell phone in his hand.

"Oh," he said, hitting End Call. "Yeah. Sorry. I, uh, put it back together last night after you went to bed. It works fine. I guess it was just a flesh wound."

"Give it to me," Meena said, holding out her hand.

"No way." Jon cast another glance through the pass-through, into the living room. Wulf wasn't there, though. He was still in the other bathroom, showering. He'd left Jon in charge, with firm instructions not to allow Meena near any telephones, computers, or exit doors out of the apartment. "You're still all . . . infected and stuff."

"Jon," Meena said firmly. She looked better in the bright sunshine that streamed through the windows than she had the night before. She had makeup on, for one thing.

And she wasn't crying anymore. She actually seemed . . . well, *perky* was the only word Jon could think of to describe her. Even though he knew she hated that word. As usual, Jack Bauer was hanging around at her side, panting.

"Don't be an idiot," Meena said. "I'm not going to call him."

She didn't have to say who *he* was. They both knew.

The vampire.

"I just want to check my messages," she said.

Jon hesitated. She really did look a lot better. Maybe she was over the guy.

The truth was, if Jon found out some girl he'd been going out with was a vampire, he'd get over her pretty fast, too.

Unless she was Taylor Mackenzie, of course.

"Well," he said. He glanced down at the cell phone. It had been vibrating like crazy all morning. Someone was being pretty persistent, trying to get hold of her.

It could have been the vampire, he knew. If it was, he could give Meena the phone, then listen in on their conversation, find out where the guy was, then let Alaric Wulf know and help kill him.

Then for sure he'd get hired by this Palatine group, or whatever they were. He'd have a whole new career! And an awesome one, too.

On the other hand, there was the whole thing where Meena was pretty sure her new boyfriend was going to kill him.

So, that was a bit of a downer.

The phone buzzed in his hand as he was standing there, debating whether or not to give it to her.

"That could be Leisha," Meena said. "She could be in labor."

"She's not due for two months," he said.

"That's just the doctor's opinion," Meena said. "Not mine."

"And your medical expertise is widely known," Jon said.

"Actually," Meena said, "it is."

Jon looked down at the phone in his hand. "It says 'Unknown Number,'" he said.

"Leisha's probably calling from work," Meena said.

"On a Saturday," Jon said.

"She's a *hairstylist,*" Meena reminded him.

Jon rolled his eyes and handed her the phone. She obviously wasn't that worried about the prince of darkness killing him. So why should he be?

Meena pressed Accept Call. "Hello?"

"What is going on out here?" a deep voice thundered from the dining room.

Jon threw Meena a desperate look. Now she'd gotten him in trouble. This definitely wasn't going to look good on his Palatine Guard job application.

"Uh, nothing," Jon said, coming out of the kitchen with the plate of flapjacks. "It's just her best friend calling. She's having a baby. Seriously, dude, I checked. Pancakes?"

Alaric Wulf looked pissed off. His blond hair was still wet from the shower, and he'd left his shirt behind somewhere, showing off a truly impressive set of deltoids and pecs, not to mention some rock-hard abs that redefined the term *six-pack*. In fact, if Jon could have gotten some muscle definition like that, he had no doubt that Taylor Mackenzie would have been eating out of his hand months ago.

On the other hand, the dude had some wicked-looking scars that were making Jon think he might want to reconsider joining him in the vampire slayer thing. Was that a *bite* wound? It looked . . . well, *gnarly* was the only word Jon could think of to describe it.

Meena, in an act of bravery for which Jon decided he would admire her forever more, held up one finger in Wulf's direction in the international gesture for *I'll be with you in just a moment* while she nodded at whoever was calling her.

Apoplectic with anger, veins standing out on his neck and forehead, Alaric Wulf stood there glaring at Meena, completely ignoring Jon. He didn't even notice the nicely set table or the fact that Jon had made bacon. Real bacon! Not even turkey. He'd had to open the windows to let out some of the stink of the grease.

"Hang . . . up . . . the . . . phone," Wulf said.

Jon glanced over at Meena, who didn't even seem to notice Alaric. Her eyebrows were knit, and she was saying into the phone, "Wait, slow down . . . where exactly are you?"

Alaric Wulf crossed the room in three long strides. Jon thought he was going to rip his sister's head off.

But all he did was reach for the phone.

Meena, however, darted behind the armchair—moving as fast as Wulf had—and demanded tartly, "Do you mind? I'm on the phone. It's *important*."

Alaric Wulf finally glanced in Jon's direction, obviously looking for an explanation.

"Uh," Jon said, "yeah. Her best friend's pregnant, and she thinks . . . it's a long story. I swear it has nothing to do with vampires. Look, I made breakfast. Why don't we sit down and have some before it gets cold? Can I make you a coffee? It's easy with Meena's coffeemaker."

Alaric growled something. Jon couldn't tell what. He didn't look happy. He stood where he was, waiting for Meena to finish her call, his arms folded across his broad, scar-strewn chest.

"I understand," Meena was saying into the phone. "No, you did the right thing. Just stay where you are. We'll be right there to get you."

A look of complete disbelief spread over Alaric Wulf's face. Meena met his gaze and narrowed her eyes at him.

"Yes, I know exactly where you are," Meena said into the phone. "We'll find you. I promise. Give us half an hour. Good-bye."

She hung up.

"We have to go," she said. "We—"

Before she could get out another word, Wulf exploded. "You were with him last night," he erupted, pointing an accusing finger in Meena's direction. "He was here!"

Meena's jaw dropped. Hers wasn't the only one. Jon stared at the vampire hunter in astonishment.

"What are you talking about?" Jon asked. "We were here all night. And she never—"

"I'm talking about *this*."

Wulf strode forward and pulled at the little red scarf Meena had tied around her neck, the one that matched her red flats.

"Ow," Meena said, looking annoyed. "Choke people much? Really, your boss is okay with your treating people like this?"

Alaric, looking way more annoyed than she did, threw a bearlike arm around her waist to keep her from darting away again. Then, with his free hand, he plucked apart the knot holding the scarf in place.

When the scarf fell away and fluttered to the ground, Jon gaped at the now familiar circular mark he saw on his sister's long, slender throat.

He would have been willing to give her the benefit of the doubt—considering it was his sister, Meena, who hated vampires—if her cheeks hadn't been the same color as the scarf at her feet.

"Holy shit, Meena," Jon heard himself blurting. "What's wrong with you?"

"You don't understand," she said, giving Wulf a kick in the shin with her heel that caused him to release her with an *oof.*

But despite the outward appearance of rebelliousness, there were tears in her enormous brown eyes.

"He's not evil. He's as worried about the killings as you guys are," she insisted to Alaric. "I know what you think he is, but he's not. He's not like his father. I think you have the wrong man."

"How did he even get in here?" Jon asked Wulf, ignoring his sister, because it was obvious she was crazy. "We were watching the door the whole time."

"The *front* door," Alaric Wulf said grimly. He hadn't taken his gaze off Meena once. "We should have been watching the balcony door, too."

"The balcony door?" Jon's voice cracked. "We're eleven stories up. What'd the guy do, fly up?"

Both Meena and Wulf looked at him, Meena sadly, Wulf with sarcasm. Jon, realizing who he was talking about, swallowed.

"Oh," he said. Then he turned back toward his sister. "I thought you were so worried about him killing us," he cried. "And you just let him in?"

"She can't help it," Wulf said. He turned abruptly, heading back toward the bathroom, apparently in search of his shirt. "She's his minion. Whether we live or die means nothing to her. As long as *he* stays with her."

Jon shot his sister an accusing look. "Jesus Christ, Meena," he said. "You meet one vampire and your deep abiding loathing for monster misogyny goes right out the window, and you turn into one of *those* girls? I thought you hated that kind of girl."

Stung, Meena sucked in her breath. "I'm not," she cried. "I'm not one of those girls. I'm not a minion. I still hate vampires. Just not Lucien. Because he isn't like the others. And I care about both of you! Well," she added with a withering glance at Alaric's departing back, "one of you."

Wulf waved a hand dismissively behind his back as he strode down the hall toward Jon's bedroom.

"It's true." Meena turned her tear-filled eyes toward Jon. "You have to believe me. I'm not a minion. If you'd just leave Lucien alone, there'd be nothing to worry about."

Jon shook his head. "I don't know, Meen. Letting the prince of darkness into the apartment, when you said he was going to kill me? And then letting him bite you? *Again?* It's very minion-like behavior, if you ask me." He lowered his voice so Alaric couldn't overhear. "And it doesn't look very good for me, you know, with this job thing."

"*Job* thing?" Meena looked bewildered.

"You know," Jon said. "If I'm going to get a job with the Palatine. I can't have a sister who's sleeping with the enemy. You have to cut it out."

Comprehension dawned. Meena's expression became sarcastic. "Oh, sorry," she said. "I forgot this whole thing was all about employment opportunities for *you,* Mr. Can't Keep It in His Pants."

Jon's jaw dropped. "*One* time," he whispered, holding up an index finger. "And I told you, it was the middle of the night! I really had to pee! How was I supposed to know a cop was going to pull up right at that exact second, in front of that exact Subway shop?"

Wulf came back, buttoning his shirt. "How much did you tell him?" he asked.

"Who?" Meena asked, blinking up at him.

Wulf rolled his eyes. "The enemy of the light."

"I didn't tell him anything," Meena said. "And stop calling him that. He's not like that."

"She told him everything," Wulf said knowingly to Jon.

Jon raised his eyebrows. "She just said she didn't—"

"Your neighbors will be moving out." Wulf finished the last of his buttons. "I hope they didn't borrow your sugar bowl, because you're never going to see it again."

"I don't know why you won't listen to me," Meena said, glaring at him. "Lucien isn't like other, er, vampires you might know. He's kind and warmhearted and generous and was horribly abused by his father, who made him what he is. He didn't have any choice. It's his brother, Dimitri, you should be going after. Did you know he tried to kill us the other night? Or he sent a colony of bats to do it for him. He wants to destroy Lucien so *he* can be the prince of darkness, or whatever it's called. And if that happens, the world is *really* going to be in trouble."

Wulf looked over at Jon, his expression bored. "I'll take that coffee now."

"Oh, sure, coming right up," Jon said, hurrying to get him a cup.

"Suck-up," Meena said to her brother accusatorily. Then, following Alaric to the mirror by her dining room table, where he'd gone to make sure he hadn't missed any spots shaving, she said, "Lucien is the one who's making sure none of the Dracul and the rest of the vampires out there kill anymore. I mean, yes, they drink human blood . . . but only from willing donors."

"Try telling that to Caitlyn," Wulf said.

"Who's Caitlyn?" Meena asked blankly.

"My name for our killer's latest victim," Wulf said, sipping the coffee Jon had rushed over to deliver to him.

"Didn't you hear what I said?" Meena asked impatiently. "Lucien's trying to figure out who's killing those girls and stop him, just like you are. Why can't you judge him for what he *does,* not what he *is*?"

"What's that supposed to mean?" Wulf had pulled out a chair to sit down at the dining room table, reaching for a piece of Jon's bacon.

"I mean, you're judging Lucien just because of what he is, which, I'll admit, is a vampire," Meena said. "But he doesn't act like one."

"Doesn't he?" Wulf inquired, his gaze going pointedly to her neck.

Meena's face flushed red as her scarf.

"That's just . . . just—" she stammered. "We were just messing around."

"*You* might have been messing around," he said, picking up a knife and fork and beginning to eat the pancakes Jon had made. "But I can assure you, it wasn't 'messing around' to him. The fact is, if you let a vampire in one time, he'll never go away. They're like an unemployed, homeless relative."

"Hey," Jon protested.

"No offense," Wulf said, taking a bite of toast.

Meena looked down at his plate. "What are you doing?"

"What does it look like I'm doing?" Wulf asked. "I have a long day ahead of me, guarding you to make sure you don't do anything else stupid. I'm obviously going to need my strength. Because I have a feeling you're going to try to do many other very stupid things."

"We don't have time for that now," Meena said, sounding exasperated. "We have to go. Unless you're up for letting me out of the apartment on my own."

Wulf lifted a single blond eyebrow. "That's hardly likely. And just where do you need to go so urgently?" he asked.

"That was Yalena on the phone just now," Meena said, looking at Jon. "She finally got away from her boyfriend. I promised I'd go and get her."

Chapter Forty-five

12:00 P.M. EST, Saturday, April 17
Shenanigans
241 West Forty-second Street
New York, New York

Alaric didn't quite understand how he'd come to be sitting in a chain restaurant called Shenanigans in Times Square at noon on a Saturday.

But if he was ever asked to offer his idea of hell on earth, it would be Shenanigans.

"I'll have a large Diet Coke," Meena was telling the waitress from behind her nine-page-long—literally, it was nine pages long—menu.

The waitress, in her green polyester pants and visor, looked disapproving. This clearly was not a big enough order to satisfy her.

Or justify their taking up a booth in one of the window seats looking out over Times Square, so Meena could watch for the arrival of this Yalena person she kept insisting they had to save.

"What about some Taco Torpedoes?" the waitress suggested. "Or the Spicy Potato Stax are on special today, twelve for five ninety-nine."

"Just the Diet Coke," Meena said with a smile. She had her red scarf back on, set at a jaunty angle. It made her look like an American actress's idea of how a French girl would dress.

Kind of like this place was some soulless corporate conglomerate's idea of how a restaurant should be.

The waitress turned to Meena's brother, Jon.

"I'll take the Torpedoes and the Stax," he said. "And also the Paprika Curly Fries and the Sticky Wings and the Onion Brick."

Meena shook her head. "You suck," she said to her brother. "I hate you." Alaric had no idea what this exchange meant. Perhaps she resented her brother for his lack of caloric restraint?

Jon smiled at his sister. "Oh, and a Coke," he said to the waitress.

The waitress beamed at him approvingly, took his menu, and smiled down at Alaric. "And you?"

"Coffee," Alaric said, handing her back the menu. It was as heavy, he suspected, as the Onion Brick. "Black."

The waitress lost her smile. "Coming right up," she said, and disappeared.

"Tell me one more time," Alaric said, leaning his elbows against the sticky tabletop. "Who is Yalena?"

Meena glared at him. It was clear he wasn't her favorite person. "She's a girl I met on the subway," she said. "She's new to this country. I gave her my number and told her to call if she got into trouble, because I could tell her boyfriend was going to try to kill her."

"Unlike with us," Jon said bitterly, gesturing to himself and Alaric. "When Meena gets one of her visions about *her* boyfriend trying to kill someone, she just invites him in and sleeps with him and lets him bite her on the neck."

Now Meena was glaring at her brother. "Lucien is only going to kill you in self-defense. If you don't try to kill *him,* then he won't have a problem with you and so won't—"

"I want to go back to talking about the girl on the subway," Alaric interrupted, placing a thumb and forefinger on the bridge of his nose and closing his eyes. "I'm tired of hearing about how wonderful Lucien is. Also the two of you fighting all the time is giving me a migraine."

Spending the night on the couch hadn't helped, either.

Nor had the fact that he'd missed decapitating Lucien Antonescu so nearly. If Holtzman ever found out about that, he'd never hear the end of it back in the office.

"Oh," Jon said with a snort. "*Us* fighting? What about you two?

You two sound like an old married couple when you start in with each other."

Alaric opened one eye and eyed the younger man. "I have my sword with me, you know. I am perfectly willing to use it here at Shenanigans. I highly doubt anyone would notice, in fact."

The brother closed his mouth and picked up the glossy cocktail menu that sat at the end of the table with the ketchup bottle and other condiments, clearly sulking. He was upset, Alaric knew, because he wanted to be a member of the Palatine, and the slightest hint of criticism from Alaric marred his dream of future employment.

Alaric knew that sooner or later he was going to have to tell the brother that his dream was never going to happen in this lifetime. Primarily because it took years of training to achieve, and Jon was too old to start that training.

But also because Alaric found Jon, like his sister, annoying.

But in entirely different ways, of course. Alaric was not, for instance, sexually attracted to the brother, as he was to the sister. A fact about which he kept berating himself. How could he be attracted to a woman who was sleeping with the master of eternal darkness? She wasn't even that attractive! She kept her hair too short for his taste, and her front teeth were a little crooked.

Plus, she had an irritating habit of jiggling her foot. She was doing it now, under the table. He could feel her shoe brushing his leg. The contact was far too intimate, considering how she'd spent the evening—making love with Dracula's son under his very nose.

Meena went on as if her brother had never interrupted. "He—Gerald, the boyfriend—took away her passport and was holding her captive, making her . . ." She looked down and coughed. "Service other men. Yalena got away somehow and called me because mine was the only number she had. She's going to meet me here. Though what she'll do when she sees you two, I don't know." Meena glared at both her brother and Alaric darkly. "She doesn't exactly trust men right now."

"Well, I don't exactly trust you, either," Alaric said, still rubbing the bridge of his nose. "Especially *now*."

"Oh, right," Meena replied, her voice dripping with sarcasm. "Because it's so likely this is all just a ruse so I can run off with my vampire lover. Or tip him off about where to find you. Like I couldn't have done that last night, when you were watching movies in the room next door. We'll see how much you still think that when she comes in here, all beat up, terrified and alone."

Alaric dropped his hand and opened both eyes to stare at her. "You act like you've done this before."

Meena shrugged. "It's not totally uncommon. Unfortunately."

"I don't understand," the brother burst out. "Is my sister a vampire now or not?"

Both Alaric and Meena turned to look at him in astonishment.

"Well," Jon said, "it's the elephant in the room. She got bit *again*. Is she or isn't she? Do we have to stake her?"

"Oh, that's very nice, Jon," Meena said, still sarcastic. "Just talk about staking me in the middle of Shenanigans."

"I already told you." Alaric's headache was not improving. "He has to bite her three times, and then she needs to drink his blood to become a vampire. This is only the second time he's bitten her. Did you drink his blood, Meena?"

"No!" she cried, looking horrified. He felt her foot stop jiggling and come to rest against his leg. He didn't think she knew his leg was his leg and not part of the table.

He ought, he knew, to move his leg away.

And yet, he didn't. He didn't know why he didn't. This was the most disturbing thing of all.

All right. He did know why.

This was the most disturbing thing of all.

He ought to get out of this assignment as soon as possible. Possibly Holtzman was right, and he did need psychological counseling.

"And I'm not going to, either," she insisted. "I happen to enjoy things like sunshine and dining at Shenanigans. Even if it *is* owned by Consumer Dynamics Inc., which means it'll probably be showing up on an episode of *Insatiable* soon, considering the way things are going," she added darkly. "And would I really be sitting here in broad daylight if I were a vampire?" She looked up at the ceiling. "I cannot believe I'm actually having this conversation. In a *Shenanigans*."

The waitress appeared and slammed Alaric's and Meena's beverages down in front of them. For Jon she had a gracious smile.

"Your Taco Torpedoes and Spicy Potato Stax will be ready soon, sir," she said.

"Thank you," Jon said, smiling back at her.

At the table beside theirs, a man wearing a black leather jacket and a pair of pleated khaki pants chuckled as the cell phone at his belt suddenly squawked with static and a child's voice was broadcast, loudly enough to be heard over the entire second floor of the restaurant: "Daddy? Are you there?"

Khaki Pants smirked and pressed a button on the side of the cell phone/walkie-talkie device and shouted, "I'm here, munchkin! I'm in Times Square!" while the woman across the table from him—who had a pair of extremely large fake breasts on prominent display in a too-small crocheted shirt beneath her mink jacket—slurped a frozen daiquiri and typed into her own cell phone with a set of long, French-tipped nails.

Alaric threw the man a warning look. Khaki Pants pretended not to notice it.

This would soon become his misfortune, Alaric decided.

"There she is," Meena said, her foot going still again and her spine straightening like a pool cue.

Alaric turned in his seat to see a girl slinking into a chair at a table for two in one darkened corner of the restaurant, far from where the sunlight streamed through the plate-glass windows looking out over Times Square.

The girl wore a pair of enormous sunglasses, even though they were indoors, which might have been suspicious in and of itself. . . .

If it weren't for the ugly purple bruise he could see creeping out from beneath the lower frame of one side of the sunglasses, indicating she was suffering from a fresh, tender-looking black eye. She wore a gray hoodie pulled up over her head, with tufts of not very attractively cut blond hair sticking out from beneath it here and there.

The thing about her that struck Alaric most of all was the shoes she wore: white pumps with enormous plastic butterflies on the toes.

She glanced around furtively from beneath the sunglasses . . . until her gaze fell upon their table.

Then she looked away quickly and picked up one of the nine-page menus, behind which she hid her battered face.

"Good God," Alaric said, appalled. The victims he normally encountered had suffered their abuse at the hands of the undead. It seemed hard to believe the person who'd done this, at least according to Meena, had actually possessed a beating heart.

"Stay here," Meena said, and laid her napkin on the tabletop. "I'll be right back."

"I'm going with you," Alaric said, rising. He made it clear with his tone that this wasn't a request.

"Just stay where you are and let me handle this," Meena snapped. "You'll only scare her."

And then she was gone.

Alaric, astonished by this outburst—really, how could such a small person lose so much blood every night and remain so . . . . *forceful?*— watched as Meena scooted out from the booth and left the two men alone while she went to join Yalena, who looked up at her when she approached . . . and immediately burst into tears. Meena moved a chair over and slipped an arm around the younger girl's shoulders, murmuring to her soothingly.

"My sister can be a real bundle of fun, can't she?" her brother reflected as he poked the ice in his drink with his straw. "Hard to see what this prince guy sees in her."

Alaric grunted, neither agreeing nor disagreeing. The truth was, he was starting to form his own theories on that particular topic. . . .

"I mean, he could have anybody." Jon went on. "Taylor Mackenzie, for instance. Why would he want a pain in the ass like my sister?"

Why indeed? Alaric thought. "She met this woman on the subway?" he asked the brother, instead of responding to his question. "And told her she had a vision she would die?"

"No," Jon said, slurping his Coke. "Meena just told her to call if she got into trouble. Meena doesn't tell people they're going to die. Nobody ever believed her when she did that. So now she just gives them advice."

Alaric looked back at Meena. "And when they don't listen to the advice?"

Jon shrugged uncomfortably. "Well . . . then they die."

Alaric shook his head. It was bad enough he was in a Shenanigans in Times Square with a woman who was sleeping with the prince of darkness. And wouldn't stop doing it.

But now he was finding out that this woman might actually really be what she said she was . . . a psychic.

And if this was really true . . . then she might prove a valuable resource to his employer.

Yes. Why not? Meena Harper—not her brother—might be just the person the Palatine needed to help in their battle against the undead.

On the one hand, having someone around who could warn them when he and his fellow guards were about to walk into a deathtrap might come in handy.

On the other hand . . . Alaric wasn't sure how much time he actually wanted to spend with Meena Harper in the future.

"Daddy, guess what?" blared the cell phone on the hip of the man at the table beside Alaric's. "We're watching *Astro Boy*!"

"That's great, buddy!" Khaki Pants shouted into his cell phone.

Alaric balled a fist.

"Here you go," the waitress cried, arriving with a heaping tray of fried foods. "Your Taco Torpedoes and your Spicy Stax, curly fries, and Onion Brick—"

"What about my Sticky Wings?" Jon asked, looking worried.

"Right here," the woman said, laying several thousand calories in a basket before Meena's brother.

"Sweet," Jon said, and began digging in hungrily. They'd had to leave before he had time to finish breakfast due to Meena's insistence that they meet Yalena on time.

Alaric eyed the food on the table in front of him. It all looked amazingly . . . good. Particularly the Sticky Wings.

Jon, apparently noting Alaric's longing gaze, said, "Dig in. Seriously. You won't believe how good it is. And you better eat it before Meena gets back over here, because there won't be anything left when she's done with it. That's why she didn't order. She was trying to be health-conscious, but it never works. She's addicted to Shenanigans. She may look small, but you wouldn't believe how much food she can put away. You should see her secret candy drawer at work. It's truly disgusting."

Alaric studied the many baskets in front of him. Then he shrugged, lifted a wing, and bit into it.

The flavors that exploded into his mouth were like nothing he'd ever experienced. The foie gras at Per Se couldn't hold a candle to it.

Behind him, Khaki Pants's cell phone beeped loudly, then roared with static. Munchkin shouted, "Daddy, Daddy, Mommy wants to know when you're coming home!"

Alaric laid down his chicken bone. Every one of his muscles tensed for what he knew was coming next. He had no choice, really.

He was going to have to wipe the floor with Khaki Pants for disrupting his dining experience and that of everyone around him. It was, simply, bad manners.

Jon wiped his face with a napkin. "No," he said, holding up a hand. "Allow me."

Alaric watched skeptically as Jon rose, stepped over to the table beside theirs, and yanked the cell phone from the belt of Khaki Pants.

"Munchkin," Jon said into the cell phone. "Can you tell your mommy that your daddy can't talk now because he's having lunch with another woman? And that the other woman has really big boobies? Be sure to tell Mommy about the lady's boobies."

"Okay," said Munchkin excitedly into the phone.

"What the hell?" burst out Khaki Pants, standing up so quickly that his chair flipped over backward.

Alaric, picking up another chicken wing, chewed, enjoying the show. . . .

At least until he noticed a man wearing a hooded sweatshirt and a Yankees baseball cap pulled low over his eyes coming up the stairs, his gaze, behind a pair of mirrored sunglasses, fixed on Meena and Yalena.

Alaric laid down his chicken wing and reached for some napkins with which to wipe his fingers.

"Now, Phil," the woman with the mink jacket said. "Don't get excited. Remember your heart."

"Maybe you ought to take your calls outside," Jon said, handing Phil his cell phone. "It'll keep you out of trouble."

"Maybe I will," Phil said in a huff as static crackled on his phone and a woman's voice came on, squawking, "Phil? Phil? What's munchkin saying about you and some woman?"

Phil pushed a button and the woman's voice was abruptly cut off. He put the phone to his ear and said, "Aw, honey, never mind. It was just a joke. Some New York nut," as he moved swiftly toward the stairs . . .

. . . brushing shoulders with the man in the baseball cap and sunglasses, who was reaching for the inside pocket of his leather jacket with a gloved hand as he moved swiftly toward Meena and Yalena's table.

Alaric swore and slid from the booth while pulling out his sword at the same time.

Jon was sidling back into the booth opposite him, looking pleased with himself.

"See?" he said to Alaric. "Some situations you can solve without swinging a sword around . . . wait. What's happening? Where are you going?"

But Alaric had already launched himself over the woman in the mink coat—who'd stayed in her seat to finish her daiquiri and texts—pulling Señor Sticky from its scabbard as he dove. Over at Yalena's table, Gerald—because of course it was Yalena's boyfriend Gerald in the ball cap and hoodie; who else could it be?—had tugged something small and black from his leather jacket and was pressing it to Meena's back, speaking to her in a low voice, his sunglasses still shading his eyes beneath the baseball cap brim.

No one in the restaurant was paying the least bit of attention to them. All eyes were now on Alaric, the crazy man in the leather trench coat, doing gymnastic flips with a sword in his hand. Only Alaric saw Meena's spine go straight as a pool cue again, her eyes wide and frightened looking.

Meanwhile, across the table, Yalena didn't seem the least bit surprised. More like relieved it wasn't *her* rib cage the gun was pressed into this time.

At least, not until Alaric came crashing down beside them.

Then he got a reaction out of Yalena. Her mouth formed a perfect little O of surprise.

Which got even bigger when Alaric seized Gerald by the neck with one hand and brought the flat of his blade smartly down on Gerald's wrist with the other, causing him to drop the pistol in pain.

Alaric looked down at the .22 Ruger on the floor with a smirk.

"Planning on doing some target practice later?" he asked Gerald.

Gerald opened his mouth and let out a hiss, revealing a set of extremely pointed incisors . . . along with a curled, pointed tongue that darted in and out of his mouth like a snake. Meena, her eyes wide with horror, jumped from her chair and hugged the wall, knocking some Shenanigans memorabilia onto the floor.

"Oh, my God," she cried. "He's—"

"Yes, he is, isn't he," Alaric said calmly, still holding the vampire by the throat. "Do me a favor, will you? Reach into my coat."

Meena lifted a shaking hand, then plunged it into the deep pocket of Alaric's trench coat.

"Got it?" he asked as he felt her slim fingers close around what was at the bottom of his pocket.

"Got it," Meena said, pulling out a small crystal vial and studying it curiously. "What is it?"

"Holy water. I want you to throw it in his face now."

The vampire hissed with even more venom upon hearing this and clawed at Alaric's arm.

Meena looked from the vial to the vampire, her expression horrified.

"I can't do that," she said, shocked.

"Yes, you can, Meena," Alaric said. "He's not a man anymore. He's a monster. Look at him. And he just tried to shoot you."

"It's not that," Meena said.

"I don't want to upset everyone in this nice restaurant by cutting his head off," Alaric said. It was true. Everyone at the tables around them had lain down their Sticky Wings and was staring, clearly confused by what was going on. "But I need to subdue him somehow. So please do as I ask and throw some holy water in his face. It's really all right. He's already dead. So you won't be hurting him."

"No," Meena said, shaking her head. "I mean, I really can't do that. That's Stefan Dominic, the new star of *Insatiable*. I knew I'd seen him before somewhere. It was that picture Yalena showed me on her cell phone. *He's Gerald.*"

"Great," Alaric said, looking heavenward.

This was, without a doubt, the worst assignment he'd ever had.

Chapter Forty-six

E mil wasn't certain how to console his weeping wife. He had never seen Mary Lou quite this upset.

"It's probably only for a little while, darling," he said as she threw armfuls of designer clothing, most of it still on the hanger, into her hard-sided Louis Vuitton suitcases. Because it was the maid's day off, there was no one to pack for her.

"I love this apartment," she sobbed. "I don't want to go. And I'm going to miss all the sample sales!"

"We'll be back in no time," Emil said.

In no way did he believe this was true. But he said it to comfort her, since she was crying so violently.

"And there'll be lots of shopping in Tokyo," he pointed out.

"T-Tokyo!" Mary Lou echoed miserably. "What's there for me in Tokyo? Nothing!"

Exactly, Emil thought to himself. *No one for you to be hosting dinner parties for or sending e-mails to.*

But he didn't dare say any of this out loud.

"You'll love it," he said instead. "And I really don't think you need to bring so many dresses. We can pick up whatever you need when we get there." He added, a little hesitantly, since he didn't want to upset her further, "Do hurry, darling. I saw the vampire hunter leaving on the elevator with the Harper girl a little while ago. They'll be back shortly, I'm sure. I don't think we have much time."

"*Meena!*" Mary Lou snarled the name like it was a curse word. "After all I did for her! For *her* to be the one to turn on us!"

Emil looked furtively at his watch.

"I don't think she had much of a choice," he said. "And you were the one who set her up with the prince. I'm not sure what you thought would happen. It's never good to mix our kind with the humans."

Mary Lou had been trying to close her suitcase lid. It wouldn't shut. Emil wasn't sure if it was this fact or his remark that caused his wife to lose what was left of her patience and scream, "*I* was human when you met me! Remember? Are you saying *we* don't mix?"

"Not at all, darling," Emil said. He reached out, flipped back the suitcase lid, and began tucking in all the loose sleeves and fur cuffs that had been sticking out. "I'm just saying, pleased as the prince is with Miss Harper—and he seems to like her very much—it stands to reason that with all the attention the dead girls have been getting in the media, the Palatine would come sniffing around. And of course, that means they'd figure out where *we* are. And now . . . well."

Mary Lou, sniffling, slumped down onto the bed next to the suitcase, her normally perfect blond hair limp. Her eye makeup was smeared as well.

"If he's going to kill us, why doesn't he just come already, then?" she demanded. "I'd rather be staked than have to leave Manhattan!"

Emil thought this was a particularly dramatic sentiment but didn't say anything, since his wife was already so overwrought with emotion. He himself was feeling somewhat at loose ends from his very early morning encounter with the prince, who'd appeared unexpectedly on his terrace, then come strolling into his living room from the balcony doors.

"My lord!" Emil had cried. "Is everything all right?"

"No," Lucien said. His shirt had been unbuttoned to the waist, showing off his lean physique. Emil wished he'd been taken when he was in such prime condition and not, as had been the case, when he'd been so close to middle age. "There's a Palatine vampire hunter next door in Miss Harper's apartment."

Emil nearly dropped the glass of human blood he'd been drinking for breakfast.

"*What?*"

"Yes," the prince had replied grimly. "I would suggest you and Mary Lou find alternate lodgings immediately."

Emil hadn't been sure he'd heard the prince correctly.

"Sire? Wouldn't it . . . shouldn't we . . ." Emil was babbling, but honestly, what else was a man supposed to do in the face of such a pronouncement? "I mean, shouldn't we just . . . kill him?"

"I'm afraid we can't," Lucien said, sinking into one of Mary Lou's favorite overstuffed living room chairs. "Meena's psychic, you know."

This statement had completely perplexed Emil. "What?" he'd asked again. Rather stupidly, he supposed. A century younger than the prince—fortunately for him, from what he'd heard concerning the things Lucien had gone through at the hands of his newly turned father—he'd never quite gotten used to the fact that he was related to royalty and was never certain how to act around him.

"She can tell how everyone is going to die," Lucien explained. "Humans, anyway. And so can I, when I've drunk from her."

He didn't look very happy about it.

Suddenly, Emil understood what the prince had been doing all night.

How extraordinary. He'd never heard of a psychic before, not a real one. Not one who could give consistent predictions.

And for Lucien to be able to make predictions now too . . . of course it would be better if he could predict something more interesting than when a human was going to die . . . such as the score in sporting events.

The prince went on. "In any event, Meena's had a vision that I'm going to kill her brother and the slayer. Obviously, we can't have that."

Emil heard this last part with astonishment.

The prince *didn't* want to kill a member of the Palatine Guard who was threatening their well-being?

Emil understood that Lucien wanted to do things differently than his father had when he'd been the lord of darkness.

And it generally made good business sense, from a publicity stand-point, not to go around killing people for food—especially women and children—something Lord Dracula had seemed never to understand.

But when a papal society was intent on wiping out your entire species, it just didn't seem like a good idea to let them.

But Emil knew better than to argue with the prince. He valued his neck too much.

"Certainly, my lord," he said.

"But I can't have you and Mary Lou being put into danger, either." Lucien went on. "So you'll both need to pack up and go. I wouldn't suggest going to Sighişoara. I think they're probably onto all that by now."

Emil listened to all of this with growing horror. They were onto Sighişoara? He'd been living there under the very noses of the Palatine for centuries.

And now, because the prince had fallen for the girl next door—who was some kind of psychic freak—he had to abandon it forever? Instead of staying and fighting?

"All right, my lord," was all Emil said, however.

Because that was all he ever said.

But it wasn't what he *wanted* to say.

"And what about your brother?" he'd asked.

"What *about* my brother?" Lucien's tone had been sharp.

Perhaps, Emil had thought, he'd gone too far.

But Dimitri, surely, would want to stay and fight.

And this was going to cause a problem.

"Well . . ." Emil knew he was going to have to choose his next words with care. "I just thought that you might want to warn your brother that the Palatine is in town, so that he and your nephew can make their escape, as well."

"And I shall say something to my brother," the prince said. "When the time is right."

Emil thought he had seen which way the wind was blowing with *that* remark.

And that was when he decided that he had best do as the prince said and get Mary Lou out of town as soon as possible.

And not just because there was a Palatine guard staying next door, or because that Palatine guard was about to be used as a pawn in the ongoing vampire war between two brothers . . .

But because there was a glint in the prince's eye that Emil had never seen there before.

And Emil had a pretty good idea what—or, more accurately, who— had put that glint there.

He would never look at Meena Harper in the same way again. If he ever saw her again, that is.

Now he turned to his wife, who was piling shoes into another suitcase, and said, "Darling. Enough. They have shoes in Tokyo."

Mary Lou looked at him with streaming eyes. "But I've had some of these for over forty years! And you know they're in style again now."

"We'll be back for them, darling," he said, laying a gentle hand on her arm.

"Are you sure?" she asked with a sniffle.

Emil thought back to the steadfast expression he'd seen on the prince's face. He didn't know what Lucien had planned.

But he was certain the prince had a plan of some kind.

And it wasn't going to be pretty, for anyone who happened to be around, when that plan got under way.

"I'm quite sure," he said to his wife. "We have to go. I think there's a battle brewing."

"You said that already," Mary Lou said, sniffling. "The Palatine . . ."

"No," Emil said. "Between the prince and his brother."

"Well, of course there is," Mary Lou said bitterly. "They've hated each other for centuries. That's why I thought if the prince met a nice girl, he might mellow out a little. And I thought Meena would be perfect for him, because of that thing she does."

Emil stared at her. "What thing is that, dear?" he asked.

She couldn't, he told himself, know. How could she? *He* hadn't known until the prince had told him himself, that morning. And he knew everything that went on in their world. Didn't he?

"You know." Mary Lou waved a hand impatiently over her head.

"She predicts how people are going to die. I thought the prince might like it. It makes her different, you know, than other girls."

"You *knew* about this?" Emil asked with a feeling of growing horror. "You *knew* Meena Harper could do this when you asked her to dinner at our home . . . with the *prince*?"

"Of course I did." Mary Lou stared at him like he was an idiot. "I ride the elevator with her nearly every day. You think I don't know what's going on in that head of hers? Well, I'll admit . . . it's a little confusing in there. But that brother of hers, he's an open book. I just put two and two together. I'll admit, I was always a little tempted to take a bite myself, just to see what it would be like. But you always said not to eat where we live. But when I found out the prince was coming, I thought, *Wouldn't it be nice if* they *got together*? A girl who can tell when everyone is going to die, and your cousin, the prince of darkness, with everything *he* can do. Together . . . well, talk about a power couple! And then if he turned her . . . well, think about the possibilities!"

"Mary Lou," Emil said. He felt as if his entrails had turned to stone. "You haven't told anyone, have you? About Meena and her ability. And about her and the prince getting together. Tell me you haven't told anyone."

"Well, no," Mary Lou said, her eyelids fluttering. "I mean, no one who *matters*. Just Linda. And Faith. Well, and Carol, from your office. And Ashley. Oh, and Becca, of course."

"Oh, God," Emil said with a groan.

Then he reached for his cell phone.

Chapter Forty-seven

7:00 P.M. EST, Saturday, April 17
Shrine of St. Clare
154 Sullivan Street
New York, New York

Meena sat at the gleaming kitchen table across from Yalena, watching her as she lifted the mug of steaming cocoa to her lips with fingers that still shook hours after her rescue. Meena wasn't sure Yalena would ever stop shaking after everything she had been through.

"More hot milk for your cocoa, dear?" Sister Gertrude asked her, hovering nearby with a pitcher.

Yalena didn't respond. It wasn't clear if she didn't understand what the nun was saying or if she was deaf from all the blows she'd received at the hands of her captors.

Or maybe she was just in shock from everything that had happened.

Meena didn't blame her. *She* was still in a little bit of shock from the way Alaric had leapt across all those tables, single-handedly subdued Stefan, then assured all the stunned lunch patrons at Shenanigans that Stefan was a meth head and that Alaric was an undercover cop who was putting him under arrest.

Meena was pretty sure if she'd been sitting there, eating Sticky Wings at Shenanigans, she'd never have believed it.

But everyone—even the waitstaff and manager, who'd offered all the customers free Onion Bricks for their inconvenience—seemed fine with it.

It wasn't until they'd started down Shenanigans' back staircase to grab a cab to St. Clare's—where, Alaric had insisted, they'd get help for Yalena and "the rest of this straightened out"—that they'd discovered two more "vamps" (as Alaric called them) waiting in the shadows at the bottom of the stairs.

They'd fled upon seeing Alaric holding Stefan at sword-point, tearing through the restaurant's kitchens and out a back door to a Town Car waiting in a darkened alley. The car, its windows tinted almost black, took off with a squeal of brakes . . . or so Jon, who'd chased after the vampires, reported. Apparently they'd been expecting only Meena, Yalena, and of course Stefan . . . not Meena, Yalena, Stefan, Meena's brother, and a hulking demon hunter from the Palatine Guard.

First Meena's boyfriend. Then her next-door neighbors. Now one of the actors on the show on which she worked.

Was *everyone* she knew going to turn out to be a vampire?

Meena had known Stefan Dominic looked familiar. She just hadn't been able to place him back at the studio. But why had Stefan—who'd turned out to be *Gerald,* of all people—tried to kidnap her?

Alaric was in another part of St. Clare's, applying holy water to different parts of Stefan Dominic's body, trying to discover the answer to that very question.

From where she sat, in the rectory kitchen, Meena could barely hear the vampire's screams.

"There you go," Sister Gertrude said soothingly, pouring more milk into Yalena's mug, even though the girl hadn't indicated she wanted more. Then the nun bent down to straighten the downy comforter she'd draped around Yalena's shoulders. "Nice and hot. Good for the body. Good for the soul."

Yalena didn't know how lucky she was to still *have* a soul.

Or maybe she did. Meena wasn't sure what the girl knew.

One thing *Meena* knew:

The way Alaric had saved Meena—and Yalena—at Shenanigans had softened her attitude toward him. There was something to be said for someone who would leap over several restaurant tables to wrap his bare hand around the throat of a vampire who was trying to kidnap you.

"Does this happen often?" she asked Abraham Holtzman, pointing in the direction from which the faint sounds of Stefan Dominic's screams could be heard. Abraham had introduced himself to Meena and Jon as Alaric Wulf's boss . He was currently pacing nervously up and down the kitchen, occasionally bumping into Sister Gertrude and saying, *Oh, I beg your pardon, Sister.*

"Good heavens, no," he said, coming to a halt in the middle of his path across the kitchen. He looked horrified. "We don't condone this sort of thing under normal circumstances. Alaric has his own methods, of course, and, well, though I can't say I actually *approve* of them, they have been shown over time to have surprising effectiveness—"

Meena held up a hand to stop him. "Say no more," she said drily. "I get the picture."

It did bother her a little, however, that her brother had volunteered so cavalierly to "help" Alaric, and several of the Franciscan friars who lived in the rectory, torture Stefan.

"Miss Harper," Abraham Holtzman said, looking slightly disturbed, "I can tell by your tone that you may not be particularly fond of Guardsman Wulf—and, by extension, the Palatine—which, for a woman in your current circumstances, is perfectly understandable."

Meena felt herself blushing. She was aware that Alaric had told his boss what her "current circumstances" were—that she was sleeping with the prince of darkness—and she was thoroughly mortified. That this total stranger (who was old enough to be her father) knew the most intimate details of her life was *not* okay.

Did Sister Gertrude know, too? Meena darted a nervous look in the older woman's direction, but she was serenely trying to get Yalena to eat a fresh-baked chocolate chip cookie from the batch she'd just pulled from the oven. (Meena had been shoveling Sister Gertrude's cookies into her mouth nonstop since the nun had led them back into the rectory's kitchen from the cab they'd all come tumbling out of—Alaric had kept Stefan Dominic smothered under his own black leather trench coat in order to protect him from the sun, and at sword-point, the entire ride downtown . . . much to the bemusement of their cabbie.)

Abraham Holtzman went on. "Whatever impression Guardsman Wulf might have given you, and I don't doubt it's been a colorful one, you should know that he's one of our most highly skilled officers. He garners more kills every year than the average guard accumulates in an entire career. That he manages to do so with zero loss of civilian life is a truly unheard-of accomplishment in our line of work." Abraham looked thoughtful. "He has a grating personal manner. I'll give you that. But considering his background, it's only to be expected."

Meena raised her eyebrows. "His background?" she asked.

"Well, the fact that he's . . ." Abraham looked uncomfortably at Sister Gertrude and Yalena and whispered, "A *bastard*."

Meena had to suppress a smile.

"In America we call that being raised by a single mom," she whispered back. "And it's actually not that big a deal. It happens to a lot of people."

"Oh, but he wasn't," Abraham said. "His mother was a drug addict who abandoned him. He grew up on the streets until he was put into a youth home, which is where the Palatine found him. Now what is this about you being some kind of psychic?" Abraham asked, before Meena had time to get over her surprise at hearing this about a man who seemed to go about life with such a chip on his shoulder. "This is very unlikely, isn't it? Perhaps Alaric misunderstood. He often does. His people skills leave much to be desired . . . understandably."

Meena bristled. What was up with men who worked for the Palatine Guard? Were they *all* completely arrogant?

"Yes," she said. "That's right. He misunderstood."

"I thought so." Abraham looked out the rectory windows and then at his watch. "The sun is starting to set. Sister, I think we'd better move Miss Yalena to a room without windows."

"That's a good idea," Sister Gertrude said. She laid gentle hands on Yalena's shoulders. "Come along, dear."

"Wait," Meena said as Yalena rose—like an obedient child—and allowed the nun to begin steering her from the room. "I don't understand. A room without windows? What do you think is going to happen when the sun sets?"

"Well," Abraham said, looking a bit uncomfortable, "I think it's very likely that after darkness falls, the Dracul will come here looking for you, Miss Harper."

"*Me?*" Meena blurted. She stared at him. "What would the Dracul want with *me?*"

"Well, that's the million-dollar question, isn't it?" Abraham said with the same sort of eagerness any other type of academic might show. He just happened to be an expert on demonology. "But there's a reason that vampire downstairs went to such elaborate lengths to stage an abduction of you during daylight hours. Very risky. He could easily have been fried alive. Someone wants you, Miss Harper, very much. Whether it's the dark lord or someone else . . ."

Meena opened her mouth to say that it was ridiculous to suggest that *Lucien* was behind the kidnapping attempt on her. True, she did remember exacting a promise from him, right before falling asleep in his arms at dawn, that he would go away and never come back . . . otherwise he was going to kill her brother and Alaric.

But kidnap her against her will so that they could be together? Never. Lucien loved her, and she him. He would *never* have sent anyone to do such a thing to her. He'd have kidnapped her himself.

Wait. No, he wouldn't.

Would he?

Abraham Holtzman, however, didn't give her the chance to say a word.

"The best thing we can do right now is batten down the hatches, as they say, and prepare for a long night. You and I can defend ourselves, of course, but this young lady here . . ." He sent a compassionate glance in Yalena's direction; she still stood in the doorway, Sister Gertrude's arm around her. "Well, she's best off safely tucked in bed, I think."

Sister Gertrude nodded, not seeming at all ruffled at the suggestion that her church might come under vampire attack now that it was getting dark out.

"I'll put some garlic on her door, for good measure," the nun said with a hearty nod.

"Excellent idea," Abraham Holtzman said. "The oldies are still the goodies."

"And I've got my Beretta semiautomatic," Sister Gertrude added cheerfully, patting her habit, "right here with the silver bullets. That ought to take out a few of those dirtbags."

Meena's eyes widened. No wonder she had such a bad feeling about all this.

These people were completely nuts.

Yalena surprised everyone by opening her mouth and trying to speak. "I—" Her blue-eyed gaze was fixed on Meena. Yalena stood in the doorway, wrapped in the absurdly huge comforter, with the stout little nun's arm around her.

"I—sorry," Yalena finally managed to say, a tear escaping from one swollen eyelid and trickling slowly down her bruised cheek. "I not want to call you, Meena. I not want to g-get you in trouble like I in trouble. But he find the card you give me. Right away, he find it. And today, for some reason, they make me call you. They say they do to me what they do to . . . the other girls if I don't. I so sorry!"

She flung both her trembling hands over her face and burst into sobs. Sister Gertrude tsk-tsked with her tongue and hugged Yalena's slight form fiercely to her bosom.

"There, there, dear," Sister Gertrude said. "They're nasty, nasty creatures. You mustn't blame yourself. You didn't know."

"I not know," Yalena sobbed into Sister Gertrude's habit. "I not know!"

Meena got up from the kitchen table and went to lay a hand on Yalena's slender back, her heart twisting for the girl.

"It's all right, Yalena," she said. "It was good that you called me. I told you to, remember? I said I'd help you, and I did." Well, technically, Alaric had. But she was the one who'd brought Alaric and his sword arm along. "But," Meena added, "I need to know . . . what other girls?"

Yalena lifted her bruised, tear-stained face from Sister Gertrude's shoulder and said, sniffling, "For the bankers. Gerald, he not a manager for actresses." Yalena looked infinitely sad. "He only wants girls to feed to the bankers."

"To *feed* to the bankers?" Meena shook her head, completely confused . . . and horrified. "Yalena, what are you talking about?"

"The bankers," Yalena said. Her eyes were wide with terror. "That they make into the vampires."

Chapter Forty-eight

Oh, my God," Meena said after Sister Gertrude had taken Yalena—sobbing too incoherently to get any more sense out of her—off to bed.

"What?" Abraham Holtzman looked down at her distractedly. "Oh, right. Sister Gertrude. Yes, she's quite an amazing woman. St. Clare, who was a contemporary of St. Francis of Assisi, founded her own order just for women, the Poor Clares. Oh—and this might be of particular interest to you, Miss Harper—St. Clare is also the patron saint of television, due to the fact that she—"

"Please," Meena said, trying not to sound impolite. "I didn't mean Sister Gertrude. I meant . . . ."

Before Meena had a chance to go on, heavy footsteps sounded in the corridor outside the kitchen. Then the swinging door burst open to reveal Alaric Wulf, a swathe of his blond hair falling over one eye.

"Is . . . is he dead?" Meena asked hesitantly. She was torn between hoping they'd killed Stefan, who'd done such terrible things to Yalena, and being horrified at herself for wishing anyone dead, even a vampire.

"Just taking a break," Alaric said. He stalked straight to the rectory's industrial-sized fridge. "I'm thirsty."

Meena stared at him as he reached for the milk, then straightened and began chugging the contents directly from the bottle, without bothering to pour it into a glass first.

Well, she supposed killing vampires *was* his job, after all. It wasn't any wonder he treated it somewhat . . . cavalierly.

And now that his boss had explained about his childhood, Meena thought she understood Alaric Wulf's lack of interpersonal skills and manners as well.

"What did he say?" Abraham Holtzman asked his fellow guardsman eagerly. "Did he talk, Wulf?"

Alaric's small mouth twisted with bitter humor. "That's a good one, Holtzman. You're filled with jocularity tonight, I see."

"Listen," Meena said, glancing back and forth between the two men. "I, uh, really appreciate everything you've done for me. Honestly, I do. But if it's all the same to you, I'm tired after a really exhausting day, and I'd really like to go now. Plus"—her eyes flashed with defiance, even though Alaric was only regarding her mildly over the milk bottle, not challenging her in any way—"and I know what you're going to say to this, so I don't even know why I'm bothering, but here goes: I really think if I could just *talk* to Lucien, on the phone, we could clear a lot of this up. Just let me call him. Some of the stuff Yalena said . . . I don't think he knows about it. And . . . well . . ." She added the last part in a rush: "Jack Bauer needs to be walked."

Still holding the milk in one hand, Alaric's glance shifted toward the windows and the growing darkness beyond them. Meena could think of only one way to describe his expression as she mentioned her dog:

He looked as if someone had kicked him in the gut.

To her surprise, he didn't mention anything about what she'd said concerning Lucien. He only murmured, as if speaking to himself, his gaze shifting away from the darkening windows, "The dog. I forgot about the dog."

"What?" Meena looked from Alaric to the windows to Abraham Holtzman, who'd also gone pale. She didn't need to be psychic to know that the tension in the room had gone up about ten notches.

"What do you mean, you forgot about the dog?" she asked. "Why do you have that look on your face?"

Before either man could respond, the swinging door to the kitchen burst open again, and her brother came in. He, however, didn't possess anything like Alaric Wulf's swagger. He was shuffling like an old man, his shoulders slumped, his expression dazed. He seemed to look straight through Meena. In fact, she wasn't sure he was even aware of her presence until he mumbled, when he came alongside her, "Meen . . . you should have been there. It . . . it was unreal."

That's when she realized he meant what had been going on in the rectory basement . . . from which she hadn't heard any screaming in a while, which was why she'd asked if Stefan was dead.

"I don't want to hear about it," she said firmly. She didn't approve of torture—not even of a vampire who'd mercilessly beaten a young girl, then forced her to call Meena to set up a fake meeting so he could attempt to kidnap her.

Killing that vampire outright? That, Meena wasn't sure she had a problem with . . . especially since the entire cab ride down to St. Clare's, Stefan Dominic had done nothing but hiss invective at her from beneath Alaric's leather trench, calling her the devil's whore and any number of other equally vile names, even though Alaric Wulf had threatened to lift the coat and let him fry to death in the sunlight streaming through the cab's windows.

But then . . . there was always a chance that, with rehabilitation—and maybe even Shoshona's love—Stefan Dominic might be able to change his evil ways. Why not?

Lucien had.

And *he* was the prince of darkness, supposedly the most evil of all the demons against whom the Palatine Guard was sworn to do battle.

So if they killed him, they'd be killing any chance at helping Stefan Dominic to become a better, kinder vampire . . . like Lucien.

"Are you going to kill him?" she asked nervously.

"I wish I could," Alaric said, looking wistful.

"Of course not, Miss Harper." Abraham Holtzman pulled a manual from the pocket of his corduroy jacket and began to thumb through it. "According to the *Palatine Guard Human Resources Handbook*," he said when he came to the page he wanted, "it is unethical to kill any demonic entity while he is our prisoner and helpless under our power. He will, of course, be tried by a Palatine officer for his crimes and properly executed if found guilty."

Meena looked over at Alaric. "Then I don't get exactly what you people do all day. I thought you hunted down demons and killed them. You never mentioned anything about a trial."

"Oh, there's always a trial," Alaric assured her, pausing with the milk bottle halfway to his lips. "I find demons very trying. That's why I always kill them whenever I find them."

Meena glanced at Abraham Holtzman, who explained quickly, "In the heat of battle, if a demon tries to kill one of our hunters, of course it's permissible for them to defend themselves."

"Well, did either of you find out what's going on?" she asked Alaric and Jon impatiently. She didn't want a lecture from the *Palatine Guard Human Resources Handbook*. And she could tell from Alaric's pained expression that he wasn't enjoying it much, either.

"He didn't say *anything*," Jon said. "And we poured that holy water on his—"

"I said don't want to know," Meena said, giving him her outstretched palm. *Stop.*

Jon didn't pay any attention, however. "They have these super healing powers, you know? It's really amazing, Meen. As soon as you do anything to them, they heal right back up, as long as you don't stake them in the heart or cut off their heads. They barely even feel it. Except for maybe a few seconds. So you don't need to worry about it. Stefan Dominic's face will be fine in time for filming. Right, Alaric?"

Alaric shrugged his heavy shoulders, clearly not wanting to be a part of this conversation, and turned his attention back to his milk bottle and a Pious League calendar on the rectory kitchen wall.

Jon continued. "Although you might want to warn Fran and Stan that they've hired a *real* vampire." He seemed to have recovered enough from whatever had gone on downstairs to give a sarcastic laugh. "Taylor might have a problem getting all up-close-and-personal with a walk-

ing corpse. But what do I know? I'm just an unemployed systems analyst—"

"What," Meena interrupted, "did you mean when you said you
forgot about my dog, Alaric?"

Alaric took his time turning away from the wall calendar and
opening the refrigerator to put the half-drunk milk bottle back where
he'd found it. She noticed that he was careful not to glance in Meena's
direction.

"Tell her, Holtzman," he said after he'd straightened.

Meena felt something cold trickle down her back. She didn't like
Alaric Wulf's tone. She couldn't describe it, but she didn't like it.

"Now, Alaric," Abraham said. "Let's not jump to rash conclusions."

Alaric's voice lashed like a whip. "When the facts are staring us in
the face?"

"It's too soon," Abraham said, "to be sure of anything without
proper—"

"Why," Alaric demanded, "would vampires attack Meena
Harper?"

Only then did his gaze shift toward her—and when it did, she was
struck, once again, by how piercing and bright blue his pupils were . . .
the color of the sky. The color of the ocean.

The color of a blue flame.

The cold trickle of fear Meena had felt down her spine turned to a
gush.

"She should be the safest woman in all of this city," Alaric said. "She's
the chosen one. The lover of the prince of darkness. No one should dare
to lay a finger on her, to touch her, for fear of his wrath. What happened
today should never have happened in a million years. And yet . . . it did
happen. I've gone over and over it in my head. Why? And I think there
is only one answer."

Abraham Holtzman made a sound. It was a whimper of protest.

Both Meena and Jon whipped their heads around to look at him.

He'd lowered the *Palatine Guard Human Resources Handbook* to stare
at Alaric.

"No, Wulf," Abraham said. "It isn't possible."

"Isn't it?" Alaric asked. "What other explanation is there, then?"

"The obvious one," Abraham said. "If it wasn't the prince himself, then a few of the Dracul have gone rogue. It happens, you know, from time to time. Like when you and Martin were attacked in that warehouse—"

"Then why is he so afraid to tell us?" Alaric demanded sharply.

Meena jumped at the curtness of his tone.

Whatever it was they were talking about, Alaric believed in what he was saying.

And he believed in it passionately enough that he wanted to disabuse his boss of any other notion he might be harboring.

"If he isn't answering to a higher authority, why was he so afraid to open his mouth and give us the name of whoever told him to put that gun in Meena's back?" Alaric thundered, his voice so loud, Meena almost imagined the pots hanging above the stove had tinkled slightly. "Tell me that, Holtzman. I used everything I had on that boy down there, and I got nothing. Nothing! It's happening, Holtzman. You might as well admit it."

Meena glanced quickly at Abraham to see how he took this news. He looked ashen faced.

The chill of fear along her spine went glacial.

"Oh, dear," the older man said. "I suppose . . . I suppose in that case, I'd better call the office."

"What are you both *talking* about?" Meena demanded. The glacier creeping up her spine had turned into a polar ice cap. "And what does any of this have to do with my going back to my apartment to walk my dog?"

Alaric blinked at her as if only just realizing she was still standing there.

"You?" he said. "You're never going back to that apartment again."

Chapter Forty-nine

8:00 P.M. EST, Saturday, April 17
Shrine of St. Clare
154 Sullivan Street
New York, New York

"W hat?" Meena cried. The single word ricocheted around the highly polished kitchen like a bullet.

"Hey." Jon held up a hand. "Let's not get ahead of ourselves. I mean, I think we should be able to decide for ourselves if we want to risk—"

"You want to decide for yourselves? Fine."

Alaric opened his jacket pocket and pulled out the photo of his partner, the one who was missing half his face, holding it out for all of them to see.

"Remember this?" he asked brutally. "*This* is what's going to happen to you if you go back to that apartment. Because they're going to be there waiting for you. And this is probably the *least* they're going to do to you."

"What?" Meena cried again, though more softly this time. "But . . . why?"

"War," Abraham Holtzman explained. "Alaric thinks we've stumbled into the middle of a vampire war. And I'm sorry to say that, given the evidence, I have to agree with him."

"A . . . vampire *war*?" Meena looked from one man to the other. She remembered Lucien's strange reaction to those very words when she'd said them herself on the countess's balcony a few nights earlier.

"That's right," Alaric said. He, unlike his boss, didn't attempt to soften his tone. There was no sugarcoating anything where Alaric Wulf was concerned. He added matter-of-factly, "And you, Meena Harper, are the flag everybody wants to capture. That's why you can never go back to your apartment."

Meena, her knees suddenly turning to water, fumbled her way toward a nearby chair.

"But . . . ," she said. "War? With who? Between who?" Then she added, "And what about Jack? My dog is in that apartment. What's going to happen to my dog?"

She knew it made no sense to be worrying about her dog. He was, after all, only a dog.

But he was all she had.

She thought she saw Alaric Wulf fling another glance at the kitchen window. Then he frowned.

What was going on with the windows? Why was everyone so obsessed with windows?

"Wait," Jon was saying. "Vampire war? Excuse me? What is all this about, exactly? And what does it have to do with my sister?"

Abraham Holtzman explained patiently. "Alaric's talking about a battle for the throne of the prince of darkness. When Dracula originally made his pact with the dark forces in order to attain life eternal in exchange for his immortal soul, he was anointed as the unholy one, the heir to the Dark Lord, the overseer of all of Satan's dealings on earth, or the mortal plane. When we dispatched Dracula, that mantle passed to his eldest son, Prince Lucien, your sister's lover."

Meena winced at the words *your sister's lover*.

"There *is* reason to believe that Lucien Dracula is a bit of an anomaly in the vampire world," Abraham went on, flipping to a well-thumbed page of the *Palatine Guard Human Resources Handbook*. "His mother, as you might know, was rumored to be an angelic creature, and some say that might possibly have—"

"Holtzman," Alaric interrupted. When Abraham looked up, he pointed at the windows. "Speed it up."

"Oh, right, right," Abraham said, closing the book, to the relief of everyone. "Well, in any case, Lucien has a half brother—"

"Dimitri," Meena said faintly. Noticing the curious glance Abraham threw her, she said, through numb lips, "Lucien told me. He doesn't like his brother very much. Or trust him."

"Yes, well, with good reason, I would say," Abraham said, nodding. "Nasty piece of work, Dimitri Antonescu, as I suppose he's calling himself now. Different mother entirely. Ambitious, grasping woman. And the son's the same, from what I've gathered. Murdered his own wife. Never been happy that the throne went to his elder brother. Never agreed with the way Lucien has been running things since their father died. Wants to take over the whole operation himself. . . ."

Jon blinked. "You think *Dimitri's* the one who—"

"Sent Stefan Dominic to try to capture your sister to use her to convince Lucien to give up the throne, or at least do something stupid so Dimitri could trap and kill him and then take over the throne? Yes," Alaric said succinctly. "That's exactly what he's saying."

"He probably found out somehow that his brother was, er, seeing you, Miss Harper," Abraham said. Meena appreciated the chivalrous delicacy with which he put it. "And that you had some connection with Yalena—"

"I gave her my business card," Meena murmured, still feeling dazed by the discovery that sleeping with Lucien Antonescu had caused her to lose her beloved dog, her apartment, and probably, since the Dracul seemed to know everything else about her, her job. . . .

Her entire life, basically.

But what about Lucien? Where was he? Did he know about any of this? Was he safe? If only they'd let her call him!

"Yes, yes, of course," Abraham was saying, excited. "They probably found her card in Yalena's things and later made the connection. Goodness. They get smarter all the time, don't they, Alaric?"

"They can read minds," Meena said, feeling sick to her stomach. "When I saw Stefan at work yesterday . . . I didn't recognize him from the picture Yalena showed me on her cell, but I knew . . . *something.* He must have sensed it . . . and my connection to Lucien. . . ."

She groaned and dropped her face into her hands. All of this was her fault. Her own fault, for being so stupid.

"Oh, well, there you go," Abraham said almost cheerfully. "That explains everything. So he must have gone to Dimitri—"

Jon interrupted. "I rode down in the elevator with that Stefan guy and his agent, or whatever he was. His name was Dimitri."

There was stunned silence for a few seconds after this. Then Alaric said slowly, "You took an elevator ride with one of the most depraved vampires in the history of time. Dimitri Antonescu—or Dracula—is widely known to be second only to his father in cruelty, perversion, and all-around moral debauchery. You're lucky to be alive."

Now it was Jon's turn to sink down into one of the kitchen chairs. "Shit," he said, his face having gone as pale as his shirt.

Meena couldn't blame him. She knew exactly how he felt.

Although not when he asked, "What about our stuff? Up in the apartment? What are we supposed to do about that, apply for FEMA aid? I doubt they're going to believe us when we say we lost a whole apartment to a bunch of warring vampires."

"Jon!" Meena cried, appalled.

"Well," Jon said, blinking at her, "we're about to lose everything we own, for Christ's sake. Think about your new tote bag. That thing was worth a couple grand, at least."

At Jon's mention of the tote bag Lucien had given her, Meena felt something erupt within her.

"This is ridiculous," she cried, leaping to her feet, though her knees were shaking. She found that she was mainly yelling at Alaric, who leaned against the kitchen counter, his arms folded across his broad chest, staring at her, his already small mouth shrunk to the size of a grape. "You *have* to let me go home!" This wasn't about a tote bag, of course. She didn't care anymore about the tote bag. This was about so much more. "Or at least let me call Lucien. He can stop this. He really can."

"But we don't want to stop it," Alaric said simply.

"*What?*" This was the craziest thing Meena had heard all day. "Why not?"

"It's Palatine policy," Abraham Holtzman explained earnestly, "to let warring vampire clans wipe each other out. So long as civilians are protected."

It took a moment for the full significance of this statement to sink in . . . but when it did, it was like a fist to the face.

So they expected her just to let Lucien be attacked by his brother and the Dracul? For her not to lift a finger to try to warn him or help?

Of course they did. They didn't care about him. Or think of him as anything but what he was:

The prince of darkness.

"So if Lucien," she said faintly, "goes to the apartment, looking for me . . ."

"That's exactly what they're hoping he'll do," Alaric said. "He's who they'll be there waiting for."

Tears filled her eyes. Alaric didn't lower his gaze from hers.

"Oh, that's just great," Meena said. Her voice was shaking as badly as her knees now. "Let the vampires wipe themselves out. But obviously no one cares what happens to my dog!"

It was as she said the word *dog* that a projectile burst through the kitchen windows, shattering glass everywhere.

Something heavy and hard hit Meena in the midsection, sending her flying to the floor. She realized belatedly that it was Alaric Wulf. He'd tackled her almost the same way only the night before.

But this time it wasn't to keep her from running away from him. It was to shield her from the flames of the Molotov cocktail that had burst against the wall.

"Are you all right?" he lifted his head to ask her, his face just inches from hers.

The impact of his body weight slamming her into the floor had completely winded her. She knew she'd be sore tomorrow, but she was otherwise unharmed. She nodded, then gasped, "Jon?"

"I'm all right!"

Peeking around Alaric's broad shoulder, she saw an arm waving out from beneath the kitchen table.

"I'm good," Jon cried. "But there's glass everywhere. And the wall is on fire."

"Everyone take cover!" Abraham had rushed to fill a pitcher at the kitchen sink to douse the flames. "Stay away from the windows. It's starting."

The swinging door burst open, and a man in a clerical collar called, "Is everyone all right? We thought we heard—oh, dear."

"Yes, yes," Abraham said. "They seem to have followed Alaric from uptown, as we feared. We need to go make sure Father Joseph has closed the chapel for the night. Evening prayer's going to have to be canceled. We can't have any civilians on the property. I suggested they put signs up saying there's been a small flood from a broken water pipe. Jon, go see how Father Bernard is doing making stakes out of last year's manger—"

"On it." Jon wiggled out from beneath the table just as Alaric lifted himself off Meena and offered a hand to help pull her up from the floor.

She took it, casting a quick glance over her shoulder at the smoldering kitchen wall as she followed Alaric out into the hallway. Nuns and friars—St. Clare's was staffed by Franciscan friars and Poor Clare sisters, the rectory behind the church with the convent just next door to it—were scrambling to get to their battle stations. Meena had never seen so many crucifixes in her life.

"Alaric," she said breathlessly, trotting after him. "*Please* just let me call Lucien. I have to talk to him right now. He'll stop them. He's their prince. They'll listen to him."

Alaric let out a grim chuckle, apparently at Meena's naïveté. "Haven't you been listening? No, they won't. Not if they've launched an all-out rebellion against him. Which, trust me, they have. In fact, now that I think about it, that's what the bodies of those dead girls were probably all about in the first place."

"What do you mean?" she demanded.

"Bait," Alaric said enigmatically.

Meena shook her head. Really, he was so frustrating sometimes. "I don't know what you're talking about. Yalena said something about bankers—"

"Bankers?" Alaric kept striding through the rectory, dodging nuns with crossbows.

"Alaric," Meena said, shaking her head. "Where are you *going*?"

This question was seconded by an all-too-familiar voice behind them.

"Wulf!" Abraham Holtzman yelled. "Where do you think you're going?"

Alaric froze, causing Meena to ram into him.

Slowly, he turned in the hallway to face his boss, who was leaning out of a doorway.

"I'm going," Alaric said with deliberation, "to get the dog."

"Dog?" Meena turned her head sharply to look up at him. "But—"

Abraham Holtzman cut her off, annoyed. "You can't be serious, Wulf. We're in the middle of a battle zone here. We need you! Besides, it's a fool's mission. You'll be walking into a trap."

"I'm used to that," Alaric said. "And you have more trained fighters here than you need. Sister Gertrude could kill a Dracul with her eyes closed. Father Bernard took out a half dozen after last year's Christmas pageant with the angel off the top of the tree."

"That's not the point, Wulf," Abraham hissed, lowering his voice when one of the novices tittered upon overhearing this. "Don't go playing the hero just to impress the girl."

Meena, realizing she was the girl he was referring to, wanted to point out how badly Abraham was misjudging the situation. Alaric Wulf hated her.

"You'll only end up getting yourself killed." Abraham went on. "And we actually need you *here,* in case you didn't notice."

"I'll be back with the dog in less than an hour," was all Alaric said, and then he disappeared through yet another swinging door.

"Stubborn fool." Abraham rolled his eyes and disappeared through his own doorway.

Meena, looking from one doorway to the other, realized belatedly that she'd made an even bigger mess than the gasoline bomb had. How did she keep doing this?

She was after Alaric like a shot.

"Wait," she called.

He was in the rectory's foyer, buckling on his scabbard. He didn't appear, from the look he threw out at her from underneath the hunk of blond hair that had once again fallen over those blue eyes of his, excited to see her. She didn't blame him.

"What do you want?" he asked.

She suddenly felt aware of his size, which was enormous. His hands, his feet . . . all of him was big, just huge. When he came into a room, he didn't just come into it, he lumbered, he banged, he *swaggered* into it.

She couldn't count how many times she'd wished over the past twenty-four hours that he had never showed up at her door.

And yet now that he'd saved her life—twice—she couldn't find the words to express how glad she was that he had. And she was supposed to be a dialogue writer.

"I'm sorry. I didn't mean I wanted *you* to go," she finally settled for saying, reaching out to lay her fingers across one of those huge, almost ungainly wrists. "You don't have to do this."

His hands, busy working the buckle to keep his sword in place, stilled. "Yes," he said to the threadbare, flowered carpet. "It's my fault. I shouldn't have forgotten the dog."

"But you didn't know, Alaric," Meena said. She curled her fingers around his wrist. His skin felt warm in all the places, she now remembered, Lucien's had always felt so strangely cool. "You didn't know any of this was going to happen. How could you have?"

"*You* knew," he said, throwing the words at her almost accusingly. And now, she saw, he *was* looking at her, those bright blue eyes searching her face. "*You* know everything before it happens."

"No." The directness of his gaze unnerved her. "Not everything. Only . . . well, you know."

"Right," he said, dropping his gaze again. "Only how people are going to die. Not dogs, though."

She shook her head. "No. Not dogs. Only people. Look—" She lifted her chin, attempting a brave smile. "Forget what I said before. Jack Bauer will be all right. You said yourself, he's a vampire dog. He'll be able to take care of himself. So stay here. Really. I want you to stay here. I'm going to. I'm going to stay. Please stay with me."

He lifted his gaze to meet hers once more, narrowing his eyes at her. "You don't need to worry," he said. "Holtzman will protect you while I'm gone."

"*Me?*" She realized he didn't understand what she was trying to say to him at all. "I'm not worried about *me*."

Now he looked confused. "But I'll be all right," he said. "And you want the dog."

"Alaric." Her chin was starting to tremble, and she was aware that her brave face was melting. "You may *not* be all right. And even though I really do love Jack Bauer, in the end, you're a person, and he's just a dog."

His gaze was unreadable. "How?" he asked her curiously.

Now she was the one who didn't understand. "I beg your pardon?"

"How does it happen?" His fingers were busy again, working his belt. "My death. You're seeing it, aren't you? You think if I go, I'm going to die. So how does it happen this time? Not in the pool. Is it still with the darkness? And the fire?"

"No," she lied. "Not at all. I see you living a really long, happy life and dying of old age in a resort community of some kind. Florida, maybe. Palm Beach?"

It was too late. He'd seen the tears in her eyes. His broad shoulders tensed, and he turned away from her, reaching for his black leather trench coat, which hung on a rack by the door.

"You're lying to me," he said. "I would never retire to Florida. Majorca, maybe. Or Antigua. But never Florida. You shouldn't lie to a guardsman to protect his feelings. The information you are able to provide to us before a mission could save our lives." His coat on, he looked down at her with those amazing blue eyes. "Never lie to me again, Meena. Swear to me."

She blinked away the tears that still clung to her eyelashes. "All right," she said hoarsely. "I swear. I see a death filled with smoke and darkness and fire for you. There. Are you happy?"

"Oh," he said, brightening. "See? This is good to know. I like this." He reached out to tap her roughly on the collarbone, then struck his own. "We need to learn to communicate more like this if we're going to be working together in the future."

"What?" She shook her head, perplexed. Her throat throbbed, both with emotion and the smoke she'd inhaled back in the kitchen. "I have no idea what you're talking about, Alaric. Why would we be working together in the future? I'm trying to tell you that if you do this, you won't *have* a future. But since you won't listen to me . . . let me go with you."

"Oh, no," he said with a humorless bark of laughter.

"But it's *my* dog you're risking your life to—"

"No." He wagged one of his massive fingers in her face. "And if I catch you following me, I'll handcuff you to something to keep you safe. Don't think I won't."

She believed him. "I know you will," she said. "But at least let me . . . here."

Impulsively, she loosened the scarf she'd been wearing around her throat.

Alaric looked down as she began tying the delicate strip of red material around his wrist, the one that she'd been holding.

"What is this?" he asked, his voice sounding . . . well, strange.

A *token,* she thought. From milady, for St. George, about to do battle with the dragon for her.

She knew she was losing what frail grip she'd once had on her sanity.

There was no chance she was going to say that milady stuff out loud to Alaric Wulf, however.

"I don't know," she said, trying not to let him see the tears that were still in her eyes. "For luck, I guess. If you really are going and really won't let me come with you."

"Oh, I'm going," he said with assurance as Meena pulled his sleeve back down over the scarf. "And alone. The Palatine leave no one behind. This includes dogs."

"This is for luck then, too," she said in a tear-clogged voice.

She rose onto her tiptoes and placed a kiss on one of Alaric's cheeks.

One dark blond eyebrow raised, his small mouth pressed even smaller than usual in . . . surprise? Disapproval?

She couldn't tell.

"Meena Harper," he said, looking down at her very intently.

"Yes?" she asked.

"This is for you," he said, and slipped something long and hard into her fingers. "Don't be afraid to use it."

Then he opened the front door to the rectory, looked around outside, and stepped through it, shutting it firmly behind him.

He was gone.

Meena examined what Alaric Wulf had placed into her hand.

It was a pointed wooden stake.

She couldn't help smiling to herself.

He was just so . . . *annoying*.

So why was she standing there crying?

"There you are."

Her brother, Jon, had come out into the hallway. He was holding several empty plastic milk jugs.

"They want someone to fill these with holy water," he explained. "I volunteered you for the job. So can you go scoop some out of the font in the baptistery?"

Meena, reaching up hastily to wipe the tears from her cheeks, slipped the stake into the back pocket of her jeans and said, "Sure."

She knew what she had to do. What she should have done long ago.

Tremulously, she asked, "Jon?"

He'd already started down the hall. At the sound of his name, he turned back. "Yeah, Meen? What?"

"Nothing. Just . . ." She shuffled toward him, letting her head hang and dragging her feet. "I'm kind of scared. Can I have a hug from my big brother?"

"Aw, of course," he said, holding his arms open wide.

Once he'd enveloped her in his embrace, he asked, over the top of her head, "Is this crazy or what? I always thought your psychic thing was weird. But *vampires*?"

"Gee, thanks, Jon," Meena said drily, her ear over his heart. "You always know just the right thing to say to make a girl feel better."

"Well," Jon said with brotherly awkwardness. "Yeah. Sorry about that. You know what I mean."

"Yeah," Meena said. She pulled away from him and gave him a tearful smile. "I do. And thanks. Sorry about getting our lives destroyed."

"No big deal." Jon ruffled her hair. "And don't worry. I'm sure Alaric will be back with Jack soon, and both of 'em will be just fine. Now go fill these up." He practically threw the milk jugs at her. "I have to go; Abraham is going to teach me the best way to cut off a vampire's head." He hurried back into the kitchen.

Meena watched him go. Then she lifted her hand. In it was her cell phone, which she'd managed to pick from the pocket of his jean jacket while he'd been hugging her.

She checked to make sure the battery was still charged.

The cell phone thrummed to life.

Perfect.

She had an important call to make.

Chapter Fifty

Lucien Antonescu had listened as calmly as possible to the information from his cousin Emil that his wife, Mary Lou, had known all along about Meena Harper's ability to predict death—had known it well before ever setting up the two of them. That it was, in fact, the *reason* she'd set them up.

That Mary Lou should have chosen for him a young woman of her acquaintance who was in possession of such an . . . *unusual* talent was flattering, to say the least.

But the fact that Mary Lou had told everyone she knew about Meena's talent, putting Meena in a position of such danger?

That Lucien couldn't accept calmly.

Lucien had already come to several decisions in the wee hours of the morning as he'd watched Meena sleep, before ever speaking to his cousin Emil.

The first was that he would not, of course, be able to return to his teaching position in Romania or to any of his homes there.

Not now that the Palatine knew who he really was.

Obviously, he was going to have to change his name.

Again.

Surprisingly, he was not as irritated by these things as he might have been had he not met Meena. The fact that she was in his life now made everything that would have once seemed unbearable a mere annoyance.

Of course, the Palatine was no longer an organization that merely hunted its prey on foot, satisfied with an old-fashioned stake to the heart, and then left it at that.

Oh, no. Not anymore.

They now used sophisticated technology to track their quarry's financial and real estate assets as well, monitoring bank accounts even in countries that criminalized the violation of their banking privacy laws, such as Switzerland and the Cayman Islands. If the Palatine could not snare the monster, they would find ways to seize his money. And they did so with a ruthlessness that would make the CIA green with envy . . . were the Palatine not such a highly secretive organization that even the CIA knew nothing of its existence.

The money, more than anything, was an issue. Starting over without any money would have been fine, had it just been himself.

But he couldn't ask it of Meena. That would be impossible.

And he wasn't going anywhere without Meena . . . despite her insistence that they no longer see each other.

She would never be safe now. Every vampire in the world would want a taste of her. Any chance to be able to experience what Lucien had—the ability to foretell the death of a human, and not by vampiric hands—would be irresistible to them. It wouldn't be irresistible for the same reasons it was to Lucien . . . it allowed him in some small way to make up for the sins of his past—such as when he'd taken away that boy's car keys, saving his own life—or even because it was just something, *anything* different after centuries of sameness.

But because it was something they might be able to use to their own advantage. Lucien had no doubt that his brother Dimitri would find a way to use Meena's gift of prophecy to prey on the human race's very real fear of mortality, and somehow profit financially from it.

Then there was the fact that Meena's blood coursing through Lucien's veins hadn't just afforded him the ability to predict how humans were going to die. It had heightened his other senses as well, in a way no other human's he'd tasted ever had, making him feel for the first time in centuries as if he were alive again.

He knew this was something he could never share with anyone. Because if this got out, Meena Harper would become demon meat . . . the most hunted mortal on earth.

The fact that Meena was his might have been protection enough under ordinary circumstances. But these weren't ordinary circumstances. The Palatine had their hands on her . . . and had found *him* out. How could he protect her properly? He couldn't even find her, let alone get in touch with her. His frantic phone calls to her had all gone straight to voice mail. Her apartment, according to Emil, whom Lucien had ordered to stay put until Meena's whereabouts could be traced, was empty, except for her little dog. It didn't, Emil had reported, look like anyone—anyone human, anyway—had been there all day. Had they abandoned the place? Surely not. Lucien would know, would sense it if something had happened to her. . . .

But he sensed nothing . . . nothing except dread and a tightness in his chest where his heart had once been. He hadn't felt anything in that spot in centuries. Not since Meena Harper had come into his life.

Then he received the call from Emil that changed everything:

A weeping and repentant Mary Lou, intent on trying to rectify her wrong and give help where she could, had seen a gossip piece while surfing the Internet that an altercation had taken place at a midtown eatery involving a man with a sword . . .

. . . and a certain popular soap opera star's best friend.

This, surely, could only have been Meena's Palatine guard.

And Dimitri's son, Stefan.

There was no other explanation.

Lucien had only had to hear the name *Dimitri* and he was in one of Emil's black cars, headed downtown for his brother's club. If he discovered that his brother had anything, anything at all, to do with Meena's disappearance . . . if he or that idiot son of his had harmed so much as a hair on her head—

There wasn't a hole on earth deep enough into which Lucien could throw them.

But when Lucien got to Concubine, it was closed.

Not that this particularly bothered Lucien. Given his mood, he merely kicked the doors in.

The club was quite a different place empty than when it was occupied. With all the lights on, and no dry ice, it lost something of its mystique. The only shine to the large room, surrounded by black velvet curtains, was the metallic top to the long bar. The place wasn't as clean as it could have been; the floor was a bit sticky.

Perhaps the cleaners hadn't yet arrived. There was no one around.

And yet Lucien, his senses heightened because of Meena, felt that there were quite a few souls around—human, and in the gravest of danger . . .

. . . and not just because of him.

"Hello?" he called. Where were all these people? Why couldn't he see them?

His voice echoed hauntingly around the dance floor, the bar, the VIP room. No one.

Nothing.

Where was his brother? Why had he felt such a powerful pull to this distasteful place if the certain source of all his problems—Dimitri—wasn't even here?

Then Lucien heard it. Heavy footsteps, coming from the front of the building. He turned expectantly.

"Can I help you?"

It was Reginald, Dimitri's three-hundred-pound bodyguard/bouncer, still wearing his gold chain with his name emblazoned proudly across it. His dark head gleamed, newly shaved.

"Hello there, Reginald," Lucien said, genuinely pleased to see him. This was going to be easy. Some humans—like Meena, for instance—were impossible to control, their minds too damaged or crowded with mental baggage. But Reginald's was a vast, open plain.

"How did you get in here?" Reginald had a Hollywood-gangster-style grip on his gun, raising it sideways to shoot at Lucien instead of straight on, using his other hand to steady it for better aim.

Lucien felt even more cheered. Poor Reginald.

"Put the gun down, son," he said. "You remember me. I was here the other night, to visit my brother."

Reginald lowered the gun obediently. "Oh, yeah," he said, recognition dawning. "You messed Mr. Dimitri up."

"That's right," Lucien said, smiling fondly at the memory. "I've come back to do it again. You wouldn't happen to know where Mr. Dimitri is right now, would you?"

Reginald shook his head, putting the gun back into the waistband of his sweatpants . . . not the most propitious place to keep a loaded firearm, in Lucien's opinion. "Naw," Reginald said. "Everybody got all excited about something and took off a little while ago and just left me here. They didn't say when they'd be back or nothing. I don't even know if I'm supposed to open up tonight or what."

"Interesting," Lucien said. "And would you happen to know what it was they got 'all excited about,' Reginald?"

"Hell, no," Reginald said. "No one tells me nothing around here."

Lucien reached into the man's brain with his own mind and probed gently. Reginald was telling the truth. He knew nothing . . . except. . .

"Reginald," Lucien said. "Are we the only people here?"

"No," Reginald admitted. Lucien could feel the man's fear. It was as sharp and as pointed as a knife. "There's the folks in the basement."

"The basement," Lucien repeated. "Would you take me to the basement, Reginald?"

Reginald's fear stabbed him. "Mr. Dimitri said none of us is supposed to go down there," Reginald protested. He did *not* want to go down to the basement.

"It's all right, Reginald," Lucien said calmly. "I'll be with you. Nothing bad will happen to you in the basement if I'm there with you."

Reginald believed him . . . but only because Lucien was there in his brain to comfort him. Reluctantly, he went to the bar to get the keys to the basement, then led Lucien to a door that he unlocked with hands that still shook, despite Lucien's presence.

Whatever was in the basement, the human employees of Concubine, who weren't supposed to know about it, not only knew about it but feared it.

Lucien followed Reginald down the narrow concrete staircase, sensing approaching death more closely with every step. He couldn't just smell it . . . he could *feel* it, oozing through his pores the way moisture seeped from the basement walls. This had been what he'd noticed when he'd entered the club: the thump of human heartbeats, quivering with life . . . and impending doom.

Was this what Meena Harper felt every day of her life, walking down the street, getting on the subway, going about her daily business?

How could she stand it?

They came to two doors. Behind one of them Lucien could hear the heartbeats thundering so loudly, he wanted to fling his hands over his ears.

Behind the other, he heard . . . nothing.

He nodded toward the door where there was only silence.

"Open it," he said to Reginald.

Reginald, holding the keys like they were a rosary, looked like he was about to cry. "I really don't want to, sir," he said. "Please don't make me."

Lucien nodded, understanding. There was only so much the human mind could take.

He lifted his foot and smashed down the heavy metal door with a single powerful kick.

Inside the darkened room, on concrete mortuary slabs, lay the seven financial analysts from TransCarta to whom his brother Dimitri had introduced him the night before.

Only they were no longer alive.

On the other hand, they weren't quite dead, either.

They were in a place between life and death. Someone had turned their stiff white shirt collars down and bitten each one neatly along the carotid artery, not once, not twice, but three times.

And along each man's mouth, Lucien saw faint traces of blood.

They were turning. They were currently in a metamorphic state. When they woke, they would be vampires.

And they'd be hungry as hell.

"Who did this?" Lucien demanded, turning to face Reginald, who, unable to control his curiosity—even terrified as he was—stood peering in past the broken door, which hung by its hinges.

"I have no idea," he said. "What the hell is wrong with those guys? Why are they just laying there like that, all bitten on the neck? Are they . . . are they—" Reginald couldn't bring himself to say the word.

"Yes," Lucien replied.

He swept from the room and back out into the hallway to face the second door, the one behind which he could hear so many heart-beats.

Reginald stared at him.

"I know you're not going to kick that door down," Reginald said. "If there were vampires behind that first door, what's going to be behind that door? Don't even *think* about—"

Lucien kicked down the second door.

Behind it blinked a half dozen young women, all very much alive, all in various states of semi-dress, stretched out across cheap mattresses, seeming very weak and confused to see so much light streaming into the room all of a sudden. The smell was not very pleasant.

None of the girls, Lucien could tell, was a vampire. Yet.

But all of them had been bitten and drained, just enough to keep them compliant.

The mystery about what the vamps next door would eat when they awoke was solved.

"Gerald?" one of the girls asked in a bewildered voice.

"Is not Gerald," another said, sounding even more bewildered.

All of them looked terrified.

Lucien turned around and signaled to Reginald.

"Get them out of here," he said. "Start taking them upstairs. Wait for me there."

"Okay," Reginald said, affable now that the mystery of the base-ment had been solved. "But what about—" He nodded his head toward the room next door.

Lucien looked around the tiny cell in which the girls had been held, clearly for quite some time, and with no toilet facilities that he could see, save for a bucket. He saw a rickety chair and smashed it to pieces.

"This will do," he said, lifting one of the chair legs and examining the pointiest end. "Now go."

While Reginald went to work corralling the girls up the stairs—

they needed a lot of assurance that it wasn't a trap and that they were being set free—Lucien set about his own task.

It was grim work. He had no idea if the men had asked to be turned or if his brother was forming some kind of indentured vampire investment banker army to handle his finances.

Knowing his brother, he guessed the latter.

In any case, these men were not going to wake immortal, with superhuman powers, and thirsting for human blood.

They were never going to wake again at all.

When Lucien was finished with his foul task, he threw the chair leg away, washed himself off as best he could—humans who had not quite turned still exuded massive amounts of blood—and turned to leave the concrete room, giving it one last glance over his shoulder.

It was exactly the last resting place he'd pictured for all of them when he'd met them at the burlesque club.

Only he'd thought they'd be dying in a parking garage, in some sort of car accident. He'd never imagined *he'd* be the instrument of their death.

Except, he told himself, that he hadn't been.

His brother was.

Dimitri knew the rules. What was he doing, turning humans and leaving them in a nightclub basement to awaken alone, then throwing them weakened human girls on which to feed?

At least now Lucien had a good idea where the bodies in the parks had been coming from.

"Reginald," he called as he came up the basement stairs.

Reginald was waiting for him in the bar. He'd given all the girls cans of soda and little bowls of nuts, as if they were VIP guests of the club. Reginald had also, Lucien saw, raided the lost and found on the girls' behalf. All of them were now fully, if somewhat whimsically, clothed.

"Yes, boss?" Reginald asked. He'd been wiping the bar as if the club was open for business and he was tending it.

"Where does Mr. Dimitri keep his safe?" Lucien asked.

"In his office," Reginald responded promptly. "Here, I'll show you."

Reginald no longer needed the slightest mental push to do Lucien's bidding. Having found a nest of soon-to-be vampires in his employer's basement, alongside their next meal, Reginald's loyalty to Mr. Dimitri seemed to have ended.

"Ladies," Lucien called to the girls. "This way, please."

The girls, chattering softly in their native languages, brought their sodas and nuts along as they followed Lucien and Reginald up the stairs to Dimitri's plush office.

"It's there," Reginald said, pointing to a mirror that hung above a large art deco desk. "Behind the mirror. He keeps loads of cash in it. In case he has to make a quick getaway."

"How fortuitous for us," Lucien said. "Stand out of the way, ladies."

He lifted a paperweight shaped like a greyhound and smashed the mirror to pieces with it.

"Dude really likes smashing shit," Reginald remarked to the girls, who looked impressed.

Lucien took hold of the door to the safe and peeled it away, dropping it to the floor with a thump.

"Whoa," he heard Reginald say. The young ladies gasped.

Lucien ignored them. He had work to do. As Reginald had stated, the safe was filled with a great deal of cash. There were also a lot of passports. Lucien reached for these and flung them to Dimitri's desk.

"Look through these," he said. "Perhaps the girls will find their own."

There was a flutter of excitement behind him as the girls did just that. Lucien continued to rifle through the safe but found nothing else that would be of any use, to him or anyone else he could think of, except a set of keys and the title and registration papers to a car.

"Reginald," he said. "What are these?"

"Oh," the young man said. "Those are to Mr. Dimitri's Lincoln Continental. He keeps it parked in a garage downtown. He lets me drive him in it sometimes. It's a black '69 Mark III. Sweet ride."

Lucien nodded. "Consider it yours," he said, and flung the keys and papers toward Reginald, who caught them expertly.

"Are you kidding me?" Reginald looked down at the keys in his hands. "But what's Mr. Dimitri going to say?"

"Not much," Lucien said, "when I get through with him. Ladies, come here, please."

When the girls had gathered around the desk, Lucien gave them each several stacks of the neat piles of hundred-dollar bills.

"Take this money," he instructed them, "and your passports, and start a new life, somewhere far away from here. Or go back to your old lives, if that's what you think will make you happy. Just forget all about what happened here. I'll take care of the people who hurt you. They won't harm anyone else again. I promise. You have nothing more to fear. Go, and be healthy and happy."

The girls, whose grasp of English was shaky, smiled—first down at the money in their hands, then at each other, and then at him.

They didn't need to know English to understand what he'd said to them.

Because he hadn't even spoken out loud. He'd said all he had to say in their minds, giving them each a gentle memory wipe.

It would be a long time before they were completely healed. Even he couldn't do that for them.

But this, he knew, was a beginning.

The money would do nothing to bring back the lives that had been lost due to his failure to control his brother's barbarism.

But for now, this was the only penance he could make.

"Reginald," he said aloud. "Take the women outside, and make sure they get safely into cabs. Have the drivers take them to JFK. They can decide from there where they want to head next."

"You got it," Reginald said.

"Then," Lucien said, "you're going to take the car and drive it to Georgia to live with your brother."

"My brother," Reginald said, looking pleased. "That's a good idea!"

"I thought so. Don't forget anything here at the club. If you do, you won't be able to come back for it. It's just going to burn."

"Burn, sir?" Reginald looked confused. "How?"

"In the fire," Lucien explained patiently. "Go now. And don't worry. No one will be left to point a finger at you, I assure you."

Reginald turned, his arms open wide, and shepherded the girls away. They all left, smiling back at Lucien gratefully . . . and a little bit worshipfully.

He looked away. Gratitude was the last thing he deserved, much less worship.

He was dousing the bodies in the basement with rum from the bar—he'd always found that 151 burned quickest and most efficiently, leaving very little tissue residue—when his cell phone buzzed.

He pulled it out and saw the name on the screen he'd been longing to see all day.

Meena Harper.

Chapter Fifty-one

9:15 P.M. EST, Saturday, April 17
Shrine of St. Clare
154 Sullivan Street
New York, New York

L ucien?" Meena cried when someone finally picked up at the other end. "Is that you?"

She had to stick a finger in her other ear in order to hear him.

That was because of all the screaming coming from the ground below her.

She supposed it was her own fault, though: she'd just lobbed a water balloon filled with holy water at a pack of vampires who'd been trying to climb the churchyard fence in order to get into the rectory.

"Meena," he said. "Are you all right?"

"Oh," she said. "I'm fine. But I'm sorry. I can barely hear you. Where are you? This is a horrible connection."

"No, *I'm* sorry," Lucien said. He sounded impossibly far away. "I'm not in a very good location for cell phone reception right now. Let me just . . . there. Can you hear me now?"

"Oh," Meena said. A wave of warmth washed over her at the sound of his voice. Suddenly, she felt as if everything was going to be okay.

Which was ridiculous, because one man couldn't possibly fix all the things that had gone wrong in the past few hours.

Even Lucien, who was no ordinary man.

"That's much better," she said. "You sounded like you were in some kind of tunnel before. So you're not at the apartment?"

"No," Lucien said. "Meena, where are *you*? Is that . . . screaming?"

"Oh," Meena said. She glanced down at the vampires beyond the churchyard fence, feeling a twinge of fear . . . and loathing.

Then she instantly felt guilty about the loathing. She couldn't quite believe how quickly she'd gone from feeling pity for these creatures who couldn't help what they were, and insisting there were surely some redeeming qualities in them, just as there were in Lucien, to callously hurling water balloons filled with a liquid that was as corrosive to them as battery acid from the rectory rooftop.

What was happening to her? What was she turning into?

She was just as much a monster as they were.

Then again, she supposed being nearly murdered tended to bring out the monster in everyone.

"Never mind about that," she said to Lucien. "They'll be all right again in a few minutes." Her brother had been right about vampiric healing powers. They were amazing. Nothing killed these things. Well, except a stake to the heart, apparently, but Meena, up on the rectory roof, hadn't been close enough to one to test this theory. Yet.

"Meena." Lucien's deep voice sounded like heaven to her ears. Especially when he said her name like that, so filled with pure, masculine love . . . and longing. "What are you talking about? Who'll be all right?"

"No one," she said. She didn't want to spoil things by having to admit that she'd just spent the past quarter of an hour dousing his kind with holy water so she could get a few minutes alone to call him. "It's good to hear your voice."

"It's good to hear you, too," he said. "You can't know what I've been going through, not knowing where you've been all this time. I've been torturing myself, thinking of all the things that might have happened to you and how I haven't been there to protect you."

"Oh," Meena said, flattening a hand to her chest. Tears filled her eyes. "Lucien, you have to stop saying that kind of stuff. You know we can't be together. It's impossible."

"You keep saying it's impossible," Lucien said. "But if there's anything I've learned in my five centuries on earth, Meena, it's that nothing is impossible. Especially to a man as much in love as I am with you."

A hand appeared over the edge of the rooftop beside Meena's foot—a vampire, trying to claw his way up the building toward her. Stifling a startled gasp, Meena pulled a squirt gun from the back pocket of her jeans, aimed, and launched a steady stream of holy water at him. He shrieked as his fingers caught fire, lost his footing, and fell fifty feet to the pavement below. Horrified, Meena turned away.

"Meena," Lucien said. "What was that?"

"That? Oh, nothing. Look, I want you to know I did get your messages. I would have called sooner, but I had to steal my phone back from my brother. He doesn't know I have it—"

As if right on cue, she heard her brother shouting from a second-story window below, "You want a piece of this? You want a piece of this? Well, then come and get it, you sick vampire pusswad!" This was followed by a small explosion.

"Meena," Lucien said. There was renewed urgency in his tone. He'd definitely, she realized, heard the explosion. "*Where are you?*"

"Oh," she said, "it doesn't matter."

A part of her just wanted to keep hearing him tell her how much he loved and missed her. Which was wrong, because she knew he was still going to kill Jon and Alaric.

"It *does* matter." He insisted. "Meena, you've got to listen to me. I think you're in serious danger."

"Really?" She tried to ignore the smell of smoke still drifting up from the rectory kitchen. Father Bernard had already called the fire department and assured them (in case any of St. Clare's neighbors happened to dial 911, he didn't want to worry about the NYFD being attacked by vampires) that the only trouble was the "broken water pipe" that had caused them to cancel evening mass in the first place. The smoke? Oh, the smoke was just from a batch of Sister Gertrude's cookies that had been left in the oven too long.

"It's funny," Meena said over the phone, "because I think *you're* in very grave danger."

"I'm serious, Meena," Lucien said. She could hear him moving on the other end of the line. It sounded, oddly enough, like he was pouring something. "I'd prefer to have this discussion in person, but with things the way they are right now . . . well, I'm just going to say it: let's go away together."

"What? You mean like . . . on a trip?"

"Yes," he said with an odd hesitancy. "Exactly. Like on a trip. Well, maybe a bit longer than the average trip. And I know what you're going to say about my killing your brother and the guard. But I won't be able to do that if we're nowhere near them, will I?"

"No." Meena had to agree. "That's true."

"And I know how you feel about your job. But surely you have some vacation time coming to you."

"Well," Meena said. She chewed her lower lip, thinking about Stefan Dominic, still tied up in the basement. The Dracul had already managed to infiltrate where she worked and, according to Alaric, where she lived, as well. Taking a vacation until things died down a little wouldn't be such a bad idea. "A couple weeks off might not hurt, now that I think about it. . . ."

"Well," he said, sounding surprised. And a lot more cheerful. "That was easy. I thought you'd be more resistant to the idea, to be honest. Can you leave now, tonight, Meena? I can be uptown in a few minutes. Do you think you can get away from the Palatine Guard? And meet me out on your little balcony? You needn't be afraid. I'll help you get across, onto Emil's terrace. Then we can leave from there."

He sounded so sure of himself. That was one of the things she loved about him. He always seemed to know exactly what he was doing, and on the few occasions when he didn't, well, that vulnerability only made her love him all the more fiercely.

"Um," she said, "meeting you on my balcony might be a bit of a problem, actually, Lucien."

"Why?"

She hadn't wanted to tell him this way. But now she had no choice. "Well, because right now I'm actually on the roof of the rectory of the Shrine of St. Clare on Sullivan Street in downtown Manhattan, just off Houston," she said into the phone. "We're not totally sure what's going on, but it seems like your brother got Stefan Dominic—the guy we hired to play the vampire on *Insatiable*, only it turns out he really *is* a vampire—to kidnap me—"

"Did he hurt you?" Lucien demanded in a voice as hard as stone.

"What?" Meena asked. "No. Well, I mean, he tried. He had a gun. But Alaric stopped him. Now we're keeping him hostage here and currently experiencing just a little bit of difficulty because a few dozen Dracul really seem to want to come inside and kill us or something—"

"*What?*"

She winced and had to hold the phone away from her face.

That's how loudly he'd erupted into her ear.

"Lucien," she said when the volume of what she supposed was his swearing—it was in Romanian, so she couldn't understand a word of it—got back to a decibel level she could bear, "I knew you were going to freak out like this, which is why I didn't—"

"Meena," he thundered. She had to hold the phone away from her face again. "*Stay exactly where you are*. I'll be right there to get you."

"No," she yelled into the phone before he could hang up. "Think about it, Lucien. It's a trap. Alaric says they'll be waiting for you at the apartment, too." Which was why she wasn't going to say a word to him about Jack Bauer. She didn't need *two* men risking their lives over her dog. "It's all just a trap to lure you out so your brother can kill you—"

"Oh, Alaric says that, does he?" Lucien roared. "Well, I don't care what *Alaric* says. Do you know who Stefan Dominic is, Meena? He's my nephew. He's Dimitri's *son.*"

"Oh," Meena said, taken aback. "So . . . you're saying you think we should let him go?"

"I'm saying I'm coming down there to get you, and you and I are leaving—"

"You mean running away," she said quietly. "Don't you?"

Lucien's voice was like ice. "We're not running away, Meena," he said. "I'm going to keep you safe. That is my first—my *only*—priority."

"Well," she said, lifting a hand and running it raggedly through her hair. Her voice caught on a sob she hadn't been expecting.

She thought she'd been doing a pretty good job of keeping it together. At least for the past half hour or so.

But now everything was starting to unravel again.

"What about Jon, Lucien?" she asked, her voice breaking. "Because he's here, too. What if we leave, and then your brother captures *him*? Do you think I could live with myself if something happened to my brother? Are you going to protect Jon, Lucien, for the rest of his life, too? Because I don't think you are. In fact," she said, and now her voice rose a little hysterically, "I still think you're going to kill him, and Alaric, too."

"Meena." Lucien sounded calm now. The storm was over. He seemed to be choosing his words with deliberate care, the way a jeweler would choose pearls to string a necklace. "I'm not going to kill anyone. Except my own brother. Not to mention my nephew. Then Jon will be safe. And so will you."

She desperately wanted to believe him. "Do you really think so?" she asked.

"Of course I do, Meena," he said. "All of this will be over very soon. Now, start thinking about where you want to go. I've always dreamed about having a place in Thailand, myself."

"Thailand," Meena said. She liked the sound of the word on his lips. "I've never been to Thailand."

"Neither have I," Lucien said. "We can discover it together."

Even as she was dreaming of sharing a thatched hut on the beach with Lucien—on stilts, like she always saw in magazines—she heard a scuttling sound. Whirling around, she saw a bat landing on the rooftop just a few feet away from her and beginning to transmogrify into its vampire host.

"Oh, no," she said with a groan, her heart booming in her chest. She raced toward it, giving the bat the most vicious kick she could, sending it shrieking off the roof . . .

. . . just as it changed into a young woman wearing jeans and a leather jacket. The girl screamed as she tumbled through the air, not changing back into a bat quickly enough to save her from falling onto the spikes of the churchyard fence below, which pierced her body in several places.

But since the spikes weren't made of wood, she just lay there, impaled and twitching, while her friends tried to pull her off.

Meena, watching all this transpire over the side of the roof, made a horrified face and looked away.

"I really hope you're right, Lucien," she said, lifting the phone back to her ear. "About all of this being over soon. Because I'm not sure how much more I can take."

There was no response.

"Lucien?" she said. She held the phone away from her face, looking down at the screen. She still had service.

Lucien, she realized, had hung up on her.

Had she said the wrong thing?

Meena jumped as her phone vibrated in her hand. He was calling back.

"Lucien?" she cried.

"Who?" A familiar voice filled her ear.

"Oh," Meena said, disappointed. "Hi, Paul. Look, I really can't talk right now."

"Whatever," Paul said. "Sorry to interrupt your Saturday-night mini-Butterfinger orgy. I just wanted to see if you'd gotten Shoshona's e-mail."

"What e-mail?" Meena asked. She needed to get downstairs to warn everyone. She understood now why the Dracul were trying so hard to get inside the rectory. It wasn't just *her* they wanted.

It was Dimitri Antonescu's son.

"We've been sold," Paul said.

Meena nearly dropped her phone. "What? What do you mean? The show?" But that made no sense. Shows couldn't be sold. Could they?

"Not the show," Paul said. "The network. Consumer Dynamics and everything it owns. This morning. To something called TransCarta."

"I never heard of it," Meena said.

"Me neither," Paul said. "I had to Google it. It's a private equities firm."

Meena stood there clutching her BlackBerry to her face. She really didn't have time to talk, like she'd told him. And yet . . . "But . . . what does this mean?"

Fired. Like everything else, she'd now lost her job, too.

"Shoshona assures everyone in her e-mail that it doesn't mean any-thing, that everything will go on as normal, that TransCarta supports

ABN and *Insatiable* wholeheartedly and looks forward to a profitable future working with us."

"*Shoshona* said all this?" Meena asked incredulously. Shoshona could hardly even string together a lunch order.

"I know," Paul said. "But Fran and Stan cosigned. And here's the weird thing: Shoshona sent the e-mail an hour before any of this was announced on CNN."

"So then how did she even know about it?" Meena wondered aloud.

It was right then that the hatch that led to the rooftop was thrown suddenly open, letting out a strip of brilliant yellow light from the rectory's third floor.

"What are you *doing* up here?" her brother, Jon, demanded. He climbed up onto the roof, dragging a crossbow after him. "What happened to my holy water brigade? It's like it suddenly dried up or something."

"Sorry," Meena said, hanging up on Paul and slipping her cell phone surreptitiously back into the pocket of her suede jacket. "I got distracted. They're starting to dive-bomb me." She looked up, scanning the night sky for winged assassins, but everything seemed quiet . . . for the moment. "Looks like they've backed off for now."

"Yeah, that's why I'm here. Abraham thinks they're repositioning, and that you better come back down. It's probably not all that safe up here anymore anyway."

"Okay," Meena said. "Look, I need to tell Abraham something. That Stefan guy? He's—"

Jon's cell phone went off.

"Who the hell could *that* be?" He fished the phone out of his pocket. "Oh, my God. It's Weinberg." To Meena's astonishment, her brother actually answered the call. "Adam," Jon crowed. "How the hell are you?"

Meena shook her head. She couldn't remember the last time she'd seen Jon in such a good mood. Maybe back when he'd been employed.

It was nice to know someone, at least, was enjoying himself on this, the worst night of her entire life.

Then Meena felt her pocket vibrate. What was going on? Someone was *texting* her? *Now?*

Casting a furtive glance at her brother—he was still having his animated conversation with Leisha's husband—Meena pulled her phone out of her pocket and glanced at the text that had just been left for her.

It was from Lucien.

Stay where you are, he'd written. *I'm coming for you.*

That was when, over in the distance, on the east side, there was the sound of an extremely large explosion.

"Jesus Christ," Jon said, glancing up. "What the hell was that?"

"I don't know," Meena said, looking in the direction from which the sound had come. "That was too loud to be a car."

"It sounded like a whole freaking building exploding," Jon said. "Oh, man, look at that."

He pointed at a bright orange glow that had begun to fill the sky in the east where the sun would have been, if it had been morning. Meena, looking at it, could think of only one thing.

Lucien. Lucien had something to do with that.

She was as sure of it as she was that she was standing there.

The pouring sound she'd heard in the background when she'd been speaking to him. Had that been gasoline?

It didn't matter.

This vampire war had just been taken to a whole new level.

"Definitely a building," Jon was saying. "Some insurance company has gotta be bumming right now." To Adam, who was still on the phone, he said, "What? Yeah, sorry, no, something on TV. Yeah, Meena and I are just chilling in the apartment right now." He made a comical face at Meena. "We're gonna maybe order in some Chinese food. . . . Do we wanna have a drink? Uh, naw, I think we're just gonna take it easy tonight, right, Meen?"

"Uh, yeah," Meena said, raising her voice so Leisha could hear her if she was there on the phone with her husband. "We're just going to stay home and chill."

"Yeah," Jon said. "So, we'll see you guys. . . ." All at once, his face went the color of ash. "Oh. You are?" he asked into the phone.

Meena stared at him. "What?" Suddenly, all her concerns about Leisha and her unborn baby came flooding back, full force. "What's wrong?"

"They're in front of your place," Jon said to her, holding the phone away from his face. He looked as if he were going to be sick. "Nine ten Park. They want to know if they can come up."

Meena felt as if the roof had suddenly shifted a little under her feet. And not because vampires were making another assault.

No, she thought. *Not Leisha and the baby. Not this way.*

Except . . . of course. Of *course* it was going to be Leisha and the baby.

And of course it was going to happen this way.

And she'd always known it was going to.

She'd just refused to see it, because it was too horrible even to contemplate.

Until now, when it was staring her straight in the face.

Chapter Fifty-two

She reached over and snatched the phone away from Jon.

"Hello, Adam?" she said. Her fingers had gone numb. She couldn't feel her fingers.

She couldn't feel anything.

Except fear.

"Oh, hi, Meena, it's your best friend's useless, unemployed husband," Adam said with his customary self-derision. "Leisha got tired of me hanging around the house all day doing nothing, so she said we had to go for a walk because it was such a nice afternoon, and we ended up in Central Park."

"Hi, Adam," Meena said. "Can I talk to—"

"Then we crossed the park and had dinner and ended up in your neighborhood," Adam said. "So Leisha suggested we stop by and see what you were doing, since apparently you don't answer any of your phones anymore—"

"Meena?" Leisha's voice, strong and vibrant, rang in Meena's ear. She'd apparently wrestled the phone away from Adam. "Hey. What is going *on* with you? I've left you, like, five messages. How was the concert? That boring, huh, that you can't even call me back to tell me about it? Anyway, can you tell Pradip to let us up? I have to pee like crazy. This kid must have taken up residency on my bladder. And don't give me that excuse about the place being messy, because at this point, I wouldn't care if you guys had dead bodies piled up on the floor. That's how bad I have to go. Your buzzer must be broken or something because Pradip says you aren't answering, but Jon just said you guys are there—"

"Leisha." Meena took a deep breath. This was a nightmare. She was living an actual nightmare. "You guys have to leave. You guys have to turn around and get away from my building. Please don't ask any questions. Just go."

"What?" Leisha was understandably bewildered. "What are you talking about? Stop playing, I really have to pee. And there isn't a Starbucks for like two blocks. And believe me, I'm not going to make it."

"Leisha."

Meena's heart was slamming into the wall of her chest. Jon, standing in front of her, was making frantic hand signals to her and whispering, "Tell them I'm running a fever. Tell them you think I have the flu and you don't want to Leisha to get it. Don't tell them the truth, Meen. You know what Alaric said about telling people the truth—"

But she didn't care about preserving the Palatine's conspiracy of silence about the existence of vampires.

All she cared about was keeping her best friend and her baby from dying.

"Remember Lucien Antonescu?" Meena asked Leisha over the phone.

"Yeah . . . ," Leisha said. "Mr. Perfect? What about him? Come on, Meena, make this quick."

"He's not so perfect," Meena said. Her voice was trembling. *All* of her was trembling.

Was it her imagination, or were the sounds of the attack on the building dying down? Where was Abraham Holtzman, shouting orders to the friars? Why couldn't Meena hear Sister Gertrude's Beretta?

"He's actually a vampire," Meena said, ignoring Jon, who'd slapped his forehead with the palm of his hand. "Okay, Leisha? He's the prince of darkness. And a whole lot of vampires are staking out my apartment right now so they can kill him. So you and Adam need to get out of there right away in case some of them see you and somehow connect you with me. Okay? So just do it. Just go."

Leisha didn't say anything for a minute.

Then she said, sounding more amused than offended, "Meena, honey, if you don't want Adam and me dropping by without calling first, all you have to do is say so. You don't have to try out any of your crazy plotlines for *Insatiable* on us like this—"

"Oh, my God, Leisha, this is not a plotline for *Insatiable*!" Meena burst out. How could this be happening to her? And why *now,* when it really mattered? "It's real! Do you remember Rob Pace, Leish? Do you remember how I told you not to get in his car? This is like that. If you don't want you and the baby to end up like Angie Harwood, you've got to do what I say."

"But you never said anything." Leisha sounded stunned. "You never—"

"I've known something was going to happen to the baby for a while, Leish," Meena continued, "but I didn't tell you because I didn't want to scare you. That was wrong of me. I should have told you. I'm an idiot. This is all my fault. All right? You've just got to believe me when I tell you now. Something bad is going to happen to the baby. You've got to get out of there."

She heard her best friend breathing on the other end of the phone. For a few seconds, that was *all* Meena could hear, except for Jon, panting heavily next to her, and the traffic noises over on Houston Street. It was silent around the churchyard. The Dracul, it appeared, had given up and gone home.

All of Meena's being, all her concentration, was focused on the soft sound of Leisha's breathing.

Then Leisha said, "Something's going to happen to the baby?" in the tiniest voice Meena had ever heard her normally loud, self-assured, brassy friend ever use.

"If you don't get out of there," Meena said, her heart wrenching in her chest, "yes."

Then, to her infinite relief, she heard Leisha say to her husband, "Go. Let's go."

"What?" Meena heard Adam say, sounding confused. "What's going on?"

"We're leaving. Meena says we have to get out of here. Go flag down a cab." Leisha had apparently forgotten to turn off the phone. She was bossing Adam around, the phone hanging loosely in her hand as she did it. "Don't just stand there. Get us a cab! There's one, get it. Get it!"

"I don't understand," Meena heard Adam say. "Why don't they want us to come up?"

"Just get in the damned cab," Leisha was saying. "I'll tell you later."

Meena felt herself beginning to relax. A sort of semi-hysterical bubble of laughter even rose in her throat. Jon, standing in front of her, mouthed, "What's going on?"

"They're leaving," Meena said and he gave her a relieved thumbs-up signal.

It was going to be all right. Leisha was going to be all right. The baby was going to be all right. All those crazy premonitions she'd been having for so long . . . they were wrong.

It had been close. Too close.

But everything was going to be all right after all.

Thank God.

"Oh, hell," Meena heard Leisha swear. "Who's this guy?"

Meena tensed up again, pressing the phone to her ear.

"What?" Jon asked, noticing her expression.

She held up a hand to silence him so she could hear. A man's voice was speaking. It sounded strangely familiar.

"Sorry," the voice said. "But was that apartment 11B you were just trying to call up to?"

"No," Leisha said hastily. "Sorry."

"Yeah," Adam said. "Actually, it was. Why do you ask?"

"Meena Harper, right?" the voice asked in a friendly way.

Oh, God, Meena thought in agony. *No. No, no, no, no . . . this can't be happening. Get out of there. Get out of there, Leish. . . .*

"No," Leisha said quickly. "We don't know her."

"Yeah, we do," Adam said. "Leish, what's wrong with you? Meena's a friend of ours. My wife's best friend, actually."

Meena sank to the gravel-strewn rooftop, the ground having suddenly pitched out from under her.

"Meena, what is it?" Jon asked, hurrying to kneel by her side. "What's going on?"

Wordlessly—she couldn't have spoken if she'd wanted to; her tongue had turned to lead in her mouth—she laid the cell phone down between them and turned on the speakerphone so that he, too, could listen to their friends being killed.

"No, she's not," Leisha was saying loudly. "I don't know anyone named Meena Harper."

"I think you do," the stranger said. He had an oddly mellifluous voice, soothing, almost . . . hypnotic. Was that what he was doing to get Adam to admit all these things? Hypnotizing him? "I think you know Meena Harper very well."

"Yes," Adam said. "Of course we do."

"Jesus Christ," Jon exclaimed, looking down at Meena with a stunned expression on his face. "Who *is* that guy? How is he doing that? Adam hates everyone. He thinks everyone in the whole world is a potential serial killer. Adam!" he shouted into the phone. "Adam! Don't listen to him!"

Meena just shook her head. Tears were streaming down her face. She murmured, "It's no use. He can't hear you. It's already done."

"What do you mean?" Jon said. He looked angry. "Did you . . . did you *know* about this?"

"I told you," she said, reaching up to wipe away some of her tears. "The baby . . ."

Jon's face blanched. "*This* is what you saw happening?"

"No, of course not." Meena covered her face with her hands. "How was I supposed to know it was going to have to do with *vampires*?"

"Maybe because you started sleeping with one?" Jon shouted down into the phone. "Adam! Adam!"

But Adam wasn't listening.

"Hey . . . aren't you that guy?" they could hear him saying in an unnaturally—for Adam—enthusiastic voice. "That guy from that soap opera? Gregory Bane. That's it! Look, Leish. It's Gregory Bane."

A wave of nausea rolled over Meena. *Gregory Bane.*

Of course. Of course Gregory Bane was a Dracul.

"Yes," the mellifluous voice said. "I'm Gregory Bane. Thanks for watching."

"What are you doing?" they heard Leisha cry. "Don't touch me. Get your hands off me. Get away from me!"

"Hey," Adam said. He sounded dazed. "That's my wife. . . ."

"Adam!" Jon shouted into the phone. "Adam! Go for his eyes! His eyes, Adam!" He whipped his head around to look at Meena. "What's wrong with him?"

"They can control people's minds," Meena said, dropping her hands away from her face and her head down onto her knees. Her tears made damp spots on the denim of her jeans. "It's not Adam's fault."

Jon was searching his pockets.

"I'm calling Alaric," he said. "I have his number. If he's still there getting Jack, maybe he can stop this—"

"It's too late," Meena whispered. She'd begun to rock herself, clutching her knees to her chest. "It's too late."

There was a scuffling sound from the cell phone, shoes on pavement. Then a sound that pierced Meena's heart:

Leisha screamed.

Then a clatter, as if the phone had fallen to the ground.

Then . . . nothing. Meena lifted the cell phone and pressed it to her ear, straining to hear a sound, any sound.

But she heard only the faint, familiar churn of traffic on Park Avenue.

"Hey," Jon said. He was still going through his pockets. "Where's your cell phone?"

Meena reached into her own pocket, keeping his phone glued to her ear, and passed her phone to her brother.

"I should have known," Jon said tensely, pressing numbers into her keypad from a slip of paper he'd fished from the pocket of his jeans. "Who've you been calling, huh? *Him*?"

"Shut up, Jon," Meena said, still pressing his phone to her ear.

"That's just great," Jon said sarcastically. "That's exactly what we need right now, your boyfriend to show up and—"

Meena held up a hand to silence him. Something was happening on the other end of Adam's phone: a scraping noise like . . .

The phone was being picked up.

Then beeps, like someone was pressing numbers on the keypad.

"Ow," Meena cried, jerking the phone away from her face. "Hello? Hello? Who's there?"

Then Adam's voice, still sounding dazed, came on. "Meena?" He seemed confused. "Is that you? I was just trying to call you."

Jon lowered the phone he was holding.

"Adam," Meena shouted. "Oh my God, Adam, are you all right?"

"Dude," Jon yelled into the phone. "Where's your wife? Where's Leisha?"

"They . . . they took her," Adam said. His voice seemed small. And it wasn't, Meena knew, because he was on a mobile phone.

He wasn't crying. Not yet.

But he would be. And soon.

"I tried to stop them," he said. "I tried, but they . . . they . . . *bit* me. I'm bleeding." Adam seemed dumbfounded by this fact. "There's blood everywhere."

Meena and Jon exchanged panicked glances.

Call Alaric, Meena mouthed to her brother. *Now.*

"Adam," Meena said into Jon's phone, "where are you? Are you still outside our building?"

"Yeah," Adam said vaguely, like he was surprised to discover this.

"Well, get inside," Meena said. She tried to sound authoritative, which wasn't easy, since she was shaking so badly. But she wanted Adam to do as she said. "Go see the doorman, Pradip. He has a first-aid kit at the desk. He'll call 911 and help you until the EMTs arrive. Go see Pradip, Adam."

"But I have to find my wife," Adam said. "They took her."

"I know they took her," Meena said, reaching up to pull at her hair in frustration. "Do you know where they took her, Adam?"

"They told me to tell you," Adam said slowly, speaking like a man under a spell or in profound shock. "They gave me a message for you . . ."

Meena glanced at her brother, who was speaking rapidly into her phone. She was relieved to see that he'd evidently managed to reach Alaric.

"What?" she asked Adam desperately. "What's the message they gave you for me, Adam?"

"They said told me to tell you that if you ever want to see Leisha again, you have to come to the church," Adam said.

"Church?" Meena shook her head, not understanding. "But I'm already *at* the church!"

"St. George's," Adam said. "They said to go to St. George's. That's where the coronation is going to be."

"Coronation?" Meena stared down at the cell phone. Now she was completely confused. "Coronation of *who*?"

"The new prince of darkness."

Chapter Fifty-three

Alaric stared at the disaster area that had once been Meena Harper's apartment.

The Dracul had been thorough, if not downright imaginative, in their destruction of it. There wasn't a piece of furniture in 11B that hadn't been smashed, slashed, or otherwise torn apart or ruined. The sofa cushions had been slit open with knives, the stuffing strewn about the place with colorful abandon. The exposed wooden sofa frame had been chopped to bits. Same with Meena's easy chair and the rest of the upholstered furniture.

The coffee table lay smashed into pieces, as did all the lamps and every bit of dishware in the kitchen. The legs from the dining room table had been stuffed through the television screen. All of Meena's books from the built-ins in the living room lay piled into the bathtub, where they'd been left to soak with the shower still running.

That had taken some true inspiration on the part of the Dracul. He couldn't help wondering which one of them had thought that one up. Destroying the beloved books of a writer?

It could only have been Dimitri. The gesture bore all the signs of his old-school, Hun-style viciousness.

Meena's bed had seen a particularly savage assault, having been attacked with what looked to have been a chain saw. On the wall above it, someone had spray-painted the word *whore* in black. The dragon symbol of the Dracul had likewise been spray-painted on walls throughout the apartment, wherever other various euphemisms for the word *prostitute* hadn't been used instead, usually spelled incorrectly.

Alaric, stepping across the broken glass and shredded clothing from Meena's closet, shook his head.

The Dracul would certainly never have to worry about being mistaken for Rhodes scholars.

There was not the slightest chance, of course, that they had left anything living in this apartment. Wherever Meena's dog was, he was undoubtedly dead. Alaric didn't even know why he was bothering to look.

Except that he wanted to see the corpse for himself. He felt that the sight would give him just that much more reason to hate the enemy and do to them the kinds of things he'd been fantasizing about doing to them since entering the apartment.

He was inspecting the contents of Meena's appliances—he wouldn't have put it past the Dracul to have broiled or, alternately, frozen the dog to death—when he heard a voice from the doorway to 11B, which he'd most definitely locked behind him.

"Yoo-hoo," a woman called. "Knock-knock. Anybody there?"

Alaric, who was of course clutching Señor Sticky in his hand, fell into a defensive stance, ready to slice off the head of the female vampire who stood in Meena's entranceway, blinking at him. She was a tall blonde wearing a fantastical outfit that included a pair of platform heels, some kind of sparkly gaucho pants, and a blouse that appeared to be made out of feathers.

If his eyes didn't deceive him, it was Mary Lou Antonescu, the socialite.

And while she appeared startled by the sight of the sword, she wasn't half as startled as he was. How had she gotten there? He hadn't heard a key turn in the lock.

Was it possible she, like the prince, had the ability to turn to mist? Had she come in from *beneath the door*?

"Oh, hey there!" she cried in a friendly way. " You must be the Palatine guard who's trying to catch the prince. You're not going to whack my head off with that thing, are you?"

Alaric stared at her in horror. If she possessed the ability to turn to mist, she must be an extraordinarily powerful vampire.

And yet she looked as if she'd just come from a shopping trip to a suburban mall.

"Why shouldn't I?" he asked.

"Because this top is Gucci, and it cost a fortune," she said. "It would be a shame to ruin it by turning me all to dust. Besides, we're on Meena's side. I saw the lights come on, and I figured it was you. I knew you'd just cut Emil's head off and ask questions later. I didn't think you'd be quite as quick to kill a lady. Are you here for the dog?"

Alaric couldn't quite believe that he was actually standing in Meena Harper's kitchen having a conversation with . . . well, with a vampire.

A vampire who was dressed to the nines in designer clothes, flinging her long-nailed hands around as she spoke like a starlet on a late-night talk show, promoting her latest Hollywood release.

Was this some kind of trick?

But vampires weren't smart enough to stoop to such tricks. Not even the Dracul. Tricks like dropping down on him from a secret air duct in the ceiling and eating half his face off, yes.

But a conversation?

This was a first.

"Yes," he said finally. He didn't lower the sword, however. "I came for the dog."

"We've got him over at our place," Mary Lou said. "He's fine. Lucien asked us to come get him after we heard about that little altercation at Shenanigans. We weren't sure it was you all, but better safe than sorry. We figured Meena might have some . . . well, unpleasant visitors, and Jack might not be safe over here."

She looked around the apartment, shaking her head.

"Such a shame," she said, tsk-tsking. "She had a sweet little place. And they just tore it all apart, didn't they? We heard them doing it, of course. But there was nothing we could do. I mean, if we didn't want to be next. We were going to leave town to get away from them—and you, of course—but then we decided to wait. I suppose we could have dumped the dog off at a kennel, but that just didn't seem right somehow."

Alaric, still keeping the sword aloft, narrowed his eyes at her. What *was* this?

"I know what's going on here," he said. "You're a succubus, aren't you? You're going to try to seduce me, then suck out my soul. Well, it won't work. I've dealt with your kind before. And I always win."

Mary Lou, surprised, threw back her golden head and laughed. It was a happy sound in an otherwise dismal place.

"A succubus," she said. "Oh, honey, that's a good one. Wait 'til I tell Emil. I've been mistaken for a lot of things in my time, but never one of those! No, sweetie, I'm a vampire, just like the rest of them. Well, not *just* like the rest of them. I'm on your side, like I said."

"Yes, well, that's not possible," Alaric said. He crept forward, Señor Sticky aimed at her throat. She, in turn, backed up until her spine was against the front door. "Humans and vampires don't mix. Vampires kill humans. And so it's my job to kill you. All of you. No matter how beautiful."

"Oh, sweetie," she said, looking pleased by the compliment. "Thank you. But not all vampires kill humans. I don't. Why, I used to be a human once. But I gave it up. You know why?"

"No," Alaric growled. "And I don't care."

"Love." She raised her heavily made-up lashes to look at him. "I fell in love with a vampire. My husband, Emil. I'm not saying he's perfect or anything. He's not. No one is. But he loves me. He loves me so much that he was willing to give up killing humans just because I asked him to . . . and that was before the prince ever became the prince and issued his command that we *all* stop killing them. When Emil did that for me, I knew I'd found the love of my life. And I was willing to give up everything I loved—my family, pecan pie, sunshine, the chance to ever have babies—just to be with *him*."

"That's too bad," Alaric said flatly. "If you'd just have contacted someone in my office instead, we could have helped you. It's our job to keep women like you from falling prey to soul-sucking demons like him. But it's too late now."

"Well," Mary Lou said, putting her fingers delicately on his sword blade to push it a few inches down and away from her neck, "it's a good thing I didn't. Because I've never regretted my decision. Emil's my everything. If you think I'd rather have babies and pie than that, all I can say is I feel sorry for you. Because you have no idea what love is."

Alaric considered her words carefully. *Did* he know what love was? His partner, Martin, had told him that he'd known he'd found his true love—the man with whom he shared the parenting of Simone—when the two of them discovered their mutual fondness for Belgian waffles and a certain German rock band from the nineties. Alaric had always found this a bit . . . odd.

It was true Alaric wasn't that familiar with the sensation of loving or of being loved. Who had he ever had in his life to love or to be loved by?

But you couldn't miss what you had never known, and so Alaric hadn't been particularly bothered by this.

Until quite recently. He'd realized this when Meena Harper had insisted on following him through the rectory and then tied that ridiculous scarf of hers around his wrist.

It was then that he had found himself almost blurting out the truth. Not all of it, of course. But the part about his idea of how she should come and work for the Palatine.

What had he been thinking? He had almost revealed something that up until that moment he had been trying to play close to his chest.

He still had the scarf tied around his wrist, even though it wasn't particularly comfortable. What man wore a scarf around his wrist? What had she even been thinking putting it there?

But she had said it was for luck. And then she had kissed him.

So he didn't dare remove it.

He had a sinking feeling that he really was a fool, just as Holtzman had accused him of being.

He looked the vampire in the eye. She said he had no idea what love was?

"What you're confusing for love," he concluded aloud, "is the release of the neurotransmitter dopamine in your brain, stimulated by the mammalian hormone oxytocin."

"I think we should just agree to disagree," Mary Lou Antonescu said. "Do you want the damned dog or not?"

Sighing, Alaric pulled the sword away and sheathed it. "I want the dog," he said. "If this is a trick, I will kill you and your husband both. And I won't make it quick."

It wasn't a trick. She had the dog locked up in a bathroom of her apartment, which was five times the size of Meena's and had been neither vandalized nor ransacked by the Dracul. Alaric found himself approving of both the tasteful and expensive décor and the timidity of the husband, Emil Antonescu, who seemed to be expecting Alaric to strike him down at any moment.

"For heaven's sake, Mary Lou," he exclaimed when his wife opened the front door to let the two of them in. "Where have you been? Didn't I warn you not to leave the—"

That's when he saw Alaric and dropped the brandy snifter he'd been holding. It fell with a crash to the parquet, glass and brandy going everywhere. Emil went as pale as . . . well, a vampire.

"Is th-that," the husband stammered, "th-the—"

"Oh, don't worry, hon," Mary Lou said. "The Dracul seem to have all gone. And this is just the Palatine guard, here to pick up Meena's dog. He promised not to hurt us. Well, he didn't promise, exactly. But I'm sure he won't. He seems all right, for a Palatine guard. Oh, look at the mess you've made, Emil. Who do you expect to clean that up? You know it's the maid's day off. Do you want a drink?" This last was directed at Alaric. "I never did get your name. What is it?"

Alaric was looking at a painting of a pretty young girl they had hanging in their foyer. The signature at the bottom said *Renoir*.

"Alaric Wulf," he said, studying the painting. "And I don't drink. I'm just here for the dog. I like this painting very much."

"Isn't that nice?" Mary Lou said about the painting. "Emil picked that up for a song from the artist when he was just an unknown. Emil has quite an eye. Are you sure you don't want anything? Not even a soda or something?"

"Nothing for me," Alaric said. Like he was going to accept a drink from a vampire. What if they put poison in it? "Just the dog, please."

"Of course. I'll be right back."

Mary Lou drifted away, leaving Alaric alone with the husband, who was standing on the far side of the spreading brandy stain on the highly polished wood floor, staring wide-eyed at him.

"I would kill you right now," Alaric said casually to Emil Antonescu, "but I promised Meena Harper I would bring her dog back in a timely fashion."

"I would kill you right now," Emil Antonescu said, hatred causing his eyes to flare red, "but my prince forbade me from it."

"Did he now?" Alaric heard this with interest. "I wonder why."

Emil shrugged. "Your people," Emil said, "have done nothing but harass my people for decades, causing us misery and heartache."

"Well, I believe your people started it," Alaric pointed out, "by dining on the blood of innocents."

"We no longer drink to kill," Emil said. "We're forbidden from it. Now we dine only on willing donors or blood purchased from blood banks. Why can't you leave us alone?"

Alaric's sword hand itched. It was incredibly difficult for him to be standing this close to a vampire and not kill it. "Perhaps," he said, "because there's no such thing as a willing donor, only human beings who are too weak willed to stand up to your freakish mind games. And your people are the ones who keep attacking mine."

"In self-defense," Emil hissed. "In self-defense only."

Alaric took a step toward him . . . and kept on stepping until they were standing only inches apart.

"It wasn't self-defense when a pack of Dracul attacked my partner and me in a warehouse outside of Berlin and nearly killed him," he snarled, glaring down at the smaller man.

"It's a shame it was only *nearly*," Emil snarled back, giving him a chest bump.

Alaric drew his sword. It came singing from its scabbard, the blade shining in the glow from the crystal chandelier hanging from the foyer's high, arched ceiling. . . .

"Here we are," Mary Lou sang. She came back dragging a highly reluctant Jack Bauer behind her on a leash. The dog fought her every step of the way, growling and struggling against the leash, his claws skidding on the polished floor.

The men parted at once, going back to their separate squares of parquet.

When Jack Bauer saw Alaric, however, he stopped fighting and bounded over to him excitedly.

Alaric stooped down and lifted the dog, who appeared to be unharmed and in perfect health.

"He looks good," he said, unable to keep the surprise from his tone.

"Of course he looks good." Emil glared at him. "We aren't savages. We wouldn't hurt a little dog."

Alaric raised an eyebrow in the vampire's direction. But Mary Lou had already given her husband a little smack across the chest.

"Oh, *Emil*!" she cried. "Alaric, don't mind him. He's just in a bad mood because you all finding out where we live means we have to move again. You know, because now you're going to try to kill us and all. And it's my fault, because I'm the one who sent that—"

"Mary Lou." Emil Antonescu locked an arm around his wife's slim waist, then dragged her to his side. "Please. Just stop talking. For once."

That's when Mary Lou's gaze fell to the sword in Alaric's hand. "Well," she said, her smile fading. "What was going on here with you two boys while I was gone?"

"Nothing," Emil said. "Nothing was going on. Mr. Wulf was just leaving. Weren't you, Mr. Wulf?"

Alaric just stood there, holding Meena Harper's squirming dog. For the first time in his career, he wasn't certain what to do.

He was sworn to kill all demons, no matter what their form.

And sometimes those forms could be very deceiving indeed.

That's what the dark side did: worked to play tricks on the human mind, to rouse compassion and sympathy to keep a man from doing what he'd been trained to do—plow a stake through the heart of whatever evil creature was before him.

But for once, Alaric wasn't certain what stood before him truly was evil.

Maybe all that chattering Meena Harper had been doing, about redemption and rehabilitation and how Lucien Antonescu wasn't like the other vampires, was getting to him.

But he actually believed these two vampires were just a couple of pathetic losers—with very good taste in home furnishings and art—who deserved to have to spend all of eternity with each other.

Could he actually feel *sorry* for them?

And the truth was . . . they *had* saved Jack Bauer from being blown up in the microwave by the Dracul.

And Meena Harper liked them.

Good God. What was *happening* to him?

"If you tell anyone about this," he said, pointing Señor Sticky at their necks, causing them both to stagger back a few steps, "I'll find you, wherever you are, and force one of you to choke on the dust of the other."

Mary Lou looked queasy. "Good heavens," she said. "We won't tell."

Alaric turned and ran from the apartment. He didn't bother with the elevator. He took the stairs, two at a time, down all eleven flights, giving Jack Bauer quite a jogging in his arms. It wasn't until he reached the bottom that he paused to think about what he'd just done:

Let two vampires go free.

He was going to regret this. It was going to come back to haunt him.

On the other hand . . .

He could always hunt them down and kill them later. How hard would it be, considering the woman's obvious taste for designer clothes?

He sheathed his sword and put Jack Bauer down on his four paws. Then he hit the exit door and walked out into the lobby.

His cell phone buzzed. He reached down to answer it.

"Alaric Wulf," he said.

"Alaric?" Jon Harper's anxious voice was on the other end of the line. "Where are you? Are you still at the building? Because we have a problem. A big problem."

Chapter Fifty-four

The subway. Of course it had to be the subway.

Well, how else was she supposed to get there? It was Saturday night, and she was downtown. There weren't any cabs.

And Meena had to get uptown as quickly as possible.

What else was she supposed to do, exactly? Sit quietly in a windowless room in the convent, like they wanted her to, and let Sister Gertrude and "the men" go uptown with Stefan Dominic and get themselves killed trying to save Leisha?

Sitting quietly in a windowless room might have been all right for Yalena, who was traumatized physically and emotionally. But that wasn't all right for Meena, who was the reason all of these people, including Leisha, were in so much danger in the first place.

Meena sat on the 6 train, trying not to make eye contact with any of the other people in her car. The last thing she needed right now was to get involved in someone else's problems.

She had plenty of her own.

Scholarly Abraham Holtzman, listening to her and Jon frantically trying to explain what they'd heard on the phone after they'd come running down from the roof to find him, had nodded gravely and said, "Yes. Yes, of course. It all makes sense. St. George's is under construction, you say?"

Jon had nodded. "Yeah. It's closed to the public while it undergoes renovation."

"When I was walking by it the night I first met—" Meena had interrupted herself. "Well, when the colony of bats attacked me, I thought one of the spires was falling down. It's in pretty bad shape."

Father Bernard, Sister Gertrude, and Abraham Holtzman had all exchanged uneasy glances when they'd heard this.

"What?" Meena had cried. "What difference does that make?" She'd already begun to regret telling any of them anything. She should have just run straight from the rectory and for the nearest train station. . . .

"A church that has gone too long unused—or unrepaired—falls into danger of becoming deconsecrated," Abraham had explained slowly. "Perfect for demon rites."

"Demon rites?" Just the words had caused the hairs on the back of Meena's neck to prickle. "Like . . . the coronation of a new prince of -darkness?"

No one had answered her. They'd already begun running around, gathering weapons for what they obviously thought was going to be some kind of apocalyptic showdown up at St. George's with the Dracul— who had all mysteriously vanished from outside of St. Clare's. None of them—not Abraham Holtzman, nor Father Bernard, nor Sister Gertrude, nor the friars and other nuns . . . nor even the novices or her brother, Jon—showed the slightest flicker of fear or even of hesitation. They were perfectly prepared, Meena saw, to fight.

And perhaps to die.

But what they didn't know—and she did—was that they were *going* to die. All of them. Every last one of them. The truth of what lay in store for them had hit her with perfect, almost stunning clarity in those few moments as she'd stood there in the rectory hallway:

Dimitri was holding her best friend—her *pregnant* best friend— captive at St. George's Cathedral and wasn't going to let her go unless Meena showed up to make the exchange.

Her own life for that of her friend.

Then when that happened, there'd be a second exchange: Meena's life for Lucien's.

After which Dimitri Antonescu, the demon half brother of Lucien

Antonescu, son of Dracula, the prince of darkness, would crown himself the new prince in the deconsecrated cathedral . . .

. . . and a reign of vampiric terror and death would spread across Manhattan, if not the world.

Meanwhile, Meena's brother; Abraham; Sister Gertrude . . . all of these good people dashing around her were going to die fighting to try to stop what Meena saw happening in her mind's eye. She envisioned exactly the same death for them, in fact, that she'd seen for Alaric Wulf when she'd looked into his future while she'd been tying her scarf around his wrist:

Darkness. Fire. Lots and lots of fire. Then . . .

Nothing. Just . . . nothing.

It was what Meena had tried to explain to Lucien that first night she'd spent with him. How being dead was never a happy ending.

Because when Meena looked into the futures of people who were going to die, all she saw was a vast pit of nothingness, stretching out before her like a huge crevasse. She stood with the toes of her shoes poking over the edge of that crevasse, so deep she couldn't even see the bottom.

She hoped there was some kind of afterlife beyond the pit of nothingness. But maybe it was better that if there was, she couldn't see it.

Because it was the nothingness that drove Meena to warn people to look out, even though they often didn't listen. It was nothingness she saw in her friends' futures that night. Their lives were barreling straight toward it.

Which was why, standing there in the rectory, she took action. She grabbed a pen and a sheet of paper and jotted a quick note; scooped up enough change for train fare from a jar by the door, since Alaric had long ago taken her wallet; and left, making sure the note would be easily discovered.

She knew they'd be upset. In fact, Alaric Wulf's explicit orders, when Jon had reached him over the phone, had been the exact opposite of what she was doing: to keep Meena as far away from St. George's Cathedral as possible.

Oh, and he'd also said that her dog was fine and that Alaric was leaving him in the safekeeping of Pradip, the doorman, for the time being.

Apparently, Meena going to St. George's was only going to hasten, not put an end to, the coming demonic apocalypse.

But none of that changed the fact that Meena knew she was the one who had caused all this.

And that she had seen what she had seen, and knew what she knew.

Which was more than Alaric Wulf, with all his experience, or Abraham Holtzman, with his *Palatine Guard Human Resources Handbook,* knew.

She was the one who had looked into the future and seen it filled with fire, darkness, and finally, slow, agonizing death for all of them.

Then, nothingness.

No. Not today.

Because if she knew anything at all, it was that that was only one version of the future.

The future could change. She could change it. She'd done it before, lots of times. She'd stopped people from hurtling over the side of that precipice more times than she could count.

She was going to do it again tonight.

And no one, not Alaric, not Lucien, not even a crazed pack of vampires, was going to stop her.

The subway train roared into the Seventy-seventh Street station. Meena's station.

She got up from her seat . . . then paused before stepping through the sliding doors when they opened. There was a couple that had been making out on the seat across from hers. They had gotten up at the same time she had. She glanced at them. . . .

And saw, in her mind's eye, both of them getting struck on the head and killed by a gigantic piece of flying blue scaffolding.

It looked suspiciously like the blue scaffolding that surrounded St. George's.

The couple had their arms around each other, still canoodling as they started to get off the train. Meena, standing in the open subway car door, held up both her hands like claws, opened her mouth, and hissed at them.

"Get back!" she shrieked. "Don't get off at this stop!"

"Shit!" the boy cried, staggering backward.

The girl looked torn between fear and embarrassment. She giggled nervously. "Dude," she said to her boyfriend. "What's wrong with her?"

"I'm a vampire!" Meena yelled, stepping off the train but staying in the doorway and still making menacing motions with her hands. "A vampire! Stay on the train!"

"Stand clear of the closing doors," the voice announced.

The train doors closed, trapping the couple safely inside. Meena immediately dropped her hands, resumed her normal posture, turned, and began walking away. She saw the boy make an obscene gesture at her as the subway car pulled past her and out of the station.

She waved at him.

Meena hurried through the station, which was empty on a Saturday night, inhaling the familiar scent of stale urine, then jogged up the steps to Seventy-seventh Street.

It wouldn't be long now. What would she do when she got there?

She didn't know, exactly. She still had the stake that Alaric had given her in her back pocket. Maybe she'd stake someone. Like Dimitri.

She'd demanded her cell phone back from Jon after he'd called Alaric. She'd texted Lucien about what had happened with Leisha.

With luck, he would already be at St. George's when she got there and everything would be taken care of. She'd walk in and find Leisha freed and perfectly fine, and Dimitri and the rest of the Dracul dusted, with stakes in their hearts. Lucien would take her tenderly in his arms, and they'd fly off to Thailand to begin their new lives together as man and wife . . . after they picked up Jack Bauer from Pradip, of course. Jon could be best man at their wedding.

Yeah, Meena thought cynically as she approached the church, its spires floodlit against the inky sky. *That so wasn't going to happen.*

The church looked abandoned . . . dead. The blue scaffolding that surrounded it was undisturbed, covered in razor wire at the top, chained with padlocks.

No one, human or vampire, was around, that Meena could see.

Had this all been some kind of sick vampire joke? Had they made her come all the way up there for nothing?

And if so . . . where *was* Leisha? How was Meena ever going to find her?

Frustrated, Meena stood there at the bottom of the steps in front of the church, exactly where Lucien had tackled her a few nights ago and saved her from what she knew now had been an attack by the Dracul. If only she could go back in time and . . .

And what? What would she have done differently?

Nothing at all. She'd have fallen in love with him all over again right then and there. Who wouldn't have? He was everything that—

"Meena!"

Startled, Meena turned around. A familiar voice was calling her name.

She turned again, at first failing to see anyone. Then finally she spotted a man sitting on the stoop of a brownstone across the street. She recognized him in the light from the streetlamps.

"Adam?" she cried. "What are you doing over there?"

As Meena hurried to cross the street to his side, however, she soon saw the answer to her question.

Adam, a white bandage around his throat, had been handcuffed to the metal railing alongside the steps to the building.

"That freak chained me here!" Adam yelled, rattling the cuffs in an effort to free himself. "He told me to stay with Pradip after he patched me up, but I followed him instead. So he threw these cuffs on me so I couldn't go into the church after him. He said it was too dangerous. What am I supposed to do now, huh, Meena? *They have my wife in there!* And I'm stuck out here. You have to help me get free, Meena. Do you have a hairpin or something? You can pick locks, right?"

Meena looked down at Adam. He was a mess. His entire shirtfront was covered in what appeared to be his own blood from the bite wound he'd sustained on his neck.

But he didn't seem to be in shock anymore. His pupils looked normal sized.

And his anger was typically Adam.

"Who left you here, Adam?" Meena asked. She actually had a pretty good idea. But she wanted to be sure. "Whose handcuffs are those?"

"That freak vampire-slayer friend of yours," Adam cried. "That's who. The one you and Jon sent to allegedly help me. Some help he was! I've been sitting out here doing nothing while my wife, Leisha, is probably being eaten alive—"

"Leisha is fine," Meena said reassuringly, laying a soothing hand on his shoulder. "I promise you. I would know if something had happened to her." Meena hoped this was true. "You said Alaric is inside the church already?"

"Yeah, he's inside the church. I told you, he left me out here while he went in with that big sword of his! He's even got a name for it. Señor Stinky or something. Meena, you've got to unlock these cuffs. I need to get in there and help find my wife. Who knows what they're doing to her?"

"You should be in a hospital," Meena murmured, absently patting him on the shoulder.

"Screw the hospital," Adam said. "I need to find my wife! It's my fault she's in there in the first place."

"No," Meena said firmly. "It's my fault."

She walked away from him, starting back across the street, toward the church. If Alaric had gotten inside, she could, too.

"Hey," Adam yelled after her, outraged. "Where are you going? You can't leave me here, too, Meena!"

"You'll be fine out there, Adam," she called over her shoulder. "Believe me. You're better off there than you would be coming with me."

"This is bullshit!" Adam shouted. "Bullshit! You get back here, Meena! You turn around and get back here, right now!"

But instead of turning around, Meena stalked right up to the scaffolding that surrounded the church. There had to be a way inside, she told herself. If Alaric had found a way, she could too.

Tentatively, she laid a hand on the cool blue wood.

No sooner had she done this than it blew apart.

Chapter Fifty-five

The force of the explosion sent Meena sprawling back against the sidewalk where she'd first lain with Lucien. It also sent razor wire and pieces of plywood flying. Meena flung up her arms to protect her eyes. Around her, car alarms went off.

Then, just as suddenly, they were silenced.

When she put her arms down and opened her eyes, it was just in time to catch one particularly huge chunk of blue painted plywood landing exactly where the young couple from the subway would have been . . . if she hadn't scared them from getting off the train.

Instead, the wood landed harmlessly on the sidewalk with a solid clunk.

"What the hell was *that*?" she heard Adam ask from the across the street.

Rising painfully to her scraped hands and knees, Meena found herself looking at the doors to the church, which had now been thrown open. A tall man who looked not unlike Lucien, except that he was a little shorter and a little heavier and wore a light gray suit with a black shirt and tie—which Meena couldn't imagine Lucien doing—stepped through the cloud of dust left behind by the explosion and peered down at her, a pleased expression on his face.

"Meena Harper, I presume?" he said. Unlike his brother, there wasn't a trace of anything European in his accent.

Meena nodded. "That's me," she said, coughing a little from all the dust. "Are you Dimitri?"

"I am," he said. He offered her his hand to help her up. Meena, her heart hammering, took it, because what else was she going to do? She had come there for a reason, and that was to free her friend and end this.

The time had come to do both.

"Sorry about that," he said apologetically. "Oh, look at your poor coat. Here, let me help you." He brushed dust and bits of plywood off the suede of her jacket. "You know, you're nothing like I expected."

"I get that a lot." she asked, still coughing. "Shorter?"

"Younger," he said. His gaze on her face was every bit as intense as his brother's had ever been. But unlike Lucien's, Dimitri's brown eyes weren't sad. No, they didn't have that kind of depth. They were as shallow as *Insatiable*'s plotlines. "But pretty!" he added gallantly. "Well, I expected that, to be honest. My brother never could resist a pretty face."

"Thanks," Meena said sarcastically as she picked her way across the debris.

She noticed that they weren't alone. Glowing, red-eyed gazes peered out at them from the shadows . . . gazes belonging, she knew, to the Dracul, Dimitri's father's faithful followers. She caught glimpses of them, expecting to see lean, leather-jacketed men who all resembled Gregory Bane and girls who looked like Taylor Mackenzie, in low-rise jeans and halter tops.

And she did spy Gregory Bane, leering at her by Dimitri's side.

But the majority of the creatures she saw peering at her looked like ordinary people, no different than anyone she would see riding the subway or standing in line at Abdullah's coffee cart in the morning, neither particularly thin or fat, young or old, fashionable or unfashionable.

And maybe that, Meena thought, her heart pounding harder than ever, was what scared her most of all.

The one thing they did have in common was that they all looked . . . hungry.

But hungry, Meena wondered, for *what,* exactly?

Dimitri was leading her into the church. Meena had never been inside St. George's before. She knew it was fairly large and had always heard it was pretty. She had seen from the outside that it had a lot of stained glass windows. The largest of them hung above the front doors to the church and was supposed to depict St. George mounted on his steed, slaying a serpentlike dragon.

But she had never even been able to tell the glass was stained because it was so badly in need of cleaning. It just looked black. Hardly any light whatsoever got into the church, even from the safety lamps attached to the spires. The only light to see by was thrown by hundreds of candles that had been lit by the Dracul . . . and these weren't votive candles, either. They were thick black candles that had been placed, wax dripping, over every available flat surface in the church, including the pews, which looked like they'd been kicked over.

The walls of the church hadn't fared any better. They'd met with the wrong end of a few dozen cans of spray paint. There were dragon symbols sprayed everywhere, including across the stained glass windows. Meena, looking up at the church's thirty-foot ceiling, saw that the choir loft had been equally decimated and was also strewn with graffiti. "Wow," she said. "You've really done wonders with the place. Who's your decorator?"

She heard a tinkly laugh and then an all-too-familiar female voice behind her said, "Me. I am."

Meena whirled around, her heart exploding in her chest.

"Hey," Shoshona said with a great big smile. "Surprise!"

Meena felt as if she'd been run over by a steamroller.

Then again, she thought, why was she so surprised? She'd always known something was going to kill Shoshona at the gym.

Why shouldn't it have been a vampire? Specifically, Dimitri Antonescu's son, Stefan, who'd only this morning been ramming a gun into Meena's ribs.

Still, Meena couldn't stop herself from staring. Shoshona looked fantastic. Her hair had never been shinier . . . or straighter.

I guess you don't need a flat-iron when you're dead, Meena thought.

"Yeah," Shoshona said, strolling up to her. "It's me. Hey . . . thanks for the bag."

Meena lowered her gaze and saw that Shoshona was holding a Marc Jacobs jewel-encrusted dragon tote.

In ruby.

Meena's ruby red Marc Jacobs jewel-encrusted dragon tote, to be exact. The one Lucien had given her.

Meena didn't know what to say. A thousand different retorts popped into her head.

But she was too stunned to say any of them out loud.

"By the way," Shoshona said, leaning in close to lay a long, manicured fingernail in the opening of Meena's white-collared shirt, just where her pulse was leaping in her throat. "Guess who's just been appointed the new cochairs of entertainment at Affiliated Broadcast Network?"

Shoshona pointed over her shoulder at a middle-aged couple in business attire, who waved enthusiastically in Meena's direction.

Shoshona's aunt and uncle.

Meena's heart sank. Not Fran and Stan, too.

Everyone Meena knew really *was* turning out to be a vampire.

But cochairs of entertainment at ABN? How was that even *possible*? All they'd ever done was create a *soap opera*.

"Oh," Shoshona said, tossing her long black silky hair. "And guess who they made president of programming at the network?" She pointed proudly at herself. "And as my first official duty in that capacity, I'm firing you, Meena. Sorry about that."

"*What?*" Meena cried. She knew she had a few more important things in her life to worry about than her job.

But her job was, in a way, her life.

"What can I say?" Shoshona asked with a shrug. "We don't really appreciate people who are prejudiced against our species. Nor do we need them making disparaging remarks about our so-called misogynistic tendencies."

"Your *species*?" Meena felt a spurt of white-hot anger dart through her. "Your *species*? Let me tell you something about your species and what I've seen you do to women—"

"That's enough, Shoshona," Dimitri said in the tone of a disapproving father as he reached out to lay a hand on Meena's shoulder and steer her away from the other girl. "I have better uses for Miss Harper's time now, I think. For instance . . ."

That's when Meena finally saw the apse at the front of the church. The sanctuary, debased with graffiti. The altar, up on the dais, broken into pieces. A statue of St. George, pushed to the floor and missing its head.

And Leisha, sitting in the only pew that had been left upright, with her hands tied in front of her and resting in her lap.

"Leish," Meena cried, relief rushing over her. She jerked her shoulder out from beneath Dimitri's grip and raced to her friend's side. "Are you all right?" Meena asked, kneeling down beside her. "Did they hurt you?"

Leisha shook her head. Her cheeks were tear-stained, her eye makeup smudged. But otherwise, she looked fine.

"I just want," she whispered to Meena, "to get the hell out of here. I hate these people. They're freaks. That girl, Shoshona, from your office? You always told me she was a total bitch, but I never knew how *much* of a bitch until tonight. And I still really have to pee."

Meena choked back a sob. *Leisha. Oh, Leisha.*

"Okay," Meena said. She reached for the cords that held Leisha's wrists and began untying them. "We'll get you out of here."

"What are they?" Leisha asked, eyeing Dimitri suspiciously over the top of Meena's head. "Like meth heads or something? You know that Gregory Bane guy from *Lust* bit Adam, don't you? He *bit* him."

Leisha, with her usual common sense, had apparently chosen to ignore the explanation Meena had given her over the phone about what was going on and come up with her own, one that she could process and understand.

"Yes," Meena said. "Yes, they're meth heads." She dropped her head to the knot that was holding her friend's hands tied together, trying to bite it apart with her teeth. She couldn't get it undone otherwise.

"Hey," she said finally, raising her head, realizing the futility of what she was doing. "Could someone give me a hand here and help me untie her? I fulfilled my part of the bargain. I'm here. You said you'd let her go if I showed up. So could someone help me?"

She glanced up at Dimitri, only to find him grinning down at her with an expression on his face that she didn't like at all.

"Oh," he said, "I can see why my brother likes you. You're so . . . trusting."

On the word *trusting,* he reached down, grabbed her by the arm, and yanked her back up to her feet, almost in a single motion. The gesture was so violent and jarring, Meena saw stars for a second or two.

"But I think we're going to keep your little friend here for a while longer," he said to her. "Because having her around will make you more accommodating to my needs. And I still need a few things from you, some of which I'd like to hurry up and get to before my brother comes along and tries to spoil things, which he's always had an unfortunate tendency to do."

Dimitri hauled her, none too gently, into the sanctuary and up onto the dais, beside the altar. Meena did not like the way the Dracul—including Shoshona and her aunt and uncle—had gathered around, as if eager for a show that was about to start.

Nor did she like what she suddenly recognized sitting on the still upright part of the altar.

It was a bowl from Meena's own apartment. The large antique one made of pewter her great-aunt Wilhelmina had left her and that Meena never used because she was worried about lead poisoning.

First the bag Lucien had given her. Then her job. Now her great-aunt's bowl. What *else* were the Dracul going to take from her?

"I understand you possess quite the power to predict the future, Meena Harper," Dimitri said in his deep voice.

Suddenly, Meena had a very bad feeling about what was about to happen.

Especially because of the way all of the Dracul were eyeing the holes Lucien had already put in her neck—which were obvious to everyone because Meena had given Alaric the scarf she'd been wearing to cover them—and then glancing down expectantly toward the large silver-colored bowl. The hungry look in their eyes seemed to increase by a hundredfold.

Dimitri was right about one thing: Meena had always been good at predicting the future. *Other people's futures.*

Never her own.

Until now.

Meena looked up at Dimitri. He was staring down at her with those flat brown eyes, in which she saw more than just a hint of blood red.

Then she glanced up at the enormous dragon symbol someone had spray-painted behind the altar.

Ever since I left you this morning, Lucien had said to her last night in her bedroom, *I've had the oddest sensation that I know how almost every human I've come into contact with is . . . is going to die. . . . I've never, ever experienced anything like this. Not until . . . well, being with you.*

Now, Meena knew exactly what the bowl was for . . . and why Dimitri had been so intent on getting her to come up to St. George's. It wasn't just because he wanted to lure his brother there, to trap and kill him.

Although certainly that would be an added bonus.

No, Dimitri wanted her for something else.

He wanted her blood, for a little precoronation precognition cocktail.

Meena flung a hand to her mouth to avoid letting out a semi-hysterical scream.

And then, before she had a chance to think twice about what she was doing, she reached into her back pocket for Alaric's stake with one hand, then used the other hand to stabilize herself on the altar while she launched her right foot, as hard as she could, into Dimitri's face.

Too bad she was only wearing flats and not her platform boots.

Still, she seemed to manage to catch him off guard, since he bent at the waist while crying out in pain, clutching his face.

There was a collective gasp from the Dracul.

Yes! She'd done it! She'd caught a vampire off guard!

She came at him with the stake while she had the advantage, determined to plunge it into his heart and end this, all of it, once and for all, forever. Save herself and her brother and her friends.

This was for Yalena and for Leisha and for what they'd done to her apartment and for whatever they intended to do to Cheryl and Taylor and everyone else at *Insatiable*. . . .

Except that Dimitri, still bent over in pain, shot out a lightning-fast hand and seized her wrist—the one holding the stake—in a grip that was like iron.

And then he began squeezing her wrist so hard that Meena, tightly as she tried to hold on, eventually had to let go. Alaric's stake fell with a clatter to the marble floor of the altar and rolled off and away, until it was out of sight.

But still, he didn't stop squeezing, even when Meena cried out in pain, collapsing to her knees in front of him and the Dracul and the altar and everyone, convinced he was going to shatter every last bone in her wrist. . . .

"Do you think because you can see death before it comes that you can outwit me, Meena Harper?" he asked her, looking down at her with eyes that glowed red as hot barbecue coals. His teeth had turned into pointed fangs, and they were suddenly entirely too near Meena's throat for comfort. "Or are the rumors true and you can read the thoughts of the dead, as well? Is that how you've managed to captivate my brother so?"

Read the thoughts of the dead? No wonder they were so desperate for her blood.

"No," she said with a gasp. "I can't read anyone's thoughts, living *or* dead. I can only how tell how someone is going to die—"

Dimitri smiled, his fangs gleaming menacingly in the candlelight. "Oh, my dear," he said. "I think you overestimate yourself. Because if that were true, why on earth would you have come here tonight?"

Her eyes filled with tears from the pain he was inflicting on her wrist and the fact that those fangs were looming closer and closer to her throat.

This is it., Meena thought, closing her eyes. *It's finally my turn to find out if there's anything beyond that nothingness . . . .*

That's when she heard someone shout Dimitri's name in warning.

And she opened her eyes to see something huge and heavy and black come swooping down on a rope from the choir loft, striking Dimitri Antonescu squarely in the chest and sending him crashing into the dragon symbol spray-painted behind the altar.

Dimitri was so surprised, he let go of Meena's wrist . . . but only just in time to keep from dragging her across the altar with him.

Alaric Wulf, releasing the rope and landing on his feet a few yards away from where Meena lay panting on the cool white marble, surveyed his sword blade.

"Damn," he said. "I missed."

Meena, more relieved than she could say to see him, sat up.

"What do you mean, you missed?" she asked. "You almost chopped my head off."

Alaric pointed at where Dimitri was rising from the crumbling rubble and had just let out a furious, wordless scream.

"I mean I missed *him*," Alaric said. Then he glanced over his shoulder. "And they don't look too happy to see me either."

The Dracul, outraged at the assault on their leader, were swarming at Alaric, hissing in protest. He lifted his blade in defensive. Meena crawled across the sanctuary floor toward him, favoring her tender wrist.

She knew it was hopeless, of course. They were both dead. There were probably a hundred Dracul against the two of them.

Still, she wasn't going to let him go down alone. There had to be something she could do.

Only what? She'd lost the stake he'd given her, her single weapon.

Alaric seemed to be thinking along the same lines.

"Did you have any kind of plan when you came sneaking in here?" he asked her as he swung his blade at the encroaching vampires.

"No," Meena said when she reached his feet. "Did you?"

"No time," he said. "Reach into my pocket. There might be some holy water or stakes left in there."

She rose to her knees, searching the pockets of his leather trench coat as he waved his sword around.

"No," she said, disappointment surging through her. "There's nothing there."

"I told you not to follow me," Alaric said. "Didn't I?"

"You did," Meena admitted. "But I couldn't sit back and let everyone die."

"*So.*"

They both looked over at Dimitri, who was standing a few feet away from them, a very discontented look on his face. He had obviously not enjoyed being kicked into a wall by a Palatine guard.

"As I think you can see, you're outnumbered." Dimitri raised a dark eyebrow. "A bit like when you and your partner were in that warehouse outside of Berlin, eh, Mr. Wulf?"

"That was you?" Alaric looked furious. "I swear, I'll rip you limb from limb for that, you—"

"Don't be so childish," Dimitri said with a laugh. "You Palatine are all the same. Arrogant. Always thinking you're one step ahead of us. But even with all your fancy modern computer equipment to track our movements and our money, we'll still find ways to slip through your fingers and prevail . . . because of your arrogance. And your stupidity. It's because of your stupidity that we're going to kill the pregnant woman now."

Meena's heart flew into her throat. The hordes of Dracul crowding around her and Alaric at the bottom of the dais parted a little, and she saw that Leisha had been pulled onto her feet. She stood with her arms being clutched on either side by Gregory Bane and Shoshona. They were both grinning a little maniacally, but Leisha didn't look too happy.

Maybe that was because Gregory Bane was hissing at her, showing off his fangs.

"Stop it," Meena said, climbing shakily back to her feet. Her wrist was throbbing, and her head wasn't feeling too good, either. "I'll give you what you want."

She limped to the altar and lifted the pewter bowl, which shone in the candlelight.

"Meena," Alaric said. His bright blue eyes shot her a warning. He shook his head at her.

No. Don't do it.

But Meena knew it wasn't any use. She had failed. Alaric had failed. Lucien obviously wasn't coming, for whatever reason, or he'd have been there by then.

It was over. It was useless.

It was done.

Her toes were on the precipice.

"Take it," she said, holding out the bowl to Dimitri. "Take it all. I don't care anymore. Just let Leisha go."

"Well, thank you." Dimitri lifted the bowl from her hands and gave her a courtly bow. "Aren't you an accommodating creature?"

Then he extracted from an inside coat pocket a dagger with a gold, elaborately jeweled hilt. This he pressed to Meena's throat. She swallowed, her heart hammering.

But all Dimitri did next was look over at Gregory Bane and Shoshona, then nod.

"You can kill the woman now," he said to them.

"*What?*" Meena twisted around just as Dimitri, still pressing the blade in the direction of her neck, seized her by the arm and began dragging her toward the altar. "*No!*"

But it was too late. The Dracul surged forward, falling hungrily upon the spot where Meena had last seen Leisha, even as Alaric leapt toward them, intent on saving her friend.

Except that Leisha wasn't there anymore. Meena blinked, thinking her eyes must be playing tricks on her in all the candlelight.

But it was true. The hungry Dracul—Fran, Stan, Shoshona, all of them—were staring at an empty spot where Leisha had been. Meena, twisting in Dimitri's grip on the dais by the altar, caught sight of a flash of movement on the far side of the church.

That's how she saw that Leisha was already in the back of the church, being rushed out the doors and into the waiting arms of her husband, Adam, by none other than . . .

Mary Lou Antonescu?

Meena would have thought that she'd imagined the whole thing in some kind of post-traumatic-stress-induced hallucination if Dimitri hadn't pointed the dagger after Mary Lou and screamed, "*Traitor!*"

The Dracul whipped around, almost as one, and launched themselves toward Mary Lou, as if intent on ripping *her* apart, as they'd been about to do to Leisha.

That's when a gust of wind rose up from nowhere and tore through the church. It was so strong that it blew out every single candle flame, causing everyone to throw an arm up over his or her eyes in order keep out all the dust it raised from the construction.

Then the wind turned and whipped back through the church again, this time in the opposite direction.

Now each and every candle wick magically reignited, the flames burning merrily again.

After the final breath of wind died down, and Meena had cautiously lowered the arm Dimitri wasn't grasping, shaken by what had just occurred, she—and everyone else in St. George's—saw that there was someone else standing on the dais beside Dimitri Antonescu. Someone who hadn't been there before that freakish wind had whipped so savagely throughout the church, dousing and then reigniting all those candles.

It was Dimitri's brother, Lucien.

The prince of darkness.

Chapter Fifty-six

Lucien didn't even glance in Meena's direction. Instead, all his powers of concentration appeared to be focused on his brother.

"Dimitri," he said. His voice, as always, was like velvet. "I understand you wanted to see me about something?"

Dimitri still had hold of Meena's arm. It was her sore arm, the wrist he'd nearly broken. Or maybe he *had* broken it. Meena didn't know.

He still held the knife, as well.

"Why, yes, Lucien," he said. His own voice purred like a kitten's. "What a pleasure it is to see you tonight. And what an entrance. But then, you always did know how to make those, didn't you?"

"Let go of her," Lucien said. Now the velvet was more like ice.

"But Miss Harper and I were only just getting acquainted," Dimitri said, casually running the point of the jeweled dagger down her bare neck. "And I want to be able to read everyone's minds and tell the future, too. I don't think it's fair that you're getting to have all the fun."

"I think you've been having quite enough fun," Lucien said coldly. "I went to Concubine earlier today, and I saw what you were keeping in the basement."

Dimitri looked surprised. He was holding Meena close enough

to him that she felt him go still. Everyone in the church—the Dracul, even Alaric, at the bottom of the dais—seemed to be watching the brothers' tense conversation intently.

"Did you?" Dimitri asked. Then he smiled so that his fangs showed again. "So you happened to stumble across part of my latest financial enterprise—"

"TransCarta," shouted a male voice from somewhere near the back of the church.

Meena, recognizing that voice, froze.

No. Oh, no.

Every head in the building swiveled to follow the sound of that voice.

Which was how everyone managed to get such a good look at Meena's brother, Jon, standing in the entrance of the church, flanked by Sister Gertrude and Abraham Holtzman, who was holding a stake to Stefan Dominic's chest. Behind them stood every friar, nun, and novice from the Shrine of St. Clare.

Meena raised her gaze to the ceiling. As if things hadn't been going badly enough. Just how awful was this night going to get?

"Oh, hello," Abraham called out cheerfully, waving to them. "Didn't mean to interrupt. Do go on. As long as no one makes a move to attack us, I'll let this fellow here live."

"Let him kill me, Father," Stefan Dominic cried, struggling in the guard's arms. "Please! I'd rather die than dishonor you in this way!"

Neither Dimitri nor Lucien looked particularly impressed by this impassioned speech. But it was at least clear that Stefan's theatrical ambitions hadn't been misdirected.

"Stefan!" Shoshona looked upset. She flung a panicky look up at Lucien and Dimitri. "Please don't let them kill him, my lords. You can't!"

But Dimitri hadn't taken his gaze off Lucien, who went on. "Yes. TransCarta is the bank where all the dead men I found in your basement used to work."

"TransCarta bought the network that owns the show I work for," Meena said with a gasp of surprise.

Although she ought, she realized belatedly, to have said *used to work for.*

"It's actually the Swiss private equity firm that Dimitri Antonescu formed last year," Jon said.

"*Trans* for Transylvania, obviously," Alaric said thoughtfully. "I don't know what *Carta* is for."

Lucien looked at his half brother with a raised eyebrow. "That would be Carta Abbey, I presume," he said. "Where you tried to kill me . . . what was it? The third time?"

Dimitri shrugged. "I thought it had a nice ring to it. A private equity firm allows one to conduct business without the usual scrutiny by the federal government or the prying eyes of *other* entities." He gave Alaric a knowing wink.

"Because they aren't publicly traded on the stock exchange or subject to any other requisite filings or disclosures," Alaric said through gritted teeth. He looked as if he couldn't believe he hadn't thought of this before.

"Absolutely." Dimitri grinned. "They're a fine way for an individual like myself who might value his privacy to expand his, er, brand . . . through, say, a television network."

Lucien frowned. "Dimitri," he said in a warning tone, "we don't *have* a brand."

"Actually, members of both the financial and the entertainment community," Dimitri said, "are quite impressed by the Dracula name and eager to experience immortality, it turns out. And consumers . . . well, their fear of death is what drives the beauty industry. By the year 2013 they're set to spend at least forty billion dollars on cosmetic surgery services alone. Well, who wouldn't want to live forever, if they could? You'd know all about that, wouldn't you, Miss Harper, in your line of work?"

Meena felt as if a cold shadow had passed over her soul.

Revenant Wrinkle Cream.

Of course. *Revenant* meant animated corpse.

"It's you," she cried in disgust, trying to break away from Dimitri's grip. "*You're* the one behind the new products they want us to feature on *Insatiable*."

"Of course," he said with a smile, easily defeating her attempts to free herself from him. "But you needn't look that way, my dear. We're no different from your former sponsor, really. We too only want to help your viewers find products that help improve their lives."

"Like the Regenerative Spa for Youthful Awakening?" Meena demanded.

"I've visited one of those," Lucien said in a voice as cold as January. "In the basement of Concubine."

"Nonsense," Dimitri said. "That was merely a prototype. You were never supposed to see it in that state, Lucien. We have plans to upgrade and expand our spas worldwide—"

"No," Lucien said, cutting him off. "Because this ends. Now."

Dimitri shrugged. "This may not be how *you* envisioned the family enterprise, Lucien, but I can assure you I've seen the financials, and the potential for growth is astrono—"

"There *is* no family enterprise," Lucien said, taking a step toward Dimitri. "And I believe the potential for growth of your enterprise is going to significantly decrease if you keep feeding defenseless girls to your newborns. Although they may enjoy the idea of looking young forever, one thing you seem never to have learned about humans over the years, Dimitri, is that they tend to dislike murder."

Meena, looking from the face of one brother to the other, was too stunned to keep up with the conversation.

Not because she was standing in a deconsecrated church with a dagger at her throat, in front of a ravenous horde of vampires.

But because she'd realized that Dimitri was right:

She *did* know all about wanting to live forever.

Not only had she spent over half her life protecting everyone she'd ever met from an untimely death, but it was what she wrote about: the insatiable thirst for life (and love) of Victoria Worthington Stone and her daughter Tabby.

But were Victoria and Tabby *really* so insatiable? All they'd ever wanted was someone to love and care for them.

Wasn't that very human need exactly what corporations like Dimitri's were taking advantage of when they hinted that women would never find that special someone unless they purchased their products in order to look a certain way? They preyed upon human insecurity the way the Dracul preyed on human life.

Suddenly, Meena realized just how twisted Lucien's brother really was.

And who the truly insatiable ones had been all along.

"If you're so eager to expand the Dracul brand but still so frightened of the Palatine that you'd go to all the trouble to form a Swiss company just so they couldn't seize your funds, why not at least hide the dead girls' bodies, Dimitri?" Lucien was asking in wonder, shaking his head. "That's what I can't understand. Exposing the bodies meant exposing everything."

Bait.

That's what Alaric had meant.

"Because he wanted to lure you here, Lucien," Meena said. It was all so clear to her now. "He was never worried about the Palatine. The dead girls were just to bring you to New York, so he could get you here and do *this*."

The coronation was just the final phase in Dimitri's master plan to turn all of America—and soon the world—into a vampire smorgasbord. The only thing standing in his way was . . .

Lucien's glance shifted away from his brother and toward her.

And when their gazes met, Meena felt something like an explosive charge go off inside her head.

She could see in his eyes how much he loved her.

And how hard it was for him not to kill his brother then and there, with his bare hands, for what Dimitri had done to her.

But he couldn't.

Not while Dimitri stood so close to her, with one arm still wrapped around her, a dagger at her neck, his fangs within such easy snapping distance.

Meena nodded. She understood. It was all right. The important thing was that she had to keep Dimitri and the Dracul from doing what they were there to do:

Kill the one impediment to their master plan. Lucien.

It was right then that a stake went whizzing from a crossbow somewhere near the doors of the church and plunged directly into the center of Lucien's back.

"Yes!" Meena heard her brother scream. "Did you see that? I got him!"

Chapter Fifty-seven

12:00 a.m. EST, Sunday, April 18
St. George's Cathedral
180 East Seventy-eighth Street
New York, New York

Meena was never exactly sure what happened after that, because it all seemed to take place in a sort of blur, like it was underwater or in a nightmare.

Or at least, that's how it seemed to her.

Lucien fell to his knees.

That she knew for certain, because she was standing only a foot or two away from him. She tried to catch him as he swayed, to keep him from pitching to the hard marble floor of the dais.

But Dimitri yanked her back.

She thought she heard someone say, "No," softly.

Then realized that someone was herself.

Then something whizzed past her head. Dracul and humans began screaming. Dimitri yanked her sore arm very hard again and shouted in her ear, "Get down!"

Then he shoved her roughly to the floor of the dais.

Meena could hear someone—it sounded like Alaric—shouting something. It sounded like, "Stop, you fool! What are you doing?"

Meena knew she should feel frightened. She knew she should feel *something,* anyway.

But she felt nothing. Nothing at all. She just lay with her cheek pressed to the cool marble, staring in the direction where she'd last seen Lucien.

She could see nothing there at all now. Not even the dust he must have crumbled into.

He's dead, she thought in the part of her brain that was still working. *He's dead, and I never got the chance to warn him that he was going to die . . . because I never got the chance to know him when he was alive in the first place. I only knew him when he was already dead.*

And now he's really, really dead.

Then she thought, *Why did I ever think that he was going to kill Alaric and Jon? He would never do something like that. He's the sweetest, most wonderful person I've ever known.*

And now he's dead.

Then she thought, *I wish I were dead, too.*

And then she was wrenched abruptly to her feet by Dimitri Antonescu.

And Meena realized that her wish was about to be granted.

"You're coming with me," Dimitri said. His face was a twisted mask of greed and hatred and something else. Something Meena had never seen before .

Evil, she thought in that part of her brain that had taken over for the rest of her mind, which seemed to have stopped working since she'd seen Lucien die.

Why, Lucien's brother is nothing but pure evil.

And then Dimitri scooped her up over his shoulder by the hips, as easily as if she were made of straw.

Now the world was suddenly turned upside down.

Not that Meena particularly cared.

But she found it interesting, as she dangled there like a limp doll, to observe that Father Bernard and Sister Gertrude and the rest of the people she'd known from St. Clare's were suddenly there among the Dracul in the apse of St. George's, fighting them with stakes and crucifixes and holy water . . . and, in the case of Abraham Holtzman, with a crossbow and a gleaming Star of David.

Interesting, but not much beyond that. Meena hoped no one would die.

But she knew they would. She'd tried to warn them that they would. They all would.

But none of them had listened. No one ever listened.

And now look at what was happening.

Oh, well. Everyone was going to die eventually. Even her.

It might as well be tonight.

"Meena!"

She heard someone call her name through all the smoke and chaos. She thought it might be Alaric.

She didn't care.

Dimitri was taking her somewhere. She didn't know where. He was probably going to bite her—and not in a pleasant way, like Lucien had—and then suck out all her blood.

Then *he'd* be the one to know when everyone was going to die.

Better him than her.

"Meena!"

Why wouldn't Alaric leave her alone? He really *was* the most annoying person on earth.

Dimitri appeared to be taking her up the steps to the choir loft. He was probably going to rape her, too, when they got up there. Wouldn't that just be the perfect end to a perfect day?

"Meena!"

Alaric was so irritating. He had never let her alone when she was alive, and now he wouldn't leave her alone when she was about to die.

Reluctantly, she lifted her head. Alaric was struggling to reach them—no doubt in order to stop Dimitri, not realizing that Meena wanted this to happen; she *wanted* to die. What did she have to live for? No job. No apartment. No Lucien—but Alaric had a vampire hanging off either arm, holding him back. It actually looked a bit comical, the way the Dracul were trying to snap at Alaric's throat.

Warding off their hissing mouths and pointed, saliva-dripping fangs, Alaric had a hand wrapped around the neck of each of them. He threw Meena a furious glance. He looked enraged with her.

"Stop being an idiot," he roared at her. "He's not dead. *Look*."

Meena looked in the direction Alaric had tipped his head. The sanctuary.

And then she saw it.

It was true.

Lucien wasn't dead. He was getting up.

Slowly. Painfully.

But he was getting up.

Meena saw more than just that in her glance, though.

She saw that the warriors from the Shrine of St. Clare were getting soundly beaten by the Dracul, who outnumbered them almost three to one. Jon may have gotten off a single lucky shot into the back of the prince of darkness, but the rest of his shots wouldn't have hit the side of a barn if he were standing next to it. Gregory Bane was giving her brother's face a pummeling, and seeming to enjoy it, if the movie-star grin he was wearing was any indication. Stefan Dominic had Sister Gertrude in a headlock. And Emil Antonescu had three or four men—who were dressed, oddly, like the kind of guys Jon had used to work with at Webber and Stern—shredding his suit jacket with their fangs, while Mary Lou tried to hold them off with a wrought iron candle sconce.

Meena flung out both arms—even the sore one—against the sides of the stairwell up which Dimitri was carrying her, grabbing the stone walls.

Dimitri wasn't expecting his formerly semicomatose victim to suddenly come to life. That was the only way Meena managed to propel herself out of his powerful grip and down from his broad shoulders, a physical maneuver that required both the element of surprise and a complete lack of fear of pain on her part . . . especially since it ended with her falling down the last few steps and landing on her tailbone.

Dimitri spun around, looking flabbergasted. She'd gone from completely limp to human projectile in a matter of seconds.

"Get away from me," Meena warned him, crab-walking as fast as she could from the bottom of the steps.

But Dimitri was already thundering down the stairs after her, his eyes glowing red as twin stoplights. Meena scrambled to her feet and whirled around to make a run for it . . .

. . . only to career directly into Alaric Wulf's wide, solid chest. He'd managed to shake off his new vampire buddies and had come running over with his sword drawn to help her.

"You're very popular with the Dracula boys," Alaric remarked drily. "They all seem to want to have you for dinner."

"Less joking," she said. Dimitri had his dagger out, the blade gleaming in the candlelight. "More head chopping. And please don't miss this time."

"Isn't this nice?" Dimitri asked Alaric as he tossed the dagger from hand to hand. "We finally get to finish what we started in Berlin. You ran off with your partner that day before we were done. It wasn't at all sporting."

"Yes," Alaric said. "Well, I had more important things to do than stick around to kill you. My partner was bleeding to death, as you might recall."

Dimitri's grin broadened.

"I know," he said. "He was delicious. I'm looking forward to another bite someday."

Alaric, his face darkening, lifted his sword.

Uh-oh, Meena thought. *This isn't good. Should he be fighting angry?* "Alaric," she said urgently. "Don't—"

That's when they all heard it: a sound like no other—certainly nothing human. But it wasn't anything vampire, either.

It came from the apse at the front of the church, where the altar sat. It was so loud it shook the building to the foundations. So loud dust floated down from the choir loft and the low ceiling that hung over Alaric's and Meena's heads.

Turning slowly, Meena was afraid of what she was about to see—but knew full well what it was. Of course it was. She was in St. George's. All her visions had been of fire. And there were crude drawings of it all over the walls.

She still couldn't believe her eyes.

But there it was.

A dragon.

On the Upper East Side.

Chapter Fifty-eight

It was crouched in the apse, its huge body and enormous wingspan filling the entire space, while its serpentine head perched on a neck that was stretched nearly the height of the thirty-foot ceiling.

Its claws made obscene scratching noises on the marble floor.

Its scales were ruby red.

Smoke poured from its nostrils.

Out of one of its shoulders poked a tiny wooden stake.

Lucien, Meena thought, feeling as if her heart had turned to ice in her chest. My God. *Lucien.*

What's happened to you? What have they done to you?

"Oh . . . my God," said Dimitri, dropping the dagger he held when he saw it.

Hearing Dimitri's voice—and then the noisy clatter of the falling knife—the dragon's head whipped in their direction . . . then dipped low to peer at them where they stood beneath the choir loft.

Meena's frozen heart gave a convulsive double beat. *Oh, God. Oh, God.* The dragon was looking at them.

A mixture of steam and what smelled like sulfur shot straight at them as the beast exhaled hot air with enough force to douse all the candles in their area.

Suddenly they were plunged into semidarkness.

But Meena could still see, thanks to the fiery glow coming from the dragon's nostrils, which loomed closer and closer to them . . . and from which she could hear a strange snuffling sound.

"Whatever you do," Alaric whispered in the dark, startling her, as he slowly reached out to lay a warm, steadying hand on the back of Meena's neck, "don't move."

"I wasn't going to," Meena whispered back. "But what's . . . happening?"

It wasn't what she wanted to ask. What she wanted to ask was, *Where is Lucien? Can he really be in there, beneath all those scales? Is that really* him?

"I don't know," Alaric replied. "I've never seen this before. But I think he's—"

Suddenly, the dragon's head reared up right next to Meena. She froze, every muscle in her body tensing. She couldn't remember ever being that paralyzed with fear in her life—not even when she'd realized Lucien was actually a vampire—as she found herself being examined by a huge, double-lidded, foot-wide eye, its many facets, each the color of a blood-red sun, casting her own terrified reflection back at her.

Calm down, she tried to tell herself. *This is* Lucien's *eye. It's going to be all right.*

But she wasn't sure that was really true since she could see no hint at all of the man she had known and loved in there. What she found herself gazing at wasn't a man at all. It was completely, entirely beast.

A giant lid slid sideways over the pupil staring at her, then opened again as the dragon peered at her—and then at Alaric, standing behind her.

Then came that huge snuffling sound again, so loud that Meena would have jumped out of her skin entirely if Alaric hadn't been keeping such a firm grip on the back of her neck.

Did he just . . . smell *me?* Meena asked herself, stunned.

Alaric squeezed the back of her neck.

She got the message. Don't talk. Don't move. Don't even breathe.

It was good advice.

Too bad Dimitri couldn't seem to follow it.

He'd found the knife somehow where he'd dropped it.

And now he made a running lunge out of the darkness at the beast, going for its giant blinking eye with a scream of pure, unadulterated hate.

This, it turned out, was a mistake. A big mistake.

" . . . pissed," Alaric said, finishing his thought about Lucien's state of mind. He shoved Meena to the floor, then threw himself on top of her. "*Stay down.*"

The fire that came bellowing out of the dragon's nose and throat in Dimitri's direction was white-hot.

It was the searing heat of the sun. It was the brimstone-filled heat from the fiery pits of hell, and it was aimed at a single target. It went shooting over their heads and bodies.

Meena had never felt heat like that before in her life and hoped she never would again.

Meena wasn't sure if Dimitri ever even knew what hit him. One minute he was there, and the next, there was only fire. . . .

And then there was only thick black smoke.

Where Dimitri had been standing was a charred, smoldering spot.

"Oh, my God," Meena heard someone saying. And then she realized it was herself. She was saying it, over and over. "Oh, my God, oh, my God."

"Stay down." She heard Alaric's deep voice in her ear. "Just stay down."

Meena caught her breath as the dragon's head dipped toward them once more. Lucien swept his gleaming red snout just inches above them, making that snuffling sound again.

He *was* smelling them. She was certain of it.

Then the head disappeared.

Lucien was turning his attention—and his breath of fire—to the people and vampires in the rest of the church.

Alaric must have realized it, too. That's why he sprang up from Meena and ran after Lucien's departing head.

She knew instantly where he was going.

And why.

"*No!*" she screamed.

And she tore off after him.

She lost him in the chaos that was ensuing outside of the sheltering roof of the choir loft.

Yes, there might have been a seventy-foot-long dragon breathing fire in one part of the church.

But in the rest of the building, there was still a vampire-versus-human war being waged. She saw the Dracul sinking their fangs into the necks of novices . . . Sister Gertrude stabbing a Dracul with a piece of pew . . . Jon firing his crossbow at point-blank range at a Dracul (and missing). Fran and Stan flipping friars over with a superhuman strength amazing for people Meena had never before seen lift anything heavier than a knish. Abraham Holtzman and Emil and Mary Lou Antonescu had formed some kind of bizarre partnership and seemed to be trying to kill as many Dracul as they could with whatever they could . . . which appeared to be not many with very little.

Meena, appalled, knew she couldn't just stand there. She had to do something to help . . . even if there *was* a dragon lumbering around, incinerating people with its breath.

Scooping up a jagged chunk of crushed pew, she grabbed the hair of the nearest vampire, who happened to be trying to sink its teeth into the throat of a hapless novice . . .

. . . and was shocked to find herself face-to-face again with Shoshona.

"Oh, right," Shoshona said, smirking at her and at the pointed chunk of wood Meena held in her fist. "Like you have the guts."

"Oh," Meena assured her, "I have the guts."

There was no way she had the guts.

This was *Shoshona*. Sure, Meena had never liked her very much. She had told herself, nearly every day for a year, that today was the day she was finally going to warn her coworker that if she didn't stop working out so much, she was going to die.

Now Meena realized that it was never the gym Shoshona had to fear.

It was Stefan Dominic, the man she'd met in it.

Still, Meena had always had every intention of saving Shoshona's life.

So was she really going to put a stake through her heart and end it? Here, now?

No. Of course not.

"Yeah." Shoshona smirked some more. "I knew it. By the way, I took something else from your apartment, besides this bag."

Shoshona unzipped the top of the red Marc Jacobs bag she still wore slung across her chest and showed Meena a glimpse of something inside.

"Thanks for all the great story ideas," she said, smirking. "Have a nice time on unemployment."

Then she turned around to look for the novice, who'd run off, crying.

Meena stared at Shoshona's slender back.

Her *laptop*? Shoshona had stolen her *laptop*?

Meena didn't have backup files of *anything* she'd kept on that laptop. Not on her work computer. Not online. Not anywhere.

Meena stalked forward, grabbed the back of Shoshona's two-hundred-dollar shirt, and spun her around to face her . . .

. . . then plunged the broken piece of pew into her chest.

Shoshona turned into a pile of dust before Meena's eyes.

On top of the dust lay the ruby red jewel-encrusted dragon tote Lucien had given to her, tangled in Shoshona's clothes. Meena picked it up, dusted it off, and slung it across her own chest.

The weight of her laptop inside it felt reassuring.

When Meena lifted her gaze again, it was to see the last person she'd ever expected: Leisha, carefully holding her belly and picking her way toward Meena through the smoke and rubble.

"Oh, my God," Meena cried. "*Leish?*"

All of Meena's worst nightmares seemed suddenly to be coming true. Her boyfriend was a vampire. She'd just killed her own boss.

And her pregnant best friend was wandering around a live battle-field with no regard for her own safety or that of her unborn child.

Meena rushed to Leisha's side.

"What are you still doing here?" Meena demanded anxiously. "I thought Mary Lou Antonescu got you out!"

"Oh, was that who that was?" Leisha looked dazed. "Well, yeah, she did. But then after she broke Adam out of those handcuffs and told him what was going on, he decided he wanted to stay to see the end of the play."

Meena raised her eyebrows. "*Play?*"

"Yeah," Leisha said. "I was kind of cool with it at first, but now I don't know, there's that *thing*—"

She pointed over Meena's shoulder. Meena turned around and there, behind her, was Lucien, his dragon head weaving back and forth as if he were looking for something—or someone—his long serpent's tongue darting in and out of his mouth. Every once in a while he opened his mouth and let out an eardrum-splitting roar.

"Now see? That just seems like overkill to me," Leisha said.

Meena's gaze slid back toward her friend. Leisha, she was pretty certain, had had her mind scrambled by a combination of shock and some kind of Dracul brainwashing. Her normally alert brown eyes looked glazed over.

"I realize it's all in good fun," Leisha complained, "but I'm pretty sure the smoke isn't good for the baby. I'm actually not feeling so hot—"

Meena reached out and grabbed her friend by both arms.

"Leisha, this isn't a play," she said, urgently. "You have to get out of here. The baby is coming early. And it's not a boy. It's a girl. I'm sorry I didn't tell you sooner. I knew, but—"

"What?" Leisha cried, flinging both her hands away. Whatever they had done to Leisha's memory, it hadn't affected her concern for her unborn child. "You knew and you didn't tell me? Meena, what's wrong with you? *How* early?"

"Early enough that Adam should have started on that baby room a long time ago," Meena said. Suddenly spying her brother over Leisha's shoulder, she cried, "Jon! Jon! Get over here."

Jon staggered over. Blood was streaming from a cut on his forehead; Gregory Bane had split it open with a fist. Jon was dirty and sweaty and looked like he was having the time of his life.

"What?" he demanded. "Oh, my God. Leisha, what are you still doing here?"

Over in the sanctuary, the dragon let out another roar.

The walls shook.

Outside the church, sirens were wailing. The NYFD and New York City police were on their way. It had only taken a vampire war and a seventy-foot dragon to get some of St. George's neighbors to call 911.

"Oh, thank God," Leisha said when she heard the sirens. "Someone needs to shoot that thing."

"No!" Meena cried. Then, seeing the expressions on the faces of her brother and friend, she said, more calmly, "Jon, I think Leisha is in labor. You need to find Adam and get them both out of here."

"*What?*" Leisha and Jon exclaimed together.

"Yes," Meena said firmly. "Leisha, I think you're having your baby now. Jon, you've got to get her and Adam into the first ambulance you see and get her away from here. *Far* away from here. Do it now, Jon. I want you to go with them. It's all your fault they're even here in the first place."

"How is it *my* fault?" Jon demanded indignantly.

"Remember that note I left down at St. Clare's?" Meena asked. "The one in which I specifically stated that anyone who followed me up here was going to die tonight?"

Jon rolled his eyes. "Oh, right. Yeah, we all saw that. But what were we supposed to do, Meen? Just let you come up here and fight these guys on your own? It looked like you were doing a real terrific job when we got here."

"You *shot* my boyfriend," Meena reminded him. "He was handling it fine, and then you shot him. And now look what's happening. The police are here, and the fire department, and innocent people are going to get hurt. And by the way, I'm pretty sure it's *you* he's looking for."

The dragon let out another one of its roars. It sounded much closer than the previous one. Jon jumped and seemed to realize Meena was right: Lucien *was* coming for him. Those huge, blood-red eyes seemed to be searching the apse for someone. . . .

Jon hastily surrendered his cocked and loaded crossbow to Meena.

"Yeah," he said guiltily. "I really am sorry about that. I was actually aiming for his brother." He took Leisha by the arm. "Relax, Leish," he said to her. "I'll have you out of here in no time. I'm pretty sure I saw Adam over by the doors. He must have been looking for you."

Leisha threw a frantic look over her shoulder at Meena as Jon led her away.

"Aren't you coming with us?" she asked.

Meena smiled and waved at her. "I want to stay to see the end of the play," she said. "Call me later and let me know where you are." She held an imaginary cell phone to her face.

Leisha nodded, then looked concerned. "The baby's really a girl? We never even talked about any girls' names."

"I've always been partial to the name Joan," Meena called after her . . .

. . . just as a Dracul spotted her standing there and began racing her way. While Jon hurried to get Leisha to safety, Meena spun to face the vampire . . .

. . . who turned out to be none other than Gregory Bane.

"Hello, Meena Harper," he said, giving her the same slow, deliberate smile that had sent so many thousands of women in the eighteen-to-forty-nine demographic into screaming fits.

Meena rolled her eyes, lifted Jon's crossbow, and shot him directly in the chest.

Then she stepped through the crumbling dust of his remains.

That's when yet another projectile went hissing through the air, missing Meena's cheek by mere inches.

A second later, the dragon let out a bellow—this one of pain—that was loud enough to shake the building's foundation. Meena, confused, looked up to see a stake sticking out of its long neck.

A stake. Another *stake*.

Someone else, other than her brother, was shooting at Lucien.

Meena spun around, trying to see who it was.

She spotted Abraham Holtzman in the center of the smoke-filled apse, a crossbow to one shoulder, reloading.

She threw down her own crossbow and flew toward him.

"Stop," she yelled at him. "You've got to stop. You're hurting him!"

"Of course I'm hurting him, Miss Harper," Abraham said matter-of-factly. "That would be the point, wouldn't it? I'm trying to distract him while Alaric—"

"But Lucien is on our side," Meena cried. "He's trying to help us! He killed Dimitri."

"Don't be ridiculous, Miss Harper. He killed his brother in order to preserve his grip on the throne," Abraham said with measured patience. "He's the prince of darkness, Satan's chosen son on earth to rule over all demon beings. I know you think you love him, my dear, but he must be destroyed in order for goodness and light to stand a chance—"

"But he's *part* of goodness and light," Meena insisted. "His mother was—"

"Miss Harper," Abraham said. "You surely can't be telling me that there's any part of *that* that isn't evil."

On the word *that,* he gestured toward the dragon, which was loosing a stream of its white fire at the bankers Meena had previously seen attacking Sister Gertrude. One minute they were there.

The next, they were gone.

"Oh, dear," Meena heard a voice close to her say. She turned her head and saw Emil and Mary Lou Antonescu standing beside her.

But they didn't look anything like they ever had when she'd seen them around their apartment building. They were both covered in soot and blood, their designer clothing torn and Mary Lou's hair in complete disarray. She was clinging to her husband, watching in utter terror as Lucien breathed fire onto the Dracul.

"Did you know about this?" Meena demanded of them. "Did you know Lucien"—she didn't even know what to say, exactly—"could . . . could . . ."

Emil turned to look down at her. His expression was grave. And a little bit sad.

And left absolutely no doubt, in Meena's mind at least, that he'd known. Oh, he'd known all along.

"The prince has always had a very bad temper," was all he said, however.

"A bad temper?" Meena cried. She gestured toward the dragon, which had dipped its long, slender neck to pick up Stefan Dominic in its mouth and was now ripping him apart, limb from limb. Meena had to cover her eyes with her hands. "You call that a *bad temper*?" she asked, with a moan.

"It's never a good idea," Emil said, "to make the prince angry. Dimitri really ought to have known better."

Meena, careful not to look in Lucien's direction, lowered her hands and asked, "Well, how do we stop it? How do we make him turn back?"

"Oh," Emil said, tightening his arm around his wife. "We can't."

Meena's jaw dropped. "What? You mean—"

This was exactly what Meena had feared when she'd stood so close to that giant eye and seen nothing in it of the man she loved . . . that Lucien would never go back to being himself again.

Not that it mattered. Meena was still going to do everything in her power to keep him from being obliterated by a combination of the NYFD, the NYPD, the Palatine, and the Dracul, whatever he was, man or beast. Or vampire.

"Oh, he'll turn back eventually, when he stops being so angry," Emil said. "In the meantime"—he glanced over his shoulder at the police officer who was now shouting into the church on a megaphone for them to put down their weapons and come out with their hands on the back of their heads—"Mary Lou and I are leaving. I would suggest you do the same, Miss Harper."

And with that, both of them disappeared before Meena's eyes. One minute they were there, and the next, there was nothing at all where they'd been standing, except twin wisps of mist.

Stunned, Meena looked back at Abraham, who was reloading his crossbow. He seemed to take what had just happened in stride. He didn't even care about having missed his opportunity to stake the Antonescus.

He was after much bigger game.

She was going to wake up soon, Meena decided. Because this all had to be a nightmare. She was going to wake up in her own room, with Jack Bauer in her arms, and it would be morning, and the sun would be shining, and everything would be okay. None of this would have happened. She would get up and go to work, and—

"Meena!" She heard Alaric calling to her from somewhere across the church. "Meena!"

Then she saw him. He was standing directly behind the dragon.

"Move!" he shouted at her, and made a get-out-of-the-way gesture with his arms, indicating that he wanted her to step away from Abraham.

And right then—in that moment—she knew exactly what he and his boss were planning to do:

Abraham would shoot at Lucien, distracting him with another stake to the neck.

Then, while Lucien was roaring over the pain of that, Alaric would run up onto the dragon's back . . .

. . . then slice off its head.

Alaric, Meena concluded, was crazy. Especially if he thought Meena was ever going to let this happen.

"You'd better do as he says, Miss Harper," Abraham said, lifting the crossbow to his shoulder and taking aim. "I know this is painful for you. But trust me, it's the best way. I promise you'll feel much better when it's all over."

As Abraham was speaking, the dragon, which had finished its latest meal, looked around. It had been weaving its head back and forth on its long, serpentine neck as if searching the apse for its next victim. But now it finally froze . . . and squared both Meena and Abraham in its sights.

Those gigantic, crystalline eyes focused directly on them, unblinkingly, like a snake's. All the hairs on the back of Meena's neck stood up as the dragon stared at her. She saw a stream of smoke release from its nostrils. The noxious odor of sulfur engulfed them a second later.

"Oh, dear," Abraham said, freezing with his finger on the crossbow's trigger. "I think—"

Meena reached up to undo one of the hooks on the messenger strap of the dragon tote. It slid down from her shoulder. Then, clasping the strap in both hands, she swung the bag as hard as she could at Abraham, the weight of her laptop inside catching him full across the back.

"What—?" he cried as he stumbled.

He didn't go down, though. He was too heavy and had far too much experience.

His shot, however, did go wild.

What happened next wasn't part of Meena's plan.

Chapter Fifty-nine

12:30 A.M. EST, Sunday, April 18
St. George's Cathedral
180 East Seventy-eighth Street
New York, New York

The tip of the dragon's long red tail shot forward, wrapped around Meena's waist, and lifted her bodily into the air.

Meena would have screamed if she could have. But she was being squeezed so tightly, she couldn't breathe.

Plus, she was too terrified to scream.

Sailing over the heads of everyone left in the apse, Meena had a dizzying view of shattered pews, smoldering walls, her dragon tote and laptop sailing off into oblivion, and finally, Alaric's stunned face . . . until she was flung back into the area where the dragon had apparently first recognized her scent—by the stairwell to the choir loft—and where he seemed to want her to stay put.

Because that's where he released her, with what she supposed a dragon might consider gentle consideration but that in actuality was a landing that caused her to go spinning back against the same wall where there was only a burned spot to show any proof that Dimitri Antonescu had ever once existed on this planet.

Too stunned to move, she lay slumped there, seeing only blackness.

"Meena!" she thought she heard someone yelling from far away.

But she felt too sick from her violent ride through the air—combined with the force with which she'd hit the wall—to respond.

Then Alaric was there, trying to pry first one, then another of her eyes open, checking her pupils, asking if she was all right.

"Go away," she said. She wanted to throw up. Her head hurt. Her arm hurt. She just wanted to go home.

She didn't have a home anymore.

"Meena, look at me."

She looked at him. She could barely see him in the smoky darkness.

But his face looked tight with concern.

"I thought you had a dragon to kill," she said.

"Well," he said, "I guess I missed my opportunity. How many fingers am I holding up?" he asked, holding up two.

"Nine," she said.

And then the worst happened. The tail returned. Meena sucked in her breath when she saw it, causing Alaric to turn and see it, too. It flashed dangerously red through the smoke, seemingly searching for something. Meena froze the minute she saw it, thinking, *Oh, no. Not again.*

It was nice that Lucien loved her so much.

But he really needed to work on his landings.

Alaric seemed to be thinking along the same lines, since he raised his sword, as if he was ready to chop Lucien's tail off at the tip if it came too close. . . .

Only this time, it turned out it wasn't Meena whom Lucien was looking for. The tail found one of the supporting pillars that held up the choir loft. It wrapped around it . . .

. . . and pulled.

"Shit," Alaric said, throwing his arms over Meena.

There wasn't time to do anything else.

Maybe if St. George's Cathedral hadn't been quite as old as it was. Maybe if it hadn't been so badly in need of renovation. Maybe if it hadn't endured so many shocks from a thirty-ton dragon roaring and breathing fire in it for the past half hour.

Maybe then its structural integrity might have held up a little better.

In any case, taking out that single pillar caused a huge section of the choir loft to come falling down.

Not *on* them. Just all around them.

Enough to effectively seal them off from everything that was happening out in the nave and apse, entombing them in a sort of dragon-made cave of wood and plaster.

Which, Meena was certain, had been Lucien's plan all along. He was tired of worrying about her getting hurt. Which was sweet, she supposed, in its way.

But she wasn't sure how much longer she was going to be able to survive the way dragons expressed their affection.

"Oh, my God." She coughed. There was a lot of dust.

And Alaric Wulf, on top of her, weighed a ton. As usual.

"Are you all right?" she asked him.

He didn't say anything at first. This was a little alarming.

"Alaric?"

The force of the cave-in had caused some plywood to shift, popping the wood off a previously boarded-up window, which now let in some dirty gray light from the street. In it, Meena could see that Alaric's face, above her, was covered in ash and plaster dust. He looked . . . odd. She couldn't figure out how.

"Alaric? Are you hurt?" she asked him.

"No," he said in a slow, somewhat thoughtful way. "I do not think so."

What was wrong with him? Why did he look that way?

Well, he was probably disappointed. He'd missed his big chance to kill Lucien, and now he'd probably never get another one. Thanks to her boyfriend's affection for her, they were stuck there until someone dug them out. It was Alaric's own fault for rushing over to see if she was all right. If he'd just stayed out in the apse. . .

"Meena," he said, looking down at her. His eyes were still as bright blue as ever. But now, she thought, they looked . . .

"Am I still going to die?" he asked.

"*What?*" He was so heavy. Why did he have to be so big? And why was he acting so strangely?

"Am I still going to die?" he asked. "Now. Tonight."

"Oh, Alaric," she said with a sigh.

And then her heart gave a heave. He *was* still going to die.

Except . . . that wasn't possible.

Lucien had thrown her in there to keep her safe. Alaric should have been safe, too. Everything should have been fine now.

But for some reason, Alaric was *still* going to die.

How could this be happening? It made no sense.

He must have read the truth in her horrified expression, since he said, "That's what I thought. That's why I'm going to do this now."

Then he lowered his head and began kissing her.

While this development was alarming—it startled her almost more than anything else that had happened to her in the past few days, and that was saying quite a lot—it wasn't nearly as alarming as the fact that Meena found that being kissed by Alaric Wulf was not unpleasurable.

Quite the opposite, in fact.

It had been a while since she'd been kissed by a man who actually had a heartbeat and blood pounding in his veins . . . two things Alaric Wulf had in abundance. She could feel both pulsing hard against her as he kissed her with slow deliberation . . . a kiss he seemed to be in no hurry to end, a kiss he seemed, if she wasn't mistaken, to have given some thought to beforehand . . . a *lot* of thought to. Alaric Wulf was kissing her like this was the last kiss he was ever going to give anyone in his life.

And when she opened her eyes and looked down, wondering just what was coursing through his body and making her feel so warm, and saw the massive gouge in his right calf, from which blood was gushing at an alarming rate, she could see why he felt like kissing her might be the last thing he'd ever do before he died. A nail or something must have sliced him there while the choir loft was collapsing, and he'd gallantly rolled over on top of her. In order to save her life. Yet again.

Talk about having a hero complex.

Why was he always trying to *do* that? Didn't he know it was only going to get him killed?

Meena swore, unceremoniously pushed him off her and onto the floor, then scrambled to stop the bleeding with her hands.

"Alaric," she said, trying to stay calm. There was so much blood. "You've been cut. You're bleeding."

"I know," he said. He didn't sound like he particularly cared. He kept staring up at her face. He seemed perfectly happy.

He'd already lost a lot of blood. It was pooling on the floor beneath them. It covered her. And him.

"We have to stop the bleeding," Meena said. "I think you nicked an artery or something." She tried to think back to all the first-aid courses she'd taken in school. Why couldn't she remember any of them now, when she needed them? "I think I need to make a tourniquet."

"You told me I was going to die," he said with a shrug. "You said it would be dark and that there would be fire. And now it's happening. You were right."

"No," she said. Her heart seemed to be racing a mile a minute. *Please,* it seemed to thump out. *Let me be wrong. Just this once. Back away from the precipice.* "I was wrong. I need your belt or something."

"No one takes Señor Sticky from me," Alaric said, grasping his sword hilt.

"Oh, my God," Meena said. "I don't want your stupid sword. I—"

Then she remembered.

"My scarf," she said. "The one I gave you. Are you still wearing it?"

He lifted his wrist and pulled back his sleeve. She was relieved to see that the red scarf she'd given him at the rectory was still there. "You mean this?" he asked. "But you gave it to me."

"Well, I need it back," she said. "Take it off. Give it to me."

His big fingers, so skilled at so many things, proved clumsy with this, fumbled with the tiny knot she'd made. "I'm very surprised at you, Meena Harper," he said, sounding childishly disappointed. "I thought you gave it to me as a present. It isn't very polite of you to take something back after you've given it to someone, you know."

Beyond the thick pile of rubble around them, Meena heard a roar—Lucien. Then the building shook. Meena closed her eyes. What was Lucien doing?

Please, she prayed. *No more death.* There'd already been so much death that night. Too much. She couldn't take any more.

Alaric heard it, too. He shook his head as he continued to fumble at the knot.

"This is why," he said, "you need to come work for the Palatine."

"What?" Her hands were wrist-deep in his blood as she pressed on his wound. "What are you *talking* about?"

"You," he said. "Don't you see, Meena? If you came to work for the Palatine Guard, you could keep things like this from happening. The demons . . . they wouldn't stand a chance if you were on our side instead of theirs."

"I'm not on the demons' side," Meena snapped. She knew it wasn't his fault. He was obviously delusional from all the blood loss. It was why he'd kissed her. He'd never have done that if he'd been in his right mind. He hated her. "I just don't see why everyone wants to kill Lucien. He—"

"Like that day when Martin and I went into that warehouse outside of Berlin," Alaric said, ignoring her, "we had no idea we were walking into a trap. But if you were working for the Palatine, you might have said, 'Hey, Alaric. Hey, Martin. There's danger there. Be careful.' And we would have been more careful. And maybe now, Martin would still be able to chew."

He held the scarf out to her, having managed to untie it.

Meena stared at him for a second.

Was he serious? Or was this part of the delusion, brought on by the massive blood loss?

Come work for the Palatine Guard? *Her?*

No. That was her brother's dream, not hers. She didn't want to be a demon hunter. She was *in love* with a demon.

Wouldn't that be a slight conflict of interest?

"I wish you would come work with us, Meena," Alaric said, his gaze fixed on hers. "I don't want to die. A heads-up from you about when to expect it would be very nice. I know everyone else would appreciate it, too."

She took the scarf from him. His eyes, even in the semi-darkness, were very blue. "I'll . . . think about it," she said.

Then she bent to concentrate on making a tourniquet with the scarf and a piece of wood she'd found in the rubble. Fortunately, she'd written the dialogue for the episode of *Insatiable* where Victoria Worthington Stone had been forced to put a tourniquet on the leg of her half brother when that plane they'd been on had gone down in the jungle of South America. Victoria had radioed a local medical clinic for instructions, and Meena had been scrupulous about getting the details exactly right, just in case any of their viewers ever happened to be in the same situation. . . .

She had never in a million years imagined *she* might be one of them.

But the tourniquet worked. The blood stopped gushing from his leg.

Either that, or the blood flow had stopped because Alaric was dead.

But when she looked down at his face, she saw that he was still gazing up at her, a thoughtful expression on his face.

"So?" he asked.

"The bad news is, you're a terrible kisser," she informed him with mock gravity. Better to use humor to make him think the situation wasn't as grave as it was than let him know the truth. "The good news is, you have time to work on your technique. You're going to live."

"No," he said. He reached for her hand, not seeming to care that it was covered in blood. His blood. "I don't mean about that. I mean about the other thing."

She shook her head. "Alaric," she said, laughing shakily. "I'm not moving to *Rome*."

He seemed to think about this. "Would your psychic powers work over Skype?" he asked finally.

Then he passed out.

He didn't let go of her hand, though. He was still holding tightly to it, in fact, hours later when firefighters broke a hole through the rubble and asked if they were all right.

"I'm fine," Meena called. "But my friend needs an ambulance. His leg is badly hurt."

"All right, ma'am," the firefighter said. "Just stay back. We'll have you both out in a minute."

"What about everyone else?" Meena asked worriedly, thinking about Lucien . . . but also, she told herself, about Abraham Holtzman and Sister Gertrude and the others. "Is everyone else all right?"

"I wouldn't know anything about that, ma'am," the firefighter said. "As far as I know, you two are the only survivors."

Chapter Sixty

Alaric was deeply unhappy.

It was bad enough that he was in the hospital.

But to make matters worse, he had been there for almost a week, and no one had thought to bring him his own things from his room at the Peninsula. His silk pajamas, or his sheep's-wool-lined slippers, or even a robe.

Nothing.

So he was stuck—in traction, no less—in a wretchedly uncomfortable hospital bed, on inferior hospital bedsheets, with one of those flat, inferior hospital-bed pillows, in a hospital gown. A hospital gown!

It didn't even properly close up the back. So if he'd wanted to take a walk around the floor (which he couldn't do because he was in traction; he'd been told he wouldn't be walking for weeks—weeks!—and they called themselves doctors), he couldn't, because he'd be exposing his backside to the whole of the ward.

And his hospital room television didn't get any premium movie channels.

And there was no minibar. Not that he could have walked to one and opened it if there had been, since he was in traction. If he wanted so much as a drink of water, he had to ring the nurse for one.

He couldn't even walk to the bathroom.

He had never been so humiliated.

Alaric would have discharged himself if they hadn't told him there was some kind of infection raging through his veins, requiring him to receive IV antibiotics. Which he wasn't even sure he believed. He'd always been extremely healthy. How could he have gotten an infection?

"Perhaps because you nearly bled to death from a severed artery in a building collapse and Miss Harper had to use her bare hands and a tourniquet made from a scarf and a stick in order to stop the bleeding and save your life?" Abraham Holtzman had suggested when Alaric had posed this question to him.

But Holtzman was only cranky, Alaric knew, because he'd lost most of his eyebrows and suffered burns on 10 percent of the rest of his body thanks to Lucien Antonescu's parting shot—which had killed most of the Dracul and singed Sister Gertrude's habit straight off.

How Alaric wished he'd been there to see that.

Not that he got any particular kick out of seeing naked nuns.

But he'd have enjoyed witnessing all of them trying to flee down into the secret catacombs that existed beneath all the Catholic churches in the city before the fire department descended onto the place with their hoses.

"It's your fault," Holtzman had said, chiding him, the first time he'd come to visit Alaric in his hospital room. "If you'd just followed through like you were supposed to and gone after the beast instead of the girl, we'd have had him. But no. You had to go see if Meena Harper was hurt. And so because of you, the prince of darkness got away. You're never going to live this one down, Wulf."

There weren't enough painkillers in the world to make a post-assignment berating from Abraham Holtzman bearable. The fact that Alaric wasn't on any because he didn't like how fuzzy they made his head feel made this even worse.

"So I was just supposed to let her lie there?" he'd demanded. "With a possible concussion, or worse? She'd just gotten thrown across the room by a dragon!"

"Lucien Dracula was never going to hurt that girl." Holtzman

obviously wasn't feeling too swell himself. He'd lost the first layer of
skin on his hands and face. He looked incredibly comical without his
eyebrows.

But of course, Alaric couldn't say anything about that. Though he
did plan on taking a couple of cell phone photos of it, just as soon as he
got the chance, and sending them to Martin, for laughs.

"You knew that," Holtzman said. "You ran after her instead of doing
your job, because you're sweet on her. I have *grave reservations* about Miss
Harper and this idea of yours of hiring her to work for us. I think it will
only lead to disaster. Especially since Lucien Dracula is still at large and
obviously in love with her himself."

"I'm not sweet on her." Alaric had never in his life heard anything
so ridiculous. But a part of him wondered, *Is it that obvious?* "But if you
can't see the advantages of having someone who—"

"Oh, I see the advantages." Holtzman took out his handkerchief
and dabbed at a spot where one of his burns was oozing. Alaric looked
away. Although he didn't suppose he looked much better himself. How
he hated hospitals! "And, unfortunately, so do our superiors, since
they've already put through the appropriate paperwork to start a special
task unit here in Manhattan, with myself in charge." He added glumly,
"They want you on it as well."

Alaric, surprised, tried not to show how happy this information
made him. Except for the part about Holtzman being in charge, of
course.

"I, of course, informed them that Miss Harper isn't the only one
about whom I have *grave reservations*." Holtzman folded his handkerchief
and put it away, fixing Alaric with an eagle-eyed stare. "I saw your behavior in the field last week, and I found it far from acceptable. If you
want to be part of this new unit, you'll first have to take that mandatory
two weeks' psychological R and R you never took after Berlin." Looking
down at Alaric's leg, Holtzman grunted, then added, "Well, I suppose
you'll have to do that in any case. But you're getting counseling as well.
Agreed?"

Alaric frowned. He could think of nothing worse than having to sit
in the office of some talking head, discussing his *feelings*.

But if it meant seeing more of Meena Harper. . . .

"Fine," Alaric said from between gritted teeth.

"Excellent. That's what I like to hear. You really shouldn't be so resistant to these policies, Alaric, they're in place for your benefit. Though this doesn't mean, of course, that I'm not going to be watching how you conduct yourself around Miss Harper closely. Although," Holtzman added, "she hasn't said yet whether or not she's going to take the job."

Alaric nearly bolted from the bed in surprise, even though he was practically attached to it by a complicated assortment of wires. "*What?*" he burst out. "Why the hell not? Didn't you offer her—"

"Oh, calm down," Holtzman said sourly. "We offered her a completely adequate package."

"Adequate?" Alaric wanted to throw something. But the only thing near enough was the television remote. He'd thrown that so many times already, the nurses had threatened not to bring it back if he threw it once more. "She's—"

"She's a *psychic*," Abraham reminded him. "It's not like she'd be out there risking her life in the field. The package we offered was reflective of that. It includes full benefits and is actually very generous, if you ask me. I can't imagine anyone who wouldn't take it, especially in this job market. Who wouldn't want to come work for the Palatine?"

"Someone," Alaric said, a little bitterly, from his hospital bed, "who's in love with the prince of darkness."

Now, just remembering the conversation with Holtzman, he wanted to throw something all over again.

At least until Meena Harper herself surprised him by walking into his hospital room.

And him wearing a hospital gown. This was just *perfect*.

"Hello," she said. Her left arm was in an air cast from elbow to wrist. In her right hand, she carried a vase filled with daisies.

Alaric had never given much thought to flowers before. In fact, he'd always thought flowers were stupid.

Until now. Now daisies were his favorite.

"Hello," he said.

Except for the air cast, Meena Harper looked good. He would have gone so far as to say that Meena Harper looked great. The bite mark on

her neck was almost completely faded. She had on some new clothes—
well, of course. Because the last time he'd seen her, she'd been covered
in blood.

His blood.

She was wearing a dress. It was short and black, and a little tight in
the chest.

He liked it very much.

She put the daisies on the windowsill. It was raining outside, and
the flowers brightened up the room a little.

Which was a miracle. He hadn't thought anything could brighten
up that hospital room.

But now he knew. Daisies could. Daisies, and Meena Harper.

"I was just here visiting my friend Leisha," she said, sitting down
in the pink vinyl chair by his bed. Pink! Vinyl. The chair was a disaster. Except when Meena Harper sat down in it while wearing the
short black dress. Because then he could see a lot of her bare legs. So,
perhaps the chair was not such a disaster after all. "She had a baby girl.
It's a little premature, but they're both going to be fine. Leisha's so
happy. She doesn't seem to remember what happened at the church.
Or outside my apartment. Adam says not to tell her. He thinks it's for
the best."

"He's probably right," Alaric said, carefully.

"True," she said, with a shrug. "Adam says he wishes he could forget
it. He and Jon are installing the baby room right now. Otherwise, the
baby will have to sleep in a drawer."

"Oh," Alaric said. He didn't know anything about babies. Except
Martin's daughter, Simone, who had been a baby once. Alaric had
thought Martin was crazy for wanting a baby. He tried to sound sup-
portive, though, just like he had around Martin, because he knew that's
how people were supposed to be about babies. "That's good."

"They're calling her Joan," Meena said. "Joanie." She was looking
all around the room . . . everywhere but at Alaric.

This, he decided, was definitely awkward.

Especially because, like Meena's friend Leisha, Alaric didn't remember what had happened at the church, either. At least, not every-

thing. He knew he'd said some things to her when the two of them had been alone together after the choir loft had collapsed.

He just couldn't remember what those things had been.

This, a doctor had told him when he'd asked her about it, was not unusual. It was because of the blood loss, she'd said. He needn't worry about it.

But Alaric did worry about it. What had he said?

He hoped he hadn't blurted out anything inappropriate. Such as his feelings for Meena Harper. That wouldn't be good at all. He didn't need her knowing how he felt about her. Not if she was going to come work with him at the Palatine. How was that going to work? How was he going to be able to work his subtle Alaric Wulf magic on her if she already knew how he felt about her?

Then the magic wouldn't be subtle at all. It would be the furthest thing from subtle.

And then the magic wouldn't work. He was already competing with the prince of darkness. What the hell else did he have but his special Alaric Wulf magic?

But maybe he hadn't said anything about liking her.

He could, of course, just *ask* her what he'd said.

But then it would sound like he was worried. And he wasn't worried. He was just . . . a little concerned.

That was all.

"Joan is a nice name," Alaric said. Then he felt stupid.

"It was my suggestion," Meena said. "After Joan of Arc." Finally, she looked him in the face. For some reason, she'd seemed reluctant before to do so. "That's a saint."

He said flatly, "I've heard of her. She was burned at the stake as a witch. I went to school, you know. I'm not a complete imbecile."

His concern over what he might or might not have said while he was delusional with blood loss was making him act a little defensive, maybe.

Meena's mouth tightened as she studied him. "I didn't come here to fight with you."

Clearly, the doctor was right. He needed to relax about the amnesia thing.

He spread open both his hands palm wide. "I'm in the hospital. All I'm fighting is an infection. Which you apparently gave me, with your unclean hands."

She smiled a little. "I know. I heard. I'm sorry about that. I was trying to save your life, you know. The way you're always saving mine. Apparently, we both have hero complexes."

"They say it's a miracle they were able to save my leg, after the way you butchered it," he lied. There, that was better. The old Alaric Wulf magic was back.

She stopped smiling and looked distressed. "Oh, really? I thought I did it right. I'm sorry. That's how they said to do it when I researched it while I was writing about it for the show. I really was trying to keep you from bleeding to death."

He was getting the distinct impression from her that he had not, in fact, blurted out his undying devotion to her while they'd been trapped behind all that rubble and he'd lain there bleeding to death.

This was a relief.

Or was it?

"It's amazing," Alaric said, leaning back against his horrible, flat hospital pillow, "the lengths you were willing to go to in order to keep me from dying."

"What?" She shook her head. "No. Just a tourniquet. That's all. And apparently, that nearly killed you. I guess you're not as big a he-man as you'd like everyone to think you are."

"And yet," he said, spreading his hands wide again, "you're here with me, and not off somewhere hiding from us Palatine with Lucien Antonescu."

She stared at him. "What does that have to do with anything? I told you, I was just visiting my friend Leisha and I thought I'd stop by—"

He shrugged. "I just find it interesting, that's all."

He had her. And she knew it. What's more, she knew he knew. He could see a pink blush suffusing her long neck, rising up out of the rather low-cut neckline of the tight black dress and traveling up her cheeks.

"We all know he's not dead, Meena," Alaric said. "He must have asked you to go away with him."

The blush turned crimson.

"Well," she said, her gaze dropping to the floor. "That's right. He did. But I said no."

Alaric's heart swelled with delight. This was his best day in the hospital yet. Everything was going great. He *definitely* hadn't done anything stupid under the choir loft. What had he even been worrying about?

"It's because you're going to come work with us after all, right?" He folded his hands behind his head, enormously pleased with himself. "I knew you were just leading Holtzman on. That's the spirit. The old man needs to be kept on his toes. You're going for more money, aren't you? And why not? You're a valuable asset to the team. Or are you trying to score a position for that brother of yours, too? He showed some surprising initiative out there in the field." Although apart from that first lucky shot, he had the worst aim of anyone Alaric had ever seen. "We could probably find something for him in the tech department. Look, if I were you, I'd try to get them to pay you a housing allowance. Where are you staying right now?"

She raised her gaze. But the blush, for some reason, was getting deeper. He could have sworn even her breasts were blushing. Which was a sight he would have been very interested to see in more detail.

"St. Clare's, if you must know," she said. "Father Bernard was kind enough to take Jon and me in after my apartment was unfortunately—"

"You didn't go look at it, did you?" he interrupted, quickly dropping his hands. He didn't want her to see her apartment. Especially the bed and what the graffiti over it said.

"No," she said. "But Jon did. And he said—"

"Don't," he said. This was very important. "Promise me you won't ever go there again. Just have someone take everything out of there and throw it away. Then sell the place. Don't ever go back."

"I'll do that," she said. "I promise. But I'm not holding out for more money, Alaric. The truth is . . . I'm not taking the job."

He felt as if someone had sliced open another vein. Maybe in his heart.

"What?" he said stupidly.

"It was very kind of Dr. Holtzman to offer," she said all in a rush.

"I'm really very flattered. But I . . . I just don't think I can do that. Go to work for . . . the people you work for. Right now."

Alaric stared at her. "But I thought you said Lucien asked you to go away with him," he said. "And you said no."

"I did say no," Meena said. She had shrunk in on herself, as if she were cold. "But that was . . . before."

"Before when?" Comprehension slowly dawned. "Wait . . . before he turned into a dragon and tried to kill us all?"

She nodded wordlessly.

"So you haven't actually *seen* him again since that night?"

She nodded again.

"So you're not actually *living* at St. Clare's," he said. Everything was becoming clear. Maybe too clear. "You're *hiding* there. You're hiding from him. Because you're scared to death of him."

"Well," she said, "I wouldn't put it quite like that."

"How else would you put it, then?" he demanded. "If you're not scared of him, what *are* you scared of? Yourself? Scared you might say *yes* if he asks you again?" Alaric could hardly believe it. But it was right there, written all over her face.

"I really don't know what you're talking about," Meena said primly. "I just came in here to say hello to you, not to get one of your lectures."

Lectures!

"But if you're going to be like this," she said, in the same tone of voice, "I'm leaving. I think they have you on too many pain meds."

She got up to leave . . . but not soon enough. Because, even bedridden, he was too fast for her. He managed to reach out and snatch up her uninjured hand in his.

He wasn't letting her go anywhere.

"I'm not on anything," he said in his kindest voice, the one he reserved for Simone and . . . well, no one else, actually. "And it's all right to be afraid, Meena."

She stood there for a second or two, looking down at his fingers holding on to hers. Then, abruptly, she sank back down into the pink vinyl chair.

"Okay," she said, raising her gaze to meet his again. Her brown eyes were wide and troubled. "You're right. I'm terrified. As soon as the sun goes down every night, I take Jack Bauer and go into one of those windowless rooms in the convent they stuck Yalena in. And I stay there. I don't come out until morning. Because I know he can't get to me in there. I mean, if he's even looking for me, which I don't know. *He turned into a dragon,* Alaric. He tried to kill us all."

"Not you," Alaric said. He couldn't believe he was actually *defending* Lucien Dracula. But amazingly, his desire to see her smiling again was stronger than his hatred for the prince. "He did his best to try to keep you from getting killed."

She gave him a sarcastic look. "He turned into a *dragon,*" she reminded him.

Alaric looked down at her hand, so small in his. She was holding on to his rather tightly.

She was afraid. She was *very* afraid.

Alaric had seen this before. People—grown men and women, other guards just like him—who'd come back from missions exactly the way Meena was right now, slinking around in abject terror, afraid of their own shadows because of the demonic horrors they'd seen in the field.

He didn't want her going off with the prince.

But he couldn't let her go on this way, either.

Even if it meant losing her.

He took a deep breath and said, "If I've learned anything in this life, Meena, it's that there are a lot of scary things out there. Sometimes *I* just want to go into a windowless room until the sun comes back up, and the scary things have gone away. But the truth is . . . those scary things aren't going to just go away on their own."

Meena, as if she sensed where he was headed with this, started to pull her hand away, shaking her head. Her eyes had filled with tears.

But he wouldn't release her fingers from his. Because she had to hear it.

No matter how much she didn't want to.

"Because it turns out I have a gift," he went on. "And that gift is that I'm good at killing scary things. So I use my gift to help others who aren't as strong as I am, in order to make the world a safer place for them. I *can't* lock myself into a windowless room until the sun comes back up, Meena. No matter how much I might want to sometimes."

She whipped her head toward him, starting to protest.

But he just held her hand and went on.

"Because my job is to face the scary things. And I think deep down, Meena, you know that's your job, too. That maybe the reason people like you and me were put here on this earth was so that everyone else—people who don't have our gifts—can sleep in their windowless rooms while we make the world a little bit safer for them."

She didn't say anything for a few seconds. Then he saw why.

She was crying.

Well . . . he hadn't meant to make her cry.

Maybe he couldn't do anything right. Maybe there was no Alaric Wulf magic. Maybe Holtzman was right, and he really did need that counseling.

After a little while she looked up and said, "I've been a fool."

"I don't think you're a fool," he said.

He wanted to say a lot of other things. But he wasn't suffering from blood loss anymore. So he kept silent.

She yanked on her hand again. This time, he let go.

She took that hand and pressed it, along with her casted hand, to her eyes, which were red with unshed tears.

"You really are annoying sometimes," she said.

Martin often told him the same thing. "I know," he said, agreeing.

"Why do you *do* this to me?" she asked, drying her eyes with the edge of his bedsheet. He doubted she'd find it very absorbent. The thread count couldn't have been very high at all.

He longed to put his arms around her, to hold her.

But he was afraid she'd slap him.

Or that Holtzman would walk in. Either would have been equally embarrassing.

And besides, he couldn't lean forward far enough to get his arms around her because of his stupid leg, which was hanging in traction.

Then, her eyes dry, she stood up.

She'd be leaving now, he supposed, his depression complete. And he had no idea if he'd ever even see her again.

Except, to his surprise, instead of leaving, she laid her uninjured hand on his chest.

"I don't suppose," she said, "we're even now, are we?"

He shook his head, not understanding what she meant.

His confusion increased when she bent down and kissed him gently on the cheek, the way she had in the rectory that night.

"Probably not," she said when she straightened. "I think I still owe you. Plus, you saved Jack, too."

Oh. She meant all the times he'd saved her life. But she didn't owe him for that. That was his job.

"You need a shave," she said, wrinkling her nose. "Tomorrow do you want me to bring you some stuff to shave with?"

"Yes," he said, his mood suddenly brightening.

She'd been the only one to offer. The *only one*.

This was why he loved her.

Plus, she'd said she was coming to visit again tomorrow.

No, it wasn't the same as saying she was going to take the job.

And maybe it was only because she was going to be visiting her friend in the maternity ward, anyway, and so it was easy for her to swing by to see him, too.

But by tomorrow, he'd have another speech ready for her, about how she belonged with the Palatine.

And when she came the next day—and she would; he knew she would—he'd have another.

And eventually, he'd wear her down. That's how the old Alaric Wulf magic worked.

And even if the Alaric Wulf magic didn't exist—Martin often said it didn't—one of these days, they were going to have to let him out of traction, and he was going to stumble into some more danger.

And then she wasn't going to be able to resist warning him to stay out of it.

And that's when he'd point out, with the kind of brilliant and in-arguable logic for which he was so widely known, that she might just as well get paid to do this for a living.

She would be powerless in the face of such superior intellectual reasoning.

"Okay," Meena said. She smiled and reached out to run her finger over some of the razor stubble on his cheek. He was careful to keep very still while she did this, so she wouldn't stop. This was another example of how the Alaric Wulf magic worked. "I'll see you tomorrow."

Unfortunately, that was when she turned around and left.

But his hospital room didn't seem nearly as unbearable to Alaric after that as it had before she'd come to pay her visit.

In fact, suddenly it felt downright cheerful.

Alaric didn't think this was the result of powerful neurotransmitters, such as dopamine, being released in his brain.

He decided it was because of the daisies.

Alaric probably would have felt completely differently if he'd had the slightest idea about *where* Meena Harper was going . . . that his speech about not sleeping in windowless rooms had convinced her, not that she had to join the Palatine Guard to help him battle the forces of evil, but that she had to go, as soon as she left the hospital, to the single place that most terrified her and to which he'd made her promise not to go at all.

Chapter Sixty-one

8:00 p.m., Friday, April 23
910 Park Avenue, Apt. 11B
New York, New York

Meena wasn't sure what made her go back to her apartment.

Everyone told her not to. Alaric, who'd been there and seen the horrific destruction for himself. Abraham Holtzman, referring to his handbook about post-traumatic stress disorder and how it would only make hers worse. Sister Gertrude, who was practical and kind about these things.

Even Jon, who'd been there, too, to see if he could salvage any of his own things.

"It's awful," he'd said with a shudder. "Trust me. You don't want to know."

But Meena *did* want to know. Ever since that night . . .

She tried not to think about that night. She didn't want to think about it because every time she started to, the tears came, and with them the conviction that Lucien was dead.

He *had* to be dead.

And then came the horrible hollow sensation in the middle of her chest. . . .

And then, just as terrible, the fear that he *wasn't* dead. What if he wasn't dead, and still loved her, and wanted them to be together?

Which was worse?

The fact that she didn't know was what made her decide she couldn't think about it at all. Just not at all.

Not thinking about it was easier than anyone might have imagined. Every time she started to think about it, she just shoved all thoughts, all memories, anything and everything connected to Lucien Antonescu from her mind and thought firmly about something else.

She kept herself so busy at St. Clare's that she didn't really have time to think about Lucien. There were the dishes to do after every meal, the pots and pans and casserole dishes piled high in the in the rectory kitchen sink. Cleaning them was Meena's penance for the burns everyone had sustained because of her. She scoured them until they gleamed, sometimes late into the night, just her, alone in the kitchen, with the sponge and her rubber gloves and the hot soapy water.

And the darkness beyond the window over the sink.

And the glowing red eyes she was convinced she could see burning through that darkness, watching her every move.

She tried not to think about the eyes, and if they were really there, or if she was just imagining them.

There was the soup kitchen to help run, the donations to the thrift shop to help sort through. (The thrift shop was where she'd found her new black dress, among many other additions to her wardrobe. She understood that the donations were meant to be sold in the store. But helping herself to one or two things as she sorted didn't seem like the biggest crime. Everything she owned had been either destroyed by the Dracul or soaked in Alaric Wulf's blood.)

But maybe she'd kept herself a little *too* busy not thinking about Lucien Antonescu (those eyes, burning through the darkness outside the kitchen windows) and what had happened that night.

Because until Alaric's speech about how wrong it was for people like them to shut themselves off from the scary things in the world instead of fighting them—and he *was* right, she knew: she absolutely believed that the two of them *were* alike, he with his sword, and she with her ability to predict danger and death—Meena had thought she'd been doing the right thing by refusing to let herself think about Lucien.

But after Alaric's eye-opening speech, she realized this was wrong.

She had a moral obligation not only to think about Lucien but to face him, and what he'd done to her and to her life.

Which was destroy it.

If he was even alive, of course. She still didn't know whether or not he was (except . . . those *eyes*). No one seemed to be able to tell her. Abraham would say only that after that last blast of white-hot fire in the church—which had knocked him and everyone else unconscious for a few seconds—he woke to find the prince gone.

"*Gone?*" Meena had asked, finding it hard to believe that a thirty-ton, seventy-foot red-winged dragon could simply disappear into thin air, the way Emil and Mary Lou Antonescu had.

"Gone," Abraham had replied with a nod.

Lucien hadn't *flown* off. The cathedral's roof, it was true, had burned down with the rest of the building, but no one had reported seeing any winged dragons taking flight across Manhattan that night. (The NYPD had put what happened at St. George's down to teen arsonists, thanks in large part to the vague statements Meena and Alaric had given them. But of course, no teen arsonists had been arrested.)

So where was he?

Maybe, Meena thought as she approached her building that rainy evening after her visit to Alaric Wulf's hospital room, her keys pressed firmly in her hand, he had simply self-imploded. That last explosion of white-hot fire, from which he had tried so assiduously to protect her, had been Lucien spontaneously combusting.

At least this way, she thought as the automatic doors to her building opened in front of her, she didn't have to worry anymore about his still loving her. And asking her, as Alaric had suggested back in his hospital room, to go away with him.

And then killing her and making her one of his kind so that they could be together forever.

"Miss Harper!" Pradip cried when he saw her. "You're back!"

"Yes," she said. She tried to summon a smile for her favorite doorman, but it wasn't easy, all things considered. "But I'm just stopping by. I won't be staying. I'm selling."

Pradip's face fell. "You, too? The Antonescus just put their place on the market." He looked glum. "You heard? They're gone already. Mr. Antonescu's business took them to Asia. Or was it India?"

Meena wasn't exactly surprised to hear this. Emil and Mary Lou might have fought on their side during the vampire war. But she didn't exactly sense that this was going to take them off the Palatine Guard's most-wanted list.

"That's too bad," she said. Then she brightened. "Maybe some rich rock star will buy my apartment and theirs and knock the wall down between them, and then have the whole eleventh floor."

Pradip just stared at her. She'd been trying to cheer them both up—having a rich rock star in the building would be a good thing.

And she could use the extra cash from the apartment sale to pay back what she owed David.

But Pradip didn't seem to find the idea as appealing as she did.

"I don't think the co-op board would approve a rock star," he told her.

Why not? Meena wanted to ask. They'd approved a couple of vampires. Instead, she said, "You're probably right. Well, okay. I'm going up."

"Good night, Miss Harper," Pradip said.

Meena managed a smile for him, then went to the elevator.

For the first time in ages, she took the ride to the eleventh floor alone. Mary Lou didn't stop the doors just as they closed to snag a ride with her, as she always had in the past. No gushing conversation about some guy from Emil's office who'd be *just perfect* for her. No suggestions as to how Meena might improve the plotlines of *Insatiable* . . . which was sad, since, with Fran, Stan, and Shoshona all missing—Paul had left a message on her cell phone that everyone was presuming they, along with Stefan Dominic, had been in an accident on the way to the Metzen-baums' Hamptons retreat and that it was only a matter of time until their vehicle was recovered, with their bodies inside it—Meena was probably in line for that promotion to head writer she'd been wanting forever.

Why not? With Shoshona gone, there was no record of her "firing." Who knew what was going to happen to ABN (and CDI) now that the CEO of its new owner was missing as well?

Then again . . . who cared?

All the tabloids were abuzz about the fact that *Lust* star Gregory Bane was missing, too. Half the women in America were in mourning.

Foul play was going to be suspected some time soon, Meena supposed.

Except that no bodies were ever going to turn up.

When the elevator reached the eleventh floor, Meena stepped out and looked around, beginning to feel the first tiny tingles of fear. Why had she thought this was such a good idea, again?

Sure, the Dracul were all supposed to be dead.

The ones who lived in Manhattan, anyway.

But what if a few of them who lived somewhere else had heard about what had happened at St. George's and had decided to look her up to get revenge? Or had stopped by for a taste of her blood, which by now vampires all over the world must have heard rumors about.

Stop, she told herself. *Alaric was right. You can't spend the rest of your life in a windowless room, Meen.*

She glanced around the hallway. Everything *looked* all right . . . normal, even.

The door to her apartment seemed okay, too. She swallowed, then walked up to it and inserted the key.

Whatever lay behind it, she told herself, she could take it. She'd been thrown across a church by a *dragon,* for God's sake. She'd staked not one but two vampires, one of whom had actually played a vampire on TV.

She could handle whatever lay in store for her in Apt. 11B.

She swung open the door, then reached for the light switch . . .

. . . and gasped.

She'd expected it to be bad.

But she hadn't expected *this*.

Someone had already come through and . . . *cleaned* her apartment. Not just cleaned it but converted it . . . into a different place entirely. The walls had been completely scraped of the Dracul graffiti and repainted a crisp eggshell white. The broken furniture and spoiled electronics had been carted away. Her sodden books, her shredded clothes, her broken dishes . . . all of that was gone, too.

All new stainless steel appliances had been installed in the kitchen. Her parquet floors had been sanded and gleamed with fresh polish. Even the fireplace's flues finally opened, though they never had before.

Her apartment looked *better* than it had at any time when she had ever lived there. It looked better than the day she and David had moved in.

Who had done all this?

Not Jon. She knew that. He had been at Leisha and Adam's all week, working on the baby's room, trying to get it done before Leisha and the baby came home from the hospital.

Not Alaric, obviously. How could he have done this while lying in bed with one leg in traction?

And Abraham Holtzman and Father Bernard and the others were missing the first layer of skin off their faces and hands.

Besides which, where would they have gotten the money?

There was only one other explanation.

And even as Meena was thinking to herself that it was impossible—*impossible,* because he was dead, he *had* to be dead (except for the fact that she could swear she felt someone's gaze on her every night through the rectory kitchen window as she did the dishes); she had almost convinced herself she *wanted* him to be dead—she turned around, and there he was, coming in from the rain through the balcony door.

Chapter Sixty-two

8:30 P.M., Friday, April 23
910 Park Avenue, Apt. 11B
New York, New York

"Hello, Meena," he said.

Drops of rain clung damply to his short dark hair.

She caught her breath, her heart giving a sudden painful thump.

She was surprised her heart even remembered *how* to beat, since seeing him there, just walking into her bedroom like that, was such a shock, she would have thought it would have gone into cardiac arrest.

He looked incredible, of course, just like always, even casually dressed in a charcoal-gray cashmere sweater and black trousers. Tall, broad-shouldered, taking up so much space in that tiny room where they'd once made such riotous, crazy love, trying to be quiet so they wouldn't arouse the suspicions of her brother and Alaric, right there in the next room . . .

He looked so dark and so handsome and so sure of himself.

He gave off no indication at all that, less than a week ago, he'd been . . .

. . . well, what he'd been.

Or done what he'd done.

"I've been waiting for you," he said, those dark brown eyes as melancholic as ever. Still, sad as those eyes might have looked, Meena didn't miss the way his gaze raked her, making her feel, as he always did, that he knew exactly what she looked like beneath the dress she was wearing. Which, of course, he did. "I was hoping you'd come back. I know you haven't wanted to see me. But I hope now we can talk—"

Abruptly, Meena's knees buckled. Just gave out beneath her. She would have collapsed to the floor—there was no furniture left in the apartment for her to grab to keep herself from smacking into the hardwood that came swooping toward her so fast—if he hadn't caught her in his strong arms, then sunk to the floor with her, cradling her body against him.

"I'm sorry, Meena," he whispered into her hair. There was a world of remorse, of pain, of hurt in his rich, low voice. "I'm so, so sorry. You have to know that I—"

"You have no *right,*" she said. She was surprised her lips and tongue worked. She felt numb all over. That's why her legs had stopped working. But apparently, though it was weak, she still had a voice. "After what you did—"

"I know," he said. He was rocking her, his forehead pressed to hers. "I know."

"You can't just come in here," Meena said. Her voice had begun to sound stronger. "And clean up my apartment like that's going to make everything better. Because it isn't. Lucien, people *died.*"

"I know," he said. He looked—and sounded—as if he were carrying around the regret of a thousand vampires from a thousand years, not just a single five-hundred-year-old one. "More people than you even know, Meena. My brother was evil. He always was. I should have killed him long ago. This was all my fault. All of it. He's gone now, though. He'll never murder anyone again."

"People got *hurt,*" she said, shaking her head. He had to understand that it wasn't enough that Dimitri was gone. *If* he was really gone . . .

"I know," he said, and lifted her wrist in its air cast and kissed it. "And I want to spend eternity making it up to you."

"It wasn't just me," Meena said, the tears in her eyes making it hard for her to see. "They kidnapped my best friend. Who was *pregnant.* They bit a chunk out of her husband's neck as he was trying to stop them. And she went into early labor because of what happened. She could have lost the baby. She almost did."

Lucien stroked her. "How can we make it up to them?" he asked. "A college savings account for the baby, perhaps? I'll open one for them and move a million dollars into it tomorrow."

"Lucien!" Meena stared up at him disbelievingly through her tears. "You can't just go around paying people off to make up for your mistakes. You burned down a *church*!"

"I know, Meena," he said. He reached up to capture some of her tears with a thumb. "But what do you want me to do? How do you expect me to make amends? I've already made an anonymous donation to the church. A sizeable one that should take care of any reparations not covered by their fire insurance—"

Meena sucked in her breath. "No. That doesn't make it right. You turned into a—"

He laid a finger over her lips to silence her before she could get the word *dragon* out. "There were mitigating circumstances," he said. "Your brother *shot* me. With a stake. In the back."

She winced. "I know," she said. He'd lowered the finger. "And you'll never know how sorry I am about that. But, Lucien—"

"Whatever else may have happened, Meena—whatever else I may have done wrong, and I'm not denying that I did many, many things wrong that night—please allow me to point out that, despite what you insisted I would do, I killed neither your brother nor that Palatine guard you're so fond of . . . despite *meticulous* efforts on their behalf to murder me. They're still both very much alive today."

Meena sucked in her breath. "Because of *me*," she said. "I saved them. I put a tourniquet on one and I sent the other to the maternity ward with my best friend. But, Lucien, I can't keep on doing that. I won't always be there. I can't keep watching the people I love almost get killed because of you. Oh, wait, excuse me. Almost get *incinerated*—"

"That's why," he said, leaning his head down to place his lips where, a minute before, his finger had been, "I suggested that we go away. Thailand. Remember?"

Meena stared up at him, her face wet, her mouth still tingling from the kiss.

She definitely didn't feel numb anymore. Not anywhere. The tears and his lips had taken care of that problem.

"I can't go to Thailand with you, Lucien," she said, starting to shake her head. How could he not understand?

"Of course you can," he said. "Why not?"

His hand was already traveling up her thigh, already slipping beneath the short skirt of her new—used—black dress.

"A . . . a million reasons," she said.

"I know you're frightened, Meena," he said in his deep voice. His dark-eyed gaze seemed to have a hypnotic pull on hers . . . the same kind of pull his fingers seemed to have on her.

She was having a hard time remembering how angry she was with him when he was touching her the way he was. How could she ever have been frightened of him? Of those lips, which were kissing her, right now, on her neck?

"And you're right to be," he went on, in his deep, low voice. "There are unspeakable horrors in the world, the likes of which you can't even begin to imagine. What happened to you that night—that day—was inexcusable. Those things—those creatures—should never have touched you. It's my fault you were ever put in a position where they were able to. And you're absolutely correct: none of what happened to you can ever be righted with a check, no matter how sizable."

"I don't want your money, Lucien," she murmured. The feel of his mouth on the skin of her neck was almost more than she could stand. She was ready to start tearing off her dress right there on the bedroom floor.

"I know that. And I will never allow you to be put in that kind of danger again," he said. The hand he'd dipped beneath her skirt had reached her panties. Now his fingers skimmed the lace trim along the inside of her thigh. "But in order for me to protect you the way I want to, you have to come live with me. So we can be together. Really be together."

"In Thailand," Meena said, her eyes closed. She'd thrown her head back against his chest, her throat arched in tantalizing invitation.

"Or wherever you want to go," he said. "It doesn't have to be Thailand." His mouth moved toward her throat.

Meena's heart thumped again. It all sounded so perfect. The two of them would go away together. Maybe to Thailand. Lucien would protect her. He could because he was so big and strong. Also rich. She wouldn't need to worry about Leisha or Jon or Adam or Alaric or the baby or anyone else she cared about getting killed.

Because she'd be gone. She'd be far away from them. She'd only have Lucien to care about.

But . . .

Something tickled the back of her mind. The same thing that had always bothered her whenever Leisha mentioned the baby. The same thing that had bothered her when Yalena had shown her a picture of her boyfriend on her cell phone. . . .

The pit of nothingness.

She opened her eyes, surprised to find that Lucien's mouth was open and on her throat.

"Wait," she said, jerking away, her pulse suddenly racing, her breath catching in her throat. "What are you doing?"

He looked down at her expressionlessly. The hand beneath her skirt stilled. "Nothing," he said carefully. "I'm not doing anything to you, Meena. Except loving you."

She reached up to touch her neck. She was relieved to find that it was dry.

But all it would take, she knew, was one more bite, and then her drinking a little of his blood. . . .

And she would become like him.

She knew it. He knew it.

Meena got to her feet, suddenly feeling as if the walls of the room were closing in on her.

Her heart was racing as fast as a rabbit's now. So fast, in fact, that she was worried it might actually fly out of her chest.

What am I doing? she asked herself. *What am I doing here?*

Alaric Wulf had warned her not to go to her old apartment. He'd told her . . . he'd made her promise she wouldn't go see it.

Had he known? Had he known that Lucien would come there to find her and that he'd do this to her?

Of course he'd known.

And she hadn't listened. Oh, God, why hadn't she *listened*? She was just like all the people who never listened to *her*.

Because only now was the very great danger she was in actually beginning to become clear to her . . . this time, she was the one on the edge of the crevasse. How was she going to get away? How was she going to get out of this?

She didn't have any weapons.

And even if she did—could she really kill the man she loved, even if it meant . . .

. . . her life?

She paced from one side of the room to the other and then back again, taking quick, shallow breaths.

"Meena," Lucien said, looking at her curiously. "What's wrong?"

"Nothing," she said. Could he read her mind?

Yes. Of course he could. Or partly, at least. He always could.

Fine, then, she decided.

Let him read it now.

She came to a stop in front of him, her toes balanced on the edge of the pit.

"I can't do that," she said. "I can't . . . do *that*."

He looked up at her from the floor where he still sat. "I don't know what you're talking about," he said.

"Oh, don't lie to me, Lucien," she said, exploding. "After everything else I've been through because of you? Your freak of a brother trying to kill me? An army of vampires trying to drain me of my blood and drink it? And you're going to sit there and *lie* to my face?"

Now he climbed to his feet, his calm demeanor gone. "Fine," he said. His large hands were fisted. There was a muscle twitching in his jaw. It was obvious he'd known exactly what she'd been talking about all along. "So what? Admit that it would make things simpler, Meena."

"Simpler?" She laughed out loud, though without humor. "If I were *dead*?"

"If you were one of us," he said, putting it in a way that he obviously found more palatable. "Then you and I could truly be together. All this talk of going to Thailand—"

"Yeah, FYI," Meena interrupted sarcastically, "I knew that was never going to happen, because you'd go up like a roman candle on the beach."

"—doesn't mean anything if you're just going to grow old before my eyes while I—"

"Oh, that's very nice," Meena said, interrupting again. "So you're just going to dump me for someone younger when I get old, like every other guy? Are you suggesting I try some Revenant Wrinkle Cream or that I check into one of Dimitri's spas—"

He reached out then and cupped her face in both his hands, looking deeply into her eyes.

"I will love you, Meena," he said fiercely, "until the end of time. I will never stop loving you. My life, before I met you, was nothing. Can you understand that? My life was nothing, meant nothing, even if I may not have known it. And then you came along, and suddenly, everything I knew, or thought I knew, was turned upside down. I will never be the same again. How could I be? You have shown me what it is to love, to feel and laugh and, yes, even to feel alive again. So whether you choose to be one with me or not, I will go on loving you, Meena, even after you are a rotting corpse in the ground. But, Meena, I would like to do whatever I can to prevent you from turning into a corpse. I think I mentioned that before."

She stared up at him, shaken.

"Yes, but, Lucien," she said, reaching up to grasp his wrists and gazing into his dark eyes, in which she thought she saw flickers of flame, "tricking me into turning into a vampire so that I won't grow old and die before your eyes? What if I don't want to *be* a vampire? Which I don't, by the way. I have a dog that hates vampires, remember? I have friends and family here in New York City who I'd like to be able to visit . . . during the day. Also, I've seen death. I really, really don't like going there. Even to visit. Even for a short while. And, Lucien." She took his hands from her face and flipped them over so that she could hold them, instead, in hers. "I have a special thing that I can do. I think you experienced it, at least on a small scale, when you drank my blood. I can tell when people are going to die . . . lately, I can tell when they're just in danger. And that means I can warn them, give them a fighting chance against death . . . or at least put it off. If you killed me and turned me into a vampire . . . I don't know if I'd have that ability anymore. I'm pretty sure my blood drying up in my veins would end that. And—"

She drew a shuddering breath.

"That, I just don't think I could live without," she said. "Because those unspeakable horrors you mentioned before, the likes of which you don't think I can imagine and that I'm pretty sure you rule over?"

He stared down at her, uncomprehending. "Yes? What about them?"

"I think they're what I'm supposed to be helping protect people from," she said. She hoped the tears that had begun to stream down her face again didn't make him think she was regretting what she was saying.

Because she wasn't. Not at all.

"I don't know for certain," she went on. "But I do know that whenever I *don't* help people . . . well, bad things happen. So . . . that's what I'm going to go do."

He shook his head. Now she was *sure* that there were flickers of flame in those dark eyes, twin embers, burning bright. Outside the apartment building, the rain, which had been falling gently before, suddenly began to pour. Thunder rumbled off in the not-so-far distance.

"Meena," he said. The embers were glowing a deep, steady red, exactly the way the dragon's eyes had. "I don't understand. What are you saying?"

"I'm saying," she said, unable to hold back a sob, "that I'm going to go work for the Palatine."

He stared down at her for a second or two.

Then he threw back his head and laughed.

When he looked at her again, the embers had turned to flames, flaring high.

"Oh, Meena," he said. "You're joking."

"I'm not joking," she said. She reached up and wiped her tears with her uninjured wrist. "The Palatine offered me a job. And I've decided that I'm taking it."

His eyes were entirely red now. The brown was gone. The dragon was taking over.

"It's not like I would ever do anything to help them go after you, Lucien." She rushed to explain. "You know that. I'll always try to do everything I can to help you. Because I love you, too. I always will. But I just can't be with you. Not if it means my friends are going to get hurt. And this job . . . it means I can finally do what I think I've always been meant to do."

"You don't *need* a job," he said with sudden savagery. He reached out and grabbed her by the waist, pulling her hard against him. Outside, lightning flared as thunder caused the building to shudder. The storm was directly overhead. "I told you that I'd take care of you."

Meena lifted her chin to look him in the eye. Those fierce dragon eyes.

"But not without killing me," she said quietly.

He looked down at her as the rain and wind outside lashed the balcony, his volatile gaze smoldering in its intensity. She thought it might consume her in its wrath and wipe her off the face of the planet entirely, the way his dragon fire had wiped out the Dracul that night.

And no one would know. No one would ever know what had become of Meena Harper.

He could do it. There was nothing to stop him.

Except her courage.

"You know," she said, swallowing hard, "when you told me the story of St. George and the dragon that night we were in the museum, Lucien, there was one thing you left out."

"What is that?"

He was keeping himself under control with an effort. She could feel his arms shaking almost as badly as her knees were as he tried valiantly not to drop his lips to her neck and do what he so badly wanted to.

"You never told me that you were the dragon," she whispered.

Thunder—or maybe it was his voice—rocked the walls of the apartment, so hard that Meena would have clapped her hands over her ears if she hadn't already thrown them defensively over her face, certain the next thing she was going to see were his fangs coming at her throat.

"I'm the prince of darkness." His voice was like a sonic boom in her ears. "What did you think that meant, Meena? Did you think that meant that . . . I . . . was . . . a . . . *saint*?"

And, just as she thought that it was going to be all over for her . . .

. . . he let her go.

She lowered her arms and stood there, shaking, just staring at him. She had never seen such sadness in anyone's eyes.

"No, Meena," he said in his normal voice. "*You're* the saint."

What did this mean? Why had he let go of her?

"Go," he said curtly, nodding toward the bedroom door.

She jumped.

"If you're going to go," he said, his voice rising, "go *now*. Before I change my mind. I think you know what will happen then."

She turned and ran from the apartment, not stopping to lock the door behind her. She ignored the elevator, not willing to wait for it, and ran down all eleven flights of stairs, unable to believe he wasn't coming after her—in bat or dragon or even man form.

She didn't slow down. Like he'd said, he could still change his mind.

She tore through the lobby, not stopping to say good-bye to Pradip. She ran out into the rain, which immediately soaked her, flagging down the first available taxi that she saw. She fell into the backseat, gasping out the address to St. Clare's to the driver.

She didn't look back.

She didn't dare.

Chapter Sixty-three

It wasn't until they were more than halfway there that Meena stopped shaking and began to believe that she'd done it.

She'd told him no.

And she was still alive.

She'd survived.

She didn't know what was going to happen next.

But she did know that the horrible empty feeling in her chest was gone. She could think about him and still breathe. She was safe.

And what's more, she had a plan. More than a plan . . . she had a *purpose,* for the first time in her life.

Maybe everything was going to be all right, just like Alaric had said. Maybe she didn't need to sleep in a windowless room anymore.

By the time the taxi pulled up in front of the rectory, it had stopped raining. The sudden storm had disappeared. She paid the driver and got out of the car, running up the steps to the front door. For once, she didn't look all around her, frightened that *he* might be waiting for her, watching, from the shadows.

Everything was dripping slightly, but Meena didn't mind. It was as if the world had been baptized, washed new, just for her. It seemed like a lovely spring evening all of a sudden. Maybe she'd even corral Jon and Yalena into going out for a drink with her. Why not?

There was nothing to be afraid of anymore.

She pressed the buzzer.

Jon was the one who let her in, his clothes covered in drywall dust from all the work he'd been doing over at Adam and Leisha's apartment.

"Hey, what took you so long?" he asked. "I thought you were just going to go see Leisha. Visiting hours ended a long time ago."

Jack Bauer—sensing, as he always did, that Meena was home—leapt off the lap of Yalena, who'd been sitting on the couch in the living room watching TV, and raced toward her, barking happily.

"How's my little man?" Meena knelt down to pet him, letting him lick her face. "Who's been a good boy? Who saved the world today?"

"Well, he didn't," Jon said bluntly. "He took a dump in Sister Gertrude's roses. She was not happy. I told her it was good fertilizer, but she was still none too pleased. Seriously, though. Where were you?"

"Did you take a dump in Sister Gertrude's roses?" Meena asked her dog, picking him up and letting him lick her face some more. She ignored her brother's question about where she'd been. "Who's the worst boy? Who's the worst boy in the whole world?"

Yalena, watching them over the back of the couch, giggled. Meena had been noticing lately that Yalena watched her brother, Jon. A *lot*. Meena wasn't sure how aware Jon was of this, though.

But she did note that tonight Jon had rolled his thrift-shop T-shirt's sleeves up very high. He usually did this, she'd learned from long experience, in order to show off his "guns," of which he was inordinately proud, whenever there was an attractive female around he wanted to impress.

And he didn't do it for just any girl.

It had to be Yalena he was trying to impress with his biceps. Who else could it have been around St. Clare's? Every other female was a novice or nun.

Meena was pleased he'd transferred his affections from Taylor Mackenzie to someone a bit more attainable.

"Fine, don't tell me where you've been," Jon was saying to Meena in a voice about an octave deeper than the one he usually used. "Abraham is looking for you. He says there's been some kind of, I don't know, disturbance in Vienna. Whatever that means. And he needs to talk to you about it." He looked at her strangely as she put Jack Bauer down, then removed her jacket and hung it on the coatrack. "Why would he need to talk to *you* about that?"

"Because," Meena said. She'd been wondering how she was going to explain this to Jon. And when. Now seemed like as good a time as any. "I'm going to start working for the Palatine."

Jon, who was drinking a soda, immediately spat out the mouthful that he'd been about to swallow. This caused Yalena, still watching them both, to giggle some more.

"Wait," he said. "*What?* What about *Insatiable?*"

"Well," Meena said with a shrug. "I'm going to quit. I think it's time I moved on. I need to start helping to make the world a safer place."

"But you already do that," Jon said. "You tell people all the time how they're going to die. Not that anyone ever believes you. What makes you think this is going to be any different?"

"Uh," Meena said, starting up the stairs with Jack Bauer at her heels, "because they're paying me? So they might actually be inclined to listen."

"Is not true no one believes her," Yalena said from the couch. "I believe her."

Jon gave Yalena a sour look. "Don't encourage her," he said. "Do you have any idea what she's put me through my whole life, practically? You know they called her You're Gonna Die Girl in high school? Try being siblings with *that.*"

Yalena just giggled yet again at that remark.

Laughing, Meena hurried the rest of the way up the stairs. She wanted to put a sweater on before going to see what Abraham needed to speak to her about. It was a little drafty in the rectory.

She opened the door to her windowless little room—she'd speak to Sister Gertrude tomorrow about moving to a new room, one *with* windows—and headed straight to the small, neatly folded stack of thrift-shop clothes on the chair by her bed.

She took the sweater off the top of the pile and was heading back out the door when she caught sight of something out of the corner of her eye. Something on the bed. It hadn't been there when she'd left for the hospital earlier. She came back into the room to see what it was, Jack Bauer trotting after her.

A letter.

There was a letter sitting tucked beneath the edge of her pillow on the bed.

Meena sat down on the bed and reached for the letter, Jack Bauer bounding up onto the mattress to lay down beside her.

Meena's fingers froze, however, when she saw the envelope's color and size.

Silver. The exact same color as the note that had been in the box Lucien had sent her. The box that had contained the tote bag with the ruby dragon slinking down the side.

The tote bag that was now, along with her laptop, in ashes up at St. George's.

Her blood seeming to freeze inside her veins, Meena looked quickly around the tiny bedroom with its bare white walls—bare except for the crucifix hanging over her bed.

No. It wasn't possible. How had he even gotten in there? It was a windowless room. The front door to the rectory—definitely a sacred threshold, the kind over which he'd assured her vampires couldn't cross unless invited—was always, always locked. And they'd repaired all the windows damaged from last week's attack. . . .

Maybe, she told herself, even as her heart began to drum so loudly in her ears that its beat was all she could hear, he'd had the note messengered, and someone—Yalena, maybe—had dropped it off in her room. . . .

But as she ripped the envelope open with shaking fingers and read his elegant, old-fashioned script, she saw that this was not what had happened. Not at all.

Meena, my darling, he'd written.

> *What I meant to say just now, though I was in too much*
> *sorrow and shock, was that I think it's right and good for you to*

*work for the Palatine. I hope they know how lucky they are to
have you.*

    *But that doesn't mean I will ever stop trying to have you
for myself. You know as well as I do, Meena, that we belong
together.*

    I hope that day will come sometime soon.

    In the meantime: truce.

                            With all the love in my heart, Lucien

Stunned, Meena stared down at the ivory notecard, on which the
ink was still not quite dry. She knew this because she'd already managed
to smear it in one tiny place with her thumb.

How had he done it? How had he managed to deliver it to her so
quickly, before, she was certain, she herself had even stepped out of
her cab?

Meena didn't know.

And she wasn't sure she *wanted* to know. All she knew for certain
was that it really had been his gaze she'd felt on her every night while
she'd been doing the dishes in the rectory kitchen. Those really had
been his eyes, watching her from the darkness.

Had he just never approached her before now because he'd suspected she wasn't ready to see him again after what had happened, and
had wanted her to have at least this one place to call her own, in which
to feel safe?

Or had he just been waiting for her to be ready, finally, to stop being
frightened and to come to him?

Of course. Of course that was what had happened.

Only instead of agreeing to become his wife when she'd finally come
to him, the way he'd expected her to, she'd done the unthinkable:

She'd crossed sides and joined the enemy.

And now he wanted her to know that wherever she went, whatever
she did for the rest of her life, she couldn't escape. Not that easily.

He would always be there in the darkness. Watching. Waiting.

To protect her, was how he would probably think of it.

And Meena didn't have the slightest doubt in her mind that he
would protect her. He'd protect her to within an inch of her life.

She looked down at the graceful, slightly antiquated handwriting.

A truce, he was calling it.

She smiled.

Then she slid the note back beneath her pillow, called to her dog, and headed downstairs to join Abraham and the others.

She wasn't afraid. Not anymore.

All she could think was that Lucien had been wrong in his first note.

She hadn't slain the dragon. Not at all.

She hoped no one ever would.

Author's Note

All of the details about the life of Vlad the Impaler (Vlad Dracula) mentioned in this book—including the suicide by drowning in the Princess's River of his first wife; the lack of knowledge of the whereabouts of his remains; and the fact that Bram Stoker borrowed his last name for the title of his classic novel—are historically accurate.

THE PALATINE GUARD WAS an actual military unit of the Vatican, formed in 1850 to defend Rome against attack from foreign invaders. Today the Palatine Guard is listed in most encyclopedias and search engines as defunct.

THE CHURCH LOCATED ON 154 Sullivan Street in New York City is called the Shrine Church of St. Anthony of Padua, not the Shrine of St. Clare. St. Anthony's really is, however, staffed by Franciscan friars. St. Clare, one of the first followers of St. Francis of Assisi, founded the Order of Poor Ladies, better known today as the Poor Clares.

ST. CLARE WAS DESIGNATED as the patron saint of television in 1958 by Pope Pius XII.

ST. MICHAEL THE ARCHANGEL, St. Joan of Arc, and St. George are the patron saints of the military.

TRAGICALLY, THERE IS NO longer a cathedral located on East Seventy-eighth Street.

THERE ARE SO MANY people to whom I owe a huge debt of thanks for their help and support while I was writing this book that if I listed all their names, the list would be longer than the book itself. So I'll just settle for saying thank you all so much! Extra special thanks go to Beth Ader, Jennifer Brown, Barbara Cabot, Benjamin Egnatz, Carrie Feron, Michele Jaffe, Laura Langlie, and Abigail McAden.

AN EXTRA-SPECIAL THANKS, TOO, to all my readers.

MEG CABOT